D0030125

Praise for Mike Lawson:

"Who knew the Speaker of the House had his own hotshot troubleshooter, an agent who can be sent out on jobs that require secrecy, political savvy, and an impressive array of physical talents? Anyone who read Lawson's *The Inside Ring*, his first thriller about Joe DeMarco, that's who."   —*Chicago Tribune*

"Seattle thriller writer Mike Lawson has quickly established himself as someone to watch. His work is a potent combination of high good humor, deft prose, and insider smarts; it's reminiscent of the late, great Ross Thomas, and that's saying something.
                        —Adam Woog, *The Seattle Times*

"Lawson writes a mean thriller and has a sense of humor that hurts."   —*The Independent* (UK)

"Lawson has a true insider's insight about real-world spinelessness, venality, and corruption that have taken the place of moral courage and true leadership on Capitol Hill . . . a fine ear for dialogue . . . [and] a good eye for irony."   —John Weisman, *The Washington Times*

Fort Nelson Public Library
Box 330
Fort Nelson, BC
V0C-1R0

FEB - - 2012

"The nice thing about Mike Lawson's Washington thrillers is that nobody is high-minded. Certainly not John Fitzpatrick Mahoney, speaker of the House . . . and as unscrupulous a politician as you'd hope to find outside a federal prison cell. Nor could you pin that high-and-holy tag on Mahoney's go-to guy, Joe DeMarco, who holes up in a subbasement office of the Capitol building and surfaces only when the speaker has some dirty business that needs to be done."
                              —Marilyn Stasio, *The New York Times*

"Mike Lawson has certainly made a claim as the best political thriller writer working today . . . I'm especially impressed with the consistently high quality of this series. The stories are not only scarily believable, but exciting and very well told. I'm a big fan."
                              —George Easter, *Deadly Pleasures*

"One of the most engaging heroes I've ever encountered."   —Tess Gerritsen

"Snappy dialogue, fantastically off-kilter characters and one extremely pissed off Chinese spy makes for non-stop reading. He's got the goods for bestsellerdom."
—Sarah Weinman, *Confessions of an Idiosyncratic Mind*

The Second Perimeter

Fort Nelson Public Library
Box 330
Fort Nelson, BC
V0C-1R0

Also by Mike Lawson

Mike Lawson

The Second Perimeter

Grove Press
New York

Copyright © 2006 by Michael A. Lawson

All rights reserved. No part of this book may be reproduced in any form or by any electronic or mechanical means, including information storage and retrieval systems, without permission in writing from the publisher, except by a reviewer, who may quote brief passages in a review. Scanning, uploading, and electronic distribution of this book or the facilitation of such without the permission of the publisher is prohibited. Please purchase only authorized electronic editions, and do not participate in or encourage electronic piracy of copyrighted materials. Your support of the author's rights is appreciated. Any member of educational institutions wishing to photocopy part or all of the work for classroom use, or anthology, should send inquiries to Grove/ Atlantic, Inc., 841 Broadway, New York, NY 10003 or permissions@groveatlantic.com.

This is a work of fiction. Names, characters, places, and incidents either are the product of the author's imagination or are used fictitiously. Any resemblance to actual persons, living or dead, events, or locales is entirely coincidental.

Published simultaneously in Canada
Printed in the United States of America

ISBN-13: 978-0-8021-4560-4

Grove Press
an imprint of Grove/Atlantic, Inc.
841 Broadway
New York, NY 10003

Distributed by Publishers Group West

www.groveatlantic.com

11 12 13 14 15   10 9 8 7 6 5 4 3 2 1

For
Tracy Howell

ACKNOWLEDGMENTS

I am deeply indebted to a number of people for their help in publishing this novel.

At the Gernert Company, Matt Williams for his hard work on all the contracts, Tracy Howell for her expertise on foreign rights, and Karen Rudnicki for her help and her patience with all my phone calls and questions.

I want to thank Abner Stein, Andrew Nurnberg, and their associates for getting the book published in so many countries overseas. Talk about European allies! One day I hope to meet all of you in person so I can thank you properly.

At Doubleday, my editor, Stacy Creamer, for the improvements she made to the manuscript, particularly the twist she added at the end. Also at Doubleday, Karla Eoff, for her outstanding work in finding all the typos, misspellings, and broken English; and Tracy Zupancis, for all her assistance to a beginner.

The person I am most grateful to is my agent, David Gernert, for agreeing to represent a new author, for his boundless enthusiasm, for the time he took to help me improve the manuscript, and for his phenomenal ability to convince others that it was a book worth publishing. David, thanks to you, I'm now doing what I've always wanted to do.

The Second Perimeter

PROLOGUE

From his office window Norton could see a Los Angeles class attack submarine moored at one of the piers. He was too far away to read the sub's hull number but he thought it was the USS *Asheville*, SSN 758. He had worked on the *Asheville* last year, spent a lot of time drinking with some of the chiefs. He stared at the sub a minute longer, then realizing he was just stalling, turned the rod and closed the venetian blinds. It was unlikely that anyone would be able to see what he was doing through a fourth-floor window but he couldn't take that chance.

Norton turned away from the window and peered over the partitions that enclosed his cubicle. It was lunchtime. There were four guys playing cribbage two cubicles over, and near the door, a secretary buffing her nails. There wasn't anybody else in the office that he could see. He had sent Mulherin up to bullshit with the secretary. Mulherin was good at bullshit. If anyone started to come down the aisle in Norton's direction, Mulherin would slow the person down and say something to warn him.

Having no further reason to delay, Norton pulled the chessboard out of his backpack. The board was thirteen inches square and an inch and a quarter thick, a little thicker than most chessboards. He pressed down on one side of the chessboard and a thin door popped open and a dozen chess pieces spilled out onto his desk. He then tipped the chessboard downward and a slim laptop computer slid out of the hollow space between the top and bottom of the chessboard.

The chessboard had been Carmody's idea.

After he used the laptop, Norton would slide it back into the hidden compartment in the chessboard, put the chessboard on top of his file cabinet, and arrange some pieces on the board to make it look as if he was playing a game with Mulherin. What a joke that was: Mulherin playing chess.

Getting the laptop into the shipyard was the riskiest part of the whole operation. Norton only needed to use it a few minutes a day, and when he did, he'd do like he was doing now—use it at lunchtime with Mulherin standing guard. But he'd been worried about bringing it in. In fact he'd been sweating so hard he was surprised one of the jarheads at the gate hadn't noticed.

Personal computers were prohibited inside the facility—only government-issue equipment was allowed—and if the marines guarding the gates had picked him that morning for one of their random security checks, and if by some chance they had discovered the laptop hidden in the chessboard, he'd have been screwed. Absolutely screwed.

But the likelihood of that happening had been small. If the terrorist threat level was high, the marines searched everything coming through the gates. Cars, knapsacks, purses, lunch boxes. Everything. But Norton had brought the laptop in when the threat level was normal and he had waited until there was a backup at the gate, a lot of people bitching that they needed to get to work, which tended to make the marines rush their searches. That had been Carmody's idea too, going in when the line was long. Carmody was a smart bastard.

Norton realized at that moment that it wasn't the marines that he'd been worried about. It was Carmody. Carmody scared the hell out of him.

I

———◆———

DeMarco pulled his car into a parking space at the Goose Creek Golf Club in Leesburg, Virginia. He got out of the car, shut the door, and had walked twenty yards before he remembered that he hadn't locked the car. He went back to the car, *jammed* down the knob to lock the door, then slammed the door harder than necessary. It bugged him, particularly this morning, that his Volvo was so damn old that it didn't have one of those cool little beeper things to lock the doors.

On his way into work DeMarco had taken a detour to a used car dealership in Arlington. He'd passed by the place a couple of days ago and had seen a silver BMW Z3 sitting on the corner of the lot, posed like a work of art. The car had sixty-four thousand miles on the odometer, the leather seats were sun-faded, and DeMarco wasn't sure he could afford it—but he wanted a convertible and he was sick to death of his Swedish box on wheels. He had just started to dicker with the salesman when Mahoney's secretary called and told him that Mahoney wanted him down at Goose Creek before he teed off at nine.

He found Mahoney on the practice green, about to attempt an eight-foot putt. DeMarco watched in silence as Mahoney squared his big body over the ball, took in a breath, and stroked the ball. He hit it straight but too hard, and the ball rimmed the cup and shot off perpendicular to its original vector.

"Son of a bitch," Mahoney muttered. "Greens're fast today."

Yeah right, DeMarco thought, *like they waxed the grass just before you got here.*

Mahoney was almost six feet tall and broad across the chest and back and butt. A substantial, hard gut gave balance to his body. He was in his sixties; his hair was white and full; his features all large and well formed; and his eyes were the watery, red-veined blue of a heavy drinker. He dropped another ball onto the grass.

"The guy I want you to meet," Mahoney said, looking down at the ball, "will be here in a minute. He just went up to the clubhouse to get us some beer." Mahoney stroked the ball smoothly and this one dropped in. "Now that's better," he said.

DeMarco knew Mahoney had been a fair athlete in high school—football, basketball, and baseball. He hadn't competed in college because he went into the marines at seventeen, and when he was discharged, his right knee shredded by shrapnel, the only sports he played had involved beer steins and coeds. But even in his sixties he exhibited the hand-eye coordination of an athlete, and in spite of his size, moved lightly on his feet.

"Here he comes now," Mahoney said, dropping a third ball onto the practice green, this one about ten feet from the cup.

Walking toward the green, carrying a small cooler designed to fit in the basket behind the seat of a golf cart, was a man about Mahoney's age. He was five eight, stocky and had a round head with a flat nose and short gray hair. As he got closer, DeMarco could see his eyes: bright blue and surrounded by a million crow's feet from squinting into the sun. He had the eyes of a fighter pilot—which he'd once been. The man was the Secretary of the Navy, Frank Hathaway.

Hathaway, in turn, studied DeMarco, probably wondering what a hard-looking guy in a suit was doing standing on the practice green. DeMarco was five eleven and had broad shoulders, big arms, and a heavy chest. He was a good-looking man—full dark hair, a strong nose, a dimple in a big chin, and blue eyes—but he looked tough, tougher than he really was. A friend had once said that DeMarco looked like a guy you'd see on *The Sopranos,* a guy standing behind Tony while Tony hit someone with a bat. DeMarco hadn't thought that funny.

Hathaway acknowledged DeMarco with a nod then said to Mahoney, "Al's in the parking lot, talking on his cell phone. He'll meet us on the first tee. Andy won't be able to make it though. His secretary called and said there's a fire drill in progress, two Saudis they caught trying to cross in from Canada, up near Buffalo." Hathaway put the cooler on the ground near the golf cart and added, "I wouldn't have Andy's job for all the tea in China."

Andy, DeMarco knew, was General Andrew Banks, Secretary of Homeland Security.

Mahoney stroked the ball toward the hole. It dropped in. "Oh, yeah," Mahoney said. Gesturing with his putter at DeMarco, Mahoney said, "Frank, this is Joe DeMarco, the guy I was telling you about."

Hathaway stuck out a small, hard hand and De-Marco shook it.

"John says you do odd jobs for Congress," Hathaway said to DeMarco.

"Yes, sir," DeMarco said.

John was John Fitzpatrick Mahoney, Speaker of the United States House of Representatives, and DeMarco worked for him—although no organizational chart showed this to be the case. DeMarco had a small office in the subbasement of the Capitol and he performed for Mahoney those tasks the

Speaker preferred not to dole out to his legitimate staff. DeMarco liked to think of himself as Mahoney's personal troubleshooter—but odd-jobs guy was accurate enough.

"There's Al," Mahoney said, pointing his blunt chin at a golf cart driven by a man so tall that his head almost touched the canvas roof of the cart. DeMarco recognized him, too: Albert Farris, a onetime forward for the Portland Trail Blazers and currently the senior senator from Oregon.

Just four guys playing a round of golf: a United States senator, the Speaker of the House, the Secretary of Homeland Security, and the Secretary of the Navy. The fact that it was a weekday morning could mean that something more was going on than a game of golf—or it could mean they all just felt like playing. You never knew.

"Joe, do you golf?" Hathaway said.

"Uh, well . . . ," DeMarco said.

"Yeah, he plays," Mahoney said as he pulled a can of beer from the cooler and popped the top.

"Well since Andy can't make it, why don't you play the front nine with us?" Hathaway said. "You ride with me and I'll tell you what I need while we're playing."

Meaning Hathaway didn't want to delay his game talking to DeMarco about whatever this odd job was.

"I'm not exactly dressed for it," DeMarco said, gesturing at his clothes. DeMarco was wearing a freshly dry-cleaned suit, a white shirt, and his favorite tie. "And I don't have any clubs," he added, already knowing that the only excuse that would work was polio.

"Aw, just take off your jacket," Mahoney said. "It's fuckin' golf, not football. And you can share Frank's clubs. Let's get goin'."

Shit. *And* he was wearing brand-new loafers and they'd cost him a hundred and fifty bucks on sale.

"Yeah, sounds great," DeMarco said. He removed his tie, folded it carefully, and put it in the inside pocket of his suit jacket. He then took off his suit jacket and placed it neatly in the little basket on the golf cart. Immediately after he did so, Mahoney put the beer cooler in the basket, squashing down his jacket.

At the first tee he was introduced to Senator Farris. Farris was six foot seven. He had no excess fat on his body and his arms still looked strong enough to rip a rebound out of an opponent's hands. During his playing days he'd been the team enforcer, the guy they sent into the game to cripple the opposition's star. Farris's best shot had been an elbow to the ribs. He had short dark hair with a small bald spot on the top of his head, big ears, a beaky nose, and an expression on his face that seemed far too serious for someone about to play a friendly game of golf.

Hathaway told Farris that Banks wouldn't be coming and that DeMarco would be riding with him.

"That's good," Farris said, "because I want Mahoney with me so I can keep an eye on him."

"Who's up?" Mahoney said, ignoring Farris's comment.

"I mean it, Mahoney," Farris said. "We're playing by the rules today. No mulligans, no gimme putts, and no, I repeat *no,* free kicks outta the rough."

"Aw," Mahoney said, "you're just sore 'cause I kicked your ass last time."

"You didn't kick my ass!" Farris yelled, then immediately looked around to make sure no one had heard him. Lowering his voice he said, "You won by one friggin' stroke and I still think you moved your ball on the tenth hole."

"Pure bullshit," Mahoney said. "Now get your skinny butt up there and tee off."

Jesus, DeMarco was thinking. *And these guys actually run the damn country.*

Farris's drive found the left side of the fairway two hundred and forty yards from the tee. Mahoney's tee shot was slightly longer, also ending up on the left edge of the fairway. Hathaway, who didn't have the bulk of the other two men, hit his shot a respectable two ten and it landed square in the middle of the fairway, as if the Titleist was a wire-guided missile.

This wasn't good.

DeMarco took a couple of practice swings with the driver he'd selected from Hathaway's bag. The grip on the club didn't feel right; it was too small for his hand, or something. "Uh, you know, I haven't played in a couple of months," DeMarco said.

"Yeah, yeah, come on, come on, take your shot," Mahoney said.

Mahoney was rushing the game and DeMarco suspected that this was a tactic to defeat Farris. Mahoney was never in a hurry. Ever. He did whatever he was doing at a pace that suited him. At his level, the next meeting didn't start until he got there.

DeMarco swung. He made good contact. It felt good. It sounded good. And the ball sliced so far to the right that it ended up on the adjacent fairway.

"Christ, Joe," Mahoney said. "You play that way, we'll be here all day."

As Hathaway drove the golf cart over to find DeMarco's ball, he said, "It's my nephew, my sister's kid. He's an engineer and he works at this navy shipyard. The thing is, he thinks some guys out there are committing fraud."

"What kind of fraud?"

"I'm not too clear on that," Hathaway said. "Something to do with some kind of bogus study and the people doing it overcharging the government. Dave, my nephew, he tried to tell his bosses what was going on, but according to my sister, they blew him off. Which is why she called me, all pissed, demanding I do something. Where the hell'd your ball go, Joe? I know it's in these trees somewhere."

DeMarco topped the ball on his next shot and it went about twenty yards. It was Hathaway's midget-sized irons, that's what the problem was. He hit a third shot and he was finally on the fairway—the right fairway.

"So anyway," Hathaway said, when they were back in the cart, "I'd just like you to check the kid's story out and tell me if he's really onto something. John says you've done stuff like this before and I wouldn't think this would be all that hard."

"I've been involved with whistle-blowers before but, well . . ."

"Yes, Joe?"

"Well, why don't you just call up somebody who works for you and ask them to look into it?"

Before Hathaway could respond there was a commotion across the fairway. Farris was yelling at Mahoney, pointing a long finger at something on the ground at Mahoney's feet. Mahoney had probably claimed that his ball was on the concrete cart path and the rules allowed him to move it. Whether his ball had actually been on the cart path was most likely Farris's issue.

"Jesus," Hathaway said, shaking his head. "Those guys are so damn competitive they take the fun out of the game. And Mahoney, well, I think he does bend the rules a bit."

No shit, DeMarco thought.

"You were asking why I didn't have somebody in my chain of command investigate this thing," Hathaway said. "The problem is, I'm the Secretary of the Navy, Joe. If I told my people to look into it, even if I told them to be discreet, in two hours there'd be twenty NCIS agents running around that shipyard questioning every swinging dick who works there. I don't want to cause that kind of ruckus based on a phone call from my sister. And, well, to tell you the truth, there's something else." Hathaway turned and looked away for a moment as if telling the truth bothered him. "You see, both my sister *and* her kid—it must be genetic—they both tend to be a little, ah, dramatic."

Now this was starting to make sense. Hathaway didn't trust his nephew and if he launched an official investigation based on a tip from a relative and the relative turned out to be wrong, Hathaway would be doubly embarrassed.

"I see," DeMarco said.

"So just check this out quietly. Okay?" Hathaway said. "Go talk to my nephew and see what he says. Interview these guys he's complaining about. If it turns out that there's something to what he's saying, I'll have facts from an independent source—Congress—and *then* I'll have it officially investigated."

"Okay," DeMarco said, not that he really had a choice.

On the sixth hole, Mahoney's and DeMarco's balls were both in the rough, approximately twenty yards apart. Farris was on the other side of the fairway looking for his ball and Hathaway, as usual, was in the center of the fairway.

Mahoney looked down at his ball—it was behind a small tree—then he looked over to where Farris was standing. "C'mere a minute," Mahoney said to DeMarco. DeMarco figured Mahoney wanted to know what he and Hathaway had been talking about.

As DeMarco approached Mahoney, he heard Farris yell, "Hey, Mahoney! What the hell are you doing over there, Mahoney?"

DeMarco looked over at Farris, and when he turned back toward Mahoney, Mahoney's ball was no longer behind the tree. Mahoney had used DeMarco to block Farris's view.

On the putting green, Farris said, "DeMarco, what did Mahoney do back there? Did he kick his ball out?"

"No, sir," DeMarco said.

"Don't you dare lie to me, DeMarco. I'm a United States senator and that fat son of a bitch is only a congressman. Now tell me the truth, son. Did he move his ball?"

"Come on, come on, let's get goin' here," Mahoney said. "And as usual, you're away, Farris."

Farris's ball was about six feet from the cup. As Farris took his putter from his bag, Mahoney said to

Hathaway, "Frank, I'll betcha a beer Farris two-putts this hole. Just like when he choked on that free throw in the playoffs in Chicago."

DeMarco saw the senator's face flush crimson but he didn't say anything. Farris took his position over his ball, adjusted his feet, took in a breath, and stroked the ball. He hit the ball on line, but too hard, and it hit the back of the cup, popped up, and came to rest two feet from the hole. Farris's lips moved in a silent curse and he glared at Mahoney. Mahoney smiled and cleaned off the head of his putter with a grass-stained towel.

When they arrived at the clubhouse after the ninth hole, DeMarco took his rumpled suit jacket out of the golf cart basket. His shirt was soaked through with sweat, there were grass stains on the cuffs of his pants, and his new shoes were scuffed and filled with sand.

"I'll give you a call as soon as I know something, Mr. Secretary," DeMarco said to Hathaway as he tried to smooth the wrinkles out of his jacket.

"Yeah, sure," Hathaway said. He wasn't listening; he was adding up his score. DeMarco could tell that Hathaway wasn't really all that concerned about fraudulent activities taking place at some shipyard. What he had wanted was a way to get his sister off his back, and now, thanks to Mahoney, he had one: Joe DeMarco, hotshot investigator from Congress.

Mahoney, his tongue sticking out the side of his mouth, was also adding up his and Farris's score on the front nine. "You shot a forty-one, Farris," Mahoney said. He paused a minute then said, "I got forty."

"You lemme see that damn card, Mahoney," Farris said.

2

Emma and Christine were sitting in white wicker chairs on Emma's patio drinking mimosas and reading the morning papers. They were a portrait of domestic contentment. Beyond the patio was Emma's English garden. DeMarco knew it was an English garden because Emma had told him so, and an English garden, as far as he could tell, was one in which the gardener planted a thousand long-stemmed flowers in no discernible pattern, all clustered together.

Emma was wearing white linen pants and a blouse that DeMarco thought of as Mexican—an off-the-shoulder number embroidered with small red-and-orange flowers. Christine, a thirty-something blonde who played cello for the National Symphony, wore a tank top and shorts. Christine had the most beautiful legs that DeMarco had ever seen, but since Christine was Emma's lover he made a point of not staring at them. In fact, his eyeballs were getting cramps from the strain of not staring.

Emma was tall and slim. She had regal features and short hair that was either gray or blonde, depending on the light. She was at least ten years older than DeMarco but in much better condition. She looked over the top of her newspaper as DeMarco approached. Her eyes were the color of the water in a Norwegian fjord—and usually just as warm. "Well, you're a mess, Joseph," she said when she saw the condition of his clothes. "What on earth have you been doing?"

"Golfing with the leaders of the free world," DeMarco said.

"Yes, that makes sense," Emma said. "Would you like something to drink? Mimosa, perhaps?"

"Orange juice would be great. No bubbly."

DeMarco took a seat next to Emma at the patio table, a seat where Emma blocked his view of Christine's legs. He thought this seating arrangement most prudent. He and Christine exchanged how-are-yous, then Christine went back to reading her paper, ignoring DeMarco as she usually did. Maybe if he played an oboe she'd find him more interesting.

"What do you know about the navy, Emma?" DeMarco asked.

"A lot, most of which I'd just as soon forget," Emma said.

DeMarco had known this before he asked the question. Although she never discussed it, Emma had worked for the Defense Intelligence Agency and she had worked at a level where the word "classified" didn't come close to defining the degree of secrecy that had applied to her activities. She claimed to have retired from the agency a few years ago, but DeMarco wasn't certain that this was really the case. Emma was the most enigmatic person he'd ever encountered—and she delighted in being so.

"How 'bout navy shipyards?" DeMarco asked.

"A little," Emma said. "Now would you like to tell me why you're asking silly questions?"

DeMarco told her about Frank Hathaway's problem and asked her a few questions about shipyards and the people who worked in them.

"I didn't know the navy had its own shipyards," DeMarco said.

"The navy operates four major shipyards in this country," Emma said in her most pedantic tone. "Most of the employees are civil service and their primary function is to overhaul and refuel nuclear-powered warships."

"Well I'll be damned," DeMarco said.

"Most assuredly," Emma muttered and poured another mimosa for herself and Christine. These girls were going to have a pretty good buzz on by lunchtime, DeMarco was thinking.

"Why's Mahoney loaning you to Hathaway for this thing anyway?" Emma asked as she handed Christine a glass.

"I dunno," DeMarco said. "He plays golf with the guy; maybe they're pals. But more than likely he wants something out of the navy for his district and figures doing Hathaway a favor can't hurt. With Mahoney, you never know. A man who drinks beer at nine in the morning is hard to predict."

"Humph," Emma said, the sound reflecting her opinion of Mahoney. "What shipyard does this engineer work at, by the way? The one in Norfolk?"

"No," DeMarco said. "One out in someplace called Bremerton, near Seattle."

When DeMarco said "Seattle," Christine's pretty blond head popped up from behind the newspaper she'd been reading. "Seattle," she said to Emma. There was a twinkle in her eyes and DeMarco could imagine what she had looked like at the age of twelve, tormenting her younger brother.

Emma smiled at her lover then said to DeMarco, "Joe, considering my vast knowledge of all things military and your limited knowledge of all things in general, I believe I should go to Bremerton with you."

DeMarco met Emma a few years ago by saving her life. Luck and timing had more to do with

the outcome of the event than any heroics on De-
Marco's part, but since that day she occasionally
helped DeMarco with his assignments. She would
provide advice, and if needed, access to various illicit experts—hackers, electronic eavesdroppers, and,
once, a safecracker—all people connected in some
way to the shadow world of the DIA. On rare occasions she'd personally assist him, but DeMarco
usually had to grovel a bit before she'd help—and
yet here she was volunteering.

"What's going on?" DeMarco said.

"It just so happens that Christine's symphony
is playing in Seattle for a couple of days, starting
the day after tomorrow," Emma said, patting one of
Christine's perfect thighs.

"Ah," DeMarco said, understanding immediately.
If Emma helped DeMarco, the Speaker's budget
would pick up the tab for her trip to Seattle. Emma
was fairly wealthy but she was also a bit of a cheap-
skate. Maybe that's why she was wealthy.

3

Carmody was at the rendezvous point at exactly eight p.m. This time the woman had picked a little-used lakeside picnic area fifteen miles from Bremerton. She picked a different place every time they met.

He knew he'd have to wait at least twenty minutes, maybe longer. She was already here, somewhere, but she'd be watching to make sure Carmody hadn't been followed. Half an hour later he saw her. She materialized out of a small stand of trees on his right-hand side and began to walk toward him. She was dressed in black—black jeans, a long-sleeved black T-shirt, black Nikes—and carried a shoulder bag. She was tall and lithe and she moved quickly but gracefully. When she entered his car, she didn't greet Carmody.

She unzipped the shoulder bag, took out a laptop computer, and turned it on.

The woman's hair was dark, cut short and spiky, the style as edgy as her personality. Carmody figured she was about forty, though it was hard to be certain. She didn't have a single wrinkle on her face and the reason for this, Carmody believed, was because she was the most unemotional person he had ever encountered. Her face never changed expression. He had never, ever seen her smile.

The laptop ready, she finally spoke to Carmody. "Give them to me," she said.

Carmody reached beneath the driver's seat and took out a flat plastic case holding an unlabeled compact disc. He handed it to her.

"Just one?" she said.

"Yeah."

She started to say something but checked herself. She put the CD into the laptop's drive. When the document opened, she scrolled down a few pages, stopped and read the words on the screen, then scrolled down a few more pages. She did this for about ten minutes, never speaking. She didn't examine the entire document, that would have taken too long, but she looked at enough of it to satisfy herself. She finally shut down the laptop and returned it to her shoulder bag.

"You have to do better than this, Carmody," she said. "In a month, you've only delivered seven items."

"We have to be careful," Carmody said. "And sometimes the material you want just isn't available, somebody else is using it, so we have to wait."

The woman's eyes locked on to Carmody's. Her eyes were black and they were the coldest, most lifeless eyes that Carmody had ever seen in either a man or a woman, eyes completely devoid of warmth and humor and humanity. Carmody doubted that she had been born with eyes like that; something in her life had caused them to be that way.

"Carmody, do you understand what's at stake here?" she said.

That wasn't really a question—it was a threat.

"Yeah, I understand," Carmody said. His big hands were gripping the steering wheel so tightly his knuckles were white. And she noticed.

Carmody watched as she walked across the grass and disappeared once again into the trees, back into the night she had come from.

4

Emma caught her flight to Seattle out of Dulles International Airport. She chose this airport not only so she could fly with Christine and the orchestra but also because from Dulles you could get a nonstop flight to Seattle. DeMarco didn't like flying out of Dulles because the airport was thirty miles from his house. Reagan National, on the other hand, was just a ten-minute cab ride away. He would have to change planes in Chicago and his flight would take an hour longer than Emma's, but if you added up total travel time, *door-to-door* travel time, his arithmetic said he was making the wiser choice.

He didn't.

His flight boarded right on schedule at nine a.m. then sat on the runway for two hours awaiting the installation of some malfunctioning part. DeMarco didn't know anything about airplanes but when the pilot explained the purpose of the part, it didn't sound terribly significant—like it was the redundant backup gizmo to the backup gizmo, the aeronautical equivalent of the seat belt indicator in your car not working.

Naturally, since his flight left Washington two hours behind schedule, he missed his connecting flight in Chicago and arrived in Seattle at three a.m. instead of five that evening as originally planned. He then had to drive another hour to reach Bremerton. Consequently he was tired and not in the best of moods the next day as he and Emma waited for Dave Whitfield, Frank Hathaway's nephew.

Whitfield had agreed to meet them in the bar of the motel where DeMarco was staying, a place that overlooked a quiet, tree-lined inlet called Oyster Bay. Emma was staying in a much more expensive establishment in Seattle with Christine. While they waited for Whitfield, Emma informed DeMarco that her trip from the East Coast had been delightful: an upgrade to first class, a good movie, and nothing but tall winds all the way. Emma annoyed him.

Dave Whitfield entered the bar as Emma was talking. Frank Hathaway had referred to his nephew as a "kid" but Whitfield appeared to be in his late thirties, a kid only from Hathaway's perspective. He was a tall, loose-jointed man; his hair was wispy blond and already fleeing his head; and he wore wire-rim glasses with square frames over intense brown eyes.

Whitfield was impressed with DeMarco's congressional identification. He was impressed—but he wasn't happy. "Man, I can't believe you're talking to me," he said. "I mean I didn't want *this* to happen. I just thought my uncle would, you know, call a few people."

"Your uncle is the Secretary of the Navy," DeMarco said.

"Yeah, I know, but sheesh. I could get in trouble for this. You guys should be talking to shipyard management, not me."

"Relax, Dave," Emma said. "We just want a little background information from you so that when we do talk to management we'll have something specific to ask. We won't even mention your name." Before Whitfield could say anything else, Emma said, "Would you like a beer?"

"Yeah, sure, I guess," Whitfield said, surprised that a government investigator would offer him a drink.

After Whitfield had gotten his beer, Emma eased him along by saying, "Why don't you tell us what you do. Let's start there."

"I'm an instructor," Whitfield said. "I—"

"Your uncle said you were an engineer," DeMarco said.

"I am. I'm a nuclear engineer. And I'm an instructor. Basically what I do is teach the new engineers how the reactor plants in the ships work."

"That's good," Emma said. "So now why don't you tell us about these concerns you have." Emma kept speaking to Whitfield in this low, soothing voice, as if he was some skittish, balding horse. DeMarco found her talking this way unnatural; Emma rarely tried to soothe.

"Okay," Whitfield said, "because somebody needs to look into this thing. Nobody at the shipyard believes me."

"So what's the problem?" DeMarco said impatiently.

"It's these two guys I used to work with. They worked at the shipyard about twenty-five years and then took an early out—meaning they retired when they were fifty-two or fifty-three instead of fifty-five. People don't normally do that because they lose a percentage of their retirement pay. Anyway, as soon as they retired, they were hired by this company to do a study on how we train our engineers. For some jobs, the training takes about two years."

"Two years!" DeMarco said.

"We're talking about *reactor plants*," Whitfield said, glaring at DeMarco. "We don't let some kid right out of college run around a nuclear submarine unless he knows what he's doing. Anyway, the company these guys went to work for told the navy—I don't know who—that they could figure out a way to complete the training in half the time for half the cost. Sounds like total bullshit to me, but somebody bought their story."

In other words, DeMarco was thinking, this company had been hired to figure out a way to do Whitfield's job better than he was doing it, meaning Whitfield was probably more than a little biased.

"But the thing is," Whitfield said, "these two guys are a couple of losers."

"Are you saying they're not *qualified* to do this study, and you think this is fraudulent?" Emma said.

"No," Whitfield said. "They're qualified, I guess. They're ex-navy, they were reactor operators on subs, and like I said they worked in the shipyard for more than twenty years. So on paper, they're qualified. But they're just . . . I don't know. *Incompetent.* Before they retired they were always in trouble for something, not paying attention to details, doing sloppy work, not showing up on time. Like I said, losers. It's hard to believe somebody would hire them."

"I'm confused, Dave," Emma said. "What exactly is it that you think they're doing that's illegal."

"I'm not sure."

"What!" DeMarco said.

"Go on, Dave," Emma said, giving DeMarco a settle-down look.

"You see," Whitfield said, "all of a sudden these guys have got gobs of money. One of them just bought a new fishing boat and the other guy, I heard him talking about getting a home-entertainment system that's worth ten grand. And one day I asked one of them how much he was getting paid working for this company. He beats around the bush for a while, but he finally tells me he's getting about twice what he used to make working for the government."

"So that's it?" DeMarco said. "You don't think these two guys oughta be doing this study and they're making more money than you."

"No, damn it, that's not what I'm saying," Whitfield snapped. "I'm saying there's something *funny* going on here. These guys just shouldn't be getting all this money for what they're doing. Something's wrong. And that's not all."

"Yeah?" DeMarco said. "What else is there?"

"They don't *act* like they're reviewing our training program. They ought to be gathering data on class sizes and training costs and reviewing curriculums, that kinda thing. But they don't seem to be doing that. They just seem to sit around a lot, bullshitting, and looking at the reactor plant manuals."

"What are those?" DeMarco said.

"They're manuals that tell you how navy reactor plants work. You understand?"

By now DeMarco thought he had a pretty good sense of Whitfield. He was the type who was *always* outraged by something; he probably called up the mayor's office and wrote passionate letters to the editor every time something got his goat.

"So," DeMarco said, "let me see if I got all this straight. You got a couple of guys you don't think are very good, who have come into some money recently that you can't explain, and they're going about this study all wrong. Is that it?"

"Yeah," Whitfield said. "Something stinks."

"Can you believe that guy?" DeMarco said to Emma after Whitfield had left. "No wonder Hathaway didn't want NCIS talking to him. I mean, did you hear one damn thing that sounded like fraud to you? *Anything?*"

"Take it easy, Joe," Emma said. "You're in a beautiful part of the country. Take a walk. Go for a drive. Tomorrow we'll meet these two people, talk to the company they work for, and get their side of the story. And we'll talk to somebody in shipyard management who's more objective than Whitfield."

Christine was going to be in Seattle for another day with the symphony and DeMarco could tell that Emma—the new, laid-back, take-it-easy Emma—had decided that torturing consultants and shipyard managers would be more fun than sitting around doing nothing.

Emma rose from her chair and said, "I have to get going. I need to catch the next ferry to Seattle to meet Christine in time for dinner."

"And after we question these guys tomorrow and don't find anything illegal going on, then what?" DeMarco said.

"Then you tell Hathaway to tell his sister to tell her son to quit being such a damn crybaby."

After Emma left, DeMarco sat sipping his beer, thinking a little more about Whitfield. He still thought the guy was a whiny flake but Emma was right: he'd worry about Whitfield tomorrow. He looked around the bar. Other than the bartender, he was the only one there. On the television set, a baseball game was playing: the Seattle Mariners versus the Toronto Blue Jays, both teams at the bottom of their respective divisions. Professional bowling was more exciting.

He walked to a supermarket two blocks from the motel, bought half a dozen car magazines, and returned to the motel bar. He'd research the auto market, become an informed consumer. He'd probably still get screwed if he bought the Beemer convertible but he could console himself with the thought that he'd done his homework. He ordered another beer—it must have been his fourth and he was starting to feel like a bloated sumo wrestler—and began to read his magazines.

He concluded that the smart thing to do—the practical thing—would be to buy a Honda or a

Toyota. *Last* year's model. These cars were rated top
of the line in terms of quality and gas mileage and
resale value, and if he could find last year's model
with less than thirty thousand miles on it, he'd be
getting a *practically* brand-new car and shave four or
five thousand off the price of a *really* brand-new car.
Yeah, that made sense. That would be smart.

The problem was he couldn't tell the difference
between a Honda and a Toyota. They looked like
they'd been designed by a computer based solely on
data from wind-tunnel tests. They were about as
sexy as an old lady's bloomers. Beemer Z3. Jaguar.
Mercedes coupe. Porsche. Those cars had va-voom.
They had sex appeal. They were created by *artists,*
not some pencil-necked engineer trying to squeeze
one more mile per gallon out of a friggin' four-
cylinder engine.

"Well, hello there," a very sultry voice said.

Thank you, Jesus, DeMarco thought, and looked
up from his magazine. The lady who had spoken
looked *hard.* The expression "forty miles of bad road"
came immediately to mind. She had crammed a size
fourteen body into a size eight dress, wore a blonde
wig that didn't match the dark mustache over her
upper lip, and her makeup looked as if it had been
applied with a trowel.

DeMarco mumbled something inarticulate,
scooped up his magazines, and headed back to his
room. Why did he always have such bad luck with

women? Why couldn't the old hooker have been a Swedish stewardess or foxy young businesswoman looking for some fun? Why didn't those sorts of fantasies ever come true for him?

Because he drove a Volvo, that's why.

5

———— ◆◆◆ ————

The offices of Carmody and Associates were in Bremerton on the corner of Pacific and Burwell, on the ground floor of a building that housed three other small enterprises: an independent insurance agent, a tax consultant, and a beauty shop with no customers. Emma knocked once on the door, then immediately opened it without waiting for an answer. Two men—sitting at a card table, drinking beer and playing gin—looked up in surprise.

Both men were in their early fifties, and both wore blue jeans and short-sleeved shirts. Pretty casual attire for consultants, DeMarco thought. One of the men was tall, had gray-brown hair in need of a trim, a scraggly mustache, skinny arms, skinny legs, and a small potbelly. The other man was short, almost bald, and had a much larger pot belly. The bald guy also had an anchor tattoo on his right forearm.

Maybe it was the tattoo, but DeMarco had the immediate impression that if these two had been born two hundred years earlier they would have been pirates.

"You need something?" the tall one said.

"Yes," Emma said. "We're doing a review for Congress. We called earlier to set up an appointment but no one returned our phone call. I guess you were just too busy," she said, looking down at the card table.

The tall man looked over at the short man. The short man made eye contact with Emma, a touch of insolence in his eyes, then turned his head toward a partially open door behind him and yelled, "Hey, boss!"

The man who came through the door was big and good-looking: six three, broad shouldered, maybe two hundred and twenty pounds. He wore gray slacks and a blue polo shirt, and his chest and biceps strained against the material of the shirt. The guy worked out. His dark hair was cut short and he had a small scar on his chin. He struck DeMarco as being tough and competent, but more like a cop or a solider than someone you'd hire to study a navy training program.

"It's that lady who called this morning," the bald man said.

The big guy was silent for a moment as he sized up DeMarco and Emma, then he relaxed and smiled. He had an engaging smile. "I'm Phil Carmody," he said, and shook hands with them. "I'm in charge of this little zoo. That's Bill Norton," he said pointing at the short, bald guy. "And that's Ned Mulherin." Mulherin nodded like a friendly puppy; Norton glared.

Carmody didn't invite DeMarco and Emma into his office, which DeMarco found odd. Instead he told Norton to grab a couple of chairs from the office and directed Mulherin to clear the cards and bottles off the card table. DeMarco noticed the way he spoke to his employees, giving curt orders, not bothering to say "please" or "thank you," having no doubt he'd be obeyed immediately. DeMarco had the impression that if Carmody had told his two guys to eat their playing cards, they'd start chewing.

"And in case you're wondering," Carmody said as Mulherin removed the beer bottles from the table, "we only bill the government for the hours we work, and these two were not on the clock."

"Right," Emma said, not bothering to hide her disbelief. DeMarco expected Carmody to protest but he didn't. He just shrugged, obviously not overly concerned about her perception of his billing practices.

When the extra chairs were in place, Carmody said, "You want anything to drink? Coke? Bottled water? Coffee?"

"No," Emma said.

"Okay, then," Carmody said. "So how 'bout showing me some ID."

DeMarco passed Carmody his congressional identification. Emma stared into Carmody's eyes for a moment, then pulled a library card from her wallet and held it up for Carmody to see. She didn't hand him the card. Emma was screwing with Carmody and DeMarco waited for his reaction, but all Carmody did was smile, his lips twitching in amusement. Unlike most people, Carmody wasn't intimidated by Emma; he seemed tickled by her attitude.

"So what can I do for you?" Carmody said.

Before DeMarco could say anything, Emma responded to Carmody's question. Emma had a tendency to assume command whenever she and DeMarco worked together. "A congressman," Emma said, "received a complaint from one of his constituents regarding how much you're charging the navy for the work you're doing."

"You flew out here because of one complaint?" Carmody said. He seemed to find that both astounding and amusing.

Emma ignored the question. "We'd like to understand what you're doing, how much you're billing, how long it will take, that sort of thing."

"That fuckin' Whitfield," Mulherin muttered.

"What did you say?" Carmody said sharply to Mulherin.

"Oh, there's this guy I used to work with and he keeps bitching about how much I'm making. I'll betcha he caused this. I mean, I explained to him—"

"That's enough," Carmody said. DeMarco knew that after they left Carmody was going to have a pointed discussion with Mr. Mulherin. To DeMarco and Emma, Carmody said, "As you probably already know, we're doing a review to streamline a shipyard training program. The current program is expensive and I have, *we* have, some ideas for how to improve it. Get the book, Norton."

Norton dashed into Carmody's office and returned with a three-ring binder. Carmody spent the next fifteen minutes going over the existing training program, what it cost, the curriculum, class sizes, class hours, that sort of thing. DeMarco didn't understand everything Carmody said but based on the questions she asked, Emma seemed to. The one thing DeMarco *did* understand was that as opposed to what Dave Whitfield had led them to believe, Carmody seemed to have acquired exactly the sort of information you'd expect him to have to do his review, and he seemed to know what he was talking about.

"We understand that your guys here," DeMarco said, gesturing toward Mulherin and Norton, "are making a lot more money than they made when they worked in the shipyard."

Carmody shrugged. "So what?" he said. Before DeMarco could respond, he said, "Look, I submitted a bid to get this job, the navy accepted my bid, and I'm paying these guys the going rate. It's not my problem that some yardbird thinks they should be paid less."

"Who awarded you the contract?" Emma asked.

Carmody hesitated, but just for a second. "NAV-SEA," he said.

"Who?" DeMarco said.

"It's not a person," Emma said. "NAVSEA is the Naval Sea Systems Command. A navy headquarters outfit back in D.C."

"Right," Carmody said. "You people could have saved yourself the trip out here. Somebody at NAV-SEA could have given you the same information I just did."

DeMarco wished he had known that before he flew out to Bremerton.

"But who specifically at NAVSEA?" Emma said. "Who's the individual that awarded you the contract?"

"I don't know," Carmody said. "Whoever handles this sort of thing back in Washington, I guess."

Carmody's response had been casual but DeMarco had been looking at his arms when he spoke. Carmody was holding a coffee cup in both hands and when he answered the last question, he squeezed the cup hard enough that the muscles in his forearms jumped. DeMarco would hate to have to arm wrestle this guy.

Emma stared at Carmody for a moment but before she could say anything else, Carmody stood up. "Hey, it's been great talking to you but I have a meeting I have to get to. All I can tell you is that the review we're doing is needed, our billing rates are not out of line, and I was low bidder on the job. If you have any more questions you need to talk to the people back in D.C. who awarded me the contract."

As they walked back toward Emma's rental car, she said, "What do you think?"

DeMarco shrugged. "I don't know. Norton and Mulherin didn't exactly strike me as rocket scientists but the study sounds legit, and as for Carmody, he seems pretty sharp."

"Yes, he does," Emma said. She paused before she added, "He reminds me of mercenaries I've known."

6

Carmody watched through the window as DeMarco and Emma walked away, then turned and stared at Mulherin. Mulherin looked like a dog waiting to be kicked, and Carmody definitely felt like kicking him. Goddamnit, what an idiot. But he'd deal with Mulherin later.

He went into his office and closed the door and took a seat at his desk. He put his right hand on the phone but he didn't pick it up.

He wasn't worried about the questions they had asked. There was nothing wrong with his contract or what he was charging the government or anything else. No, it wasn't the questions that worried him—it was the people asking the questions.

First, if somebody had really written their con-gressman to complain about his contract, the con-gressman would have handed off the complaint to the GAO or the Naval Inspector General. He wouldn't have sent congressional staffers out here to deal with it.

And then there was DeMarco. There was some-thing about him, a toughness to him, that didn't match his mission. Carinody had been exposed to House staff people in the past and they were usually eager young kids, not some hard case like DeMarco. DeMarco's ID had looked legit so he might be some kind of political operator—but he sure as hell wasn't a guy you sent out to check on a nickel-and-dime navy contract.

But the woman was the real problem. Carmody had met her once before, ten or twelve years ago. She was someone you didn't forget. He didn't remember her name though—and that little game she'd played with the library card had kept him from finding it out—but he knew *what* she was even if he didn't know *who* she was. Fortunately, she hadn't recog-nized him, which wasn't surprising considering the conditions under which they'd met. But whether she recognized him or not, the fact that she was here could mean real trouble.

His hand was still resting on the phone. He knew he should make the call. The problem was that he could never predict how she was going to react. Or overreact. He finally took his hand off the phone. He'd wait. If they came back again and if they asked different questions, then he'd call her.

Goddamnit. He felt like killing Mulherin.

7

DeMarco and Emma were having lunch, Emma picking at a tuna salad while DeMarco consumed a cheeseburger the size of a catcher's mitt.

The navy dominated the city of Bremerton and the county in which it was located. In addition to the shipyard in Bremerton, which employed about ten thousand people, there was the Naval Submarine Base located in Bangor, Washington, and the Undersea Warfare Center in Keyport, Washington. The place where they were dining reflected the community's support—and financial dependence—on the navy. The walls were covered with photographs of submarines bursting from the water and fighters taking off from the decks of aircraft carriers. Two tables away from Emma and DeMarco sat a gentleman who wore a dark blue baseball cap emblazoned with the words U.S. NAVY RETIRED—a totally redundant statement as the man looked old enough to have sailed with John Paul Jones.

"Why would Carmody lie about not knowing the person who had awarded his contract?" DeMarco said.

"So you thought so, too," Emma said.

"Yeah. But why's he lying?"

"I'm not sure."

They sat there chewing in silence for a minute before DeMarco said, "Maybe he wasn't really the low bidder and he gave a kickback to the guy who awarded him the contract. So maybe Whitfield's right."

"I don't know," Emma said. "I suppose that's possible, but the bidding process is usually pretty transparent."

"Or maybe Carmody's just being a prick," DeMarco said. "Since he didn't give us a name, he knows that's going to cause us to waste time tracking down the contract guy, and that'll be time we don't spend looking at him."

"Yeah, but he could be doing that," Emma said, "even if everything's on the up-and-up, just to get us out of his hair." Emma pushed aside her salad, only half of it gone. No wonder the woman never gained an ounce. "At any rate," she said, "we—meaning *you*—need to find out who awarded Carmody's contract. I'd suggest you start by—"

Emma was interrupted by the ringing of De-Marco's cell phone.

"Hello," DeMarco said.

"Hey," Mahoney said, sounding abnormally cheerful. "I'm flyin' out there. In fact I'm on the plane right now."

Thanks to space-age technology, Mahoney could now jerk DeMarco's chain from thirty thousand feet.

"Why are you coming here?" DeMarco said.

"Ah, there's a guy out there we're runnin' against the Republican in the fourth district. The Republican's been there forever so Norm and I are gonna give a couple speeches tonight, pry open some wallets, give our guy a boost. But after that . . ."

"Norm?" DeMarco said.

"Norm Dicks, Joe. The congressman from the Sixth. You're right there in his backyard."

DeMarco knew Norm Dicks; he liked the guy. Unlike Mahoney, he was a straight shooter.

"Anyway," Mahoney was saying, "tonight I'll make a speech, but in the morning, I'm gonna go catch a salmon."

"What?"

"There's a guy out there, a contributor, and he's gonna take me out on his boat. We'll do a little business . . ."

But not much.

". . . and then I'll catch me a great big fish. He said he hooked into a fifty-pound king last week."

"Really," DeMarco said.

"Yeah," Mahoney said. "So you need to pick me up tomorrow morning at my hotel. Get the details from Mavis. A fifty pound king, Joe, can you believe it!" Mahoney hung up.

"Great," DeMarco muttered as he clipped his cell phone back onto his belt.

"What?" Emma said.

"That was Mahoney. He's coming out here to go fishing and I have to play chauffeur tomorrow."

Emma shrugged, the gesture meaning: that's what you get for working for Mahoney.

"Maybe, uh, you could start looking for this contract guy while I'm taking care of Mahoney."

Emma arched an eyebrow. This time the silent message was that she was more likely to marry Burt Reynolds.

"I think tomorrow, while you're drivin' Mr. Daisy," Emma said, "Christine and I will pay a visit to a spa near Snoqualmie Falls. They do seaweed facials and give hot rock massages. This thing with Dave Whitfield can definitely wait a day."

DeMarco didn't know what a hot rock massage was, but he had an immediate, vivid image of Christine lying bareassed on a massage table, her legs and butt glistening with baby oil.

8

---◆◆◆---

DeMarco was a walking corpse.

Mahoney's secretary had told him to pick up Mahoney at six a.m. at the Sheraton in downtown Seattle, which meant that DeMarco had to leave Bremerton at four thirty to get there on time. When DeMarco said that he couldn't believe that the Speaker would be up at that hour, Mavis had responded: "I know. He just works too hard sometimes." Mahoney had everybody fooled.

But at six on the nose, Mahoney walked into the lobby with a big grin on his Irish face. He looked like a husky ten-year-old going on his first fishing trip. He wore Bermuda shorts that reached his dimpled knees, a sun-faded polo shirt stretched tight over his gut, and scuffed tennis shoes with baggy white socks. On his big head sat a Boston Red Sox baseball cap and he was carrying a nylon bag that DeMarco assumed contained whatever else he needed for the trip: sun-block, a jacket—and a fifth of bourbon in case they didn't have his brand on board.

The boat taking Mahoney fishing was moored at a marina on Shilshoe Bay. It was sixty feet long and had more antennae on the bridge than a navy destroyer. The owner of the boat was a very rich guy, Alex somebody, who had invented cell phones or cell-phone towers or maybe it was cell-phone cases. DeMarco hadn't been listening when Mahoney told him. In addition to the rich guy there was a man who skippered the boat and a deckhand whose only function was to cater to Mahoney's every need.

DeMarco turned to leave after he had handed Mahoney's bag up to the deckhand, but Mahoney said, "Where you going? You're coming, too. You need to tell me what you found out on this thing with Hathaway's nephew."

Not again, DeMarco thought. This was just like the golf game. He wasn't wearing a suit today—he was dressed casually in a short-sleeved shirt, khaki pants, and Top-Siders—but they weren't clothes he wanted to get fish guts all over. Plus he didn't have a hat to keep the sun off his head or a windbreaker in case it got chilly out on the water. He told Mahoney this.

"Ah, don't worry about it. They probably got stuff here on the boat you can use. Don't you, Alex?" Mahoney said to the rich guy.

"Oh, I'm sure we do," Alex said.

DeMarco could tell that Alex didn't have a clue.

———❧———

It took an hour to transit from the marina to the area where the fish supposedly were. DeMarco was enjoying the ride, looking at the Olympic Mountains to the west, when his cell phone rang.

"Mr. DeMarco, it's Dave Whit . . ."

The cell-phone signal was weak and DeMarco couldn't hear half of what Whitfield was saying.

"What?" DeMarco shouted.

"It's Dave Whit . . . those two guys . . . I was . . ."

"Dave, I can't hear you," DeMarco yelled into his phone.

"I said, I think . . .

"Dave! I can't hear you!" DeMarco shouted.

Then DeMarco could hear nothing but dead air and he hung up.

The deckhand said to DeMarco, "If you need to talk to that guy you can go up to the bridge and use one of Alex's phones. He's got stuff up there that can reach the moon."

"Nah, that's okay," DeMarco said. "I'll just call him after we get back to the marina." He doubted if Whitfield had anything new to tell him, and at any rate, there wasn't much he could do while stuck on a boat in the middle of Puget Sound.

DeMarco would spend a lot of time in the days to come regretting that decision.

———◆◆◆———

The deckhand had set up three poles in three downriggers and the downriggers were set for three different depths to triple Mahoney's chances of catching a salmon.

"Now if one of them hits," the deckhand said to Mahoney, "you gotta set the hook. We're using barbless hooks, and if you don't set it right, the hook's gonna come right outta the fish's mouth." He showed Mahoney the motion he was looking for.

"Yeah, yeah," Mahoney said. "I've fished before. And why are we usin' barbless hooks, anyway?"

"It's the law," the deckhand said.

"Well, shit, who's gonna know?" Mahoney said.

After half an hour of trolling, Mahoney said, "Where the hell are the damn salmon? I thought you said there were fish out here, Alex."

Alex, the rich guy, didn't hear him; he was on a phone, making more money.

"We'll get one, sir, don't worry," the deckhand said. "The fish-finder's showing all kinds of fish down there. We just gotta figure out what they're hittin' on." Before Mahoney could complain further, the deckhand said. "Would you like another beer?"

As Mahoney waited impatiently to catch a fish, DeMarco briefed him on what he and Emma had learned in Bremerton. Mahoney's only response had been a disinterested shrug and the comment: "The whole thing sounds pretty chicken shit to me."

Five minutes later a salmon hit and the dialogue between Mahoney and the deckhand went something like this:

Mahoney: "Holy shit! I got the bastard."

Deckhand: "Keep your tip up. Keep the tip up!"

Mahoney: "Son of a bitch! It's a big one. Son of a bitch!"

Deckhand: "Loosen your drag. Loosen your drag! You're gonna lose him."

Mahoney: "Aw, fuck! Did I lose him? Did I lose him?"

Deckhand: "No, he's running toward us. Reel, reel! Reel faster!"

Mahoney fought the fish for twenty minutes. His face turned an unhealthy shade of purple as he reeled, and DeMarco could see the tendons popping out on his big freckled forearms. He finally got the fish up to the side of the boat. It was big and still had a lot of fight left in it. Mahoney was so excited that he was cursing incoherently at this point, and just as the deckhand was netting the fish, he gave a jerk on the line—and the fish came off the hook. Fortunately, the deckhand was good and already had the net under the fish. As the hook popped out of the salmon's mouth, the deck hand swung the net upward, enveloping the fish in nylon mesh. The salmon hit the deck of the boat with a wet flop and thrashed around until the deckhand smacked it several times with a billy club—splattering blood all over DeMarco's khaki pants.

A really ugly ending to the life of a beautiful fish, DeMarco thought.

"I got him!" Mahoney screamed, two arms in the air like he'd just scored a touchdown.

The deckhand looked over at Mahoney like he wanted to kill him. He had almost gone overboard netting the fish, and the way he was holding his back it looked as if he'd strained something getting the salmon into the boat.

While Mahoney celebrated his victory with his fifth beer of the day—it was ten a.m.—DeMarco watched the deckhand weigh the fish. The scale read forty-two pounds.

"Fifty-two pounds!" the deckhand called out to Mahoney and winked at DeMarco.

Alex asked Mahoney if he'd like to catch another one.

"Nah," Mahoney said. "One's enough."

Now this surprised DeMarco. Mahoney, he always figured, came from the same stock as those who had almost made the buffalo extinct.

"What about you, Mr. DeMarco?" Alex said. "Would you like to catch one?" DeMarco figured Alex wasn't being nice, he just wanted to spend more time bending Mahoney's ear. And since DeMarco's pants were already a mess, why not?

"Sure," DeMarco said at the same time Mahoney said, "We don't have time. I gotta plane to catch. I'm meetin' with the president tonight."

Even the rich guy seemed impressed by that.

On the way back to the marina, Mahoney and Alex sat in the cabin, Alex looking serious as they talked. Mahoney kept nodding his head, an equally serious expression on his face. Alex didn't know it, but Mahoney wasn't listening to a word he said. Mahoney had the ability to pretend to be intently engaged in a conversation with a potential contributor while his mind played back the fish—or the woman—he'd just landed.

Mahoney made arrangements with the deckhand to ship his *fifty-five* pound salmon back to D.C. The fish had miraculously gained three pounds in the last hour; God knows what size it would be by the time Mahoney reached the East Coast. As DeMarco was driving Mahoney to the airport, DeMarco's cell phone rang again. He wondered if it was Dave Whitfield calling back. It wasn't, it was Emma.

"Joe," she said, "Dave Whitfield's been killed."

"Oh, Christ," DeMarco said.

"What?" Mahoney said, hearing DeMarco's tone of voice.

"He had a four-year-old son, Joe," Emma said.

DeMarco said good-bye to Emma and turned to tell Mahoney the news but at that moment Mahoney's cell phone rang. It was the Secretary of the Navy, Frank Hathaway.

9

"Sir," the marine said, "I need to check that bag."

Norton couldn't believe it. Tonight, of all nights. They didn't usually check things going *out* the gates, and if he had left at the same time all the other day-shift workers had, they never would have stopped him. But he was going out late because of what Carmody had told him to do—and because of what had happened today—and now the damn marine at the gate, a nineteen-year-old kid bored out of his skull, had decided to fuck with him.

"Uh, yeah sure," Norton said. There was no point arguing with the marine; you *can't* argue with marines. He put his backpack on the little table near the gate and unconsciously hitched up his pants. When he realized what he was doing, he stopped immediately. He had to get a grip on himself.

"Would you please open the bag, sir," the marine said.

Norton opened the backpack and the marine peered inside. Inside the backpack was a paperback book, a pair of sunglasses, a brown bag containing the remains of Norton's lunch, and a chessboard. The marine removed the lunch bag from the backpack, peered inside, then set it aside. Then he reached for the chessboard.

Oh please, God, Norton thought.

The marine hefted the chessboard in his hand. "This thing's pretty heavy," he said. "What's it made out of?"

Before Norton could answer, a voice behind him said, "You search that bastard good, Corporal. He works for me and I want to make sure he's not stealing me blind."

Carmody placed a big hand on the back of Norton's neck and gave it a squeeze like he was being friendly. The squeeze wasn't friendly.

To the marine, Carmody said, "In fact, you oughta put on some gloves, son, and probe this boy's orifices. The only problem is, he might enjoy it."

The young marine smiled—he couldn't stop himself—then quickly rearranged his face back into a serious expression.

"Sir," he said to Carmody, "if you could please step . . ."

Carmody glanced at the marine's name tag. "Heesacker," he said. "Did you have an older brother, flew choppers in Iraq in '92?"

"Uh, no, sir," the marine said.

"Well, you're the spittin' image of a guy named Heesacker I knew over there."

"You were in the corps, sir?" the marine said.

Norton saw the marine was still holding the damn chessboard.

"Nah," Carmody said. "SEALs."

The young marine almost saluted. SEALs were his gods; a SEAL was what he wanted to be.

The marine shoved the chessboard back into Norton's backpack and replaced the lunch bag he'd removed. To Norton, he said, "You have a good evening, sir." Looking directly into Carmody's eyes, he added, "Both of you."

Carmody and Norton walked together for a block, neither man speaking. Norton was afraid to speak. When they reached the lot where Norton's car was parked, Carmody said, "Did you get them?"

"Yeah," Norton said, and he reached into the back of his baggy pants and pulled out two square plastic cases containing unlabeled CDs.

"Give me the laptop, too," Carmody said.

Norton quickly unzipped his backpack and handed the chessboard to Carmody.

Carmody stared at Norton for a second, and then he put his face close to Norton's and said very softly, "Somebody died today because you fucked up. The next time you fuck up, guess who's gonna die?"

———— ◆◆◆ ————

Carmody stood in the center of an old steel bridge called the Manette Bridge. From where he was standing he could see the shipyard less than a mile away. The drydocks were lit by banks of lights—like those used for night games in old ballparks—so work could proceed around the clock.

Carmody looked around, made sure there were no cars coming from either direction, and dropped the chessboard into the water below him. He had thought about just hiding the laptop but had decided not to take the risk. He'd get another when they needed one, which probably wouldn't be for quite a while.

He placed his forearms on the bridge rail and looked down into the water.

This whole thing was coming apart; it was time to shut it down. But he knew she wouldn't do that. He looked at his watch. He had to get going. The rendezvous was in less than two hours.

———— ◆◆◆ ————

She made him drive a long way from Bremerton for the meeting, past Green Mountain, up a winding road that changed from pavement to gravel and ended at a clear-cut section of forest surrounded by a lonely ring of still-standing trees. She also kept him waiting longer than normal before she approached his car, taking twice as much time to make sure he hadn't been followed.

She entered the car and he was surprised at the way she was dressed. She normally wore the sort of clothes a cat burglar would wear, dark jeans and a long-sleeved dark T-shirt. But tonight she was wearing a low-cut black cocktail dress, a dress which showed off very good legs. On her feet were sexy, impractical high heels that must have been tough to walk in in the area where they were parked. She even had on perfume. The rendezvous must have caused her to interrupt or cancel whatever plans she'd had for the evening, but Carmody couldn't imagine her having a social life. He had no idea what she did when they were apart; he had always thought of her as a beautiful vampire lying in a coffin waiting until the sun disappeared.

As usual she began without any sort of greeting. "What will you do now?" she said.

"Wait. Just lay back and wait."

She stared at him a moment then nodded.

"Did he talk to anyone before he left the shipyard?"

"I don't know."

"You have to control those fools," she said.

"Hey! I didn't recruit them," Carmody said.

"They're your responsibility," she snapped.

She was right about that.

"How long do you think we'll have to wait?"

Carmody shrugged. "Maybe a month."

She paused a beat then nodded. One thing Carmody liked about her—maybe the only thing—is that she didn't waste time nagging at him, telling him that she wasn't happy with the delay.

Apparently having nothing more to ask him, or further instructions to give him, she opened the door and started to leave the car.

"There's something else you need to know," Carmody said.

10

Dave Whitfield had been stabbed to death.

He had called DeMarco's cell phone at exactly 8:10 a.m. and had left the shipyard twenty-eight minutes later. No one knew for sure why he had left when he did or where he was going, but DeMarco had an idea. DeMarco figured that when Whitfield had not been able to communicate with him by cell phone when he was on the fishing boat, Whitfield had left the shipyard to go to DeMarco's motel, thinking that at that hour DeMarco might still be there, if not in his room, then maybe having breakfast.

Whitfield's car had been parked in a small lot three blocks from the shipyard. The lot had space for six or seven cars, and to reach the lot, Whitfield had to walk down an alley. The parking lot itself was the backyard of a private home; the home owner had concluded long ago that charging shipyard workers eight bucks a day for parking was more enjoyable than mowing a lawn. The parking lot was visible only to people walking down the alley and to the owner of the lot if he happened to be looking out one of his back windows.

Whitfield had been killed in the parking lot, and based on the temperature of his liver and other factors that came to light later, the time of death was established at approximately nine a.m. He had been stabbed once and the weapon used, presumably a long-bladed knife, had entered his rib cage, slid between his ribs, and severed his aorta. After he was killed, his wallet and watch were taken and his body was shoved under his car. The body wasn't discovered until noon when another shipyard worker went to the parking lot during his lunch break.

In the two days following the killing, Frank Hathaway showed exactly how much muscle an angry Secretary of the Navy could flex. A squad of investigators from NCIS descended on the shipyard like winged furies and a large navy poker was jammed up the local police chief's ass to prod him into action. Two FBI agents were also diverted from the Bureau's Seattle office to Bremerton. The FBI's jurisdiction was questionable as the killing had occurred on city—vice federal—property, but since

Hathaway was the one demanding action they had decided to engage.

DeMarco and Emma were interviewed several times. As they had no reason not to cooperate they told the assorted groups of cops what they knew. The last phone call DeMarco had received from Whitfield was naturally of particular interest but the only thing DeMarco could tell them was that he thought Whitfield had been talking about Norton and Mulherin, but nothing Whitfield had said, or that DeMarco had heard over the poor connection, had led him to conclude that Whitfield had discovered anything that would be a motive for murder.

"Look," DeMarco told the investigators, "this whole thing with Whitfield was him thinking these two guys were doing a shitty job and making more money than they should have. I don't know why he called me, but we didn't find any evidence that anything illegal was going on, and we sure as hell didn't find anything worth killing somebody over."

Norton, Mulherin, and Carmody were interrogated by navy and federal investigators and by city detectives. Alibis were asked for and verified. Whitfield's coworkers and neighbors were questioned, evidence was collected from the scene of the crime, and the neighborhood where Whitfield had been killed was canvassed by teams of cynical cops.

Norton and Mulherin were cleared almost immediately. At the time of Whitfield's death, they had been inside the shipyard and were seen by approximately twenty people. On top of alibis provided by multiple eyewitnesses, the two men also had an electronic alibi: to enter or exit the shipyard, employees had to swipe their badges through bar-code readers installed at all the shipyard gates. The bar-code readers provided the exact time Whitfield had left the shipyard and verified that Mulherin and Norton had entered the shipyard at 7:00 a.m. and remained there all day, Mulherin leaving at 3:59 p.m. and Norton at 5:30 p.m.

Phil Carmody was also eliminated as a murder suspect, although his alibi was not as airtight as that of his employees. He had been having breakfast at the time of the killing and the restaurant where he had eaten was only five minutes by car from the parking lot where Dave Whitfield had died. But for Carmody to have killed Whitfield, he would have to have been missing from the restaurant for almost fifteen minutes—five minutes to get to the parking lot, two or three minutes to kill Whitfield and hide his body, and five minutes to get back to the restaurant. The waitress who had waited on Carmody didn't think there was any fifteen-minute period when he was out of her sight, and she remembered refilling his coffee cup at least twice while he was eating. The waitress did say that Carmody had been seated near the rear exit of the restaurant.

Mahoney, as DeMarco had expected, irrationally blamed him for Whitfield's death.

"What the fuck did you do, Joe?" Mahoney had screamed. "Goddamnit, all Hathaway wanted was for you to check out some pissant navy contract thing, and the next thing you know, his nephew's dead. You musta done something."

DeMarco wasn't sure that he'd done anything to cause Whitfield's death, but not returning Whitfield's phone call that morning had been a mistake. As he had told the cops, he had no *facts* to connect Whitfield's death with Norton's and Mulherin's activities, but the timing of the phone call was disturbing. DeMarco couldn't leave Bremerton until he could explain why Dave Whitfield had been killed.

Emma, who could have left had she wanted to, also decided to stay. Something was bothering her— something other than the fact that Dave Whitfield had been killed—but she wouldn't tell DeMarco what it was.

Forty-eight hours after Dave Whitfield died, the Bremerton cops arrested a man for his murder.

II

Jerry Brunstad, Bremerton's chief of police, was a paunchy man with a sunburned face, too much dyed-black hair, and long sideburns; DeMarco thought he looked like an Elvis impersonator with a badge. Brunstad's blue uniform shirt was snug across his belly and when he raised his right arm to use the pointer, a shirttail came out the back of his pants. He was using the pointer to direct attention to a white board that listed the evidence his men had acquired on Dave Whitfield's killer. His audience consisted of seven people: Richard Miller, who was in charge of security at the shipyard; two FBI agents; two NCIS agents; and Emma and DeMarco. It had taken a phone call from the Speaker's office for Emma and DeMarco to be allowed to attend the briefing.

According to Chief Brunstad, Whitfield had been murdered by a man named Thomas "Cowboy" Conran. Conran was an easily recognizable, thirty-nine-year-old street person. He was six foot four, scarecrow thin, and always wore a battered black cowboy hat pulled down low on his forehead, making him look like a demented, undernourished Tim McGraw. Conran had been diagnosed as a schizophrenic in his teens and when he was off his meds—which was almost all the time—was known to act in an irrational, often violent manner.

"Shipyard badge readers," Brunstad said, "recorded Whitfield going out the State Street gate at 8:38 and it takes about ten minutes to walk from the gate to where his car was parked. We walked the route. A witness saw Cowboy walking down the alley at 8:55. The witness said he was sure of the time because he was waiting for a buddy to pick him up and his buddy was late. From the window of his house, the witness couldn't see the parking lot where Whitfield was killed, but he could see Cowboy leaving the alley."

"Who was the witness?" an FBI agent asked. The agent was a woman with short dark hair, warm brown eyes, and a trim figure. She was as cute as a button, DeMarco thought, and she had outstanding ankles. And the lady agent had noticed DeMarco, too. When she first came into the conference room she'd glanced at everybody, the way a person does when entering a room filled with strangers, but it had seemed to DeMarco that her gaze had lingered longer on him. DeMarco wondered if the lingering look was because she found him devilishly handsome.

"A guy named Mark Berg," Brunstad said, answering the FBI lady's question. "He's an out-of-work carpenter."

The agent wrote this down. "Why did Mr. Berg wait until now to tell you about Conran?" she asked.

"He was over in Spokane visiting a cousin. Like I said, he was waiting for his ride the day he saw Cowboy and he left for Spokane right after he saw him. He didn't hear about Whitfield's murder until he got back last night."

The FBI agent also included this information in her notebook. She had written down virtually every word that Brunstad had uttered, making DeMarco conclude: great ankles but maybe just a little anal.

"Anyway," Brunstad said, "after we interviewed the witness, we went looking for Cowboy and in his backpack we found Whitfield's wallet and watch. We also found a knife with a six-inch blade. There was blood on the blade and the ME says the shape of the blade matches Whitfield's wound. We've sent the knife to a lab to see if the blood matches Whitfield's DNA. We'll know in a couple of days."

"Whitfield was stabbed from the front," Emma said. "Why would he let this street person get so close to him?"

"I don't know," Brunstad said. "Maybe Cowboy was asking Whitfield for a handout. He's a big guy, he backs Whitfield up against his car, and when Whitfield doesn't give him any money, he gets mad and stabs him." One of Brunstad's cops nodded in approval of his boss's reasoning.

"Had Mr. Conran spent any of Whitfield's money or used his credit cards?" Emma asked.

"He definitely didn't use the credit cards," the chief said. "We checked. As for the money that was in Whitfield's wallet, we don't know how much he had to begin with, but there was still cash in the wallet when we arrested Cowboy."

"Humph," Emma said.

"So what does this Cowboy character say?" one of the NCIS agents asked.

"He says gibberish," Brunstad said. "We've questioned him but he just prattles on about weird stuff. You can't get a direct answer to anything. We're trying to get his lawyer to let us force-feed Cowboy his meds but his lawyer's playin' games with us. But right now, even without a confession, Cowboy looks pretty good for this thing."

Brunstad's presentation ended a few minutes later. Emma told DeMarco she needed to make a phone call and left him sitting there in the briefing room.

DeMarco wondered who she was calling. He noticed the cute FBI agent had walked up to look at the crime scene photos taped on the wall near the white board. DeMarco decided he, too, was interested in the evidence.

"Gotta pretty good case against Mr. Cowboy," DeMarco said to the agent.

"Yeah, almost too good," the agent said.

It was the way she said "yeah." Pure New York. "Brooklyn?" DeMarco said.

"No, smart guy. Queens. You don't remember me, do you?"

"I know you?" DeMarco said.

"Sorta. My brother was Nick Carlucci."

"You're kidding!" DeMarco said. Nick Carlucci had been an acquaintance of DeMarco's in high school. He'd never been a close friend because De-Marco's mother wouldn't allow DeMarco to pal around with him after Nick was arrested for stealing a car. DeMarco's father may have worked for a mobster but that didn't mean that Mrs. DeMarco would permit her son to associate with criminals.

"So how's Nick doing?" DeMarco said.

"Never mind," the agent said. DeMarco guessed that meant that ol' Nick hadn't gone on to Yale and become a doctor.

DeMarco vaguely remembered her now, recalling that Nick had a younger sister, a skinny little kid with a sharp mouth. What the hell was her name?

"My name's Diane," Diane said, apparently having the same ability all women had—which was to read DeMarco's mind as if there was an electronic reader-board on his forehead.

"So what agency are you with?" she asked. "NCIS?"

"No. Congress."

"Congress? What's Congress got to do with this?"

Emma returned to the conference room before DeMarco could answer. She stood in the doorway and made an impatient come-on-let's-go motion.

"It's complicated," DeMarco said to Diane Carlucci.

"Oh, yeah?" Diane said. Again, the New York "yeah," this time communicating: like *anything* you had to say could be complicated.

Emma waved at DeMarco again; he could tell she was getting pissed.

"Yeah," DeMarco said, "it's so complicated it would take me a whole dinner to explain it to you."

Diane Carlucci smiled. He liked that smile. She took a card out of the pocket of her suit jacket and said, "Why don't you call me later today. If this thing's under control, dinner tonight might be okay, you being from Congress and all."

There was nothing like a girl from the old neighborhood.

DeMarco started over toward Emma, who was still standing in the doorway. He was halfway there when she said, "Hurry up!" then turned and walked away.

DeMarco hustled to catch up with her. "So you don't think the bum did it," DeMarco said to Emma.

"I think Mr. Conran's only crime is being mentally ill," Emma said.

"Who'd you call?" DeMarco asked.

"I noticed you talking to that young lady from the FBI," Emma said. "Comparing case notes?"

"Funny thing," DeMarco said. "She was raised in my old neighborhood. I knew her brother."

"Yeah, funny thing," Emma said. "Another funny thing is how she looks like your ex-wife."

DeMarco's wife had divorced him a few years ago. She'd had an affair with his cousin, and then stripped him of most of his assets. In spite of what she'd done, he still wasn't completely over her and he had a tendency to be attracted to women who looked just like her. And Emma knew it.

"Aw, she does not," DeMarco said.

I 2

Emma had decided that she wanted to see the facility where Mulherin and Norton worked when they were inside the shipyard—the area where Whitfield had been just before his death. Richard Miller, the shipyard's head of security who had been at the briefing, had already left the police chief's office and was just getting into his car when Emma stopped him.

Miller had a head like a stubby cinder block: a square-shaped face topped by brush-cut gray hair. He had probably been a burly guy in his youth but at age fifty all the muscles had collapsed into a tire of fat around his waist. When Emma told Miller what she wanted, he told her that he had better things to do than walk her around the shipyard, at which point Emma took a card out of her purse and handed it to him.

"Call that number, Mr. Miller," she said. "A phone will ring in the Pentagon and someone with stars on his shoulders will explain to you why you want to be nice to me. Now I'm going to get a cup of coffee but I'll be back in five minutes."

Fifteen minutes later, Emma, DeMarco, and Miller were inside the shipyard, walking toward the training facility. As they walked, Miller kept glancing over at Emma; whatever he'd been told by the man in the Pentagon had made an impression.

To reach the training facility they had to traverse almost the entire length of the shipyard. The place was enormous and everything in it—the buildings, the equipment, the drydocks—was enormous. Miller said the shipyard's machine shop was the biggest such facility west of the Mississippi River, and DeMarco believed him.

Four of the shipyard's drydocks held submarines being overhauled and one drydock held two submarines that were being dismantled. The sixth drydock, the largest one, was empty, but big wooden blocks were laid out in a pattern for a ship to set down on. A big ship—a Nimitz class aircraft carrier.

Miller allowed them to look into a drydock holding a Trident submarine. A Trident submarine is five hundred and sixty feet long—almost the length of two football fields—and carries more weapons of mass destruction than most countries have in their entire arsenal. A Trident is a sleek, sinister-looking killing machine, and it wasn't hard for DeMarco to imagine it sitting motionless beneath the waves, a missile hatch silently opening—and then the entire world being set on fire. But "Gee that thing's big" was the only thing he said out loud and Emma just looked at him—like he was the first idiot to master understatement.

Miller introduced them to Dave Whitfield's boss, the person in charge of training the shipyard's nuclear engineers. She was a handsome, dark-haired woman in her forties named Jane Shipley and she was even taller than Emma. Shipley showed them her domain, which consisted of several class rooms, study areas for the trainees, and the ubiquitous corporate cubicles where instructors and other personnel pounded away on computers.

Shipley pointed out the cubicle where Mulherin and Norton worked. It was located on the front wall of the building and looked just like all the other cubicles: two desks, two chairs, two phones, two computers, one filing cabinet. DeMarco could tell that Emma wanted to yank open all the drawers, but she restrained herself.

There was also a large walk-in vault at the rear of the training area, the type of vault you would find in a bank. DeMarco could see blueprints and big books—books the size of Bibles or phone books—on shelves inside the vault. A woman—half guard, half librarian—was posted at a desk near the vault.

"What do you keep in there?" DeMarco asked Shipley.

"Drawings of ships' systems and components. The big books are reactor and steam plant manuals."

DeMarco remembered what Dave Whitfield had said: the reactor plant manuals told you how the ships' reactors worked.

Emma looked at the vault, then did a slow turn to take in the rest of the training complex. To Shipley, she said, "You have a lot of classified information in this facility, don't you?"

"Well, sure," Shipley said. "Our engineers are trained primarily on three different classes of ships: Nimitz class air craft carriers, Trident submarines, and Los Angeles class attack submarines. We can't go running all around the shipyard every time we have to prepare a class or teach a course."

"I know," Emma said. "But there's so *much* information here, all in one place." Before Shipley could respond, Emma said, "Are the manuals, those reactor plant manuals, are they on CDs?"

Miller hesitated. "Yeah," he said. "It's the most efficient way to update them when they're revised."

"CREM," Emma said.

It had sounded to DeMarco like Emma was either clearing her throat or uttering a heretofore unknown curse word.

"What did you say?" DeMarco said.

"CREM. They have CREM," Emma said. Now the word sounded like a sexually transmitted disease. "Controlled removable electronic media. In other words, CDs and floppy disks that contain classified information. CDs that can be stolen and copied and e-mailed. CREM is a security officer's nightmare, isn't it, Mr. Miller?"

Miller's mouth took a hard set, bristling at Emma's comment. "We control our classified material tighter than anybody in the business, lady," he said. "Particularly since Los Alamos."

In July 2004, Emma explained to DeMarco later, two classified CDs were reported missing at the Los Alamos National Laboratory's Weapons Physics Directorate—a place that designs and experiments with nuclear bombs. This was the same facility that the Chinese had supposedly infiltrated in the 1990s, making off with design information related to thermonuclear warheads. The CDs lost at Los Alamos in 2004 may simply have been misplaced—stuck in the wrong file drawer or safe—or accidentally destroyed. Subsequent investigations showed that the people at the laboratory, most of them egghead scientists with skyscraper IQs, were incredibly absent-minded when it came to controlling classified material. Or maybe the CDs weren't lost or destroyed—maybe they were mailed to North Korea or Iran or some other equally unfriendly party.

Because of what had happened at Los Alamos, the shipyard was ultracareful when it came to removable media. Miller explained that when an individual checked out a classified CD from the vault, the number of the CD was recorded—just like when you checked out a book from the library—and at the end of the day, the CD had to be returned to the vault. An inventory was done every day to make sure all the CDs had been returned—and if one was found missing, Miller's security force went to high alert. The problem was CDs could be copied and their contents e-mailed. When Emma said this, both Miller and Shipley responded immediately.

"No way," they said, simultaneously. They explained that the shipyard's computers were designed to prevent copying classified CDs and the shipyard's firewall prevented classified material from being e-mailed out of the yard.

"Humph," was Emma's response. "And Mulherin and Norton, I suppose they have access to these classified CDs?"

"Yes," Shipley said.

"And do they use your computers or their own?"

"You can't bring personal computers into the yard," Shipley said. "So their contract specified that they be given a work space here in the training facility and computers and phones. You saw their office. They needed the computers because a lot of the training materials—class outlines, course materials, exams—are on CDs or a secure network. But like I said, you can't burn copies of classified CDs on our computers."

"I see," Emma said.

Shipley shook her head and said, "Mulherin and Norton are a couple of eight balls. I wouldn't hire them to clean my blackboards. Why anybody would pay these guys to review my training program is beyond me."

"You know Dave Whitfield thought there was something, ah, *funny* about the work Mulherin and Norton were doing," DeMarco said. He didn't want to use the word "fraudulent."

"Yeah, I know," Shipley said. "He complained to me about it." She hesitated, then added, "Look, I think this review Carmody's doing is a waste of time, and I've already told you what I think of Mulherin and Norton, but there isn't anything illegal going on like Dave seemed to think. He was upset because these guys were making more money than he was, but . . . well, that's just the way Dave was."

"What about Carmody?" Emma asked. "Does he spend much time here?"

"No," Shipley said. "He comes up here once in a while—to check on Norton and Mulherin, I guess— but he spends most of his time on the subs."

"Doing what?" Emma said.

"Part of the training is the book stuff," Shipley said, "which we do here, and part is shipboard.

Carmody is supposedly watching the shipboard training, but my guys say that he seems to spend most of his time just bullshitting with the sailors."

"But he's on board the submarines a lot," Emma said. "On his own."

"Yeah," Shipley said. "Is there a problem with that?"

I 3

Emma led DeMarco to a café on Bremerton's water front. The place smelled of incense and flowers and served fifty varieties of herbal tea. The cheerful lady who ran the café sported John Lennon–style wire-rim glasses and had straight, gray hair that reached the small of her back. She wore what DeMarco thought of as a granny dress, a long shapeless thing as glamorous as a flour sack that touched the tops of her Birkenstock sandals. DeMarco had thought that hippies were extinct, but apparently not.

Emma ordered an exotic tea, something with ginseng in it. DeMarco asked for coffee, then a Coke, then a plain old Lipton's and each time was informed by the woman—not only a hippie but a health Nazi—that she didn't stock such beverages. He settled for a glass of water; the happy Nazi put a slice of lemon in it.

They took seats near a window where they could see the ferry terminal and watch the jumbo ferries from Seattle dock at the terminal in Bremerton.

"I think Whitfield may have been right about Mulherin and Norton," Emma said.

"That they're committing some kind of fraud?"

"Not fraud," Emma said. "Something else."

"What else? What are you talking about?"

"Let's look at everything Dave Whitfield said from a different perspective. He said Mulherin and Norton, two guys in debt, suddenly retire early and come into a lot of money and start buying things. Then you consider *where* they've been working, in a training facility loaded with classified materials. And then right after Whitfield calls you about them, he's killed. So maybe Whitfield saw Mulherin or Norton doing something or overheard something and—"

"Espionage? Is that what you're saying, Emma?"

Emma nodded her head slowly.

DeMarco had never been near a spy in his life, at least not that he knew of. His normal assignments involved wayward politicians and greedy bureaucrats and being the middleman for deals that Mahoney didn't want his fingerprints on. "You might be right," he said to Emma, "but you saw the security in that place."

The shipyard's perimeter was protected by tall fences topped with barbed wire; boats armed with machine guns patrolled the waterfront to keep watercraft—watercraft potentially filled with explosives—from approaching the drydocks or ships that were moored at the piers; armed guards manned entry gates and patrolled the grounds, and cameras were located in strategic spots. And these were just the security measures that were visible.

People entering the shipyard were carefully controlled. The employees, the ones who worked on the nuclear ships, had to have a security clearance and they wore badges that had their pictures on the front and a magnetic strip on the back, like the strip on the back of a credit card. To enter the shipyard, workers had to show their badges to guards stationed at the gates and swipe the badges through bar-code readers to further confirm they were allowed to enter. Miller, the shipyard security chief, had said that random searches of backpacks and lunch boxes and vehicles were performed at all times, and if the national or regional threat level increased, *everybody* was searched, from the shipyard commander's wife on down to the guy who mopped the cafeteria floor.

"Let me tell you something about security systems," Emma said to DeMarco. "Most systems—including the one at this shipyard—are primarily designed to keep the bad guys *out*. But once a worker has been vetted for a security clearance and given a badge, he's *in*. And once he's in, he's trusted, and he has access to classified information, and most important, he knows how such information is protected." Emma paused to sip her tea, then added, "And espionage isn't the only possibility."

"What else is there?"

"Sabotage. There are currently four nuclear-powered submarines being overhauled at the shipyard. Sabotaging one of these ships would have significant repercussions. Not only the cost to repair whatever was damaged, but fleet operations would be disrupted if a vessel had to be taken out of service for a significant amount of time, and work on all the other ships being overhauled would be delayed."

"It's kinda hard to picture Mulherin and Norton as spies. I mean these guys, they're just—"

"Remember Aldrich Ames?" Emma asked.

"The CIA guy?" DeMarco said.

"Right," Emma said. "Ames was probably the most damaging mole ever to penetrate a U.S. intelligence service. He was an alcoholic and poorly thought of by his coworkers. He was turned down for promotions, not all that bright, and openly flaunted the money he received from the Russians. In spite of all that, he fed CIA information to the KGB for almost ten years, and ten native Russians providing intelligence to the CIA died because of him. When you think about it, Mulherin and Norton bear a rather large resemblance to Aldrich Ames."

"What about Carmody?"

"We don't know anything about Phil Carmody," Emma said and her lips compressed into a stubborn line that said they soon would.

"Hell, even if they are spies, according to that tall gal up in the training area, what's-her-name, Shipley, it'd be pretty hard to sneak anything classified out of that place. You sure as hell can't sneak one of those big damn books out of that vault."

"I know," Emma said.

They sat in silence a moment until DeMarco said, "If all those security systems don't keep the spies out, how *do* they get 'em?"

"The first opportunity," Emma said, "is the background checks performed when they issue a man or a woman a security clearance. That's the time to see if they're in financial trouble or susceptible to blackmail. But that's not how spies are usually caught." Emma gestured toward the shipyard, the eastern end of which was visible from the tea house. "All that security—the fences, the cameras, the safes, the cyber locks—that's the *physical* perimeter that protects the facility and its secrets. But there's a second perimeter that's just as visible but not as apparent—a *human* perimeter. The employees. Employees like Dave Whitfield watching their coworkers, looking for odd behavior, looking for something that *stinks,* as poor Dave put it. It's the second perimeter that catches the spies."

Emma tipped her cup back and swallowed the remainder of her horrible, healthy tea. "There's somebody I need to talk to," she said. "I'll see you later."

14

"I need some help here, Bill," Emma said.

Bill Smith—his real name—worked for Emma's old outfit. He was five foot nine, slim, had curly dark hair, and wore glasses with heavy black frames. He didn't look like an international spy; he looked, to his great dismay, very much like the older brother of a guy who did a national TV commercial, one that had been running for more than three years. He and Emma were sitting in a Denny's restaurant and Emma winced as Smith poured half a pint of raspberry syrup over his waffles.

"I can't do it, Emma," Smith said. "We're more short-handed right now than we were during the Cold War." Before Emma could object, he held out a forkful of waffle, red syrup running down the handle of the fork. "Wanna bite?" he said.

"God, no," Emma said. "I'm telling you, Bill, these guys are up to something. I can *feel* it."

"Have you talked to the Feebies about this feeling of yours?"

"Yes. The Bureau assigned two young agents to Whitfield's murder. The one in charge is not only greener than grass, he's handling a caseload that would break a donkey's back. He thinks the likelihood of espionage is pretty far-fetched . . ."

"Which you have to agree it is," Smith said.

". . . and he says he doesn't have sufficient probable cause to get warrants to look into these guys' finances or search their homes."

"Probable cause," Smith said and made a sound that was half snort, half laugh. In Bill Smith's normal line of work, probable cause was rarely, if ever, an impediment.

"And as for Whitfield's murder, he says they're starting to think that poor schizophrenic really did it."

"Well maybe he did do it."

"He didn't," Emma said. Emma, as the old saying went, was sometimes wrong but never uncertain.

"So what do you want?" Smith said.

"I want someone from research to check these people out, particularly Carmody. And I want to borrow a computer guy to tell me how they could trick the shipyard's IT security. And I need a team, just a small one. I want these guys followed for a while and their houses searched. I particularly want Carmody's place sniffed for explosives and spyware."

"Jesus Christ, Emma. Maybe you'd like a helicopter, too?"

"I'm serious, Bill. It really makes me nervous that he spends his time on board the ships."

Smith sighed. Emma was a force of nature. "Look," he said, "the research we can do. You just won't get priority. The computer stuff, there's an NSA guy we borrow sometimes when we're overloaded. Maybe we can convince them to spare him for a conference call. But a team's out of the question. I'd have to bring guys back from overseas to do what you want. You gotta believe me, Emma: communism was a piece of cake compared to this terrorism stuff."

"*Listen* to me," Emma said. "They're inside a naval shipyard that overhauls nuclear-powered warships!"

"I hear you, Emma, but I can't do it. Sorry."

Emma sat back in her chair

"Well in that case, Bill, I'd suggest that you kick this up the line so that when something bad happens, your ass will be covered."

"Now that wasn't called for, Emma."

15

———◆◆◆———

Emma reclined on the bed in her motel room, waiting for the phone to ring. She was feeling lonely and grumpy. After Christine went back to D.C. with the symphony, Emma had moved into the same motel where DeMarco was staying in Bremerton. It was clean and functional and conveniently located—and, in Emma's opinion, only slightly better than a cardboard box. Emma was used to five-star accommodations.

Emma had worked for the DIA for almost thirty years. She never discussed with anyone what she did while working for the agency but in her time she had slept in mountain caves without even a blanket for warmth; she had survived by eating grubs and uncooked bitter roots; she had been bitten on the ear by a scorpion and had once acquired an exotic fungus between her toes. She had suffered these hardships without complaint or self-pity—yet here she was feeling extremely peeved because the water pressure in the motel's shower was so low it took five minutes to rinse the shampoo from her short hair.

The phone next to the bed rang.

"Yes," Emma said.

"It's Peterson in research?'

"Go ahead."

"I'll start with Norton and Mulherin. They have a history of indebtedness. Their employment records are spotty—lots of supervisor comments about tardiness, insubordination, sloppy work, etc. Before they retired they filed grievances every other month about something: lack of promotion, age discrimination, unfair shift assignments. That sorta whiny crap. Both are divorced and both have kids they don't support. Neither has a criminal record, unless you count the DUI Mulherin got six years ago. They're just a couple of fuckups."

Just a couple of fuckups. That seemed to be the consensus opinion as that was at least the third time that Emma had heard that phrase, or a variation of it, used to describe the pair. So why had Carmody hired them?

"Is that it?" Emma said.

"No. I checked their bank records. Six months ago both men came into some money, a hundred thousand dollars each. This was just before they retired from the yard and started working for Carmody."

"What was the source of the hundred thousand?"

"Carmody's company. I guess it was some kind of signing bonus."

Emma snorted. "Would you pay these two a signing bonus?"

"I don't think so."

"And where did Carmody get the money from?"

"He bought a house in San Diego when he was stationed there back in the nineties. He rented the place out when he wasn't there. Seven months ago he sold the house and used the profit from the sale to start up his consulting company and to pay Norton and Mulherin. But there's something fishy about the sale. He was paid almost three times what the house was worth. A development company bought the house and I haven't been able to trace where they get their money from. I could do it eventually, Emma, but they told me I couldn't spend any more time on this."

"Could someone be funneling money through the development company?"

"Sure. It's big, it's global, and it's got income flows from a dozen different directions. It'd be perfect for funding foreign ops."

"You need to find the source of Carmody's money."

"I'm sorry, Emma, I can't. Not now, and not unless you get something solid."

Emma was silent for a moment.

"What about Carmody?"

"He's a totally different breed than Mulherin and Norton. He started off as a navy nuc, trained as a reactor operator in Idaho Falls, then served on both attack boats and boomers. His record was spotless. Good fit reps, commendations, fast track for promotion. He was being considered for officer candidate school when he decided to leave the nucs."

"What happened?"

"Nothing happened. He was twenty-four years old—he enlisted at eighteen—and after six years he was tired of submarines and decided he wanted to be a SEAL. The nucs weren't happy about him leaving but he said if they didn't transfer him, he'd quit, and he was just too good for the navy to lose. And the SEALs really wanted him, a big young guy with a technical background. He was a dream candidate."

"How'd he do in the SEALs?"

"Great, until right before he quit. He's one of those guys that has his medals stored in a government lockbox because he can't tell anyone why he got the medals. Kinda like you, Emma."

Emma ignored the compliment. "What happened before he quit?"

"He was in . . . someplace, and . . . well . . . something went wrong. One SEAL was killed and Carmody got the blame."

Emma could tell that Peterson was reading from a report and not telling her everything—or anything.

"Come on, Peterson," she said. "What kind of op and what did Carmody do?"

"Sorry, Emma, I can't say. The point is, Carmody had to make a decision in the middle of a firefight and he made the wrong decision. In hindsight, that is. You know how it is; you've been there before. Anyway, Carmody was the NCMFIC and he took the hit."

NCMFIC was military-speak for noncommissioned motherfucker in charge.

"Did they bust him out of the SEALs?"

"No. This guy was a star. They put a letter in his file and were going to make him repeat some training—basically a slap on the wrist—but he quit before they could."

"So when he left the navy, he was pissed."

"The records don't say. His stated reason for leaving was to pursue work in the private sector. He may have been bitter, but you don't get that impression. I mean there's no nasty letters to his CO in his file, no demands for hearings. It looks like he was just ready to move on after six years of putting his ass on the line for minimum wage."

"Do you know what he did after he left the SEALs?"

"Sort of. I don't have a lot of detail but he was in Hong Kong for almost seven years. He got out of the navy in '96, bummed around Europe for a year, then he took a job at a utility company outside of Toledo that operates a nuclear power plant there. But in '98 he quit the job at the utility company—it was probably too much like being back on a sub—and goes to Hong Kong where he lands a job with an outfit that provides security for big shots and their businesses and their families over there. I don't know if Carmody was a bodyguard or some other kind of security consultant, but being an ex-SEAL he could have been either. Then the company he worked for in Hong Kong relocated to Thailand in 2003. This was six years after Hong Kong was returned to the Chinese so I imagine by then private enterprise in Hong Kong was starting to feel the heat from the old-timers in Beijing. The problem is, we have no record of what Carmody did after the security company relocated, but he stayed in Hong Kong until he came up with the shipyard training thing last year."

"That's quite a career change," Emma said, "from hired muscle in Hong Kong to training consultant in the States. I wonder why he didn't relocate to Thailand with his old company."

"Beats me," Peterson said.

Emma thanked Peterson and started to hang up, but before she did, the researcher said, "Emma, this guy Carmody is smart and if he's gone bad, he's dangerous. I've heard you're kinda on your own out there. You be careful, ya hear?"

Emma put down the phone and stared for a minute at the picture on the wall across from her bed. It was an oil painting of Mount Rainier rising above magenta-colored clouds, and it was hideous. She wondered if there was a company somewhere called Ugly Art, and if every motel in the country purchased from them.

She thought for a moment, made another phone call, then called DeMarco's room. There was no answer. Where the hell was he?

"So tell me," Diane Carlucci said, "how'd you land a job with Congress?"

DeMarco had asked a number of people for a nice place to take a lady to dinner and was directed to one in the little town of Winslow on Bainbridge Island. For a small-town restaurant it was pretty pricey, but DeMarco didn't care. The view was good, the food was good, and Diane Carlucci was very comfortable to be with. There was no first-date awkwardness, no straining to find something to say—until now.

DeMarco hesitated. "I guess you know about my old man?"

Diane Carlucci nodded.

"Well," DeMarco said, "he made it kind of hard to get a job after law school. Firms weren't kicking down the door to hire the son of a guy who worked for a mobster and killed people for a living."

"I can imagine," Diane said. She hesitated and said, "You know I met your dad once. I liked him."

"Yeah, he was a likable guy," DeMarco said. "He was a good father, too. He just didn't make the best career choice."

"So how'd you get a job with Congress?" Diane asked again.

"I have a godmother, a friend of my mom's I call Aunt Connie. She worked in D.C. when she was young and she had some pull with somebody. She talked to him and got me the job."

What DeMarco had just said was the truth. It wasn't the whole truth but it was the truth. "And you," DeMarco said, "how do you like—"

"No, we're not through with you yet," Diane said. "I heard you were married, that you married—"

"Yeah, I did, and now I'm divorced."

"I knew that. I heard that she left you for—"

"Yeah, my cousin."

"The one who works for—"

"Right. Why haven't you guys arrested him yet?"

Diane Carlucci laughed. She had a great laugh.

"So now can we talk about you?" DeMarco said.

DeMarco was the only customer in the motel bar.

He'd enjoyed dinner with Diane and had been sorry the evening had ended so early—seven thirty—but Diane was the dedicated type. She had told DeMarco that she needed to get back to her motel, review her case notes, and prepare for tomorrow. She and her partner had found out that Whitfield, who all agreed was a rather contentious fellow, was engaged in a property dispute with a neighbor, a man who had anger-management problems, which meant he tended to beat the hell out of people when he got upset. Although Diane's partner still thought the homeless guy looked pretty good for Whitfield's murder, Diane wanted to verify the neighbor's alibi, which was a girlfriend with a drug habit.

DeMarco didn't suggest that he accompany Diane back to her room for a nightcap. He wanted to, but he didn't. He knew a nice Catholic girl from the old neighborhood wasn't going to sleep with him on the first date. So now he sat, feeling horny and depressed, halfheartedly watching the Mariners get creamed by the Yankees. He glanced up at the television just as Jeter knocked the ball almost into the railroad yard behind Safeco Field and heard the bartender mutter, "Fuckin' Yankees"

DeMarco realized at that moment that he was no longer alone, that he was in the company of a brother. He and the bartender—a man with a severely peeling, sunburned nose—belonged to the largest, unhappiest fraternity in America: the Benevolent Order of Jealous Yankee Bashers. For the next half hour they repeated the sad litany of the brotherhood: Steinbrenner bought the World Series every year; Joe Torre looked like a dour leprechaun and was just as lucky. And so on. Members of the Order could bitch about the Yankees for hours. The bartender had just begun to decry the immorality of the Yankees acquiring Alex Rodriguez from the Texas Rangers when he looked over DeMarco's shoulder and muttered, "Oh, shit."

DeMarco followed the bartender's line of sight and saw that he was looking at Emma. She had stopped at the entrance to the bar and was looking into her purse. She rummaged in her purse a moment—even Emma had the female tendency to overstuff her handbag—then turned and walked away as if she had forgotten something.

"What's the problem?" DeMarco said.

"That broad. She was in here last night and orders a martini to take back to her room. I had to make it three times before she was happy. Geez, what a ballbuster. Oh hell, here she comes."

Emma walked over to the bar, nodded curtly to the bartender, and said to DeMarco, "I should have known this was where you'd be. Let's go get some dinner."

"I just ate," DeMarco said.

"Then you can watch me eat. We need to talk. Settle up your bill and meet me at my car." With that she turned and walked away, completely confident that DeMarco would follow. Emma could be a very irritating person.

"Sorry," the bartender said to DeMarco after Emma left, "didn't know she was your friend."

"Nothing to apologize for," DeMarco said. "She is a ballbuster. The biggest, baddest one you'll ever meet. How much do I owe you?"

———◆◆◆———

Emma, like DeMarco, had questioned the locals for the name of a decent eatery and had been directed to a place on a scenic bay called Dyes Inlet. DeMarco said it was even nicer than the spot where he'd taken Diane, but as soon as Emma stepped through the entrance she sniffed the air and said, "I smell cigarette smoke. I thought they'd outlawed smoking in restaurants in this state."

Outlawed? She made it sound as if smoking was a Class A felony. DeMarco himself couldn't smell a thing but Emma's sensitive nose had apparently detected a solitary, illicit nicotine molecule polluting the atmosphere near the door.

"Maybe they have a gas mask you can borrow," DeMarco said.

This earned him an arched eyebrow for his im-
pertinence, but he was fortunately spared a lecture
on the lethal nature of secondhand smoke. Emma
did ask the hostess for an outside table on the deck
of the restaurant, where a slight breeze ensured the
purity of her air supply. DeMarco liked the deckside
view. He'd heard that orca whales occasionally swam
into the inlets of Puget Sound, and that's what he
wanted to see: a great big orca flying out of the water.

Their waiter—a gangly kid whose name tag said
NATHAN—asked what they wanted to drink. Emma
described the perfect vodka martini, exactly how it
should be made, the exact proportion of both ingredients. The kid nodded while she talked but the only
thing he wrote down on his pad was "V. Martini."
Poor bastard, DeMarco thought; he was going to be
schlepping martinis back and forth from the bar all
night long.

"And for you, sir?" Nathan asked DeMarco.

"Uh, I'll have a martini, too. Make it just like
hers."

"Very good, sir."

The waiter turned to leave but DeMarco said,
"Hey, do you ever see orcas over here?"

"Orcas?"

"Yeah, you know, killer whales. Those black ones
with the white spots."

"I know what an orca is, sir, but they rarely
come in this far." When Nathan saw the look of

disappointment on DeMarco's face he said, "But you might see salmon jumping, and over there," Nathan pointed, "is an eagle's nest. That big tree, just to the left of the house with the red roof? Do you see it?"

DeMarco looked over to where the waiter was pointing but couldn't see anything but tree branches and sky in the fading daylight. Big deal, he thought, a bird's nest, but all he said to the waiter was, "Yeah. Cool."

After their drinks were served—to DeMarco's amazement Emma declared hers to be just right— Emma told DeMarco what she had learned from the DIA researcher.

"So now what?" DeMarco asked her.

"Well," Emma said, "if Bill Smith won't help then I guess we have to help ourselves."

"Yeah, that's what I thought you were going to say," DeMarco said.

16

Emma was picking the lock on Phil Carmody's back door.

Fortunately, Carmody had a big fence around his backyard. As long as nobody had seen them go through the back gate, they were probably okay. Provided Carmody didn't come back home. Provided he didn't have some kind of security system. Provided one of his neighbors didn't see them through the windows walking around inside of Carmody's house. DeMarco could just see himself: hands cuffed behind his back, a cop pushing his head down as they put him into a squad car.

And then the dog started making noise, little whimpering sounds like it was hungry or had to shit.

When DeMarco first saw the German shepherd in the backseat, he hadn't wanted to get into Emma's car. DeMarco wasn't a big dog fan—too many stories about pit bulls gnawing off people's arms—and the German shepherd was *huge*. He could just see it: they'd be driving down the road, and one minute the dog would be sitting there, its big snout sticking out of the window; and the next minute it'd be taking a bite out of DeMarco's skull because his hair resembled rabbit fur.

"Shut up," DeMarco hissed at the dog. The dog didn't obey of course; it just kept making the whimpering noise. He felt like jerking on the leash, but was afraid that might piss it off. "Shut up," he hissed again at the dog. "And why couldn't you get some kinda machine for this?" DeMarco whispered to Emma. "They make machines for this, don't they?"

"There," Emma said, and she pushed the door open. Turning toward DeMarco she said, "A good dog is more reliable than most portable machines and they're faster. Now come on. We'll start on the second floor and work our way down."

"Should we close the blinds?"

"No," Emma said and started up the stairs.

They knew Carmody had rented the house and DeMarco assumed it had come furnished—haphazardly furnished. The place was neat enough, but you could sense that it was just a temporary residence for its occupant. There were no personal touches, no family photographs, no memorabilia from Carmody's time in the service. It was a place where the man slept and ate and not much more.

The second floor of the house had two small bedrooms and a bath. As Emma opened drawers and looked into closets, DeMarco walked around the rooms and let the dog poke its snout wherever it wanted. At least it wasn't whimpering anymore; in fact it looked like it was having a pretty good time. DeMarco hoped it didn't raise its leg and pee on something to mark its territory.

They finished searching the second floor in forty minutes then went back to the first floor. Emma was thorough, and the kitchen was particularly time-consuming as she pulled things out of the freezer and poked around inside of boxes of cereal and rice. DeMarco was surprised the dog didn't try to eat a roast when Emma put a leftover one on the counter. He had to admit the critter was pretty well trained.

DeMarco checked his watch. They'd been inside the house an hour and a half.

"Come on," Emma said, "let's do the basement."

"Aren't you going to put that stuff back?" De-Marco asked, pointing his chin at the food sitting on the counter.

"No," Emma said. "He's going to know we've been here anyway."

DeMarco was afraid the basement would take for-ever. Basements are where people store boxes and boxes of old crap they don't need but are too lazy to sort through and throw away. But the basement of Phil Carmody's rented house was small and almost barren. A hot water heater and a furnace took up half the space, and Carmody had a set of free weights and a bench-press bench in the middle of the room. DeMarco mentally tallied the weights on the bar and concluded that Carmody bench-pressed three hundred and fifty pounds.

There was an old Formica-topped kitchen table along one wall and above the table was a Peg-Board containing hand tools. Clamped to the table was a small vise, the sort fly fishermen use to tie flies, and a magnifying glass on a movable arm was mounted over the vise. On the table was a model sailing ship—a four-masted man-of-war under full sail. It appeared the model was ninety percent constructed, with only a few parts remaining to be painted. DeMarco could imagine Carmody sitting here alone at night, in the dimly lit basement of his silent house, slowly constructing the model. It was an image of a lonely man killing time—not a man passionate about a hobby.

As Emma stood in the center of the room deciding where to begin her search, DeMarco pulled the dog over to the table to take a closer look at the model. It had a zillion parts, little ropes and pulleys and cleats, and DeMarco didn't see a smudge of glue anywhere. He was wondering if he had enough patience to build something like this when the dog went berserk. It started barking at the top of its lungs and straining against the leash to get at a shoe box underneath the table.

"Jesus!" DeMarco said. "Shut the fuck up! Shut the fuck up!" he hissed at the dog. He didn't know why he was whispering since the dog could be heard a mile away.

Emma came over and patted the dog on the head and said, "Good girl, that's a good girl," and she pulled a doggy treat out of her pocket and fed it to the dog. DeMarco wondered how come she had the doggy treats instead of him. The dog immediately stopped barking, but it continued to push its nose against the box.

Moving the dog's head out of the way, Emma pulled the box out from under the table and placed it on the tabletop next to the model. It was sealed in two places with clear packing tape. She studied the box for a few minutes, shrugged, and picked up an X-Acto knife that was lying near the model.

"Hey!" DeMarco said. "What are you doing? What if that's a letter bomb or package bomb or something like that?"

"Look at the dust," Emma said. "This box has been sitting here for quite a while."

"So?" DeMarco said. "That just means it could be a highly unstable package bomb."

Emma shook her head, dismissing DeMarco's objections, and carefully sliced the packing tape and slowly opened the shoe box.

"Shit," Emma said.

DeMarco looked down into the box. It contained a water pistol, a top, a couple of Matchbox cars, and a yo-yo. And a dozen bottle rockets.

———◆———

It took them twice as long to search Mulherin's place. The guy's house wasn't any bigger than Carmody's but Mulherin had lived there a long time—and he was both a slob and a pack rat. His basement, unlike Carmody's, contained so many boxes and bins and cartons that there was barely room to move. Mulherin also had a garage, and it too was filled with junk, so much junk that there wasn't space to park a car. Even Emma, the woman who never admitted to the impossible, admitted it was going to be impossible for them to search Mulherin's house thoroughly in less than two days—and all they had was about four hours.

The dog reacted twice to objects in the house: a case of marine flares in the garage stored next to a two-gallon can of gasoline, and a box of shotgun shells in the pocket of a moth-eaten hunting vest. The shotgun shells looked so old that DeMarco was afraid they might explode in his hand.

When they finished searching, even the dog looked tired.

"Now what?" DeMarco said when they were back in the car. "It's too late to check Norton's place."

"He lives in an apartment. It won't take long."

"Emma, it's almost four o'clock. They said these guys hardly ever work later than four and usually leave earlier to avoid the traffic."

"We've got time," Emma insisted, her lips set in that don't-argue-with-me line.

———◆———

Norton had a two-bedroom apartment. The living room was dominated by a television with a fifty-inch screen and there were more auxiliary components than DeMarco had ever seen connected to the set. He counted six speakers in different spots around the small room.

Unlike Mulherin, Norton was neater than De-Marco's mother—and that was very neat. There were no unwashed dishes in the sink, no unmade bed, no clothes on the bedroom floor. All the boxes on the upper shelf of his closet were neatly labeled as to their contents. Now that, DeMarco thought, was weird.

"If this guy isn't arrested," DeMarco said, "I'm gonna see if he wants to be my maid."

Emma ignored him and went directly to the kitchen and began opening drawers.

"Let's go, partner," DeMarco said to the dog and tugged on its leash and started walking the animal around the living room. For some reason the dog was panting now; its tongue was about a foot long.

When they opened the door to the second bedroom, Emma said, "My, my."

Against one wall was a long table. On the table was a flat-screen monitor, a laser printer, and a state-of-the-art scanner—those were the items that DeMarco recognized. What had most likely elicited the "my, my" from Emma were the half dozen other devices that DeMarco didn't recognize. Above the table was a bookshelf filled with computer books and computer magazines; the magazines were filed in chronological order. Beneath the table was a red Craftsman toolbox on casters and it housed small hand tools and electronic components.

Emma walked over to the table, picked up an object lying there, and said, "Huh."

"What's that?" DeMarco said.

"A section of fiber-optic cable. It can be attached to a miniature camera or video recorder."

"Ah," DeMarco said. "One of those things that weirdos poke through a little hole in a bathroom wall so they can watch women pee.' Norton struck him as the Peeping Tom type.

"That's one use for it," Emma said. "Another possibility is Carmody walking around a nuclear submarine with one of these cables up his sleeve, taking pictures of anything he wants and nobody noticing."

Emma took a digital camera out of her packet pocket and began to photograph the computer equipment and the books on the shelf above the table. After she finished photographing the equipment, she sat down at the table and turned on the computer.

"Let's see what he's got in this thing," she said.

DeMarco looked at his watch. "Emma, we gotta get going," he said.

Emma ignored him and DeMarco soon heard the little tune that Microsoft Windows plays when a computer starts up.

"Damn it," Emma muttered a moment later. "It's password protected, and judging by all the sophisticated crap this guy has, I wouldn't be surprised if some of the programs were encrypted. I'm going to need a pro to find out what's in this machine."

Now Emma looked at her watch. "It's getting late," she said.

"No shit," DeMarco said. Geez, she could be annoying.

"Take Lucy outside and stand watch. I saw an owner's manual for a laptop, but I can't find the laptop. I want to spend a little more time looking for it. If Norton shows up, call me."

DeMarco thought Lucy was a really dumb name for a German shepherd, even a female one. German shepherds should have names like Bullet, Fang, or Killer. They should have rabid doggy-slobber dripping from their fangs. Lucy, DeMarco now realized after having spent the day with her, was just a big, friendly puppy with a sensitive nose. She was an embarrassment to the breed, and the name confirmed it.

DeMarco picked a spot to wait near the entrance to the apartment building and ten minutes later Norton drove into the adjacent garage. DeMarco immediately called Emma on the cell phone.

"Stall him for five minutes," Emma said and hung up before DeMarco could complain.

Goddamnit, DeMarco thought, he needed to come up with some reason for being here. Maybe he could tell Norton he'd taken a job as a dog walker.

Norton exited the garage. He was holding a knapsack in one hand.

DeMarco walked up to him and said, "Mr. Norton, I need to talk to you."

Norton looked confused for a moment, before he recognized DeMarco. "I'm not talkin' to you," he said.

"It'll only take a minute."

"Nope. You got any questions, you talk to Carmody."

Norton started to move around DeMarco, but when he did, Lucy barked. It was a scary sound and Norton stopped immediately.

"If that thing bites me, I swear to God, I'll sue your ass," Norton said.

DeMarco looked down at Lucy. *Now* she looked like a German shepherd. Her teeth were exposed, she was straining against the leash, and her eyes were focused on Norton's knapsack. Norton again started to walk around DeMarco but when he did the dog lunged at him and barked again, making Norton take a step back, his eyes wide with fear. "Jesus Christ! You call that fuckin' thing off," Norton said. "You hear? I'm not kiddin',"

"What's in the knapsack, Mr. Norton?" DeMarco said.

"None of your business. Now call that motherfucker off."

"Norton, I bought this dog from a buddy of mine who works for the DEA. She's trained to sniff out drugs."

"Drugs?" Norton sail. "I don't have any drugs."

"Show me what's in the knapsack. If you don't, I'm calling the police and we're all going to wait here until they arrive."

"I'm not showing you shit. And I'll say it again: if that bitch bites me, I'll sue you."

"You'll be suing me with half your butt in a bandage," DeMarco said.

Over Norton's shoulder, DeMarco saw the door to the apartment building open and Emma exit. She made a let's-go gesture at DeMarco and kept walking toward where their car was parked.

"All right, goddamnit," Norton said to DeMarco. He unzipped the knapsack and held it out so DeMarco could look inside it. There were two small bags. One contained potting soil and the other fertilizer. DeMarco had seen a couple of red plants—geraniums, he thought—on the small balcony of Norton's apartment.

"You happy now?" Norton said.

"Yeah," DeMarco said and walked away, practically dragging Lucy with the leash. Stupid dog. It couldn't tell the difference between chicken shit and a bomb.

<hr />

"Fertilizer can *be* an explosive," Emma said. "What do you think they used to blow up the federal building in Oklahoma?"

"I know *that*," DeMarco said, "but McVeigh had a damn truckload of the stuff, not a one-pound bag."

Emma wasn't listening. She was talking baby talk to Lucy. "You're a good girl. Yes you are. Yes you are," she said. As she spoke, Emma thumped her right hand against the mutt's thick rib cage. It sounded like she was beating on a drum, but the dog seemed to like it. Dogs are weird, DeMarco thought.

"So now what?" he said. They were back on Highway 3, heading south. Emma was driving and Lucy was once again in the backseat, her head stuck happily out the window. Lucy belonged to the Transportation Security Administration at the Seattle-Tacoma Airport. Emma's pals at the DIA had arranged for her to borrow the animal, and she and DeMarco were now returning the dog to its handler.

"I need to get into Carmody's office," she said.

"That's gonna be tough. It's in the middle of downtown Bremerton and there are people walking around there all the time."

"Yeah," Emma said, already thinking about how she was going to break in.

"We're going to get our asses arrested for sure," DeMarco said.

"*You* won't," Emma said. "I want you to go back to D.C."

17

DeMarco was getting pretty damn annoyed with the United States Navy. He was now into his second hour of looking for whomever had awarded Carmody the shipyard training contract and he seemed no closer to finding this person than when he started. If he'd owned an aircraft carrier, he would have picked a fight with the navy.

He had been told by Carmody that Carmody's contract was administered by someone who worked at NAVSEA—the Naval Sea Systems Command. NAVSEA was located in the Washington Navy Yard in southeast D.C. The Washington Navy Yard had once been a real shipyard but the repair facilities had been closed years ago and its current function was to provide office space for navy headquarters personnel and their minions.

It took DeMarco half an hour to get past security after which he learned that NAVSEA was a gigantic bureaucracy consisting of hundreds of people working on all aspects of navy business: weapons, ship construction, overhauls, personnel, logistics, and on and on and on. The number of cogs in this bureaucratic juggernaut was endless, and the people in the various departments seemed to know nothing other than their own function.

So DeMarco walked from office to office, from building to building, searching for the group that dealt with naval shipyard training. He asked his question for the fiftieth time to a secretary, a sturdy, androgynous creature with short hair and a faint mustache. He thought the secretary was female but he wasn't sure. "Is there anybody here," he asked politely, "who knows anything about a contract for a training study at the shipyard in Bremerton?"

"Yeah," she—or he—said. "Go see Gary. Down the hall there."

Gary was a skinny, nervous kid with a mild facial tic. He looked about twenty years old and was sitting behind a desk that overflowed with paper. The capacity of his in basket had been exceeded days ago. This might have explained the tic; the kid seemed so overwhelmed by his workload that DeMarco could imagine him having a nervous breakdown when the next piece of paper landed on his desk.

"Bill Berry was in charge of that contract," Gary said to DeMarco. "He handled all that sorta stuff at the shipyards."

"So can I talk to Berry?" DeMarco asked.

Gary's phone rang before he could answer DeMarco's question. "Yes, sir. Yes, sir. I'll be right there," Gary said into the phone and hung up. "Jesus," he said. "That was the *admiral*. He wants to see me."

The way Gary said "the admiral" it sounded like the man was seated at the right hand of God—-or maybe he outranked God.

"All I want to know is where this guy Berry is," DeMarco said.

Gary wasn't listening. He had pulled open a drawer in his desk and was rifling through it. "Hold on a minute," he said to DeMarco. He searched, flipping tabs on manila file folders as fast as his index finger could move. "Damn it!" he wailed. "Where is it?" A moment later he said, "There you are!" as if speaking to a pet that had been hiding under the bed, and he pulled a graph from a tattered folder. DeMarco noticed the graph had a yellow Post-it sticker on it, and on the Post-it someone had scrawled the word "Bullshit" with a red felt-tip pen.

"Bill Berry?" DeMarco said. "Can you *please* tell me where he is?"

Gary tore the Post-it off the graph, shoved the graph into a new file folder, and patted down a cowlick on the back of his head.

"Bill Berry's dead," he said to DeMarco as he walked away.

———◆◆◆———

Bill Berry had died in an automobile accident the day after Dave Whitfield was killed. He missed a curve and his car had plunged down a steep, wooded embankment on Spout Run in Arlington, Virginia. His blood alcohol content at the time of his death had been a whopping .25.

"But are you sure it was an accident, Sheriff?" DeMarco said.

It had taken some effort to get the Arlington County sheriff to agree to talk to him about Bill Berry's death. When he'd first arrived at the sheriff's office, he was told that unless he had some official status—such as being Bill Berry's lawyer or a lawyer who worked for Berry's insurance company—they weren't going to tell him anything. DeMarco had been forced to call the Speaker and tell Mahoney that the sheriff was being mean to him.

"Shit," Mahoney had said. "What's this fuckin' guy's name?"

Half an hour later the sheriff escorted DeMarco back to his office.

"What do you mean, am I sure it was an accident?" the sheriff said. "The damn guy was drunk and he ran his car off the road. What the hell else could it have been?"

"Sheriff," DeMarco said, "I can't tell you the spe-
cifics, but Mr. Berry could have been involved in
something bad. He could have been murdered."

"Jesus Christ," the sheriff said. "So what do you
think happened, bud? You think somebody messed
with the brakes on the guy's car? Or maybe rammed
him and pushed him off the road?"

"That's what I'm trying to find out, Sheriff."

"Berry's car bounced down a hill. He bit one tree
head on, broadsided another one, then the car rolled
over a couple of times before it ended up on its top
in someone's backyard. The car was a mess, the body
was a mess, and there's no way I can tell if anybody
did something to it."

"Can't you—"

"Television," the sheriff said, shaking his big, bald
head. "I'll just bet you've been watching TV, one
of them dumbass CSI shows. You've probably seen
'em strip some car down to the frame, and then the
hero goes: 'Hey, we've got a scratch here that came
from a hacksaw made in Tijuana.' Well let me tell
you something, pal. In real life, a county sheriff's
department doesn't have the budget or the expertise
to do shit like that. We looked over the car as best
we could and didn't see anything inconsistent with a
drunk runnin' his car off the road. Now since you're
apparently some kinda big shot, maybe what you
oughta do is call up the FBI and have *them* check
out Berry's car."

———◆◆◆———

Bill Berry's widow was a small plump woman in her early fifties. She had unremarkable features, a soft chin, and lifeless brown hair. She was as drab as a sparrow except for her glasses: the frames were fire-engine red and too big for her face. DeMarco bet that one of her friends had talked her into the frames, telling her they made her look young and with-it. They didn't.

"He handled everything," she told DeMarco. "The bills, the insurance policies, the bank accounts. I don't know where anything is, and when I do find something, I don't know what it means."

"It must be pretty hard," DeMarco said. "And I'm sorry to intrude, but I need to know a few things about your husband."

"Why?" she said. She wasn't being belligerent; she was just bewildered. A week after her husband's death she found everything bewildering.

"He had a government insurance policy, Mrs. Berry. We just need to make sure of a few things before we sign off on it."

"He did?" Mrs. Berry said.

Berry had had a standard government life insurance policy that paid his widow one year of his salary. DeMarco had determined this when he had looked at Berry's personnel record. So DeMarco knew that Berry had had an insurance policy and was glad his wife now did, too. He also knew that her husband had thirty-seven thousand dollars in a credit union in Crystal City—and it was not a joint account. The account had been opened about the same time as Carmody was given the training contract at the shipyard. The initial deposit into the account had been fifty thousand dollars.

"What was your husband doing the night he died, Mrs. Berry?" DeMarco asked.

"Having dinner with some people from out of town," she said. "He was always doing that. Guys would fly in from one of the shipyards for meetings and later they'd go out for dinner and drinks."

"Do you know who he was having dinner with that night?"

"No. He may have told me their names, but I don't remember."

"Did your husband ever mention a man named Phil Carmody? He lives in Bremerton, Washington."

"I don't think so," she said, shaking her head several times. Every time DeMarco asked another question to which she didn't know the answer, the world became a stranger, more frightening place.

"Mrs. Berry, did you know that your husband deposited fifty thousand dollars in a bank in Crystal City a few months ago?"

DeMarco knew what she was going to say before she said it.

"What?" she said. "Where did the money come from?"

Mahoney was at the Old Ebbitt Grill having dinner
with four union leaders. Autoworkers union, De-
Marco thought, but it could have been steelworkers
or Teamsters. It didn't really matter.

DeMarco looked at the five men sitting at the
table, stuffing rare steak into their mouths, sipping
bourbon between bites. Mahoney fit right in with
the union guys: they were all big, beefy men with
red faces; they were all loud and crude; and they all
had eyes that hinted at intellects out of proportion
to their years of schooling and the grades they had
acquired while in school. DeMarco suspected that
if Mahoney hadn't been a member of Congress he
would have been a labor leader.

The Speaker saw DeMarco standing at the entrance to the dining room. He stood, picked up his
tumbler of bourbon, swallowed whatever remained
in the glass, then said something that made his companions roar with laughter. He slapped one man on
the back and made his way toward DeMarco. Despite
the amount of alcohol he had consumed, Mahoney
moved between the tables gracefully, never bump-
ing into a chair, never jostling the elbow of another
diner. Mahoney, the dancing bear, a wide-bodied
Fred Astaire.

Mahoney led DeMarco outside the restaurant so
he could light up the half-smoked cigar he pulled

from the right-hand pocket of his suit coat. He lit the cigar, blew smoke at the moon, and looked across the street at the massive structure that housed the U.S. Treasury Department. Floodlights lit up the white walls of the building, making it look like a monument—or a very large tomb.

It was almost nine but DeMarco could see lights burning in two windows on the third floor of the building. He could imagine a small group of people in the lighted room, staring bleary-eyed at each other as they tried to balance the nation's checkbook.

"Those guys are scared, Joe," Mahoney said. He was talking about the union leaders, not the people in the Treasury Department. "There was a time when a kid with a high-school diploma, a kid whose hands worked better than his mouth, could have a good future in this country. He could get a job at GM or Ford or Boeing, become a machinist or a welder or a toolmaker, and in thirty years he'd have a house and two cars and maybe a boat and be able to put his kids through college. Those days are gone, and those guys are scared. And I'm scared, too, because I can't figure out what the hell to do about it."

Mahoney had many faults; DeMarco knew this all too well. He drank too much, he cheated on his wife, and he bent the rules with abandon. He was selfish and self-centered and vain and inconsiderate. But he cared about the people of this country, and the ones he cared about the most wore steel-toed boots and hard hats.

"Shit," Mahoney said, still thinking about the union leaders. He took in a breath and trained his drinker's eyes on DeMarco. "So whaddya got?"

DeMarco told him.

"Goddamnit, Joe," he said, sounding tired, "why can't it be just the way it seems? Why can't this bum have killed Hathaway's nephew? Why can't this slug Berry have had a few drinks and drove himself into a tree? Why does it have to be spies, for Christ's fuckin' sake?"

"Maybe it's not," DeMarco said, "but right now too many things don't add up. The money in Berry's bank account. Whitfield's last phone call saying these two clucks were up to something. The timing of Whitfield's death. And this guy Carmody—he just doesn't fit the mold of a training consultant."

"So why would they—whoever the hell *they* is— kill Berry? Whitfield I can understand, maybe. He saw something he shouldn't have so they killed him. But why Berry?"

"I called Emma and asked her the same question. She thinks that whoever's running this thing may be wrapping up loose ends, trying to protect Carmody and his men."

"Emma," Mahoney said, shaking his big head. "Because she's an ex-spook she sees spooks under every rock." Mahoney shook his head again, and a white lock fell down onto his forehead, almost into his eyes. He looked like a big angry sheepdog. "So what do you want me to do?" he asked DeMarco.

"Nothing. I just thought I'd better let you know what was happening. And I have to go back out to Bremerton."

"Great. I don't have enough problems, I got you giving me mysteries to worry about, and then you're not going to be here in case I need you."

"We have to get to the bottom of this thing, boss. If Emma's right—"

"Yeah, yeah, I know," Mahoney said. "Go back to Bremerton."

Mahoney tossed his cigar stub toward the gutter and a passing woman gave him a dirty look for littering—or maybe just for being a large, sloppy drunk. Mahoney smiled at the woman, a smile that said: Go screw yourself, honey.

"I gotta get back inside," Mahoney said. "If I can't help those guys, I can at least buy 'em enough booze to make 'em forget their problems for one night."

DeMarco would have bet his pension that the union guys were picking up the tab—but he could have been wrong. With Mahoney you just never knew.

18

We're at a dead end here," DeMarco said.

He and Emma were sitting in a car, parked half a block away from Carmody's office in Bremerton. They'd been parked in the spot for more than an hour. Emma sat behind the steering wheel, sunglasses masking her eyes and her thoughts.

"I know," Emma said.

But that didn't keep DeMarco from telling her what she knew. "We have nothing to show that these guys are doing anything illegal. We can't pin Whitfield's murder on them. We didn't find anything in their houses. *You* didn't find anything in Carmody's office. And this Berry, back in D.C., he's dead so even if he was involved in something, he's not going to tell us."

"I was thinking some more about Berry," Emma said. "I'm inclined to think his death really was an accident."

"Oh? Why's that?"

"It occurred to me that if they—"

"Who's they?"

"—that if they wanted to keep Carmody and his guys in place out here for any length of time, they would need Berry to maintain their contract. With him dead they might have a hard time continuing to work here."

"Who's they?" DeMarco asked again.

"I don't know, but somebody is running this operation. We know Mulherin, Norton, and Carmody didn't kill Whitfield. We know Whitfield saw or heard something because he called you, and after he called you somebody killed him. This means that Carmody contacted somebody, somebody close by, and told that person that they'd been busted by Whitfield. And the person Carmody contacted acted very quickly to eliminate Whitfield. Which means there's *somebody* on the ground out here running things."

"Okay, fine," DeMarco said. "Let's assume that Carmody and the pirates really are—"

"The pirates?"

"Mulherin and Norton."

Emma laughed. "That fits," she said.

"Anyway, let's say you're right and these guys are spies or terrorists or whatever. Do you think they're going to do something stupid now, so soon after Whitfield's death?"

"No. They might not do anything for weeks, maybe months. I wouldn't, if I was running this."

"That's what I was afraid you were gonna say." DeMarco wasn't a patient man; nothing drove him nuttier than just sitting and waiting. "So let's give 'em a shove," he said.

Emma sat there a minute, tapping a manicured nail on the steering wheel. "Of the three of them," she said, "who do you think is the weakest link?"

"Weakest link how?" DeMarco said.

"The one likely to crack first. The one most likely to panic if we squeeze him."

"Mulherin," DeMarco said without hesitation.

"Why?"

"Carmody just seems like a tough bastard, ex-SEAL and all that. Norton, he's got—I don't know— *discipline*. Like the way his apartment's so neat. And he might be smart. You know, all the computer stuff."

"Yes," Emma said, "and the first time we met them, I noticed Mulherin got all bug-eyed on us when we stepped into Carmody's office and looked over at Norton for support. So I agree, Mulherin's the one."

"So how do you wanna squeeze his skinny ass?" DeMarco said.

19

―――◆◆◆―――

Ned Mulherin was sitting in the back of his boat drinking a beer, listening to a Mariners game on the radio. The boat was a twenty-one-foot Trophy and was moored at the marina in Brownsville, a town a few miles from Bremerton. For the last two hours he'd been installing new electric downriggers on his boat—no more hand cranking up a ten-pound ball of lead when he went salmon fishing, no sirree. Except for the fact that the Mariners were behind three runs in the second inning, he was feeling pretty good. Then he saw the guy walking down the pier, the hard case who'd come to Carmody's office, and he stopped feeling so good.

"You remember me, Mulherin?" DeMarco said.

"Yeah. You're that guy from Congress, the one that Whitfield sicced on us."

"That's right," DeMarco said, "and we need to have a little talk."

Emma had decided to let DeMarco brace Mulherin. She had something else to do, but even if she hadn't been otherwise engaged, she thought DeMarco would be more effective with Mulherin. The reason for this was something she called the "Godfather factor."

DeMarco's late father had been an enforcer for a New York mob boss—and DeMarco looked just like his father. He had thick shoulders and heavy arms and big hands. He had a big, square, dimpled chin. And when his mouth took a certain set, and if he let his eyes go cold and flat . . . well, the end result was a hard-looking guy but one who was polite and well educated, a guy who spoke in a soft, rational tone of voice, and all the time he's talking you're thinking that if you don't do exactly what he says, you're gonna wake up with a horse's head in your bed. The Godfather factor would start moving Mulherin in the direction Emma desired.

"We don't need to talk about anything," Mulherin said. "Ever since Whitfield got killed, I've had nothing but people talking to me. FBI guys. NCIS guys. Bremerton cops. They've all been asking me questions. And I'll tell you the same thing I told them: I don't know anything about Whitfield's murder and this job we're doing for the navy's legit. Now beat it. I'm workin' here."

DeMarco shook his head gravely, as if Mulherin was making a big mistake. "I don't want to talk about Dave Whitfield, Mulherin."

"Then what do you wanna talk about?"

"Money. I want to know how you managed a financial miracle."

"Huh?"

"Six months ago you were sixty thousand dollars in debt. Today you are debt free and have a new fishing boat. We need to discuss how that happened."

"How do you know about my finances?" Mulherin said. "You have to have a warrant to—"

"The FBI needs warrants, Mulherin. Me, I just call a few people."

"You can't—"

"Ned, you wouldn't *believe* what I can do. When it comes to terrorism, the government has rather broad powers."

"Terrorism! What the hell are you talking about?"

"Have you heard of the Patriot Act?"

"The Patriot Act? What—"

"Yeah, I love the Patriot Act," DeMarco said. "Someplace there in the fine print it says a person suspected of terrorism—"

"What fucking terrorism!"

"—can be thrown in jail and detained indefinitely. And once in custody, that person is not allowed access to counsel and may sit in a cell for months while the government interrogates him. And who knows what happens during these interrogations. What's your pain threshold, Ned?"

"You're goddamn nuts!" Mulherin said. "I'm not—"

"Ned, I'm the only hope you have."

"Hope? Hope for what?"

"Ned, we know you're not the guy in charge. Who would ever put you in charge of anything? But we'll catch your friends eventually, and when we do, you'll go down with them. It's only a matter of time. And the only one who's *not* going to spend a long time in a federal prison is the one who helps us develop our case. When it comes to crime, Ned, the first rat's the winner."

Mulherin looked down at DeMarco from the deck of his boat, his lips trembling with both fear and anger. Finally, he said, "You stay the hell away from me. You got no right . . ." Mulherin spun around and passed through a sliding wooden door into the sleeping section of his boat, and shut and locked the door. It was hot inside the sleeping section of the boat. He hoped DeMarco wouldn't hang around outside his boat for too long.

He didn't.

An hour after talking to DeMarco, Mulherin drove his Ford Explorer into the parking lot of the Clearwater Casino, a tribal casino located forty minutes from Bremerton.

Emma and DeMarco had followed Mulherin to the casino in separate cars. Emma called DeMarco on his cell phone and told him to wait in the parking lot. She then sat a few minutes to give Mullherin time to get settled in the casino. Before leaving her car, she donned a black wig—glossy, synthetic hair touching her shoulders—and covered her lips with a thick layer of bright red lipstick. She glanced into the rearview mirror and winced at what she saw there, but with a cigarette dangling from her lips she'd fit right in with the slot-machine addicts in the casino.

The casino was much bigger and grander than Emma had imagined. The Indians were giving Las Vegas a run for their money. She made a slow tour of the place, walking down the aisles between card tables and crap tables and noisy slot machines, looking for Mulherin. She found him sitting alone in a dark bar that faced an empty stage. She picked a slot machine where she could watch him and fed a twenty-dollar ticket into the machine.

Ten minutes later, Norton entered the bar and joined Mulherin at the table. Five minutes after that Carmody walked in. Emma had been hoping a fourth person would join them, but that didn't happen.

Mulherin and Norton ordered beers while Carmody declined the waitress's offer. The men began to talk and at one point Carmody jabbed a big finger at Mulherin's face to make a point and Emma saw Mulherin sit back in his chair, a chastised expression on his face.

Moments later, Carmody rose from his chair and began to walk toward the casino exit. Emma noticed she'd won fifty dollars from the slot machine—she'd always been lucky—but she didn't have time to cash out. The next slot-playing grandma who sat in the chair was going to think she'd died and gone to gambler's heaven.

As Emma followed Carmody from the casino, she made a quick call to DeMarco. Carmody turned and looked behind him once as he crossed the casino parking lot to his car, but all he saw was a woman with long dark hair, her head down, digging into her purse for her keys. Emma was behind Carmody as his car left the casino parking lot. As she was driving away, she saw DeMarco enter the casino.

───◆◆◆───

DeMarco found Norton and Mulherin where Emma had said they'd be, drinking beer near the empty stage. He was about to approach their table, when he saw Norton stand. Norton said something to Mulherin—something DeMarco assumed wasn't kind—because Mulherin gave Norton's departing back the finger.

Mulherin sat drinking a few minutes by himself, a petulant expression on his long face, the expression of a man who had just received an ass chewing that he didn't think he deserved. Mulherin finished his beer, ordered another one, then walked over to a craps table and started losing money.

Mulherin had just placed a red five-dollar chip in the section of the craps table called the "Field." The Field was essentially a sucker's bet, a one-roll, even-money bet on all the numbers on the dice that had the least chance of hitting. Only novices—and morons—played the Field.

DeMarco walked up next to Mulherin and placed a big hand on Mulherin's shoulder. "Dumb bet, Ned," DeMarco said. "You read any book on craps, it'll tell you that."

"What the hell are you doing here?" Mulherin said. "Are you following me?" Mulherin tried to pull away from the hand on his shoulder, but DeMarco just squeezed and pulled Mulherin closer.

"Yep," DeMarco said.

"You can't—"

"That wasn't smart, Ned, running to Carmody right after we talked. You're gonna make him nervous. He's gonna think you can't hold your water. I don't think you want a guy like Carmody thinking things like that, Ned."

The craps table wasn't busy, only three other players, and the pit boss had been watching the exchange between Mulherin and DeMarco. He couldn't hear what DeMarco was saying, but he could see DeMarco's hand on Mulherin's shoulder and could tell that Mulherin was scared. The pit boss—a man intimately familiar with the problems of bad gamblers—wondered if DeMarco was a guy trying to collect a debt.

"Sir," the pit boss said to Mulherin, "is this gentleman bothering you?"

Mulherin got an expression on his face similar to that of a drowning man who'd just been thrown a rope. "Yeah," he said. "He's, he's . . ."

"Sir," the pit boss said to DeMarco, "I'm going to have to ask you to leave." The pit boss didn't care if Mulherin owed some loan shark money. Mulherin was the player, and right now he was in the Indians' casino losing his money.

"Sure," DeMarco said to the pit boss. He took his hand off Mulherin's shoulder and gave him a friendly slap on the back, a hard little thump that rocked Mulherin forward. "I can always talk to ol' Ned here later. I know where he lives."

<hr>

As Emma drove, she wiped the lipstick from her mouth with a Kleenex and took off the wig. She

replaced the wig with a dark blue Calvin Klein baseball cap. Carmody drove less than five miles from the
casino before he pulled off the highway and took the
access road to a small state park, the Faye Bainbridge
State Park.

Emma wasn't certain but she figured the park
had only one exit, and that Carmody would have
to leave the park by the same road that he'd entered.
Whatever the case, she knew it would be unwise to
follow Carmody into the park in her car as he would
be almost certain to see her. So she pulled off to the
side of the access road and pushed the switch to start
the emergency flashers. It would appear as if her car
had broken down and she had gone to find a phone
to call for aid. She locked the car and sprinted down
the access road in the direction Carmody's car had
gone. She saw a flash of red ahead of her: Carmody's
Taurus. It wasn't moving. She left the access road and
veered off into the woods surrounding the parking
area. She moved carefully through the woods until
she found a small, thick stand of trees where she
could hide and still see Carmody's car.

Carmody was just sitting in his car, and as Emma
watched, he rolled down the windows to let in some
air and adjusted his seat to a partially reclining position as if he expected to be there for a while.

Emma was hoping Carmody had come to the
park to meet his control. She knew *somebody* was
controlling this operation—assuming there was an

operation. Mulherin had done what she had expected him to do: he had reported to Carmody immediately after DeMarco had talked to him. Now she was hoping Carmody would take the next step and report to his control—and then Emma would follow that person.

Carmody appeared to be sleeping in his car. Emma wondered momentarily if he'd just decided to come to the park to take a nap, but that seemed unlikely. After he'd been there exactly one hour, she saw Carmody raise his arm and look at his wristwatch. Then he readjusted his seat and started his car.

Emma watched from her place in the trees as he drove out of the park, then she ran back to her car, cursing under her breath. She was going to lose him.

———◆———

The Asian woman had arrived at the rendezvous point fifteen minutes before Carmody. As she always did, she would wait for a while before approaching his car. She had waited half an hour, and had been about to come out of the woods when a movement in the bushes *behind* Carmody's car caught her eye. She took a pair of binoculars out of her shoulder bag and focused on the spot. She didn't see anything for almost ten minutes, then the bushes moved again, and a face appeared in the lenses of her binoculars. The woman inhaled sharply; she had to bite her lower lip to keep from crying out.

She just sat and watched for twenty minutes, doing nothing, remaining absolutely still. And it was hard for her to stay still because she was literally trembling with rage. If she had had a gun with her she might have shot the woman in the bushes right then. Finally, she saw Carmody start his car and drive away, and then she watched as the woman ran out of the bushes, most likely going back to her car to follow Carmody.

A moment later the Asian woman stepped from her hiding place. She knew that most people thought of her as cold and unemotional—and she was. Her emotions had been cauterized a long time ago. But if anyone had been there to see her at that moment they would have had no trouble at all reading the hatred burning in her eyes.

20

DeMarco was still bird-dogging Mulherin.

He was sitting in his rental car, parked half a block from Mulherin's house. He was pretty certain where Mulherin was going this evening. He had found out that Mulherin was a member of the Elks, and tonight was the Elks' weekly Texas hold'em poker tournament, which Mulherin never missed. Sure enough, at six forty-five, the front door of Mulherin's cluttered house swung open and he appeared wearing a sport jacket, a dress shirt sans tie, gray slacks, and loafers. The guy was dressed so nicely that DeMarco wondered if he might be meeting an Elkette at his club.

Mulherin climbed into a Ford Explorer and backed down his driveway. Because he was fiddling with his car radio, he didn't notice DeMarco when he drove right past him. DeMarco made a U-turn and followed, letting Mulherin get a block ahead of him.

A mile from his house, Mulherin and DeMarco passed through an industrial area. There was a large warehouse on one side of the street and on the other side were buildings that advertised welding and auto body repair and marine diesel services. The businesses were closed for the day and there were no pedestrians on the street. DeMarco glanced over at a sign advertising used crab pots for sale and wondered what a crab pot was—something you caught 'em in or something you cooked 'em in? When he turned his head to face forward, he saw a black Honda sedan with tinted windows in his rearview mirror. The Honda was gaining on him, moving fast, and blew past DeMarco, then past Mulherin's Explorer. The Honda was fifty yards in front of Mulherin's vehicle when the driver hit his brakes and simultaneously turned the car sideways, blocking Mulherin's path. Mulherin slammed on his brakes to avoid broadsiding the Honda, the rear of the Explorer fishtailing as he did so.

"Jesus!" DeMarco said and stopped his car. He was a half a block away from Mulherin's vehicle.

Two men exited the Honda. Both were Asian, both over six feet tall, and they looked very fit. They wore jeans and white T-shirts that were tight to their bodies—and they were both holding pistols in their hands, and silencers were attached to the barrels of the pistols.

The men raised their weapons. Mulherin shrieked in fright, put his car into reverse, and started to back up, but before he had traveled ten yards one of the men fired bullets into the Explorer's front tires. The other man fired at the same time, a single shot that went through Mulherin's front windshield, missing Mulherin's face by less than a foot. Before the men could fire again, and with a speed that surprised both DeMarco and the shooters, Mulherin flung open his door and began running down the road—toward DeMarco.

DeMarco immediately stepped on the gas pedal and closed the distance between him and the fleeing Mulherin. The Asians, instead of chasing after Mulherin, took up shooting positions—legs spread, a two-handed grip on their weapons—and fired at Mulherin. Two bullets struck the asphalt near Mulherin's feet, another ricocheted off a garbage can sitting on the sidewalk. Mulherin screamed, "Help! Jesus Christ, help me!" Mulherin at this point was running so fast he was having a hard time maintaining his balance and he stumbled, almost falling— which was a good thing as this made him a harder target.

DeMarco, by this time, had reached Mulherin. He stopped his car, flung open the passenger-side door, and screamed, "Mulherin, get in!"

Mulherin leaped into DeMarco's car and immediately put his head down so it was below the level of the windshield. DeMarco put his car in reverse and jammed down the gas pedal. As he was backing away, going at least forty miles an hour in reverse, the shooters fired their weapons. One bullet hit the mirror on the driver's side door, and blew it completely off the car. The other bullet hit DeMarco's front windshield, punched a neat hole through the windshield, then shattered the rear window into a thousand pieces.

"Son of a bitch!" DeMarco screamed.

DeMarco didn't know how to do one of those fancy driving maneuvers where you spin a car going full speed in reverse so it ends up pointed in the opposite direction. So he did the only thing he could do. He stayed in reverse until he reached the next intersection, hit the brakes, jammed the transmission into drive, and turned the corner. As he was turning, he looked up the street: the Asians were running back toward their Honda. DeMarco pushed the car up to sixty and stayed at that speed until he reached a busy street with lots of vehicles and pedestrians around.

"What the fuck's going on?" Mulherin said.

DeMarco didn't answer; he was looking for the black Honda. He didn't see it.

"We need to call the cops," Mulherin said.

"Shut up," DeMarco said. "And keep your head down where nobody can see it."

"But who the hell were those guys?" Mulherin said.

"You know damn good and well who they were," DeMarco said.

"What?" Mulherin said.

DeMarco ignored Mulherin and took out his cell phone and punched a speed-dial button. "Emma, it's Joe," he said into the phone. "They tried to pop Mulherin."

DeMarco was silent for a moment then said, "Okay. It'll take me ten or fifteen minutes to get there."

"Where are we going?" Mulherin said.

"Someplace where your useless ass will be protected. Now keep your head down and your mouth shut."

DeMarco drove around for a brief period to make sure the Honda wasn't nearby, then got onto Highway 3. Four miles later he took the exit for the Naval Submarine Base. He drove up to the security gate and showed his ID to the guard. The guard must have known that he was coming because he didn't ask to see Mulherin's ID nor did he ask about the bullet hole in the front windshield. DeMarco drove half a mile until he came to a windowless, single-story building. There was no name on the outside of the building, just a three-digit number.

"What are we doing at the sub base?" Mulherin asked.

"Come on," DeMarco said and exited his car and walked toward the building. Mulherin hesitated a moment, then followed. They entered the building, walked down a narrow, brightly lit hallway until they came to an open door. The room contained a small wooden table and two wooden chairs. The only thing on the cinder-block walls of the room was a government-issue clock. Emma was sitting alone at the table, and on the table was a pitcher of water, two glasses, and a tape recorder.

"Hello, Mr. Mulherin," Emma said.

"Am I under arrest?" Mulherin asked.

"No," Emma said, "you're a material witness under protective custody."

"I want a lawyer," Mulherin said.

"What happened?" Emma said to DeMarco, ignoring Mulherin's demand. He told her how the men, both Asians, had shot up Mulherin's car, nearly killing him. "If I hadn't been following him, they would have nailed his ass," DeMarco said.

"I want a lawyer," Mulherin said again.

"No," Emma said. "A lawyer is not an option available to you. Either you tell me what you've been doing or we'll take you back to your house where you'll most likely be killed. What's it going to be?"

Mulherin hesitated. He must have felt something on his face because he reached up at that moment and touched his cheek. There was a small cut on his cheek that was bleeding slightly; the cut had been caused by glass fragments from the bullet that had struck his front windshield. Mulherin looked in wonder at the blood on his fingertips then sat down at the table.

"Where's the restroom?" DeMarco asked.

"Down the hall," Emma said in an irritated tone.

Like *she* never had to pee, DeMarco was thinking.

DeMarco left the interrogation room and walked down a narrow hallway. As he passed one room, he heard people talking and pushed open the door. There were two men in the room, one seated behind a desk, one in a chair in front of the desk. Both men had their feet up on the desk and were drinking Cokes. It was the two men who had tried to kill Mulherin.

"You motherfuckers!" DeMarco said.

The two men started laughing.

"You wanna Coke?" one of the men said. "Come on, have a Coke."

The two men had earlier identified themselves as Jim and Tom Wang, the Wang brothers. DeMarco assumed their names were not Wang and that they weren't brothers. Fucking spies all had a weird sense of humor. Neither of the men sounded Asian; they spoke as if they had been raised in California or some other part of the United States that didn't imprint an identifiable accent on its citizens.

"No, I don't wanna damn Coke. I wanna know if you're nuts!"

"Hey," Jim Wang said, "Emma said to make it look good."

"That one shot," DeMarco said, "the one you put through the windshield? It missed my head by about two fuckin' inches!"

"No it didn't," the other Wang said. "I missed you by a foot. It was an easy shot. I was nowhere close to hitting you."

"My ass, you weren't," DeMarco said, which just made the Wangs laugh some more. These were two sadistic bastards, DeMarco thought.

"And you shot the *shit* out of my car," DeMarco said. "It's a rental, goddamnit, and I didn't get the insurance."

"You didn't get the insurance?" Tom Wang said. "Oh, man, that's gonna cost you. Maybe your own insurance will cover it."

"Bullet holes! You think my insurance covers fuckin' bullet holes in rental cars?"

This caused the Wangs to go into convulsions.

Emma was guessing that Carmody was most likely working for the Chinese. It could have been somebody else—Russians, maybe Iranians or North Koreans, or even the Indians—but Emma figured the best bet was the Chinese. The Russians, these days, were in the midst of such political and economic chaos that they were having a hard time just keeping their fleet afloat, whereas the Chinese were building up their fleet, determined to become a real naval power. And thus the Wang brothers, two Chinese Americans.

"Who are they?" DeMarco had asked when he had been introduced to the Wangs. "Military? FBI? Who?"

"Military. Guys from my old outfit," Emma had said.

"I thought your old outfit wasn't going to provide any manpower."

"They weren't, so I called somebody higher up the food chain than Bill Smith, somebody who owes me."

DeMarco wondered if Emma had blackmailed one of her ex-bosses. Probably.

"But I was told," Emma had said, "that if this didn't pan out, we wouldn't be getting any more help."

After cursing the Wangs one last time, DeMarco visited the restroom and then returned to the room where Emma was questioning Mulherin. Mulherin was still seated at the table, looking down at it. De-Marco had heard the term "mulish" before, but had never seen an expression on a man's face that so aptly met that description.

Emma, arms crossed over her chest, sat looking at Mulherin, her blue eyes chips of ice. She didn't look any happier than Mulherin. She glanced up at DeMarco when he entered the room.

"Mr. Mulherin," Emma said to DeMarco, "insists that he and his friends have been doing nothing illegal and that he has no idea why anyone would want to kill him. I've explained to Mr. Mulherin—repeatedly—that his control has decided to wrap up their little operation, and that includes getting rid of loose ends like him. Mr. Mulherin, however, lives in some sort of fantasy world. He thinks he's going to go back home and this will all be over, like it never happened, like it was some sort of bad dream. Mr. Mulherin is dumber than a rock."

Mulherin didn't even look up when Emma insulted him.

"Mulherin," DeMarco said, "who do you think those guys were? Carjackers with silenced weapons?"

"I wanna go," Mulherin said.

"I give up," Emma said. "Joe, take this fool back to his house. Drop him off right at his front door and leave him there."

"Hey, wait a minute!" Mulherin said. "Maybe you could take me to . . . uh . . . how 'bout the ferry terminal?"

"No," Emma said. "You are going home and you are on your own. Joe, after you get rid of him, meet me back at the motel." Emma rose from her chair and walked from the room.

On the drive back to his house, Mulherin sat in the passenger seat staring down into his lap. DeMarco could guess what was going through his mind. Could he trust Carmody and Norton? What would he do when he got home? Where would he run to?

When they reached Mulherin's house, Mulherin looked around, wild-eyed.

"What if they're waiting for me in my house?" Mulherin said.

"Beat it," DeMarco said.

"Why can't you just take me to the ferry terminal?" Mulherin said.

"Because I want those guys to shoot your traitorous ass off," DeMarco said. "Now either tell me what you're up to or get the hell out of the car."

Mulherin looked over at DeMarco for a moment, small eyes begging for mercy, then he opened the car door and sprinted for his house.

Emma's plan had failed.

Emma was sitting in the motel bar at a small table that overlooked Oyster Bay. She probably saw DeMarco walk into the room but she didn't acknowledge him. DeMarco went to the bar and asked the bartender for a beer. The bartender, his Yankee-bashing pal, had been rather cool toward him since discovering he was with Emma. DeMarco joined Emma at the table where they sat in silence for several minutes before Emma said, "I couldn't budge the dumb shit. Maybe he thinks Carmody will protect him. Or maybe he's just more afraid of Carmody than he is of us."

"So now what?" DeMarco asked.

Emma just shook her head.

DeMarco saw she was drinking a Manhattan instead of her usual martini; maybe that was the beverage she consumed on those rare occasions when she failed.

"Why not try again?" DeMarco said. "Right away. Mulherin's stubborn but he's scared. Why not have those two psychopaths you hired blow up his car or put a bunch of rifle shots through his front window?"

"For one thing, the Wangs are going back to San Diego tonight. The agency said this was a one-shot deal. The other thing is, I don't think it will work. Mulherin's going to tell Carmody what happened, and Carmody is going to explain to him that hired killers wouldn't have missed him with half a dozen shots. Carmody is going to figure out in a New York minute that this was a setup."

21

The Asian woman emerged from the water and walked toward the rocky beach.

She was wearing a black neoprene diving suit to insulate her body from the cold waters of Puget Sound. As she walked, she pulled a diver's mask and snorkel from her head. Knee-deep in the water, she balanced on one leg at a time and removed her flippers, then walked onto the beach, oblivious to the rocks and oyster shells beneath her bare feet. She dropped the flippers, mask, and snorkel on the ground, then unhooked the tool belt on her waist and let it drop to the ground next to the rest of her gear.

She turned in a slow circle to make sure she was alone. The windows of the closest house, half a mile away, were dark as would be expected at two a.m. She pulled the diving hood off her head and brushed her fingers through her short hair. Her hair shined in the starlight as if coated with oil. She sat down on the beach next to her gear, unzipped a water tight pocket, and took out a pack of cigarettes and a lighter. She lit a cigarette, blew smoke skyward, and looked out across the water at a full moon. A hunter's moon.

Emma, the woman thought. After all these years. All these horrible years.

She smiled then, her teeth white and even. She hadn't smiled—not a real smile—in a long time. She smiled now, though, because she had a plan. She wouldn't be humiliated again. She wouldn't lose again.

22

Norton gripped the shaft of the barbless hook between his thumb and forefinger, then shook it a
couple of times until the twelve-inch salmon came
off the hook.

"Damn shakers," he said. "They're about all that's
bitin' out here."

"Yeah, but them downriggers are working slicker
than shit," Mulherin said. "Drop the lines down to
one twenty, and we'll make another pass."

The two men were fishing off Possession Point on
the southern tip of Whidbey Island. Mulherin was
at the wheel of the fishing boat, a beer in his fist, a
Seattle Mariners hat on his head. He wore jeans and
a T-shirt and on the T-shirt were the words: I BELIEVE

IN FILLET AND RELEASE. Mulherin wore the T-shirt every time he fished and it was spotted with fish-blood stains that were impervious to detergent.

Mulherin had caught an eight-pound silver and a twenty-pound king but Norton had yet to hook into anything of legal size. For reasons that Norton could never understand, Mulherin always caught more fish than he did even when they were fishing from the same boat at the same depth using the same bait. It really pissed him off.

Norton put another plug-cut herring on his hook and dropped the bait to the depth Mulherin had specified. He wore fish-bloodied jeans and an old T-shirt that stretched tight over his gut. He checked the drag on his reel then walked over to the cooler and took out another beer.

"I hope we got enough beer," he said, sounding genuinely concerned. They had started off with a case of twenty-four cans when they left the marina at six a.m. but it looked like half their supply was gone, and it was only nine. Fuckin' Mulherin, Norton thought, the guy drank like a fish.

"We'll get some more in Everett," Mulherin said.

"Why the hell did Carmody want us to meet him over there anyway?"

"Who cares? It works out perfect. We fish 'til eleven, catch a buncha salmon, then head on over to Everett for a nice lunch. I'm tellin' you, Norton, this is the life."

"You didn't think it was the life last night. You were so scared you were ready to crap your pants."

"No I wasn't."

"The hell you weren't. Until Carmody told you what was going on, you were ready to run for fuckin' Mexico."

Mulherin nodded his head. "Well you would have been scared, too, if guys had been shooting bullets at your head." Mulherin paused, then added, "I can't believe our own government would do something like that."

Norton just shook his head. Mulherin was such an idiot.

"You all set?" Mulherin asked. He had shut off the engine while Norton was rebaiting his line.

"Yeah," Norton said.

Mulherin hit the ignition button to restart the big inboard motor, but the engine didn't catch. He hit it again; the engine still didn't fire.

"Son of a bitch," Mulherin said. "Fucker sounds like it's flooded, but it can't be."

Mulherin hit the ignition button again.

23

Coast Guard Lieutenant Amanda Minelli was young, early twenties, and petite, no more than five foot three. And the blue coveralls she wore were a little baggy on her slender frame, making her seem even smaller. But Emma knew it would be a mistake to assume there was anything fragile about Minelli. At her rank, she probably commanded the rescue boat that went out when the wind was fifty knots and the waves thirty feet high, and rescued fishermen too dumb to heed the weather reports. Amanda Minelli likely had more courage than men three times her size. Emma was just disappointed she couldn't tell her more.

"What's left of the boat is in five hundred feet of water," Minelli said. "At that depth, it'll be a major effort to inspect the wreckage and the chance of finding anything conclusive is pretty small."

"If it was a shaped charge you'll be able to tell," Emma said.

"Yeah," Minelli said, "but the debris will be spread out all over the place. And it could have been an accident. This guy, Mulherin, we talked to his neighbors. According to one of them, he was one of those incompetent do-it-yourselfers. He'd just finished installing electric downriggers on his boat and not too long ago he replaced an alternator. If he used an automotive alternator instead of a marine one, he could have blown himself up."

"Why's that?" DeMarco said.

"Because marine alternators are made with spark suppressors; automotive ones aren't And Mulherin's boat used gas not diesel. Gas is more explosive than diesel. So if Mulherin had a fuel leak, even a small one, and he used a rebuilt alternator taken off some truck, he could have blown himself to kingdom come just to save a few bucks."

"But you *are* getting a dive team over here," Emma said.

"Yeah," Minelli said. "Navy deep-dive guys from San Diego. They have a saturation dive suite and an ROV."

"An ROV?" DeMarco said.

"A remote operating vehicle. A robot, in other words, with mechanical arms and cameras. At the depth that fishing boat is at, we're not talking scuba diving."

"When will the dive team get here?" Emma asked.

"Maybe next Thursday," Minelli said. "They're on some other mission, I guess." She looked down at the paper in her hand, then back up at Emma, and said, "With the clout you seem to have, maybe you can change the navy's priorities, but I sure as hell can't."

"No," Emma said. "Next Thursday will be fine. I'm already sure this wasn't an accident. It would just be nice to have it confirmed."

"When these divers go down, can they search the boat?" DeMarco said.

"For what?" Minelli said.

"Anything that belongs to the U.S. Navy and looks like it might be classified," DeMarco said.

Minelli didn't say anything for a minute. "I think maybe you guys oughta tell me a little more about what's going on here," she said.

24

———◆———

I'll have the blackened halibut, a Caesar salad, and half a baked potato," Emma said.

"We can't sell you half a potato, ma'am," the waiter said.

Emma closed her eyes briefly, then said very slowly, "Then sell me the whole potato, but just before you bring my dinner, take half the potato off the plate. *You* can eat the half you don't bring me."

"I can't . . . Yes, ma'am," the waiter said.

"And a Grey Goose martini, up, with a twist," Emma said.

"Will that be a whole martini or half a martini, ma'am?" the waiter said.

Emma's eyes flashed at the waiter but when she saw the small smile curving his lips, she smiled back. "You got me," Emma said.

"Yes, ma'am," the waiter said and turned to De-Marco. "And you, sir, what would you like?"

After their drinks arrived, Emma said, "This doesn't feel right?'

"What do you mean?" DeMarco said.

"Killing Norton and Mulherin. Why now? It's the *timing* that bothers me," Emma said. "Killing those guys the day after we questioned Mulherin draws attention to them. It puts a spotlight on the whole operation and it's going to make the navy and the Bureau dig harder to find out what they were doing. And that's the last thing a good control would want.

"I mean," Emma said, "why didn't they wait a while? We didn't have anything definite on them. Hell, you and I were the only ones who even believed they were spying—until this happened."

"I don't know," DeMarco said. "We scared Mulherin pretty good. So maybe it's just like you told him when we ran that bluff: whoever's running this thing realizes he's finished here and he's closing down the operation. Carmody's probably dead, too."

Phil Carmody had disappeared. After DeMarco and Emma had visited the Coast Guard, they went to Carmody's home and office, but couldn't find him. Emma alerted the FBI and asked them to start looking for Carmody and was curtly informed that the Bureau was already on the hunt, thank you very much, and that they didn't need any advice from a couple of civilians. God help them, DeMarco thought, if the Feebies found out what he and Emma had done to spook Mulherin.

Emma shrugged in response to DeMarco's comment about Carmody being dead. "Maybe he is," she said, "but I doubt it. Carmody would be a lot harder to kill than the pirates."

They sat in silence until their dinners arrived. The blackened halibut was really good. DeMarco wondered if they'd give him the recipe. As they ate, they talked briefly about what to do about the homeless guy, "Cowboy" Conran, who had been arrested for killing Dave Whitfield. The DNA tests had been completed on the knife found in the bum's backpack and Whitfield's DNA had been on the blade, giving the Bremerton cops the last bit of evidence that they needed to nail the poor schizo bastard. It still bothered Emma that Whitfield had been knifed while facing his opponent. "No way," she said, "would a guy as perpetually on edge as Whitfield let Conran get that close to him. A friend or a woman I could understand, but not some guy who smells like the inside of a tennis shoe."

"That FBI agent, the lady, she—"

"You mean the agent who looks like your ex?" Emma said.

DeMarco ignored that. "She was looking at one of Whitfield's neighbors," he said. "Maybe she's on the right track."

"No," Emma said. "*We're* on the right track. But if we can't prove that somebody associated with Carmody killed Whitfield, Conran could be convicted." She paused then added, "Although I suppose Mulherin and Norton getting blown into the afterlife and Carmody disappearing will cast some doubt on the prosecutor's case."

"Yeah, right," DeMarco said. "I'm sure the United States Navy is going to tell some public defender that Conran's best defense is the embarrassing possibility that one of their shipyards was penetrated by a bunch of spies."

Emma muttered, "So young and so cynical," then checked her watch and turned to look in the direction of the front door. And at that moment Bill Smith walked in.

After Smith had been introduced to DeMarco—just a name, no title—Smith flagged down a waiter. "Irish coffee," he said to the waiter, "with lots of whipped cream."

The waiter stared a moment at Smith, studying his face, before saying, "Yes, sir." The waiter turned to get Smith's drink, then turned back and opened his mouth to speak.

"Don't you dare say it," Smith said. "Just bring me the drink."

"Yes, sir," the waiter said. DeMarco saw the waiter talking to the bartender, pointing a finger at Smith. Both men started laughing.

"I thought you weren't helping us anymore," DeMarco said.

"That changed when Mulherin and Norton went to that great fishing hole in the sky," Smith said. "Now *everybody's* helping you. And I've got some news for you guys: Carmody was stopped by the highway patrol south of Eugene, Oregon, an hour ago."

"You're kidding," Emma said. "A cop caught Carmody?"

"I said the highway patrol *stopped* him. They didn't catch him."

25

---◆◆◆---

Carmody had been going ninety miles an hour. Occasionally he'd push the speed up to a hundred. He passed a dozen cars. He tailgated the cars before he passed them, he honked *as* he passed, and after he passed, he would swerve his vehicle over the lane markers, doing his best impression of a drunk behind the wheel.

Finally it happened. Behind him, almost half a mile back, he could see blue-and-red lights flashing. Thank God for cell phones. He slowed down to allow the highway patrolman to catch up to him but he didn't stop; he wanted to be closer to a freeway exit. The officer turned on his siren when Carmody didn't pull over immediately, and when Carmody still kept going, he pulled up next to Carmody's car and made an irate motion for him to get off the highway. Carmody looked ahead. The next exit was only a quarter mile away, so he applied his brakes and stopped his car on the shoulder of the highway.

Since the cop had been chasing him for at least ten minutes, Carmody figured that the officer had had ample time to get his license plate number and radio in to see if the car was stolen or if the driver had any outstanding warrants. The cop would have his name and so would the people in the highway patrol's communication center.

The officer exited his vehicle, slamming the door. He was pissed. Carmody opened his door and the cop yelled, "Sir, stay in your vehicle. Do *not* get out. And put your hands on the steering wheel."

"Wha . . . ?" Carmody said, and stepped out of his car.

"Sir! Get back in your vehicle. Now." The cop placed his hand on his service weapon but didn't unholster the gun.

Carmody took a step toward the cop, then fell to one side as if he'd lost his balance, then leaned against the side of his car, rocking unsteadily. He muttered "Dizzy," and closed his eyes.

"Sir, walk to the front of your vehicle and put your hands on the hood." The cop looked behind him. He was probably afraid that if Carmody tried to walk he'd end up in the middle of the highway and get hit. But Carmody didn't move. He just continued to lean against his car, his eyes closed, swaying, feigning a drunk on the verge of passing out.

He heard the cop mutter, "Shit."

The cop was now close enough to touch Carmody. He reached out and took hold of Carmody's upper arm, intending to walk Carmody to the front of his vehicle so neither of them would get run over. But when he touched Carmody, Carmody pivoted on his left foot and drove his fist into the cop's solar plexus. The cop grunted in pain and bent over, and when he did, Carmody struck the back of his neck with the side of his right hand.

Carmody reached down and felt the pulse in the cop's throat. It was strong and the cop was young and looked like he was in good shape. He shouldn't be out for more than a couple of minutes. Carmody grabbed the man's wrists and dragged him between the two cars so the cop's body was hidden by his patrol car. Carmody started to leave, then it occurred to him that if somebody hit the cop's car from the rear, the cop could get hurt. He went back and pulled the unconscious man to the side of the road, positioning him four or five feet from his patrol car.

Carmody got back into his vehicle and took the exit just ahead of him. Five minutes later he found a small shopping mall and parked his car next to another vehicle that was a good distance from the stores and other cars. He took a screwdriver out of his glove compartment and in two minutes, switched license plates with the vehicle he had parked next to.

26

Emma and DeMarco sat in a small conference room in the FBI's temporary headquarters in Bremerton. In the conference room with them were the two FBI agents who had originally been assigned to Dave Whitfield's murder. Diane Carlucci was one of those agents. The other agent, the agent in charge, was a young man named Darren Thayer. Thayer was probably in his thirties, but with his wide-eyed, unlined face he could have passed for a college senior. To make matters worse, he had a cowlick, freckles, and protruding ears. DeMarco just knew that his fellow agents called him Kid or Opie, and no matter how smart and how brave Darren Thayer was, his looks would condemn him to being treated like a rookie for half his career.

DeMarco had asked the FBI for an update on their efforts to capture Carmody. Thayer knew that DeMarco and Emma had no authority to ask him to do anything, yet at the same time he knew they had clout back in D.C. And since Thayer wasn't making any progress on the case anyway, he figured why not talk to them, they might help him. It was rare to find an FBI agent willing to talk to outsiders, much less one willing to admit that he needed help. DeMarco knew that just like his youthful face, Darren Thayer would eventually outgrow these good habits.

Thayer was saying, "Carmody used an ATM in Winnemucca, Nevada, yesterday, one with a surveillance camera. Twelve hours later, he checked into a motel in Buffalo, Wyoming, using one of his credit cards. We got in touch with the locals there and asked them to detain him, but by the time they got to the motel, he'd split. They said it didn't even look like he'd used the room."

"And I suppose you have no idea where he's going or what he's driving," DeMarco said.

"No," Thayer said. "He abandoned his own car in Nevada after he used the ATM. We don't know what he's using for transportation."

"Do you have an atlas here?" Emma asked Thayer. "A Rand McNally. A U.S. road atlas."

"I'll get one," Diane Carlucci said.

DeMarco, dog that he was, watched Diane's butt as she walked over to a nearby desk. Nice butt.

When Diane turned back with the atlas in her hand, she gave DeMarco a little wink and a smile. Nice smile. Emma had accused DeMarco of asking for the meeting just because he wanted to see Diane again. DeMarco, naturally, pretended to be offended that Emma would think he'd act so unprofessionally.

Emma took the atlas from Diane, opened it to a page that showed the entire country, and studied it for a couple of minutes. "Carmody's moving in a circle," she said. "South to Oregon, east into Nevada, then north to Buffalo, Wyoming. It almost looks like he's looping back here. But why in the hell would he be using his credit cards and bank machines? He has to know we can use those things to locate him."

"Maybe he doesn't have any other source of money," Thayer said.

"Maybe," Emma said, "but Phil Carmody is a very bright guy, Agent Thayer. So if this very bright guy didn't have credit cards under a false name why didn't he just go to his bank before he fled Bremerton and get all the cash he had in his account? And why did he go out of his way to punch a highway patrolman, an action that he must have known would be broadcast to every cop shop in the tristate area? There's something odd going on here. It's like every ten or twelve hours Carmody is letting us know right where he is— or where he *was*—and all the law enforcement guys go swarming to that spot and by then he's gone, of course."

Emma looked at the map again. "I'll bet you the next sighting of him will be in western Montana, northern Idaho, or eastern Washington. I'm sure he's coming back this way."

"But why?" Diane Carlucci said. DeMarco could tell that Diane was impressed by Emma.

"I don't know," Emma said. "I don't know what the hell he's doing."

"I have an idea," DeMarco said. He'd been silent up until this point. Catching spies wasn't his normal line of work.

"What?" Emma said.

"He's creating a diversion."

"Ah," Emma said, understanding immediately.

"A diversion?" Thayer said, not being as quick as Emma.

"Yeah," DeMarco said. "There could be something else going on, maybe right here in Bremerton, right under our noses. You guys—the FBI, the cops, navy security—right now, you're all focused on Carmody, trying to figure out what he did at the shipyard, trying to catch him, trying to guess where he's gonna go next. It's like magic, Thayer: while you're watching the right hand, the left hand's doing the trick?'

"Who's the left hand?" Thayer said.

"Carmody's boss, his control," Emma said.

"But what's the trick?" Thayer said.

27

———◆———

She hated sex.

It hadn't always been this way. There had been a time when she had lived for it, when she could hardly wait to have *him* inside her. But he was gone and this man—the man lying on her—was not him and those days were long past. Now sex was nothing more than a tool of her trade—a repulsive, degrading, sweaty tool. But an effective tool.

She could tell the man was almost finished. Fortunately he was fairly quick, and at his age, he could usually only manage to perform once during their brief, clandestine encounters. She stroked his back mechanically and managed a few moans of feigned passion. She needed to keep him enraptured just a few days longer. Finally she heard him grunt in release. Thank God. He murmured a few things into her ear, things she didn't hear, things she didn't care about. She let him breathe heavily for a moment then pushed up gently to let him know she wanted him off her. He was considerate if nothing else, and he rolled off her body.

As he went through the predictable litany of how good it had been, how he had never known anyone like her, she rose from the bed. She looked down at him, smiled in a way she hoped seemed affectionate, and ruffled his hair like he was a puppy. As she turned toward the bathroom to wash him from her, the smile vanished and her face became the unemotional mask it usually was. From the bed she heard him say, "Walk slower. Please. You have the most beautiful ass I've ever seen." She gave her butt a little shake, feeling stupid as she did so, and entered the bathroom and closed the door.

Inside the bathroom, she stood naked, her hands on the sink, and looked into the mirror. Her short, spiky hair looked particularly wild as the man had been running his soft hands through it for the last half hour. She stared at the face in the mirror and black, empty eyes looked back at her.

She couldn't do this work any longer. She just couldn't. But if she was successful, if she could carry out her plan, she would not have to. *She* could become one of those in charge. She could be the one who assigned beautiful women to fuck for their country. But to gain such power her plan had to work. Because of the woman named Emma, she had been forced to terminate the shipyard operation sooner than she had wanted. The operation hadn't been a total success but neither had it been a complete failure. At least she didn't think so; she could only hope that her superiors saw it that way as well.

But it was the man lying on the bed in the other room who really mattered. What Washburn could do and what he knew was more important than everything Carmody had taken from the shipyard—and Washburn was firmly under her control.

Soon she'd move into the final phase, the phase that only she and Carmody knew about, the phase of the plan she had hidden from her superiors. And Carmody, as she had expected, was doing what he'd been told and doing it well. She didn't need sex to control Carmody.

She nodded to the face in the mirror. Yes, it was all going per plan and in the end she'd have everything she desired.

———◆———

She took a shower and by the time she finished, Washburn was fully dressed and sitting on the edge of the bed. She left the bathroom wearing only a towel. She could tell by the expression on Washburn's face that he was once again having second thoughts. He did this every time they met, and every time she had to convince him again that if he wanted to be with her—forever, she'd said—he must follow through with his promise.

Her country was building up its submarine fleet. They'd recently acquired four Kilo-class nuclear submarines from the Russians and they had started to construct some diesel-electric boats, boats that were incredibly quiet, so quiet that they *might* be able to avoid the American submarines that patrolled continuously off their shores.

The great advantage the Americans had over the world's other navies was *silence*: American submarines were so quiet they could not be readily detected by enemy sonar. At the same time, the Americans' ability to find and track other submarines was superior to everyone else's. Her navy wanted the same advantage: they wanted quiet, undetectable submarines and they wanted the technology to locate the enemy's boats.

American submarines were occasionally used to launch Tomahawk missiles at Al Qaeda training camps and they provided protection for the giant American carriers, but the primary mission of American submarines was gathering intelligence. There was a book called *Blind Man's Bluff* written in 1998; the book was required reading for her country's intelligence agencies. The book told how in 1971, *thirty-five years ago,* an American submarine had snuck into the Sea of Okhotsk off the Russian coast and tapped into Russian military phone cables. In thirty-five years the Americans' talent for intercepting satellite and radio signals and breaching communication systems had improved dramatically. For her country to collect intelligence as the Americans did, and to be able to compete with the American fleet if it ever came to war, they needed the acoustic technology of their enemy—and John Washburn, the man she had just made love to, was one of the keys to acquiring this technology.

Washburn was an expert on noise—submarine noise. Sonar capabilities. Noise-quieting techniques. Acoustic detection systems. Her superiors wanted this man and the files he could obtain and everything inside his head—and *she* would give him to them. He knew the limits of the U.S. Navy's current equipment and how to defeat it. With Washburn's knowledge, they would find the American submarines lurking off their shores, and their submarines would be able to lie in silence off the American coast.

She had met Washburn three months ago, at the same time she was setting up Carmody's operation. She met him by rear-ending his car. He had gotten out of his vehicle, slamming his door, looking irate, but when he saw her—how lovely she was—he immediately asked if she was all right. When she had said that she needed a drink to calm her nerves, he quickly agreed to buy her one.

She had drawn him slowly and carefully into her net using her beauty as a lure. It was something she'd done many times before, and compared to some past conquests, Washburn was an easy target. His wife was an overweight woman of fifty-six, the same age as Washburn. And according to Washburn, his wife was not only unattractive but bossy and bitchy and every other thing that men say about the women they are wed to but no longer desire. He also had two children, teenage girls, who were unmanageable and unlovable. For years he'd thought about divorcing his bloated hag of a wife but he knew that if he did, she'd take everything from him: his home, his savings, and half his pension. If that happened, he'd never be able to retire, he said. He'd have to work until he died.

So she gave him the escape hatch he wanted.

She had initially planned to blackmail him: have sex with him, take photographs, and threaten to expose him to both his wife and his government. But then she discovered a better weapon: obsession. Obsession was much more effective than blackmail.

She understood obsession because she'd once been obsessed with a man. Obsession was when you couldn't go five minutes without thinking of the one you loved. Obsession was when you would do *anything*, tell any lie, commit any transgression, to be with that person. Obsession was when a man's heart—and his balls—overrode his brain. Obsession was what made an intelligent, rational man like John Washburn become reckless and irrational, throwing aside love of country and love of family to be with the one he thought he must have or he would die. John Washburn, after three months, was obsessed with her.

And she had convinced him that the only way he could have her was to leave the country and take with him the information her superiors wanted. If he did that, he could have it all. He could have her, a home on a beautiful beach, and enough cash that they'd never have to work again.

She admitted she was a spy, but she didn't tell him who she worked for. She said she worked for a private consortium who sold intelligence to several countries, including America's allies. She even told him of her original plan to blackmail him. Sometimes the truth could be effective for gaining trust. But she also lied to him: she told him she loved him. And he believed her.

Washburn was not an unattractive man. He was tall and slender, with chiseled features and a fine head of gray hair. He'd had affairs in the past; women had fallen in love with him before. His ego convinced him that she wanted him as much as he wanted her.

She said that she had devised a way for him to disappear, a way so he wouldn't be pursued. And after he left the country she would meet him to begin their new life. The truth, of course, was that he *would* leave the country, but he would be met by agents from

her division. Then her country's scientists would take
the files he had copied and they would grill him for
months and pick his brain clean. He'd stay alive as
long as he proved useful to them—but he wouldn't
be living like a king on waterfront property.

But now Washburn was hesitating again, asking
again if there wasn't a different way. Couldn't they
just flee together? he whined. Couldn't they just run
away from everything, he from his wife, she from
her employers? Did he have to betray his country?
So again she explained to him the impracticality of
what he was saying: if he didn't do what she wanted,
they would have no money. They would be poor and
on the run forever. No, her way was the only way, she
said gently. If he left and took the files her employers
wanted, they would have money to burn and a grand
place to live, but most important, they would have
each other. She knew that for this particular man the
promise of wealth had been a factor in turning him
but that the money was not as important to him as
being with her. He was obsessed—and she had to
keep him that way.

Washburn was still sitting on the bed. She let the
towel drop slowly from her body and then knelt in
front of him.

She hated sex.

28

─────◆─────

Bill Smith of the DIA, who had no jurisdiction what-
soever in capturing Carmody and his cohorts, had
arranged for the meeting to be held. Smith was not
in attendance at the meeting; he was the wizard behind the curtain. He was always behind the curtain.

The attendees of the meeting were FBI agents
Darren Thayer and Diane Carlucci; Emma and De-
Marco; and the security officers for the four major
naval installations in the Pacific Northwest: the shipyard in Bremerton, the Trident submarine base at
Bangor, the Naval Undersea Warfare Center at Keyport, and the Whidbey Island Naval Air Station. For
Emma, there was something about the meeting that
struck her as vaguely familiar, but she didn't know

what it was, and after a moment she disregarded the feeling as just a puzzling occurrence of déjà vu.

A small amount of time was wasted before they got down to business because one of the security officers asked who Emma and DeMarco were. Agent Thayer clarified the issue by saying, "Uh, Bureau consultants." Then he added, with a jerk of his head toward Emma, "She's ex-DIA." This made the security officers sit up a bit straighter.

Thayer began the meeting with an update on Carmody. Carmody, Thayer said, was still eluding the FBI and had last been spotted near Spokane, Washington. As Emma had previously said, the ex-SEAL seemed to be going in a circle and it appeared he was still headed back to where he had started. In Spokane, he was caught on a surveillance camera stealing a motorcycle from a Harley-Davidson dealership. Idaho cops found the motorcycle abandoned in the driveway of an expensive home in Coeur d'Alene, thirty-five miles *east* of Spokane. Emma said she thought this was just another bit of misdirection on Carmody's part. Her guess was that after he ditched the motorcycle in a place where it was sure to be noticed and reported, he had most likely stolen another vehicle and was once again headed west.

"We think," Thayer said to the security guys, "that a foreign government, we don't know which one, has been running an espionage operation at the shipyard and—"

"Hey, we don't know that for a fact yet, sonny," Richard Miller, the square-headed security chief at the shipyard, said. "We've looked around the area where Mulherin and Norton worked and we can't find anything missing. So there's no evidence our security was ever breached and you shouldn't go around saying shit like that."

When young Agent Thayer started to sputter, Emma said, "Mr. Miller, the fact that nothing's missing doesn't mean they didn't get something." Miller started to protest again, but Emma raised her hand to silence him. "Look," she said, "this meeting is not about what Carmody and his guys may or may not have taken from the shipyard, so you can calm down. What we're worried about—I mean what the FBI is worried about—is that there may be another operation of some kind going on out here, and what Carmody is currently doing is distracting us from seeing that other operation."

"What kind of operation?" Miller said.

"We don't know," Emma said, "but your bases—the operations at those bases, information stored at those bases—are all potential targets."

"Yeah, but what are we supposed to do?" the security officer from the Trident submarine base said. Before Emma could answer, the officer said, "I mean, we can increase gate checks, station people in sensitive areas, increase controls for checking out classified material. Is that what you want?"

"No," Emma said. "If we're right, this is an operation already in progress. This government, whichever one it is, has *already* penetrated you. What you need to do is look for anything unusual, anything out of the ordinary."

"But like what?" the Trident security officer said again.

"For example," Emma said, "has anyone reported any suspicious activity to you? This whole thing started with Dave Whitfield saying that Carmody's supposed training study looked 'funny.' So have any of your people reported anything out of the norm, something you may have dismissed as being inconsequential? Has anything unusual happened at your bases related to security, such as an unexplainable security system malfunction? Has anybody in a critical position quit recently or suddenly become rich?"

"No," Miller said emphatically.

The security officers from the Trident base and the naval air station just shook their heads, but the man from the Undersea Warfare Center said, "Uh, there is one thing I can think of."

"What's that?" Emma said.

"Well, we had a guy drown yesterday afternoon. The guy was a civilian scientist, an expert on submarine acoustic stuff—you know, noise-quieting technology, sonar systems, towed and fixed arrays. That sort of thing. Anyway, he went fishing yesterday afternoon, by himself, and they found his boat overturned. The guy's missing, presumed dead."

"Any ideas what caused the boat to flip?" De-Marco asked.

"Yeah. In case you didn't notice yesterday, it was windier than shit. The Coast Guard had issued small-boat warnings for Puget Sound, but according to this guy's wife—his name's Washburn, by the way—he said to hell with it, that he was going fishing. His wife said he had a real bug up his ass about going, like he was gonna die if he didn't catch a salmon."

"Is the Coast Guard looking for his body?" Emma said.

"Sure. Ever since they found the boat last night."

Emma looked intently into the eyes of the Un-dersea Warfare Center security officer and said, "You need to search this man's office and see if anything's missing. Immediately." Before the security officer could respond, Emma turned to Thayer and Car-lucci. "This scientist may have died in a fishing ac-cident but you can't take the chance. This is too much of a coincidence, an expert like him disappearing at the same time Carmody is playing tag with us all over the country. You need to assume Washburn has been turned and is fleeing the country. Get his picture to every airport and train station and border crossing in the region as fast as possible. My guess is that while the Coast Guard is still searching for his body, he'll fly out of one of the international airports in the area—Seattle, Portland, Vancouver—and he'll have a passport with a false name. So you need to get his picture to the Transportation Security Administration fast and have them start looking at surveillance tapes and watching passengers."

"I dunno," Thayer said. "I mean before we get everybody all stirred up, I think we should—"

Diane Carlucci rose from her seat. "I'll call TSA now and you," she said to the Undersea Warfare Center security officer, "need to get me Washburn's picture right away."

That's my girl, DeMarco thought.

29

━━━◆━━━

In a Ramada Inn located twenty minutes away from the Portland International Airport, John Washburn sat in a room, on the edge of the bed, looking mournfully over at her. She was going through his carry-on luggage for a second time, making sure he had nothing in it that would cause it to be opened by security. She had just tossed out a set of fingernail clippers, even though she knew such an item was not prohibited.

"I just don't understand why you can't come with me," he said.

It was about the tenth time he'd said this, and she wanted to scream. Controlling her anger, she said, "I've told you why I can't. There's something I must

do before I leave and it's better if we travel separately."
She tried to make her voice sound loving when she
added, "But in just two days, my dear, I'll be with
you in Manila. Only two days."

In two days she would be nowhere near Manila,
but *somebody* would meet John Washburn there.

Washburn put his head in his hands. "I still wonder if I'm doing the right thing," he said. "I mean,
you know how I feel about you, but—"

"Stop it!" she screamed. "You're *committed*! It's too
late to back out now. You've been reported missing.
They're looking for your body. You can't go back. In
two hours you're getting on a plane and you're flying
out of here. Do you understand?"

Washburn's eyes grew wide. She'd never raised her
voice to him before.

She took a breath. She only needed to control
him a little longer. She just needed to get him to
the airport and on a plane. She walked over to him
and took his face in her hands. "You love me, don't
you?" she said.

It was so hard for her to feign looking tenderly
into his face when what she really wanted to do was
twist her hands and snap his neck.

"You know I do," he said.

"Then be strong. And think about us. Think about
us lying in bed, making love. Think about the home
we'll own, the cars we'll drive, the places we'll one

day see together. Think about the years of bliss we have ahead of us."

Then she bent down and gently kissed his lips.

She would be *so* glad when he was on that plane. She never wanted to touch him again.

30

DeMarco was sitting in the bar of the motel where he'd been staying ever since coming to Bremerton. His room was beginning to feel like a prison cell. He was watching a ball game on TV, and in the long intervals between pitches, he was flipping through a newspaper, looking at used car prices, trying to find out what BMW Z3s went for in this area. He had called the dealership in Arlington yesterday and the silver Z he'd been looking at was still on the lot. They had to be asking too much for the damn car.

Emma was also in the bar, at a corner table talking to her daughter on her cell phone. Emma was an enigmatic cipher who skillfully avoided any attempt to penetrate her past, but one of the few things that

DeMarco did know about her was that she had a child. Emma was gay and DeMarco didn't know if her daughter was her biological offspring or adopted. He had no idea how she had managed motherhood during her high-powered career at the DIA. The one thing he did know was that she was fiercely protective of her child, something she had demonstrated with gusto last year when a man had been stalking her daughter. One of these days DeMarco was going to get her drunk enough to tell him how she came to be a mom.

Currently, DeMarco and Emma had absolutely nothing to do but sit and wait for something to happen. The FBI was still chasing Phil Carmody and the scientist from the Undersea Warfare Center had not been found, either dead or alive. They still had no idea who was controlling Carmody nor any clues to lead them to that person. They still had no evidence that classified material had actually been taken from the shipyard. And they still had no idea as to who had really murdered Dave Whitfield. When you added up all those zeros, you got zero. So they were sitting in a bar, killing time, waiting for something to break.

In the fourth inning of the ball game, two things happened. The first was that a guy bunted and the Mariners' catcher swooped up the ball and threw it to first—and hit the batter right in the back of the head. The Mariners needed a new catcher. The other thing that happened was that Bill Smith came into the bar.

Smith walked over to the table where Emma was seated and waved an arm for DeMarco to join him there. Emma looked up at the two men in annoyance, said into her phone, "I love you and I'll talk to you later," then hung up.

"Yes?" she said to Smith.

"They got the bastard," Smith said.

"Which bastard?" Emma asked.

"The noise guy, the scientist. He was trying to catch a plane in Portland. He was headed for Manila."

"What did he say?" DeMarco asked.

"Zip," Smith said. "He puked all over the floor when they put the cuffs on him and said all he was doing was ditching his wife and kids, but when they asked why he had a false passport, he asked for a lawyer." Smith shook his head. "I'd like to go down there and attach a wire to his dick."

"Did he have anything on him, anything classified?" Emma asked.

"No. Nothing. And they can't find anything missing from his office."

"Which means nothing," Emma said. "He could have copied his files and manuals and given the copies to whoever's running him."

"Yeah," Smith said. "They gotta make him talk."

"I wouldn't if I was him," DeMarco said. "Right now the only crime he can be convicted of is having a false passport. And faking his death, I guess."

"Did they see anyone with him at the airport?" Emma asked.

"No," Smith said, "but they're looking at tapes right now. I think I'm gonna . . ."

Smith's phone rang. He listened for a moment, said thanks, hung up, and smiled broadly. "I guess this is our lucky day," he said. "That was Dudley. Carmody's checked into a Hyatt in Vancouver, B.C., and right now he's just sitting in his room. Dudley's watching him."

"Who's Dudley?" DeMarco said.

"Does the FBI know he's in Vancouver?" Emma said.

Smith smiled again, this time a small, crafty smile. "Not yet," he said.

"Who's Dudley?" DeMarco asked again.

"Bill's absurd name for his intelligence contact in the Mounties," Emma said.

"Well you gotta admit he looks like Dudley, Emma. You oughta see this guy, Joe," Smith said to DeMarco. "Wavy blond hair, big square chin."

"He's about five foot six," Emma said.

"So who said Dudley Dooright was tall?" Smith said. "How can you tell, him sittin' on his horse or standin' next to little Nell?"

"This conversation is ridiculous," Emma said.

"I'm heading up north right away," Smith said. "I want to be there when the Canadians take him."

"I'm going with you," Emma said.

"Now, Emma, I don't think that's really necessary."

"Maybe not, but I don't like the smell of this. Something's wrong here, Bill. Carmody's managed to evade every law enforcement agency in the western United States for almost a week, and now we find him sitting in a hotel room. Something's wrong. So I'm going with you and if you don't let me go, I'll call Mary."

"What in the hell have you got on her, Emma? Did you guys, uh, you know, play field hockey together at a Catholic girls' school?"

"No, and you're a jackass."

Smith pushed his glasses up on his nose and rose from the table. "I'm gonna call somebody and get us a helicopter."

"Aren't you going to call the FBI?" Emma asked.

"In a little while," Smith said, his sly smile again curving his lips.

"A helicopter," DeMarco said. "Wow." He'd never flown in one before.

31

She had been at the airport when they captured Washburn.

She had been there to make sure he didn't back out, fearful that at the last moment the weakling would change his mind. She had stood off to one side, near the security checkpoint, a floppy, broad-brimmed hat hiding her face from the surveillance cameras. Her eyes had *burned* into Washburn's back as he stood in line, as if by her will alone she could propel him forward. She had been forced to spin around once when the fool had looked back at her—something she'd told him not to do—a frightened, lovesick expression on his face. Later she could only pray that she had moved fast enough or that none of the cameras had been in a position to follow Washburn's line of sight.

She had watched, holding her breath, as he walked at last through the metal detector and picked up his carry-on luggage. She had just exhaled in relief, thinking "mission accomplished," when two white-shirted TSA officers came up to him and took him by the arms. The last image she had of John Washburn was him on his knees, vomiting, as they placed the handcuffs on his wrists.

She walked away quickly, not looking back. It took all her resolve not to run. She went to the parking lot, got into her car, paid her parking fee, and left the airport. As she did each of these things, she did not allow herself to think about what had just happened. She forced her mind to focus only on the immediate task of escape.

Two miles from the airport she found a place where she could pull off the road and park behind a building and not be visible to passing cars. She exited her car and slammed the door shut. And then slammed it shut again. And slammed it again. And slammed it again. She was in such a red rage that if someone had come upon her at that moment she would have beaten the person to death.

How had it happened? How had Emma done it? How could she *possibly* have known about Washburn? She slammed her fists on the roof of the car. She would have wept, she was so frustrated, but weeping was something she seemed no longer able to do. She had cried away all her tears a long time ago.

Then she closed her eyes and took a breath. All was not lost. She had the files Carmody had copied, and although she hadn't delivered Washburn, she had Washburn's files. And by now Carmody should be in Vancouver. The most critical part of her plan was still intact.

She would give her government something much more important than what she had obtained from both Carmody and Washburn combined.

32

Smith wasn't happy about Emma and DeMarco accompanying him in the helicopter, but he didn't have the energy to argue with Emma anymore. He did make it clear to her that she and DeMarco had to stay in the background when they took Carmody. Emma didn't protest but Smith knew that meant nothing. Emma would do whatever Emma wanted to do. He wondered again what the hell she had on Mary.

On the trip to Vancouver, Emma sat and brooded. She mentioned again to Smith that none of this was making sense. Carmody shouldn't have crossed an international border where his ID would be examined and possibly recorded, and he sure as hell shouldn't have checked into a hotel using a credit card in his own name.

"I'm telling you, Bill," she said, "this guy isn't stupid or suicidal. You better be damn careful because this could be some sort of setup."

"Setup for what, Emma?"

"I don't know," she said. And after that she didn't say a word.

DeMarco was enjoying himself. He didn't like heights, be it standing on an eight-foot stepladder or looking down from the balcony of a twenty-story building. He didn't like flying in big passenger planes either, particularly in turbulent skies; if the plane hit some sort of stratospheric speed bump, he'd clutch the armrests in a white-knuckled grip for minutes afterward. But the helicopter was different somehow, more like a ride at an amusement park. He liked traveling just a few thousand feet above the ground, zipping over the landscape, the low altitude seeming to exaggerate the speed.

He wasn't too sure, though, that he liked that the pilot was female. She was a navy lieutenant, tall and slim like Emma, and pretty in a tomboyish way. She was very formal and professional and seemed completely competent—but he still didn't like that she was a woman. Sexist? Definitely. Illogical? Clearly. Most women he knew were better drivers than the men he knew; women tended not to be hot dogs when they got behind the wheel of a machine, whether the machine was a car, an airplane, or a golf cart. Still . . .

It also bothered him that he had to wear a funny little helmet with big ear-guards. He knew he looked goofy in it—he knew this because Smith looked *really* goofy in his. He didn't know why he had to wear the helmet in the first place; it sure as hell wouldn't keep him alive if the lady pilot steered the helicopter into a mountain. When he asked Emma the purpose of the headwear, she ignored him. He noticed Emma didn't look as silly in her helmet; she looked like a cranky Amelia Earhart.

The helicopter dropped them off near the freight terminal at the Vancouver airport. DeMarco thanked the helicopter pilot for the great ride as he was disembarking. She responded with a curt nod and a formal "Thank you, sir," then she winked at him. Whoa!

Two RCMP cars were waiting for them, and standing near one of the cars was a short man in a blue suit. He had wavy blond hair and an ultramanly chin. This had to be Dudley, though Smith introduced the man as Chief Superintendent Robert Morton, Royal Canadian Mounted Police.

"He's still in his room," Morton said to Smith. "He's made no calls nor has he received any. He's just sitting there, reading."

"You got a camera in his room already?" Smith said.

Morton nodded. "We drilled through the wall of the adjoining room twenty minutes after we located him and put a fiber-optic camera in place."

They arrived at the Hyatt, took the elevator up to Carmody's floor, and entered the hotel room adjacent to his. The room was occupied by a SWAT team, four big men wearing body armor and helmets with plastic face shields. Automatic pistols and flash-bang grenades hung from their webbing, and three of them carried short-barreled weapons that looked to DeMarco like sawed-off shotguns. The fourth man was holding a piece of pipe that was about four feet long and three inches in diameter. The pipe had a plate welded to one end and handles welded on top. A door knocker, DeMarco assumed.

Also seated in the room, practically hidden by the SWAT team, was a bald man wearing headphones and looking at a small black-and-white television. DeMarco looked at the screen. Carmody was lying on the bed, reading a paperback.

"What are you men doing here?" Morton said to the SWAT team commander.

"We were told you planned to arrest a spy, sir. We're here to assist."

"The man hasn't committed a crime," Morton said, "at least not one we're aware of. All he's done is cross the border."

"So you're not going to arrest him?" the SWAT boss said. He sounded disappointed. He and his guys probably hadn't kicked down a door in weeks. This was Vancouver, not L.A.

Ignoring the SWAT team, Morton turned to the man with the headphones who was monitoring the television. "Have you seen any sign of a weapon, Mr. Taylor?" Morton said.

"No, sir," Taylor said.

"Thank you, Mr. Taylor," Morton said. DeMarco loved Morton's manners.

"So do you want us to get him?" the SWAT commander said.

Morton glanced down at the door knocker, then raised his eyes to the SWAT team leader. "No, Sergeant, I don't want to have to pay the owners of this establishment for a new door. I'm going to knock on Mr. Carmody's door and tell him that I would appreciate it if he would accompany me to headquarters. Patrolman Janzing will assist me. Your men can stand by and if Mr. Taylor informs you that Carmody has pulled out a machine gun, then you can have your fun. Come along, Janzing."

DeMarco heard Morton knock on the door to Carmody's room and watched Carmody's reaction on the surveillance monitor. Carmody didn't jerk in surprise or spin his head about looking for a non-existent back door to the room. He didn't do anything to indicate he might be a man on the run. He lay there motionless for a moment looking at the door and when Morton knocked a second time, he calmly placed the book he had been reading on the nightstand, rose from the bed, and walked slowly to the door and opened it.

"Yes?" Carmody said to Morton. DeMarco saw him glance over Morton's head, at Patrolman Janzing who was standing behind Morton. Janzing had his right hand on his holstered gun.

Morton held up his identification. "I'm Chief Superintendent Morton, Mr. Carmody. RCMP. And I would like you to come with me please."

Carmody stood there silently for a moment. If he was worried at all, DeMarco couldn't see it.

"Why?" Carmody said.

"Two of your associates have been killed, as I'm sure you know. A Mr. Mulherin and a Mr. Norton. The Americans have asked us to detain you."

"And if I refuse to go with you?" Carmody said.

"I'm afraid I'd have to insist," Morton said.

Carmody smiled at Morton's response; so did DeMarco. "Let me put my shoes on," Carmody said.

"This just isn't right," Emma muttered.

◆◆◆

Headquarters for the Royal Canadian Mounted Police for the province of British Columbia is in an unobtrusive six-building complex in a quiet residential area near Queen Elizabeth Park. The largest building is a long, low, sand-colored rectangular box, in appearance not unlike the elementary school directly across the street. DeMarco was guessing, however, that the grade school didn't have an interrogation room with a one-way mirror.

Emma and DeMarco watched as Carmody was led into the room by a uniformed cop. Smith and Morton were already in the room, seated side by side at a small table. There was an old-fashioned two-reel tape recorder in the middle of the table.

"Please sit down, Mr. Carmody," Morton said.

Before sitting, Carmody looked slowly around the interrogation room, then looked directly at the mirror and nodded as if acknowledging whoever was on the other side watching.

There was something about Carmody's attitude that bothered DeMarco. For most citizens, a police interrogation was an unsettling experience and people either acted outraged because they've been detained or fearful because they might be incarcerated for something that they had or had not done. But not Carmody. He reminded DeMarco of a man sitting at a low-stakes blackjack table, a guy just killing some time, not particularly caring if he wins or loses. If he was any more relaxed he'd be whistling.

"Mr. Carmody," Morton said, "we wanted to talk to you because—"

"Can I have a cigarette?" Carmody said.

"No," Smith said.

"I'm sorry, Mr. Carmody," Morton said, "but neither Bill nor I smoke. I'll call out for one of the lads to bring you some cigarettes shortly."

DeMarco smiled. He really got a kick out of Morton.

"This is Mr. Smith," Morton said, gesturing toward Smith. "He represents—"

"We were stealing classified information from the shipyard and selling it," Carmody said to Smith. Carmody had figured out without being told that Smith worked for the U.S. government. "I'll tell you exactly what we took, how we did it, and I'll give you my control. In return, I want immunity."

Carmody made the admission casually—he could have been talking about last night's box score—and both Smith and Morton sat back in their chairs, momentarily stunned.

"What in the hell is he doing?" Emma said.

"What?" DeMarco said.

They were both whispering, afraid their voices would be heard in the interrogation room.

"Why is he confessing?" Emma hissed. "We don't have anything solid against him. We don't have anything at all. What in the hell's he doing?" Emma said again.

On the other side of the mirror, Smith had recovered from the shock of Carmody's opening statement and now screamed, "Immunity! You're out of your mind!"

"I don't think so," Carmody said. "If I don't tell you what we took, the navy will never know how badly it's been compromised. And if I don't tell you how we did it, you'll spend thousands of man-hours trying to figure it out, disrupting the hell out of shipyard operations. So I'll save the navy lots of time and money by telling you everything. And I'll give you at least one spy: my control. But I want immunity—and a cigarette."

Smith was silent for a moment as he studied Carmody. "Has it occurred to you, Carmody," he said, "that we just might *make* you talk? Defendants' rights, when it comes to national security, have changed in the last few years."

Carmody nodded his head. "Yeah, I suppose you could do that. But you're working against a time limit here, even if you don't know it, and I think a lot of time will have passed before you make me talk. I've also contacted a lawyer—an ACLU bitch whose blood boils whenever she hears the words 'Patriot Act.' I've told her that if she doesn't hear from me every twenty-four hours, she's to go to the press and tell them how an American citizen—a decorated veteran—has been disappeared by his own government."

"He's lying," Emma muttered.

"You're lying," Smith said.

Carmody shrugged.

"Who are you working for?" Smith said.

"Immunity?" Carmody said.

"Maybe," Smith said. "But first I want to know who you're working for."

"The North Koreans. And that's all you get until I get what I want."

33

The senior FBI guy was big—offensive-tackle big—and he was mad. His name was Glen Harris. He was six six, two fifty when he watched his diet, and had hands big enough to palm a basketball. His brown hair was a Bureau-approved length, his mustache neatly trimmed, and his jaw was clenched so tight that he was having a hard time speaking.

In the room with Harris were Diane Carlucci and Darren Thayer, the two young FBI agents who had been in Bremerton; Richard Miller, head of shipyard security; and two NCIS agents—the same two who had been at the briefing the Bremerton chief of police had held after apprehending Dave Whitfield's supposed killer. Also present were Bill Smith, Emma,

DeMarco, and Chief Superintendent Morton of the Royal Canadian Mounted Police. It was a large crowd and they were all seated around an oval-shaped table in one of the RCMP's conference rooms.

"You know goddamn good and well, Smith," Harris was saying, "that you have no jurisdiction in this thing. The DIA doesn't arrest spies, particularly spies operating in the United States. You should have called us the minute you had a lead on Carmody, and you damn well know it."

"Time was of the essence," Smith said.

"Bullshit!" Harris screamed. "All it would have taken was a damn phone call. This whole thing's an organizational cluster fuck and I'm tired of it. Like you guys, what in the hell do you think you're doing here?" he said, pointing at the NCIS agents.

"What do you mean, what are we doing here?" one of the NCIS agents said. "We're talking about navy security. We have to know—"

"But you have no jurisdiction at this point. Have you got that?"

"Yeah," the NCIS guy said, "but—"

"And you," Harris said, pointing at Emma, "you're retired, for Christ's sake." Emma gave him back a blank stare. "And you," he said, now pointing at DeMarco, "as near as I can tell you're some kinda political gunslinger. Nobody can figure out what you do or who you work for. I called Washington and told 'em I wanted both your asses shipped out of here, ASAP, and the next thing I know the Speaker of the House is talking to the director. The Speaker! I don't know why you people have so much pull, but I'm telling you that from this point forward, this is a Bureau operation. Have you all got that?"

Diane Carlucci was sitting off to Harris's right as he ranted, eyes downcast, trying not to make eye contact with DeMarco—and trying not to smile.

"Calm down, Glen, before you have a stroke," Smith said. "We all agree it's your show from here on in. Okay?"

But Harris wasn't through. "This is the kinda shit the 9-11 Commission was trying to put a stop to. Federal agencies stepping all over each other, not sharin' information, grandstanding to get the credit. And Jesus Christ, Smith, immunity! You didn't have the authority to promise him immunity."

Smith shrugged. "I told him we'd give him immunity to get him to talk. And you're right, I don't have the authority. So later on if you decide not to give him immunity, you can tell him that."

Harris started to respond, then thought about what Smith had said. "Yeah, maybe so," he muttered. But he wasn't through yet. "And why can't we move this guy back to the States?" Harris asked Morton.

"You can if you wish, Mr. Harris," Morton said calmly. "It makes no difference to me. But I will point out that Mr. Carmody said that if he was extradited, he might be less forthcoming."

Harris shook his head. "Jesus, what a mess."

No one in the room responded. "Okay," Harris said after a moment. "I'm gonna bring this guy in and have him give us a statement. I could kick all of you out of the room but you'd just go call your bosses and bitch, so I'm gonna let you sit in on this. For the moment. I'll ask the questions, and you will all sit there and be quiet. Are we clear?"

Everybody nodded—except Emma.

———◆◆◆———

Carmody was led into the conference room. He wore leg irons and his hands were cuffed in front of him. A chain linked the handcuffs to a wide leather belt around his waist. He was dressed in a blue jumpsuit, and the jumpsuit had the word PRISONER stenciled on the back so he wouldn't be confused with a janitor.

DeMarco couldn't help but think that Carmody, even manacled and dressed in jail coveralls, didn't look like a spy. Spies were supposed to be little, weaselly-looking guys with beady eyes and weak chins. Carmody looked like Hollywood's version of what he'd once been: an ex–navy SEAL. Handsome but hard, athletic and muscular. He looked like a *hero*, the guy you'd want standing next to you in a firefight. But looks, DeMarco guessed, and as his mother always said, can be deceiving.

Carmody took a seat in a chair at the head of the conference table and took a pack of cigarettes out of his pocket. The chain securing the handcuffs to the belt made it difficult for him to raise the cigarette to his lips.

"Put that cigarette away," Harris said.

Carmody winked at Harris and lit the cigarette with a match. Before Harris could say anything else, Carmody exhaled the smoke and said, "We've been giving the North Koreans everything we could on the reactor plant systems on all classes of nuc ships: Nimitz class carriers, attack boats, Tridents. They don't want to build nuc boats, they just want the reactor technology. We snuck a laptop into the training facility and made copies of CDs that contain the reactor plant manuals. We've—"

"Jesus Christ," Miller said, his face blanching white. "How did you—"

"Shut up," Harris said, looking at Miller.

Morton rose from his chair and brought Carmody an ashtray.

"In addition to the CDs we copied," Carmody said, "we answered any technical questions they had."

"Give me an example," Harris said.

Carmody shrugged. "The manuals give you a general description of how the reactors operate—system pressures, temperatures, design parameters, that sort of thing—but they don't always give you the nitty-gritty, on particular components. Say the manuals talk about a certain pump. The Koreans—their scientists, I guess—would ask us for the materials the pump is made from, who makes it, how it works. That sort of thing. So we'd get the information, write it down, make sketches if we had to, and give it to my control."

"Oh my God," Miller said. DeMarco felt sorry for Miller. Somebody was going to be a scapegoat for the gigantic hole that Carmody and his pals had punched into navy security—in fact there would probably be a large number of scapegoats—but Miller was definitely going to be the head goat. DeMarco wondered how close to retirement Miller was; he hoped he was real close.

"How did you suck Mulherin and Norton into this thing?" Harris asked.

"A talent spotter found them," Carmody said, "and I offered them enough to make them happy. It didn't take all that much."

Everybody in the room nodded, apparently understanding what Carmody meant. DeMarco didn't, but Emma explained it to him later. Intelligence agencies often posted people near military installations, people who were charming and had a gift for gab. Often these people were good-looking women. The talent spotter's job was to find people like Mulherin and Norton, people in debt, carrying a grudge, who could be turned into traitors.

"Why did you spend so much time down on the boats?" Emma said.

Harris's head spun toward Emma, his eyes blazing, but before he could say anything, Carmody said, "I got other stuff. The sailors would talk about ship operating schedules; missions they'd been on; intelligence acquired on missions. I spent a lot of time just bullshitting with the enlisted guys, buying them drinks, picking up information."

Miller put his head in his hands.

"And how did they get you to cooperate?" Harris asked.

"Money," Carmody said. "They contacted me while I was living in Hong Kong and made me the offer."

"So all it took to get you to betray your country was a little money," Harris said, his voice disdainful.

"No, it took a lot of money," Carmody said.

"How did you pass on the information? Were you mailing it, e-mailing it, using dead drops, what?" Harris said.

"I delivered it in person. I didn't trust the Koreans to pay me, so I'd meet my control here in Vancouver and hand him a package. Before the meeting, we'd agree on a price."

"Why Vancouver?" Morton asked. His tone implied that he was rather annoyed that the Americans had allowed this mess to ooze across the border.

"Because it's not in the United States. And Vancouver has a large Asian community. My control felt safer here."

"Seattle has a large Asian community as well," Harris said. "Why didn't you meet there?"

"I don't know. This was where he wanted to meet, so this is where we met."

"Who killed Mulherin and Norton?" Harris said.

"My control, I guess. If he didn't do it personally, he had someone do it. I didn't kill them."

"But why did he kill them?" Harris asked.

Carmody pointed a finger at Emma. "Her. She guessed what we were doing at the shipyard and then she rocked Mulherin pretty good with that fake assassination attempt she pulled."

"What!" Harris said, whipping his head toward Emma.

"I'll tell you later," Smith said, looking sheepish.

Carmody looked from one man to the other, smiled slightly, then continued speaking. "Mulherin was pretty high-strung to begin with and after the thing she pulled, my control was afraid Mulherin would give the whole game away if she rattled him again. So my control decided to terminate the op— and Mulherin and Norton at the same time."

"You're lying your ass off," Emma said.

"Lady," Harris said to Emma, his tone of voice warning her to be quiet. "And what do you know about a submarine noise expert from the Undersea Warfare Center named John Washburn?"

"Who?" Carmody said, looking genuinely confused. "I don't know anyone by that name."

"Bullshit," Harris said. "He was part of your operation."

"Believe what you want," Carmody said, "but I don't know who you're talking about. The only people I worked with were Mulherin, Norton, and my control."

"Then why did you run around the western United States for a week, leaving clues a blind man could have followed?" Harris said.

"My control told me to run, to avoid capture, until we could meet in Vancouver. That's all I was doing."

"You were using credit cards in your own name, getting your picture taken by surveillance cameras. You expect us to believe you're that inept?" Emma said.

Carmody shrugged. "What can I tell you?" he said. "I've never been a spy before."

Emma started to say something, then just shook her head.

"I think you're lyin', bud," Harris said, "about that little road trip you took, but what I really want to know is how, exactly, you're going to give us your control."

"I called him after Mulherin and Norton were killed," Carmody said. "I told him that I had no intention of letting him pop me, too, and that I had one last package for him. A big one. I said I needed money and a passport to disappear. So we agreed to meet here in Vancouver this week to make the exchange."

"Did it occur to you, Carmody," Harris said, "that your control might meet with you, take your information, and kill you anyway?"

"Yeah that did occur to me," Carmody said, "and I was trying to figure out a way to keep that from happening. But now I don't need to figure anything out because you're gonna protect me."

———◆◆◆———

"I love waffles," Smith said as he shoved a forkful into his mouth. "My wife never makes 'em. She says it's too much trouble to clean the waffle iron. And this place, I swear to God, they make the best waffles in North America. No matter where you go, Cleveland, Baltimore, Vancouver—the same texture, the same taste. It's amazing."

"They probably use the same batter and the same waffle irons in all their restaurants," DeMarco said.

"I think it's more than that," Smith said. "I think it's their quality control."

"They're *waffles,* for Christ's sake," Emma said. "They're not making Ferraris."

DeMarco, Emma, and Smith were in an IHOP—an International House of Pancakes. DeMarco thought the waffles were pretty good, too. And the bacon and the eggs and the hash browns. If he finished everything on his plate he wouldn't have to eat for the next three days. Maybe he'd hibernate.

Emma was having coffee and half a grapefruit. Before Smith could say anything more about the cuisine, she said, "Carmody's scamming us, Bill."

"How?" Smith said.

"For one thing, the North Koreans have about twenty subs but none are nuclear powered. Them stealing U.S. navy reactor technology is like a guy with a bicycle stealing an owner's manual for a Porsche. The Chinese, the Russians, even the Indians, I could believe. But the North Koreans, I don't think so."

"Carmody said they wanted the technology for landbased reactors."

"Yeah, I know what he said," Emma said. "And he's lying."

"I don't know," Smith said. "Maybe the North Koreans—"

"No!" Emma said. "I'm not buying any of it. I'm not buying it's the North Koreans, I'm not buying Carmody getting caught the way he was, and I'm not buying him giving everything up so easily."

"Well, I can see why he confessed," Smith said. "What else was he going to do?"

"And he is getting immunity," DeMarco said.

"I doubt he's gonna get immunity," Smith said, his eyes twinkling behind the lenses of his glasses.

"You gave the guy signed papers," DeMarco said.

"So what?" he said. "We're talking national security here, not carjacking."

"Jesus, remind me if I'm ever arrested not to believe the government."

"You work for the government, you dummy," Smith said. "Why would you, of all people, believe the government?"

"Will you two shut up," Emma said. "I'm telling you, Bill, he shouldn't have confessed. We had no, absolutely *no,* evidence of espionage. Zero. If we tried to take this case to court—without Carmody's confession—we wouldn't be able to find a lawyer willing to prosecute."

"What can I tell you, Emma? The guy's scared."

"Does he *look* scared to you, Bill, this ex–navy SEAL? I'm telling you, we're missing a piece here."

Smith shrugged and poured more syrup on his waffles. DeMarco thought if he put any more syrup on his plate the waffles would float.

"Did you guys believe Carmody when he said he didn't know Washburn?" DeMarco said.

"Yeah," Emma said. "I think his control was running two independent ops and there was no reason for Carmody to know about Washburn. The only link between Carmody and Washburn was Carmody's road trip. Carmody's control was using Carmody to distract us while he—or she—was trying to sneak Washburn out of the country."

"Or *she*?" Smith said. "Do you think—"

"Has Washburn given anything up yet?" DeMarco asked Smith.

"No. I called the FBI this morning and they said the bastard's hangin' in there, not sayin' a word. But they'll break him eventually. You know," Smith said to Emma, "instead of sitting there stewing, you oughta be feeling pretty good here. You stumble onto an operation, bust it up, and we find out what Carmody gave 'em and how he did it. And then you see through the Carmody smoke screen and we nab Washburn. So you're a hero, a heroine, whatever. The *worst* thing that can happen at this point is we don't get Carmody's control. So lighten up and eat your damn grapefruit."

Smith took a couple more bites of his waffle before saying, "You two oughta go back to Washington. This really is a Bureau show from here on in." With a little cackle, he added, "Now that we've handed it to them on a friggin' platter. But there isn't anything else to do now except scoop up Carmody's boss."

"I can't leave yet," DeMarco said, surprising both Smith and Emma.

"Why not?" Smith said.

"I have to find out what happened to Dave Whitfield. There's a pissed-off Secretary of the Navy who wants to know why his nephew died. And in case you've forgotten, there's that poor schizophrenic bastard in a jail cell in Bremerton that's going to be convicted of killing Whitfield unless somebody tells them he didn't do it."

34

What part of 'no' don't you understand?" Glen Harris said.

Diane Carlucci was behind the big FBI agent, head down, studying a transcript of Carmody's interrogation. DeMarco saw that she was making little notes in the margin of the paper, probably jotting down all the things they wanted to ask him in the next round. The woman was super anal, but damn she was cute. She was also ignoring DeMarco. She wasn't about to help him buck her boss, and he couldn't really blame her.

"I only want this one thing clarified, and then I'll get out of your hair," DeMarco said.

"*We'll* get it clarified," Harris said. "And when we do, we'll let you know."

"Nope," DeMarco said. "I want to talk to him now."

Harris put his big hands on the edge of his desk and stood up. He was seven inches taller than DeMarco.

"And what are you gonna do if I don't let you talk to him?"

Call daddy, DeMarco thought. He didn't say that, instead he said, "Do you think your director likes getting calls from the Speaker of the House?" De-Marco looked at his watch. "Right now, Mahoney's probably half in the bag. He's almost always half in the bag. If I call him and tell him you're stonewalling me . . . Well, Mahoney's a mean drunk." Actually he wasn't, but Harris didn't know this.

Harris clenched his jaw. The guy was going to have problems with his molars if he didn't quit doing that, DeMarco thought.

Harris's broad shoulders slumped in surrender. "I hate this political crap. A year ago I had an offer to be chief of police in Laramie, where I grew up. The director *personally* asked me to stay because of the terrorist threat. I should have told him to go to hell." Before DeMarco could express his sympathy—or at least feign sympathy—Harris said to Diane Car-lucci, "Carlucci, you're with this guy when he talks to Carmody."

"Yes, sir," Diane said.

As DeMarco turned to leave the room, Harris said, "DeMarco. That name's familiar. I was stationed up in New York, my second tour, and there was a mob guy up there named DeMarco. He got killed the month I started. Any relation?"

"No," DeMarco said.

Diane Carlucci studied her shoes.

"So are you really going back to D.C. after you talk to Carmody?" Diane asked as they walked toward Carmody's cell.

"Yeah. But maybe we could have dinner tonight."

"I don't think so, Joe. I still have a future in the Bureau and right now having dinner with you, as far as Glen Harris is concerned, would be fraternizing with the enemy."

"Screw him."

"Easy for you to say, being the . . . What did Glen say you were? A political gunslinger?"

"Well, Glen's wrong about that, too. So whaddya say? Why don't you sneak out of the dorm after Harris does bed check and meet me for a drink?"

Diane laughed at the bed check remark, but said, "No way. But I have good news for you, sweetie. In less than a month I'm being rotated back to Washington for some training. I'll be there and down at Quantico for about six months."

That was good news, DeMarco thought. That was *really* good news.

———◆◆◆———

Carmody was lying on the bunk in his cell, staring at the ceiling. He seemed pensive to DeMarco, displaying none of the smart-ass demeanor he'd exhibited during his interrogation. No, pensive wasn't quite it. Sad, that was it. He seemed sad. He had the eyes of a man staring into his past, remembering better times and brighter days. Then it occurred to DeMarco that he was reading too much into Carmody's expression. The guy was in jail; of course he looked sad.

Just then Carmody realized DeMarco and Diane Carlucci were standing outside his cell. He rose effortlessly to a sitting position and stood up. "Can I help you?" he said, the let's-play twinkle back in his eyes.

"Yeah," DeMarco said. "I just want to know one thing. Who killed Dave Whitfield?"

The expression in Carmody's eyes changed. "It was too bad about him, and I mean that. That should never have happened." DeMarco sensed Carmody was being sincere.

"So why did it?"

"Whitfield was fixated on Mulherin and Norton; he was always watching them. The morning he was killed, he overheard Norton talking to Mulherin about burning a CD."

"So who killed him?"

"My control. Norton called me and told me they'd been busted by Whitfield, and I called my control."

DeMarco believed him. "And the witness, the guy who saw Conran walking down the alley? Was he telling the truth?"

"No, I paid him. Go back and squeeze him and he'll tell you." Carmody paused. "On second thought, he might not tell you. My control may have taken care of him, too, by now."

There was that flicker again in Carmody's eyes. The possible death of the lying witness bothered him, DeMarco could tell.

"Okay," DeMarco said, "that's all I wanted to know. Wait a minute, that guy Berry back in D.C., the guy who awarded you the training contract? Did you have him killed too?"

"No," Carmody said. "He was a drunk. He just ran his car off the road."

"But you did bribe him to give you the contract," DeMarco said.

"Yeah," Carmody said.

DeMarco couldn't think of anything else to ask him. "You want to ask anything, Diane?" he said.

Diane shook her head no.

DeMarco turned to leave then stopped and turned back to face Carmody.

"Who were the bottle rockets for?" he asked.

"What?" Carmody said, confused by the question.

"When we searched your place we found a box in your basement containing some toys and bottle rockets. Who were they for?"

"Oh, that," Carmody said. "They were for my nephew. I forgot to mail the package."

Diane Carlucci looked at DeMarco then over at Carmody. She pulled out a small notebook and wrote something down.

35

DeMarco stopped by Emma's room to tell her good-bye before he left Vancouver.

After he had met with Carmody at the jail, De-Marco had called Mahoney to fill him in on what was happening.

"Yeah, you might as well come on home," Mahoney had said. "The FBI will get this North Korean spy, controller, whatever the fuck he is, and then they'll spend the next six or seven months question-ing him and Carmody. I got stuff for you to do back here."

DeMarco was relieved. Even though he wanted to spend more time with Diane, he was tired of liv-ing out of a suit case. But Emma apparently wasn't.

"You really should come with me," DeMarco said to her. "It's an FBI show from here on in. There's nothing else for you to do."

The day after tomorrow, Carmody was to meet his control and hand over a package of classified information. At that point the FBI, with the assistance of the Canadians, would swoop in and grab the North Korean agent. The FBI had wanted the meeting to take place on U.S. soil to avoid complications with the Canadians, but Carmody said the time and place of the meeting were already set and he wasn't able to contact his control to change it.

"I'm not leaving until this is finished," Emma said. Before DeMarco could argue further, she added, "What time does your plane leave for D.C.?"

"Midnight," DeMarco said. Since Diane wouldn't have dinner with him he saw no reason to stick around until tomorrow.

"You're going to have to hustle to make it."

DeMarco's rental car was still in Bremerton. He had to get from Vancouver to Bremerton to pick up the car, and then get to SeaTac airport for his flight to D.C. He had tried to get Smith to send him back to Bremerton in a helicopter, but Smith had laughed in his face. So he was flying commercial from Vancouver to SeaTac, taking a shuttle bus to Bremerton where'd he pick up the rental car and then drive back to SeaTac. Which reminded him . . .

"Is there any way you can get Smith to pick up the tab for the damage the Wang brothers did to my rental car?"

Emma laughed.

Great, DeMarco thought. He bet the damn Wangs had done a thousand bucks' worth of damage to the car. If his insurance didn't cover it, he was going to pad the hell out of his expense account.

"Is the FBI going to let you in on the bust?" DeMarco asked.

"Nope," Emma said. "I'll be observing from a safe distance. That's all Harris will let me do, and he's not too happy about that."

"Emma, Harris may be a horse's ass but I think he can handle this."

"Maybe so," Emma said, "but there's something wrong here and I'm not leaving until I find out what it is."

"Well, I gotta get goin'," DeMarco said, and turned to leave the room. His hand was on the doorknob when Emma's phone rang. She answered the phone and made a gesture for DeMarco to wait. He heard her say, "Oh, my God. How could that have happened?" She listened a few more minutes and hung up.

"That was Bill Smith," she said. "John Washburn committed suicide."

"Shit," DeMarco said. "Did he talk first?"

"No."

"How did he kill himself?"

"A ballpoint pen. He got the damn pen from his lawyer, and after the lights were out, he gouged his wrists with the tip of the thing until he opened up his veins."

DeMarco winced at the image.

"Goddamnit!" Emma said. "Now we don't know what the son of a bitch took or who's running him. Whoever's running this—and it's *not* the Koreans—is one lucky SOB."

She didn't tell DeMarco that she'd had the sensation that someone had been following her for the last two days.

36

Mahoney's secretary was not at her desk. In fact the only one in the office was a kid, probably an intern, who looked about sixteen years old. She was busy flipping pages in a bill that was twice the size of a D.C. phone book and she didn't even look up as DeMarco entered the room. Every phone in the office was ringing.

There was clearly a legislative scramble in progress, and Mahoney, the general, had dispersed his troops. DeMarco walked down the corridor to the Speaker's office. When he stuck his head in the door and saw Mahoney had a visitor, he turned to leave, to wait until Mahoney's guest was gone, but Mahoney said, "Come on in, Joe. We're almost done here."

DeMarco stepped into the office and remained standing. Mahoney's visitor glanced over his shoulder to see who was behind him, clearly irritated at the interruption. Or maybe, since he was with Mahoney, he was irritated before DeMarco got there.

The man with Mahoney was James Whitlock. He was a frail-looking six-footer with thin arms, a thin neck, and a concave chest. He wore a poorly fitting gray suit, glasses with bifocal lenses, and a bow tie. The expression on his face could best be described as fussy. He had "nitpicker" written all over him.

If you placed James Whitlock's photograph on a table with five other photographs, and then asked ten strangers to pick out the man who was most likely the House parliamentarian, all ten people would point at Whitlock's picture without hesitating. And they would be right.

The operating rules for Congress are complex. They are so complex that few people other than James Whitlock understood them all. One time DeMarco, for reasons he couldn't remember, looked up the definition of a quorum. Sounds pretty simple: you gotta have X number of politicians to make a decision. Right? Wrong. The rules for what constituted a quorum went on for sixty pages and, judging by the footnotes and references, sixty pages of regulations barely scratched the surface.

So like in any other game—be it baseball or politics—an understanding of the regulations gives a player an advantage. The Speaker knew most of the rules—he'd been around so long that he'd absorbed them by osmosis as opposed to study—but there were occasions, and apparently this was one of them, where Mahoney was attempting to use some obscure parliamentary convention to gain an advantage.

"So you think this'll work, Jimmy?" Mahoney said.

DeMarco saw Whitlock wince at the "Jimmy." He was a James not a Jimmy.

"It's not a matter of it *working*, Mr. Speaker," Whitlock said. "Rules are rules. Procedures are procedures. I've merely given you the correct interpretation of this particular rule."

"If the rules weren't so fuckin' convoluted they wouldn't need to be interpreted," Mahoney grumbled.

"Sir, we've discussed this before. The procedures are perfectly logical, based on history and precedent and the Constitution. You just need to—"

"Yeah, right," Mahoney said. "But this'll work, right? Bradshaw won't be able to amend the bill unless—"

"Yes, sir. It will *work*," Whitlock said, "if you insist on putting it that way."

"Well, okay," Mahoney said. "Thanks for coming, Jimmy. As always, I appreciate it. By the way, do you still drink that god-awful Spanish sherry?"

Whitlock smiled, his lips pursing as if he'd just sucked a lemon. "I do, Mr. Speaker," he said. "A small glass every night after dinner."

Mahoney picked up a pen and made a note to send Whitlock a case of his favorite sherry.

After Whitlock left, Mahoney said to DeMarco, "That guy's indispensable. He's bailed me out more times than you can believe. Even Perry doesn't understand the rules like him."

Perry was Perry Wallace, Mahoney's chief of staff.

"And that Whitlock, he's something else. I'll bet you're thinkin', with his bow tie and that priggish expression that's always on his face, that he's some sort of old maid, a bird-watcher, a stamp collector, something like that. Don't you?"

"I suppose," DeMarco said, "but I've never talked to the man."

"Well, ol' Jimmy has a wife who's twenty years younger than him and she's got more curves than a bad mountain road. And from everything I've heard . . ."

And Mahoney heard everything.

". . . they're a happy couple. And he's got a bigger gun collection than the head of the IRA."

DeMarco wondered if Mahoney meant the NRA.

Mahoney lit a cigar and poured from the Stanley thermos he kept on his desk. The aroma of rich coffee, old bourbon, and expensive tobacco filled the room.

"So the FBI's busting up this spy ring today," Mahoney said.

"Yeah," DeMarco said. He looked at his watch.

"It might be over by now. It's already twelve thirty in Vancouver."

"I talked to Frank Hathaway. He's still pretty upset with you, about his nephew, but at least now he knows why it happened. He's gonna arrange for some kinda medal to be given to Whitfield's wife when this is all over."

"That's good," DeMarco said.

"No it's not, but it's the best he can do." Mahoney sipped his bourbon-laced coffee and reflected on life's inequities—for about two seconds. "And your pal, Emma," he said, "she still thinks something funny's goin' on out there?"

"Yeah, but she doesn't know what. She's just hanging around until they wrap it up."

"If I was those FBI guys, I'd listen to Emma."

"Me, too," DeMarco said. "So why'd you want to see me?"

"Aw, there's this guy, a state house guy, back home. I've known him forever and he's been acting squirrelly lately. There've been three times in the last couple of months where he's voted the wrong way. The last time he did it, I called his ass up and asked him what the hell he thought he was doing, and he gives me some bullshit about voting his conscience. He doesn't have a conscience. I want you to find out what's going on."

"Okay," DeMarco said.

"He probably put his hand—or his dick—in the wrong cookie jar and somebody from the other side caught him and now they're telling him how to vote. So you need to get up there and straighten his ass out."

"What's his name?" DeMarco said. He'd been hoping to spend a few days in D.C. before heading out again, but at least this trip he'd know what he was dealing with: a stupid politician, not a bunch of spies.

<hr />

DeMarco descended the stairway from Mahoney's office to the great rotunda, then pushed his way through groups of tourists to reach another set of stairs. He heard a tour guide, for the zillionth time, say that it was the Italian Brumidi who had painted the ceiling one hundred and eighty feet above their heads, a painting in which Washington looked more like Zeus than the Virginia farmer that he'd been. De-Marco finally reached *his* staircase—the one leading to the subbasement, to his office near the emergency diesel generator room.

There was a reason DeMarco dwelled beneath ground: he was not an official member of Mahoney's staff. His father's notoriety had prevented DeMarco from being hired by a reputable law firm when he graduated from college, and as he'd told Diane Carlucci, his godmother, dear Aunt Connie, had used her influence to help him get his civil service job. What he had not told Diane was the reason his godmother had influence: she had once had an affair with Mahoney. And the Speaker, though willing to provide DeMarco employment to appease an old lover, did not, however, want an official connection to the son of a Mafia hood. So DeMarco was given a small drab space in the subbasement, a meaningless title (*Counsel Pro Tem for Liaison Affairs*), and a position in the legislative branch of government that showed up on no organizational chart associated with the Speaker of the House.

DeMarco passed his office door and walked twenty feet farther down the corridor to another office. Sitting at a desk, his broad brow furrowed in concentration, was a large black man with a glistening bald head studying a spreadsheet about two feet square. The man was Curtis Jackson; he supervised the Capitol's often maligned janitors.

Jackson looked up at DeMarco, then back down at the spreadsheet, and said, "I gotta give these guys all these different shifts these days. Some of 'em come to work at six, some at seven, some at nine. They're takin' night classes, or they gotta get their brats to day care, or they gotta drop off their damn wives at work. And *I* gotta plan around *their* damn schedules. When I started out, the boss said, 'Boy, you're workin' swing shift,' and that was *it*. There wasn't any of this odd-shift, flextime bullshit. In those days you were just damn glad to have a job."

"Nobody knows da troubles I seen," DeMarco half sang.

"Yeah, and fuck you, too. What do you want?"

"You know a good mechanic, one that won't charge me a hundred bucks an hour?"

'Why? That piece of crap you drive break down again?"

"No. I'm thinkin' about buying this used car, a BMW Z3, and—"

"You? A sports car?"

"Yeah. What's so strange about that?" DeMarco asked.

Jackson shrugged. "I don't know. I just have a hard time seeing you in a little convertible, the wind blowing through your hair. Or better yet, you wearin' one of them little flat caps. No, you're more a sedan kinda guy."

"Am not."

"Huh," Jackson said.

DeMarco didn't know what that meant.

"Anyway," DeMarco said, "the car, the Z, has sixty-four thousand miles on it, and I want somebody to look it over, somebody who knows what he's doing."

"Yeah, I know a guy," Jackson said. "He works nights here."

"You sure he knows his way around new cars, you know, the ones with all these electronic ignitions and catalytic converters and stuff?"

"He used to steal cars before he found Jesus, Joe. He knows what to look for."

Nothing like having friends in low places.

———◆◆◆———

DeMarco walked out of the Capitol and onto the terrace that overlooked the Washington Mall. He needed to pick up some shirts from the cleaners and go home and pack. And maybe he'd stop by and look at the Z again, torture the salesman a little more. He was about ten paces from the building exit when his cell phone signaled that he had a voice message waiting. DeMarco had noticed that since 9/11 his cell phone got spotty reception inside the Capitol. He didn't know if there was some mundane explanation for this or if the security wizards were jamming signals aimed at the building.

He punched buttons until he was able to hear his voice mail. There was just one message and it was from Emma, but the message was odd. It didn't start with "Hello" or some other greeting. He heard Emma's voice say, "You've gone rogue, haven't you, Li Mei?" Another voice, a female's, said, "Did you think I'd forget? Ever? Now put your hands on the steering wheel." Then the same woman said something in what sounded to DeMarco like Chinese, but it could have been Korean or Japanese or some other Asian language. Then there was the sound of a car door slamming shut, and afterward, nothing but the sound of traffic on a busy street.

37

━━━━◆◆◆━━━━

I need to talk to Bill Smith, right away," DeMarco said into his cell phone. "He's in Vancouver, B.C."

From his position on the terrace DeMarco could see the Washington Monument, the flags encircling its base, the tourists flowing around it. In his current state of mind it occurred to him that the monument was a perfect target for a terrorist. If it was destroyed it would be like the twin towers collapsing again, reinforcing the image of 9/11 already burned into DeMarco's brain.

"We don't have a Bill Smith in our directory," the DIA operator said.

"You listen to me, goddamnit," DeMarco said. "if Smith doesn't call me in fifteen minutes, I'm calling the *Washington Post* and telling them how the DIA withheld information from the FBI in Bremerton. Fifteen fuckin' minutes, you hear me?"

Smith called back in ten.

"What happened to Emma?" DeMarco said.

"How do you know something happened to her?" Smith said.

"I got a weird voice mail from her. It sounded like she was being kidnapped." Or killed, DeMarco mentally added, but he refused to say that out loud.

"I need to hear that voice mail."

"Screw what you need. Tell me what happened."

———◆———

Carmody had told the FBI that he always met his North Korean controller in a restaurant on East Pender Street, in the heart of Vancouver's Chinatown.

East Pender Street has the appearance of an open-air market. On the sidewalks on both sides of the street are carts laden with fish and vegetables, and the fish—carp and catfish and perch—are so fresh that some are still wiggling. Displayed in crates and baskets are Oriental spices and exotic dried foods, things like white lotus seed, wolfberry, and black fungus. The customers are mostly Chinese, though a few tourists are usually present, pointing with wonderment at things they can't name and are probably afraid to eat.

The restaurant where Carmody met his controller was in the middle of the block, on the first floor of a two-story building. Roasted ducks, fat dripping from headless torsos, hung on hooks in the window of the restaurant. The restaurant itself was long and narrow, with ten or twelve tables placed closely together, separated by a narrow aisle. The back door of the restaurant exited into an alley littered with black plastic trash bags. Green Dumpsters were stationed about every twenty yards down the alley.

Harris had decided to arrest the Korean on the street outside the restaurant after the pickup had been made. This way the Korean spy would be in possession of classified material at the time of his arrest. He would have preferred to have arrested him inside the restaurant but the restaurant's clientele was almost exclusively Asian; Harris figured four or five big white cops eating with forks instead of chopsticks might scare the spy off. Morton wasn't thrilled about the arrest being made on a crowded street where civilians would be at risk if gunplay ensued, but he agreed with Harris that it would be difficult to place many of their people inside the restaurant.

Jurisdiction for the arrest was a mess. Not only were the Royal Canadian Mounted Police and the FBI involved, but since the arrest was taking place within the city limits of Vancouver, the Vancouver Metropolitan Police were also participants. Technically it would be a Canadian bust, but Morton, who had no stake in the outcome, was willing to let Harris run the operation and take all the credit—and all the blame if it went wrong. The rules for the joint U.S.-Canadian operation had been worked out like an international trade treaty the night before by a small flock of lawyers.

Each FBI agent was paired with a Canadian cop. Six men were hidden on the street in front of the restaurant, two cops were inside the restaurant, and two more were in the alley behind the restaurant. Darren Thayer was the FBI agent Harris had posted in the alley. All the cops wore U.S.-issue communication gear and were able to hear each other, talk to each other, and take direction from Harris. Harris was confident that ten trained cops should be enough to capture one unsuspecting spy.

Bill Smith was seated in a teahouse directly across from the Chinese restaurant. He had no official role in the arrest. Emma was parked in a car half a block away from the restaurant, at the corner of East Pender and Main. From her car she could see the front entrance to the restaurant but she couldn't see the alley behind the restaurant. Smith had invited Emma to sit with him in the teahouse but she'd refused. Emma was still nervous about the meet and wanted to be in her car. Smith assumed that this was so she could give chase if anyone needed chasing—which he thought was damn unlikely considering the number of cops involved. But Emma was stubborn. Boy, was she stubborn.

Diane Carlucci and a Canadian cop named Hunter were posted inside the restaurant. They were posing as a dining couple and were seated at the table closest to Carmody's, the two tables separated by the restaurant's narrow aisle. Diane and her partner weren't expected to make the arrest; they were just there to observe the exchange, to make sure Carmody didn't try to escape or warn the North Korean, and to alert Harris when the Korean was leaving.

Carmody was the only other Caucasian in the restaurant. Even though Diane knew that he had spent several years in Hong Kong, she was still surprised when he addressed the head waiter in what sounded like fluent Chinese. Diane also observed that Carmody didn't appear to be the least bit nervous and he seemed to genuinely enjoy his meal when it arrived.

Carmody said he'd been instructed by his control to sit at a table near the back of the restaurant. Harris hadn't liked this because behind Carmody's table was a short hallway, about ten feet long, that led to the restrooms and the back exit. Harris had wanted Carmody to sit near a window at the front of the restaurant so he could be observed by the cops outside, but Carmody said that the back table was where he had always sat and where he'd been told to sit. He said the Korean would be suspicious if he wasn't seated there.

Harris had checked the back exit the day before. It had a push bar to open it from the inside but it didn't have a fire alarm bar across it and it wasn't locked, so customers could enter and exit the restaurant via the alleyway. The cops Harris had stationed in the alley would stop the North Korean should he decide to exit that way, although Carmody said that had never happened in the past.

Carmody, Diane, and Hunter were seated in the restaurant fifteen minutes before Carmody was scheduled to meet his controller. On the table in front of Carmody was a white plastic bag from a local drugstore chain that contained the information he was to give his control. The North Korean, according to Carmody, would bring an identical bag. The CDs inside the plastic bag actually did contain a small amount of classified data—better evidence to present at a trial—but it was information Carmody had already passed on. Harris was hoping Carmody's control wouldn't bring a laptop to the meeting to verify the contents of the CDs; Carmody said that he never had in the past.

The appointed time came and no one approached Carmody. This didn't alarm Harris; it was typical tradecraft for an agent arriving for a meeting to take some time to check out the rendezvous site. Harris did a communication check with his agents. They all responded; they were all ready.

Fifty minutes after the appointed hour, Diane heard Harris say, "Woman entering the restaurant." The woman was the third customer to enter the restaurant since Diane and her partner had been seated. The agents were all expecting a short Korean in his fifties who would most likely be wearing a black beret. "Shit," Harris said, "I'm beginning to think this thing isn't going to go down today, but stay on your toes."

Diane was thinking that the Korean had better show up pretty soon. She and her partner had finished their lunch some time ago, and their waiter was beginning to bug them to pay up. She glanced at the woman who had just entered the restaurant. She was Asian, tall, and wore large sunglasses. Her hair was hidden by a baseball cap. Diane admired the woman's figure and watched as she walked directly and without hesitation toward the back of the restaurant, straight toward the table where Carmody was seated. Diane figured the woman was planning to use the restroom before sitting down to eat.

Everything that happened next happened in about ten seconds, maybe less.

Five paces from Carmody, without slowing down, the Asian woman pulled a pistol out from under the windbreaker she was wearing. She raised the pistol as she walked, ultimately bringing it to bear on Carmody's head.

Diane saw the weapon emerge from beneath the woman's jacket. She yelled "Gun!" to her partner and started to reach for the .40 caliber automatic that was in the holster on her hip, beneath her coat. She should have thumbed her mic and told Harris what was happening but her first instinct was to go for her weapon.

Carmody, the ex-SEAL, reacted the quickest. The table he was sitting at was a small pedestal table with a thick Formica top. He saw the Asian woman's pistol as it cleared her windbreaker and he immediately picked up the small table by the pedestal—food and plates flying everywhere—and raised it to shield his head and torso.

The woman fired two shots at Carmody just as he was bringing the table up to protect himself. Both shots penetrated the table and splinters blew back into Carmody's face, but neither shot hit him.

Hunter had turned his head toward the shooter to see what was happening when Diane had yelled "Gun." By the time he turned, the woman was already firing at Carmody. Hunter started to stand and simultaneously began to reach for his weapon.

Diane's gun cleared her holster as the woman fired at Carmody.

The Asian woman shot Diane's partner in the side of the head before he could draw his weapon. She was two feet from him as she fired. Hunter's blood splattered on Diane's face.

Diane raised her weapon to fire, but the woman swung her pistol toward Diane and fired twice, hitting Diane in the chest. Diane flew backward, her chair tipping over. Her gun came out of her hand as the back of her head hit the floor.

The plastic drugstore bag containing the CD was lying on the floor near Carmody's overturned table. The woman scooped up the bag without breaking stride. As she went by Carmody, who was now on the floor and huddled behind the overturned table, she fired at him again, just a quick shot in passing. Diane heard Carmody cry out in pain.

The woman proceeded down the short hallway, now running full out in long strides. She slammed through the back door.

Diane, who was wearing a Kevlar vest, felt as if she'd been kicked in the chest by a mule. She shook off the shock and pain, and screamed into her mic, "Harris! The woman in the baseball cap. She shot Carmody and Hunter. She's in the alley. Thayer, she's in the alley. Thayer, she's coming your way." Harris started yelling but Diane kept talking. "Hunter's down. Hunter's hit bad," she screamed.

Carmody flung the table off him as Diane was talking. He and Diane made eye contact. Diane saw blood coming from a shallow wound on the side of Carmody's neck. Diane's eyes scanned the floor for her weapon. Her gun was closer to Carmody than it was to her. Still lying on the floor, she lunged for her weapon, but Carmody reached it first. He stood up and aimed Diane's service weapon at her unprotected head.

Diane knew Carmody was going to kill her—but he didn't. Instead he said very quietly, "Stay there and don't follow me." Then he ran toward the back door and pushed through it.

Diane struggled to get to her feet, slipping once in the blood that had come from her partner's head, and stood up. She checked the carotid artery in Hunter's throat; he was dead. She started toward the back door but stopped and pivoted, reached down, and took Hunter's gun from his shoulder holster—then she ran for the back door. She hit the door hard, her arm out in front of her like she was straight-arming a tackler, and bounced back. Carmody had blocked the door from the outside. She found out later he had shoved a Dumpster in front of it.

Diane noticed for the first time that Harris's voice was inside her head. He was screaming the names of the two agents in the alley. He was screaming for other agents to get to the back of the restaurant, to block off the alley's exits. He was screaming like his career was on fire.

Diane ran to the front of the restaurant and out the front door. To reach the alley, she had to go fifty yards to the end of the block, turn the corner, and then go another twenty yards to the mouth of the alley. She saw Harris and two other agents turn the corner, sprinting toward the entrance to the alley. Diane began to run.

The sidewalk was crowded with civilians, shoppers, and produce vendors. They had just seen a group of armed men come rushing out of nearby buildings and vans, and now they saw Diane running toward them, yelling "Federal agent," a pistol in her hand. The civilians began to scatter, screaming, knocking over carts and baskets. Dead fish spilled onto the sidewalk.

By the time Diane reached the mouth of the alley, Harris and two other agents were standing at the back door of the Chinese restaurant. Diane sprinted toward Harris; she could see Harris yelling into his mic—she could see his mouth moving—but she didn't hear what he was saying. She didn't hear him because she was looking at the bodies of the two men who had been guarding the alley. One of them was Darren Thayer. He was lying behind a Dumpster, his body partially covered by black plastic trash bags. He and his Canadian partner had both been shot once in the forehead.

"Morton," Harris was screaming, "get squad cars here fast. Have them surround the block. Set up roadblocks. Seal off the buildings on both sides of the alley. You," Harris said pointing at one of the agents, "you stay with me. You," he said pointing to the second agent, "go help seal off these buildings. They have to be inside one of them."

The backs of two-story buildings lined the alley on both sides. As Carmody and the Asian woman had disappeared so quickly, Harris assumed they had to have entered one of the buildings and were now hiding inside. Or maybe they'd gone into one of the buildings and had already exited onto the street that ran parallel to East Pender.

"Let's go," Harris said to the agent who remained with him. Harris and the agent began walking down the alley, guns in their hands, checking doors to see which ones were unlocked.

Diane began to follow Harris, but he turned, his face livid, and said to her, "You just stay here and guard the scene. I'll talk to you later."

"Yes, sir," Diane said. She tried to holster her weapon but it didn't fit in her holster. Then she remembered she was holding Hunter's gun.

"Mr. Harris," she yelled.

"What!" Harris said.

"Carmody's got my weapon. He's armed."

"Jesus Christ, Carlucci, did you do one damn thing right today?" Harris said, then began talking into his mic again as he proceeded down the alley.

Diane, holding Hunter's gun limply in her hand, walked over to the two cops lying by the Dumpster. She knew Harris had already verified that the men were dead, but she knelt anyway and felt for a pulse in their throats. There wasn't one. Diane didn't know the Canadian cop but she had worked with Darren Thayer for the last seven months. She knew he had two kids, the oldest one was seven. She knew his wife's name was Janet. She looked down at his too young face, his funny ears, the freckles so stark against his dead, pale face.

Diane Carlucci started to cry.

"The FBI and the Canadians, they've been running around for two hours now, trying to find Carmody and the shooter," Smith said to DeMarco, "but they're gone. Based on a statement from one witness, a Chinese lady who's about a hundred years old, it looks like the woman took off on a motorbike. We think she drove the bike down the alley, parked her bike, and shot the two cops in the alley. Then she walked around the block, pretty as you please, entered the restaurant, and tried to kill Carmody.

"Carmody, he disappeared like smoke. He had to have gone into one of the buildings off the alley, then God knows where he went. No one can believe it, this big damn white guy in a Chinese neighborhood, and somehow he manages to evaporate. We think Carmody—"

"Never mind Carmody," DeMarco said. "What happened to Emma?"

"I was helping Harris and his guys look for the woman and Carmody, and I didn't even think about Emma for a while. When I did think of her, I was wondering if maybe she'd followed the shooter or Carmody. I ran over to where her car had been parked and I see the car's still there but Emma's gone. Her purse was lying on the front seat and her cell phone was on the floor."

"Didn't any of the FBI guys on the street see what happened to her?"

"No. They were all watching the restaurant, not looking up the street where she was parked. Until you called, I was hoping she'd followed Carmody on foot, but if she had, she would have taken her cell phone. And now you tell me she's been kidnapped. I need to hear that voice mail, DeMarco."

———◆———

Within fifteen minutes, one of Bill Smith's associates from the DIA drove over to the Capitol and picked up DeMarco's cell phone. DeMarco went home, packed a bag, and bought an airline ticket to Vancouver. He didn't know if he'd need the ticket, but he wanted to be ready. Then he waited by his phone for a call from Smith. DeMarco had told Smith that if Smith cut him out of the investigation he was going to the press, the Speaker, and any other person he could think of to cause the DIA and the FBI the greatest embarrassment he possibly could. Smith told DeMarco to calm down, said that Emma was a friend and that he would do everything he could to find her. DeMarco just screamed at Smith that if he didn't hear from him in an hour he was going to the press, the Speaker, and . . .

While DeMarco was waiting, he found the cell-phone number that Diane Carlucci had given him.

"I heard what happened in Vancouver today," he said when she answered the phone. "How are you doing?"

"Not good," she said. "She killed a guy sitting a foot from me, Joe. I can still feel his blood on my face." She hesitated, then said, "She would have killed me, too, if I hadn't been wearing a vest. I've never seen anybody as fast as her."

"But you're okay," DeMarco said, "not hurt or anything?"

"I have a bruise on my chest the size of a dinner plate, but I'm not hurt, not physically. But I can't stop shaking." And then she started crying, and said, "And I can't stop crying, goddamnit."

"It's okay," DeMarco said, knowing that sounded stupid but not knowing what else to say.

"It's not okay! She killed Darren."

"Who?" DeMarco said.

"Darren Thayer! My partner!"

DeMarco had never known Thayer's first name. And he couldn't imagine the earnest-looking, jug-eared young guy dead. "I'm sorry," he said. "But it's not your fault, Diane."

"Yeah, well that shit Harris acts like it is. He's trying to find somebody to blame for this mess and I'm the one in his sights. Said I should have stopped her from leaving the restaurant."

"Harris is dreaming if he thinks he's gonna lay this off on you. He was the guy in charge."

"Yeah, but you don't know Glen Harris."

She was crying again, and DeMarco didn't blame her. "Are you still being transferred out here?" DeMarco said.

Diane gave a bitter laugh. "Oh, yeah. Maybe even sooner than I expected. Harris wants me off his team, says I can definitely use some training."

DeMarco couldn't think of anything to say to make her feel any better. But if Harris tried to fuck up her career, he was gonna talk to Mahoney. "Well, I'm glad you're moving back here," he said. "Even if it's only for a little while. Really glad."

"Me, too, Joe," she said softly. "Me, too."

Half an hour after he spoke to Diane, he was summoned over to the Pentagon where he was taken to a small room on the C-ring. In the room was an Asian wearing an army uniform with a major's insignia on the shoulders. On the table in front of the major was a telephone speaker box. Bill Smith was on the other end of the phone in Vancouver.

"What did the tape say, the foreign part?" DeMarco asked.

The major said, "It said: 'Do it now. Quickly.'"

Do what now? DeMarco wondered. "Emma called the woman Li Mei," DeMarco said. "Who is she?"

Smith hesitated. He hesitated too long.

"Smith," DeMarco said, "don't you dare give me some bullshit about need to know. I'm not gonna tell you again: either you bring me in on this thing or you clowns can hold a press conference."

"Li Mei was a Chinese agent who Emma burned in Hawaii twenty years ago," Smith said.

38

Honolulu, Hawaii—Twenty Years Ago

Emma was the last person to arrive for the meeting. Already seated at the table was a navy captain, an army colonel, and an air force major.

At the head of the table was a middle-aged civilian. Emma knew him—and she didn't like him. His name was Blake Hanover and he worked for the CIA. Emma could imagine how he'd looked when the cold warriors had recruited him: Harvard-crew burly, thick blond hair, chiseled chin—and that superior, the-world-is-my-oyster gleam in his eyes. Now, twenty-five years later, the golden good looks were gone and he was just another cynical, mid-level spy—a jaded, chain-smoking, alcoholic spy.

"Nice you could make it," Hanover said to Emma. Emma looked at her watch then back at Hanover. She was right on time and he knew it.

"This lady works for the DIA," Hanover said to the military officers, "our *junior* partners in this little venture." Emma didn't bother to respond to Hanover's gibe and she avoided the hand-shaking ritual by placing her purse under the table and taking off her suit jacket as introductions were being made. The men in uniform all seemed uncomfortable when she assessed them with her pale blue eyes.

"Okay, boys and girls," Hanover said, "here's what we've got. Two days ago a guy was getting on a plane to Hong Kong. The DEA had been watching him for a while because of all the trips he makes and the places he goes. Well the guy gets to the airport and the narcos pull his bag off the plane and search it, but as soon as they saw what was in it, they had the good sense to call the right people. This guy, this courier, may also be involved in drugs but what he had in his suitcase was a . . . a *stew* of military intelligence. He had a top-secret message to CINCPACFLT that gave the exact location of a sub stationed in the East China Sea. He had a maintenance manual for an F-15 fighter containing a complete description of the fighter's electronic countermeasures system. The manual was marked as coming from Hickam Air Force Base. A photograph of the reactor plant control console for a nuclear submarine was also in the suitcase. The specific sub has been undergoing a refit at the sub base at Pearl Harbor for the last two months. And finally, there was a list of six army personnel above the rank of major who were recently transferred from the 25th Infantry Division at Schofield Barracks to Taiwan to train the Taiwanese army. In addition to these men's names was a summary of their financial positions and outstanding loans. In other words, information to show which of these men might be most susceptible to being bribed."

The uniformed attendees all muttered various curses. Emma said nothing.

"Jesus," the army colonel said, "it's a good thing we got this sumbitch before this stuff got out."

"It got out," Hanover said. "We let it go."

"You what!" the navy captain said.

"The most sensitive piece of information the courier had was the location of the sub off the Chinese coast and the sub's CO was notified immediately. We replaced the photograph of the reactor plant control console with one belonging to a British boat."

"Bet the Brits'll love that when they find out," the navy captain muttered.

"The air force countermeasures manual was almost a decade old and we decided to let them have it, except for two pages we razored out. And as for the names of the guys from Schofield Barracks, well we'll just have a little talk with them."

"Why'd you let the courier go?" the army colonel asked.

"Because, Colonel, we need to know who gave him this stuff and who he was delivering it to. When the courier arrived in Hong Kong—by the way, we got his bag there before he did; those F-15s are good for something—he eventually meets up with an agent from the Chinese embassy. So we know who's running the operation: the Chinese. But what we don't know is who in Hawaii is collecting this information. Do you all understand what I'm saying here?"

Everybody nodded.

"Tell them anyway," Emma said. These men were too senior to admit they didn't understand something.

"What this means," Hanover said, "is that there's a Chinese spy here in Hawaii, or more likely a *team* of Chinese spies, and they've somehow managed to simultaneously penetrate four military commands on this island, including the headquarters of the fucking Pacific Fleet. And it means we either have Americans in four different commands giving classified material to the Chinese or we actually have Chinese agents embedded in these commands acquiring intelligence."

"Why didn't you just arrest the courier and make him tell you who gave him the stuff?" the air force major said.

"Because the information was most likely delivered to the courier by a cutout. In other words, it's highly unlikely that he has any idea who the spies are. If we had arrested the courier, or if the package had never reached Hong Kong, then the Chinese would have known we were on to them and their guys here in Hawaii would have either disappeared or just gone underground for a while. Bottom line is, we need to find out who's running this op in Hawaii, we need to know who they've turned, and we need to find out before too many more suitcases full of classified data leave this island."

"So what do you want us to do?" the navy captain said.

"Nothing. That's the whole point of this meeting, gentlemen. You are all responsible for security at your respective bases, but what I *don't* want you to do is run home and start questioning people or changing security procedures. I want you to stay watchful and keep me informed, but that's it. You are to take no action that is out of the ordinary. The main thing I want is for you to do whatever I tell you."

"Now wait just a goddamn minute, you arrogant prick," the navy captain said. "I don't work for you, and if there's a spy on my base—"

"Captain," Hanover said, "my director has talked to the president and he in turn has talked to the chairman of the Joint Chiefs. The military out here has been penetrated so badly—I mean, you people are leaking like a fucking *sieve*—that the president wants *us* running the show. Got it?"

"Why isn't the FBI involved in this?" Emma said.

"Because we don't want them involved," Hanover said, lighting another cigarette. "The only reason *you're* involved is the Joint Chiefs made a fuss, and to appease 'em, my boss agreed to include you. The other thing is we need a gal for part of this. You're the gal."

Hanover and Emma were sitting at the beachside bar of the Royal Hawaiian Hotel. The pink-painted structure on Waikiki was Emma's favorite hotel on Oahu. She loved the open-air corridors and faded Persian rugs and the tropical garden surrounding the place. She didn't like being there with Hanover, but he had said that he needed a drink after the meeting and this was where he wanted to come. From where they sat, they could see brown-skinned surfboarders paddling out to catch the next wave, ever optimistic that the next wave would be *the* wave. Every time Hanover's eyes followed the lithe body of a bikini-clad teenage girl walking by, Emma wanted to take his cigarette and put it out in one of his eyes.

"We've got something I didn't tell those guys," Hanover said. "The message on the position of the sub, it was handled by only four people. One of those people is a warrant officer who works in the message center. She's got two kids and her husband took off for the mainland six months ago. Three weeks ago this gal was about to have her car repossessed. Now she's caught up on her payments and last week she bought a new TV."

"Are you *sure* she's involved?"

"No. But she's the best possibility we've got. Anybody in two squadrons at Hickam could have snuck that countermeasures manual off the base. The photo of the reactor plant control console, there are at least fifty people at the sub base who could have taken it, not to mention half the crew of the sub itself. And that list of army guys being transferred to Taiwan, that could have come from anyone in personnel, housing, or payroll over at Schofield Barracks. Our best bet is the warrant officer."

Emma had to agree, although she was naturally skeptical of any conclusion arrived at by the CIA. They had a history of getting things wrong.

"In . . ." Hanover stopped and looked at his watch, a navy diver's watch. Emma wondered how he had gotten it. "In forty minutes the warrant officer and her two kids are gonna get killed in an accident on the Pali Highway. At least that's what the papers will report tomorrow."

Emma knew what he was going to say next.

"You're the warrant officer's replacement," Hanover said. "Your uniform should be in your room by now. Tomorrow we'll start making sure that everybody knows you're a complete flake. We had to tell the lady in charge of the message center who you really are but she had a son who died in Vietnam and we're sure she's okay. She's our head gossip-spreader. Two days from now everyone within half a mile of your new desk will know that you were recently in a drug rehab program and that at your last base you had creditors beating on your CO's door because you didn't pay your bills." Hanover's lips stretched and he added, "And we're letting it out that you're a slut, too."

Emma just stared at Hanover until the stupid grin disappeared from his face.

"You need to develop a sense of humor," Hanover said. When Emma still didn't respond, he shrugged and plucked the olive out of his martini with thick fingers and popped it into his mouth. "We think that whoever's running this thing," he said while chewing, "will check you out because the most sensitive place they've penetrated is the Pacific Fleet's message center."

Emma noticed the young Chinese woman two days after she began working at the message center.

Emma, in her persona as flake in residence, had shown up late both days for work, her uniform poorly pressed, and her eyes red-veined from alcohol or drugs. To get that red-eyed look, Emma had mixed a small amount of contact lens cleaning solution with saline and then dropped it in her eyes right before entering the office. The eyedrops stung like crazy.

The Chinese woman was in her early twenties, lovely, tall, and perfectly proportioned. She caught Emma's attention not because she was Chinese—half the population of Hawaii is Asian—but because she didn't have the proper badge for being in the building she was in. Since she was being escorted by another woman who *did* have proper clearance, she wasn't technically in violation of any security procedure, but the fact that she was in a restricted area was enough to make Emma notice her. The other reason she noticed her was because of her beauty. No, not just her beauty. Her *vitality*. The young woman just *hummed* with energy. Later, Emma noticed her sitting outside at a picnic bench with three women having lunch. One of the women, also Chinese, worked in the message center with Emma.

The young Chinese woman approached Emma two days later. Emma had taken to stopping at the officers club every night after work. She did this for two reasons: first, because such behavior was in keeping with her reputation as a boozer; and second, because officers clubs have historically been a good place for foreign agents to recruit potential traitors. The only drawback was that she had to keep fending off amorous navy drunks.

When Emma entered the club she saw the young Chinese woman at the bar flirting with a navy commander. The commander was homely and pudgy and balding, and Emma knew that never before in his life had he been with anyone so lovely. Emma made a point of wandering past the commander on her way to the ladies' room, and as she did, she memorized the name on his badge and his unit insignia.

Fifteen minutes later the young woman gave the commander a little kiss on the cheek, which left him open-mouthed and stunned, and walked over to Emma's table. She introduced herself as May Chen. She didn't have a trace of an accent and sounded as if she was U.S. born and bred. She told Emma she had been friends with the woman in the message center whom Emma had replaced.

It took no time at all for May Chen to become Emma's new best friend. And Emma, in keeping with her cover, drank too much, called her boss a bitch, and said how much she hated the fuckin' navy. She made it very clear that her paycheck didn't come close to matching the cost of living in Hawaii.

While they talked, Emma was again impressed by how beautiful the young woman was: small, delicate ears; flawless, golden complexion; perfect rosebud lips. China doll, she thought, as she sat across from May Chen. There was also this *sparkle* in May's dark eyes and Emma had the impression that this young woman—if she was a spy—was enjoying her mission as if it was the most exciting game she'd ever played.

She was absolutely *high* from the thrill of what she was doing.

Within a week, Emma established that May Chen had a boyfriend, also Chinese. The boyfriend wasn't classically handsome but he was striking; he had a hawkish, angular face you tended to notice and the build of a gymnast, those men you see holding on to the rings, their arms perpendicular to their bodies, their muscles barely quivering as they maintain the position for minutes. To do that takes not only strength but the mental toughness to ignore tendons and ligaments screaming in agony.

The couple didn't live together but they met most nights at one or the other's apartment. When they were together, they couldn't keep their hands off each other. And like May Chen, the young man gave off the same vibration—as if he too was having the time of his young life.

The CIA researcher was a sour-faced man who sucked his teeth. Between the teeth sucking and the smoke from Hanover's ever present cigarette, Emma wanted to scream.

"Both of them have excellent covers," he said, "and they go pretty deep. Birth certificates and social security numbers that belong to dead people whose names they've taken, high-school diplomas from places in California and Washington State, pictures in high-school yearbooks that even look like them. Naturally, their supposed parents are dead and they moved away from their supposed hometowns a long time ago so you can't talk to anyone who's known them in the last five years. If all you did was a cursory background check on these two, you wouldn't spot a thing. I did more than a cursory check of course."

"But who are they?" Emma said.

"The guy, we don't have a clue. But the woman, she's Red Army. She played on their Olympic volleyball team and it was pure luck we found that out. One of my assistants is a volleyball nut because her daughter plays. The Chinese team played an exposition match in D.C., and my assistant remembered her because of her defense. So we went through about twenty hours of tapes from the last Olympics, and sure enough, it was her. Her real name is Li Mei Shen."

———— ◆◆◆ ————

The first time they met, Emma had made it clear to Li Mei that she couldn't live on her salary, then two days later she told her new friend that she was now in *extremis* because they were going to start garnishing her wages to pay back her creditors. The next day Li Mei made her approach.

She was in *such* a hurry, Emma thought. The fact that Emma was a good actress and came across as disgruntled and corruptible may have been the reason

Li Mei moved so quickly: she saw Emma as an easy target and not one requiring much patience or finesse. But it wasn't just that. This young woman and her boyfriend—Emma had been watching the boyfriend, too—were like two kids who had been let loose in a candy store. They were moving at breakneck speed, caution be damned, just grabbing *handfuls* of intelligence. And they were having a blast while they did it.

The previous night, Emma had watched Li Mei and her boyfriend dance at a club. They were both athletic and graceful and completely in sync with the music and one another. They may have been spies but they had looked just like all the other twenty-year-olds writhing to the music, and they had danced until they shined with sweat and the promise of sex to come. They had gone to the club right after Li Mei's boyfriend had met an air force staff sergeant from Hickam and taken a manila envelope from him.

So now Emma sat with Li Mei at the officers club at what had become their usual table, and while Emma drank, Li Mei made her pitch. She told Emma that she belonged to a group of peace activists that would pay for messages related to the movements of nuclear submarines in the Pacific. The peace-activist angle was given so that if Emma—the Emma who worked in the message center—had a conscience, she could assuage that conscience with the belief that she was working for the noble cause of global harmony.

Emma would never forget the way Li Mei looked that evening. Her long black hair had been combed into artful disarray, and a lock would occasionally fall forward and play peekaboo with one of her bright eyes until a graceful hand would sweep it back into place. She had worn a casual, eye-catching outfit, the type favored by the beach girls of Waikiki: a short pink skirt, a midriff-baring lime green blouse, and flip-flops that were covered with some sort of sparkling substance. She had looked so young and fresh. So alive. Emma couldn't help but like her—and feel bad for her at the same time.

It should have gone down easily. There was no reason for anyone to have died.

That day, Li Mei had gone to a bank and filled a briefcase with material from a safe-deposit box. The box was where they kept the material they had acquired until it was time to give it to the courier. One of the items in the box was a bogus encrypted message that Emma had given Li Mei the day before. The content of the false message was so important that Hanover figured the Chinese would want to get it out of the country immediately. During the last three weeks, Hanover's surveillance team had identified five U.S. servicemen who had provided classified material to Li Mei and her partner. These five people and the courier would be picked up at the same time they arrested the Chinese spies.

A six-man takedown team would make the arrest. Emma insisted that she be allowed to be part of the team. Hanover made some crack about her not getting in the way of the "pros" but he eventually agreed, acting like he was humoring her. The team members were all CIA civilians and Emma didn't trust them. They had the right equipment and probably had had the right training, but they acted like high-school jocks before a big game, horsing around and joking during the preoperational briefing. They didn't have the discipline that Emma was used to seeing when working with military teams.

It was almost funny, the thing that turned the operation into a disaster. Funny, but afterward no one laughed, not even the CIA jocks.

Li Mei lived in a duplex off Lumiaina Street in Pearl City. The idea was to wait until three a.m. when Li Mei and her partner would be sleeping in one another's arms. Emma and two CIA agents would take the front door, and the other three guys would come in through the rear. As the rear-entry team was approaching Li Mei's back door they had to pass under the windows of the connecting apartment, and the windows were open. As one of the team members crawled under Li Mei's neighbor's window, a parrot the neighbor kept in a cage near the window went berserk. It began squawking, its screams ripping apart the night. The funny part was that the parrot was squawking, "Tiny bubbles! Tiny bubbles!"

The CIA team leader made the decision to go in right away, while Li Mei and her partner were hopefully coming out of the fog of sleep, still trying to figure out why the parrot was screaming. The team leader made a bad decision. By the time the CIA team broke through the doors, Li Mei and her lover were in the central hallway of the small apartment, standing back-to-back with guns in their hands and a line of sight to both entrances.

Li Mei shot the first two men who came through the back door. She shot one in the throat and one in the forehead. Li Mei's partner shot the first guy who came through the front door and then he shot Emma. Twice. The first shot hit her body armor, the other went through her left bicep. Emma was returning fire as she was shot the second time.

Emma shot Li Mei's lover in the face, though she'd been aiming for his shoulder.

Li Mei saw her lover fall and spun toward him involuntarily, and the third member of the rear-entry team, the only one still alive, was able to leap over his teammates' bodies and butt stroke her in the head before she could get off another shot.

The objective of the operation had been to capture both spies alive.

The operation had been a disaster.

Hanover told Emma that she would be Li Mei's primary interrogator.

When Emma told him to go to hell, Hanover had said, "First of all, honey, it's already been cleared with your bosses. We figure you'll probably have the best rapport with the Chinese gal, you being female. The second thing is, you're not good for much else at the moment with your arm still in a sling."

A doctor on CIA payroll was brought in to assist in the interrogation, meaning he would be the one who would torture Li Mei with drugs and sleep deprivation and carefully controlled pain. The doctor never showed any emotion while he did his work; Li Mei was no more human to him than a medical-school practice cadaver. When Emma protested to Hanover about the doctor's methods, Hanover told her to shut up and do her job.

And Emma did. God help her, she did. Emma was still a young woman when this occurred, barely ten years older than Li Mei. She didn't have, at this point, the self-assurance she would later acquire but she knew in her heart that what the CIA was doing was wrong—and yet she did what she was told.

That was the last time during her career that Emma *ever* did something that she was ashamed of.

In five weeks, they drained Li Mei dry. They found out who she had turned and what information she had taken, and as a bonus, they rolled up another

Chinese team operating on the mainland. Nobody thought it unusual that Li Mei was vomiting every morning when they took her from her cell. Considering the drugs he had given her, the doctor felt that was a mild side effect.

The playfulness and vitality that Emma had once seen in Li Mei disappeared the day her lover died. Now all that remained in those once sparkling eyes was hatred—and all that hatred was focused on Emma. Emma had set her up; Emma had killed her lover; and Emma was the one who questioned her until she could no longer remember what she had said. Emma had never thought it possible to actually *feel* hatred, but when Li Mei looked at her it was as if there were white-hot beams emanating from her eyes, twin lasers burning holes into Emma's soul.

Six weeks after being captured, Li Mei was exchanged for a U.S. "tourist" who just happened to have a camera that looked like a pack of cigarettes and who had been taking pictures of people entering a laboratory in Zhejiang Province.

Before returning Li Mei to the Chinese, the CIA doctor gave her a complete physical; the U.S. government wanted it on record that she had remained in perfect health while in American custody. During the physical the doctor discovered why Li Mei had been vomiting during the interrogation sessions: she was pregnant.

When Emma heard that, *she* threw up.

39

DeMarco left the Pentagon and rushed back to Mahoney's office.

"I have to talk to him," DeMarco said. "Now."

Mavis, Mahoney's secretary, raised an eyebrow at DeMarco's tone. DeMarco was usually polite—and laid back. And he never came to Mahoney's offices unless he was summoned. Now here he stood, glowering, his big hands on the edge of her desk like he might tear the top off. He really turned her on.

"He's busy, Joe. There's something big going on and he's with Perry right now," she said. Seeing the look on DeMarco's face, she said, "I'll let you know as soon as he's free."

"Don't bother," DeMarco said, and started back toward Mahoney's office.

"Joe!" Mavis said. "Joe! What do you think you're doing?"

DeMarco opened the door to Mahoney's office without knocking. Mahoney was behind his desk, his feet up, his tie undone. Sitting in front of his desk was a fat man wearing red suspenders over a wrinkled white shirt. The man's suspenders matched his tie.

The man was Perry Wallace, Mahoney's chief of staff.

Most of Mahoney's staff members were young-sters—bright, hard-working kids in their twenties or early thirties. Most of them had degrees in law or political science. Congressional staff work didn't pay very well but these smart youngsters took the job to have something shiny to put on their résumés, to learn how Washington really worked, as a spring-board toward their own political careers. Perry Wallace was an exception; he had been with Mahoney twenty-five years.

Wallace was one of the smartest and hardest-working people DeMarco knew. He was also one of the most obnoxious. He could read about ten thousand words a minute, and he never forgot any of the words he read. He knew every politician of any importance throughout the United States, and exactly what buttons to push to get those politicians to move in the direction the Speaker desired. Ninety percent of the decisions Mahoney made were based on recommendations from Perry Wallace.

"What the hell . . . ," Mahoney said when De-Marco burst into the room.

"Beat it, Perry," DeMarco said to Wallace.

Wallace just smiled—it was a mean little smile—and he didn't budge.

"I need to talk to you," DeMarco said to Mahoney. "It's about the . . . the thing out in Bremerton. It's important."

"Go on, Perry," Mahoney said. "Go get some dinner or something. And you," Mahoney said, pointing a thick finger at DeMarco's face, "this better be the most important fuckin' thing you've ever had to tell me."

Perry Wallace slowly raised his bulk from his chair and picked up a stack of papers from the corner of Mahoney's desk. He shook his head at DeMarco—the head shake was one of pity not annoyance—and then lumbered slowly from the office. DeMarco knew that at some time in the future, Wallace would make his life miserable for this breach of etiquette.

"So what is it?" Mahoney said after Wallace left the room.

DeMarco told him.

"Jesus," Mahoney said when he finished. "So what do you want me to do?"

"I want you to shake up the world. I want you to make sure the DIA and the FBI are doing everything they can to find her."

Mahoney didn't particularly care for Emma. She struck him as being the self-righteous type, and she always looked at him as if she found him morally wanting. But she was DeMarco's pal, and she'd helped DeMarco on more than one occasion on Mahoney's behalf. Like last year down in Georgia, when she'd saved DeMarco's bacon. Most important, Mahoney couldn't see a political downside to getting involved.

"Okay," he said. "I'll give a couple guys over at the Pentagon a call. Justice, too."

"Thanks," DeMarco said. "And I need to go back out to Vancouver to look for her."

"Nah, that'd be a waste of time," Mahoney said. "If you got the whole fuckin' government tryin' to find her, what are you gonna add? Plus, I got things for you to do. Like that state house guy back home, which is where you're supposed to be headed right now."

"I have to try and find her," DeMarco said. "She's my friend. And maybe if I'd stayed out there with her, this wouldn't have happened."

"That's crap. If you'd been with her, you'd just be dead or missing now yourself. You forget going back out there. Go do your own job and I promise I'll keep the heat on the spies."

"I'm going out there."

Mahoney's big face flushed red. "Now you listen to me, goddamnit. You do what I tell you, or you can start lookin' for someplace else to work."

"I'll see you later," DeMarco said and walked out of the Speaker's office.

40

Emma's legs were rubber. Her brain was mush. They'd injected her with drugs when they took her from her car, and in the last twelve hours she'd been injected two more times. She was in a small room, approximately eight by ten, and the only furniture in the room was a twin-size bed. She couldn't hear city noises, so she assumed she was either in the country or a quiet residential neighborhood. The one window in the room had a square of plywood nailed over it but there was still plenty of light. In fact there was too much light in the room. The light came from an overhead fixture with an abnormally bright bulb and there was a wire cage protecting the bulb. She could probably break the bulb if she wanted but the effort to do so was just . . . just too much.

They'd taken her so easily that she was embarrassed. When it happened, she'd been sitting in her car half a block from the restaurant on East Pender Street. From her car she had been able to see the front of the restaurant but not the rear, and Harris's agents were invisible, staged in nearby buildings and a panel van. Emma remembered checking her watch; Carmody's controller should have arrived fifteen minutes ago.

It had been a warm morning and her car windows had been rolled down. She had been sitting there, holding her cell phone in her hand, between her legs, thinking about calling Harris. There was one man, a stocky Asian, looking into the window of a kite store across the street from the restaurant where Carmody was waiting. The man had been there an unusually long time and he kept glancing over his shoulder at the restaurant. Emma was on edge—she knew something was wrong with the meet—and she was thinking of alerting Harris to the kite shopper, although she imagined Harris's agents had already spotted the guy.

At that moment a Range Rover had pulled up next to her car and the vehicle blocked her view of the restaurant. She had been about to get out of her car so she could continue to watch the restaurant when a woman put her head into the passenger-side window of Emma's car. Emma saw the gun in the woman's hand before she saw the woman's face. As soon as she saw the gun she pushed the send button on her telephone three times; her phone would automatically dial the last person she'd spoken to: DeMarco.

She wasn't sure her voice would be audible with the phone in the position it was, on the seat between her legs, but it was her only chance. She had identified Li Mei for DeMarco's sake and made the comment about her being a rogue agent. That would help Smith's people—assuming DeMarco answered his phone, assuming her voice was audible, assuming Li Mei didn't see the phone. The phone call wouldn't keep Emma alive but at least Smith would know who had killed her.

At the same time Li Mei had pointed the gun at her, a man appeared at the driver's-side window of Emma's car. Even if Harris's people had turned to look in Emma's direction, with the Range Rover in the position it was in, she would not have been visible. Both the man and Li Mei appeared to be leaning casually into the car, like a couple talking to a friend. The man had a hypodermic needle in his hand and he pressed it against Emma's throat. Li Mei said something in Chinese, and the man shifted the needle from her throat to her upper left arm. With Li Mei's gun pointed at her, Emma didn't move when the man pushed down the plunger on the hypodermic. It took about sixty seconds for the drug to have an effect, and when the man opened Emma's door to escort her from her car to the Range Rover, she went with him as docilely as a child. She had just enough awareness to push her cell phone to the floor of the car as she exited. If Li Mei and her partner hadn't been so focused on looking out for Harris's agents, they would have seen the phone lying on the floor mat. Emma passed out seconds after entering the SUV.

And so now here she was, locked in a room in an unknown location, her mind and body turned to pudding by narcotics. She decided to try to get up, and with great effort managed to push herself to a sitting position on the edge of the bed, her feet touching the floor. Her next job was to push herself to a standing position. She was almost certain if she tried to stand she'd fall on her face, but she had to try. As she was commanding her muscles to move, the door opened and Li Mei entered the room.

41

DeMarco pushed open the door to the office that Smith was using in Vancouver. Smith was on the phone but when he saw DeMarco—or the expression on DeMarco's unshaven face—he told whoever he was talking to that he'd call back.

"Tell me what's happening," DeMarco said without preamble.

"You want some coffee? You look like you could use some."

"No, I don't want any damn . . ." DeMarco stopped and pinched the bridge of his nose. "Yeah," he said, "some coffee would be good."

"That red-eye's a bitch, ain't it?" Smith said as he handed DeMarco a cup of tepid coffee in a Styrofoam cup.

"Yeah. Now tell me what's going on."

"Well, we're doing everything that can be done to find her. The FBI's involved and so are the Canadians. Thank God for Dudley."

"Yeah, but what *exactly* are you doing?"

"All the usual stuff," Smith said. "The lab rats have gone over Emma's car looking for fingerprints, fibers, that sorta thing. They got zip. The Bureau listened to that message on your cell phone using all their high-tech shit to see if they could pick up anything. Again zip. The Canadians questioned people in the area where Emma's car was found. They got something. One witness saw two people talking to Emma—a man and a woman—and they saw Emma leave her car and get into a dark green SUV with the two people. But that's all. No model or license plate on the SUV, no clear description of the man with Li Mei. The witness wasn't even sure if the man was Asian.

"So now," Smith said, "we're watching airports and cruise ships and train stations and borders. We have their pictures—Emma's, Carmody's, and Li Mei's— plastered all over the place. For Carmody, we're using the mug shots we took when we arrested him here in Canada. For Li Mei, we found a photo of her from the Olympic Games, it's more than twenty years old, but we had some artist age the picture. It was the best we could do." Smith took off his black-frame glasses and rubbed his eyes. Without the glasses he looked older. "I gotta tell you, Joe," he said, "the odds aren't in our favor. If I was them, and I wanted to get Emma out of Vancouver, I'd put her in a cargo container and load her onto an outbound ship. She's probably gone already."

"Oh, man," DeMarco said. "Don't say that."

"Sorry, but it'd be almost impossible to stop them if that's what they did. But the good news is that we don't think the Chinese government's involved in this thing."

"What are you talking about?" DeMarco said.

"Sit down, DeMarco. Quit pacin' my office and I'll tell you what we think happened here." After DeMarco had taken a seat, Smith cleared his throat and took in breath like a man about to give a speech. "Okay," he said, "it's like this. Li Mei was controlling the shipyard op and at the same time she was turning John Washburn. She's a beautiful woman and we're guessing she screwed ol' John's brains out to turn him. Probably offered him money, too. So anyway, she's got two ops going and they're going great. She's getting stuff on nuc ships from Carmody and she's getting ready to get Washburn out of the country, back to China, where they can empty out his head. She probably got files from Washburn, too. Okay?"

DeMarco made a move-it-along gesture with his hand—he knew all this—but Smith continued with his summary.

"Then you and Emma show up at the shipyard. You're there lookin' into what you think is some little whistle-blower contract thing, but then you figure out that Carmody and his boys are really spies. You don't have anything solid, but you spook Mulherin which makes Li Mei think that you *really* know something. Now you gotta remember, Li Mei's dealt with Emma before. Emma's beat her before. She knows how good Emma is.

"So Li Mei decides to shut down the shipyard op and concentrate on Washburn. She kills Mulherin and Norton and sends Carmody running around the country. This gets everybody—FBI, NCIS, navy security—focused on *Carmody,* trying to figure out what he took, trying to find him. And while everybody's looking for Carmody, she fakes Washburn's death, hoping nobody'll notice until she gets him on a plane. But then Emma gets lucky again. She finds out Washburn's missing, gets airport security looking for him, and TSA nabs him. Li Mei has Washburn's files but Washburn, *he's* not going anywhere. Emma's beaten her again.

"And so Li Mei decides to take Emma. It's no longer just business—it's personal, too. She uses Carmody for bait and sends him up here to Vancouver and lets us catch him, knowing Emma will follow."

"But Emma's retired," DeMarco said.

"But Li Mei doesn't know that," Smith said. "The fact is, Li Mei got lucky, too. It happens. Sometimes the bad guys get lucky. Emma didn't have to come up here but she did, just like Li Mei wanted."

"But why Vancouver? If she wanted to kill or kidnap Emma, why didn't she just do it in Bremerton?"

"She could have," Smith said, "but we think there're three reasons she didn't. One, she may not have had the time when she was in Bremerton because she was busy trying to get Washburn out of town. Two, and more important, Canada ain't the United States. So if Li Mei does the snatch up here we're not as effective as we'd be back home. What we have instead is a two-government tango: jurisdictions all screwed up and our guys not completely in charge, having to coordinate everything with the Canucks. So she does it up here partly just to slow us down, to make it harder for us."

"And the third reason?"

"The third reason is we think she had assets up here, contacts she didn't have in the States. Like the guys who helped her snatch Emma."

"I'm not following you," DeMarco said. "She works for the Chinese government. They could have provided the assets she needed in the U.S. just as easily as up here. And they could have provided extra people to deal with Emma while Li Mei was worrying about Washburn."

"Like I said, Joe, we don't think the Chinese government was involved in this thing with Emma. You heard what Emma said on that voice mail: she said that Li Mei's gone rogue, and we think Emma was right."

"I don't know what all this 'gone rogue' crap means."

"It means Li Mei did this thing on her own. Governments don't pull this kinda shit, DeMarco. Believe it or not, there're a few rules that apply to international espionage. The Chinese government wouldn't kidnap a retired American agent. Hell, they don't even capture *active* American agents unless the agents are on their turf. And they sure as hell don't go around killing FBI agents and Canadian cops. At least normally they don't."

"But in case the Chinese government is involved," Smith said, "Dudley has his people watching their embassy on Granville Street. They know most of the intelligence agents who work there—as opposed to diplomats and trade reps and cooks—and they're watching those guys in case one of them runs to Li Mei."

"I still don't get it," DeMarco said. "If all Li Mei wanted was revenge for what happened in Hawaii, why didn't she just kill Emma? Why kidnap her?"

"Yeah, well, we think . . ." Then Smith stopped.

"Come on, Smith. What?"

"Joe, I hate to tell you this, but we think that since Li Mei didn't get everything she wanted in Bremerton she decided to give her bosses something extra: everything inside Emma's head. Emma worked for us for almost thirty years and she had a security clearance higher than God's. So Li Mei can kill two birds with one stone, as the ol' saying goes. She can have her revenge on Emma and at the same time make her bosses a present out of all the classified stuff that Emma knows. And again, keep in mind that Li Mei doesn't know Emma's retired, so Li Mei thinks she's going to be getting current info."

DeMarco didn't say anything for a moment, then he said, "You're telling me she plans to torture Emma to get her to talk."

"Sorry, Joe, but that's a possibility."

"Jesus," DeMarco said. The word "torture" instantly flooded his mind with too many images from too many movies. Just to stop what he was thinking, he got up and poured himself another cup of bad coffee. "Okay," he said, sitting back down. "So what's the story with Carmody?"

"There is no story. He obviously worked with Li Mei to set this up. He allowed himself to be caught and then led us to that restaurant in Chinatown with a ring through our noses."

"But why would Carmody take that kind of risk, allowing himself to be captured the way he did?"

Smith shrugged. "Because Li Mei told him to. He works for her; she's his boss. And Li Mei probably told him she planned to spring him and he was just as surprised as we were when she tried to blow him away."

"But why would she try to kill him?"

Smith shrugged again. If he didn't quit doing that, DeMarco was going to hit him.

"Probably because Carmody could ID her," Smith said. "You gotta remember something else: Li Mei doesn't know that Emma identified her on that cell-phone call to you. She'd told Carmody to tell us that this was a North Korean op. Li Mei figured if she killed Carmody, not only couldn't he ID her but we'd go on thinking it was the North Koreans that had penetrated the shipyard, that it was the North Koreans that tried to get Washburn, and that *they* were the ones that snatched Emma. That was one of the smartest things she tried to do—use Carmody to lay all this on the Koreans. But once she had Emma, Carmody became a liability. An expendable one. Li Mei Shen is one cold-blooded, murderous bitch.

"And I'll tell you something else," Smith said. "This woman is incredibly bright and if she had balls, they'd be the size of cantaloupes. She decided from the get-go that she was going to snatch Emma and get rid of Carmody at the same time. Now she's probably been following Emma, so she knew Emma was here in Vancouver, and she knew the setup at the restaurant where Carmody would be, but she had no idea where Emma would be. Emma could have been with me or in the restaurant or with the cops. So Li Mei gets there early—we don't know what she looks like, so she was probably walking around watching the whole time Harris was setting up—and then in about an hour and a half she figures out a way to get Emma and shoot Carmody and escape. She's so good, she's scary."

Scary? A woman who had killed six people, three of them cops, and all Smith could say was that she was *scary*.

42

Li Mei saw Emma sitting on the edge of the bed, a dazed, unfocused look in her eyes. She waited until Emma looked directly at her then took one long stride across the room and slapped her face. Blood began to trickle from Emma's lower lip.

"That was for . . . everything," Li Mei said. Her eyes were unusually bright—insanely bright.

"What . . . ," Emma said—or tried to say. The word came out "Whaa." She had been trying to say "What do you intend to do with me," but "Whaa" was all she could manage.

Li Mei smiled at Emma's helplessness, then she grabbed Emma by the hair and forced her head back. Emma wondered if she was going to kill her right then.

"Later, I'm going to tell you the story of my life, the life *you* gave me. But not now; now it's time to go to work. We're going to spend the next week talking. You're going to tell me everything you've done during your career. You're going to talk to me about agents you've known and which ones are still in place. You're going to talk about ongoing operations and the technology your country's currently using. In particular, you're going to talk about how deeply my country's been penetrated, by who and how. You're going to talk a lot about that."

"I'm re . . ."

Li Mei stepped back and opened the door and called out, "Loc! Bao! Come here" A large Chinese man entered the room followed by a smaller Chinese man. The small one was the one who had injected Emma as she sat in her car; the big one had driven the Range Rover.

"The big one's Bao," Li Mei said to Emma. "Loc is the mean one."

Bao was about six four, balding, with a round face, a round gut, big arms, and heavy shoulders. His eyes were almost round, too. It was hard to read the expression on his face but he seemed uncomfortable, as if he didn't want to be where he was.

Loc, on the other hand, looked eager. He was two inches shorter than both Li Mei and Emma, skinny, his face pock marked from old acne scars. His eyes were narrow and hooded and when he smiled at

Emma, she could see that almost all of his teeth had silver fillings.

"I considered just turning Loc loose on you," Li Mei said. "Letting him pull out nails and gouge out eyes and connect wires to your tits. I think I would have enjoyed that, but that sort of interrogation takes too long. And it's messy. All that blood and shit and piss all over the place. So we're going to do to you what you did to me, Emma. We're going to do this the CIA way. No sleep and lots of drugs. We're going to pump you *full* of drugs, and drugs have changed a lot in twenty years. The drugs we've given you so far were designed to keep you awake but docile. Now we're going to give you something to make you, ah, what's the word? Manic, that's it. You're going to be coming out of your *skin* in fifteen minutes."

Li Mei said something in Chinese and both men moved toward Emma. Bao took hold of her shoulders while Loc opened a small case he'd been holding in his right hand and took out a hypodermic needle. Emma tried to pull loose from the grip Bao had on her shoulders but her limbs wouldn't respond to the signals she was sending from her brain. Loc grasped Emma's left arm at the wrist and began to move the hypodermic toward a vein in her forearm. Emma tried to pull her arm away, and when Loc couldn't keep her arm still, he cursed then slapped her with the back of his hand. Emma's head snapped back and her nose began to bleed. Loc started to hit her a second time but Li Mei said something in Chinese and Bao put his right arm around Emma's throat, increased the pressure until she began to have difficulty breathing, then used his left hand to hold her arm still. Bao was strong and his grip on her arm was like a vise biting into her flesh. Her arm immobilized, Loc injected the drugs into a vein. He pushed the hypodermic's plunger down fast and hard, and the drugs burned like liquid fire as they flowed into her bloodstream. Loc smiled as Emma grimaced in agony, his face close to hers, looking into her eyes. He seemed to be feeding off the pain he was causing her.

"We'll give that stuff some time to work," Li Mei said, "then we'll begin." She started to leave the room then spun around and said, "You have no idea how I suffered because of you." There were tears in her bright, black eyes when she said the words.

At least Emma thought the tears were in Li Mei's eyes—they could have been in her own.

43

Smith had told DeMarco that the Chinese government wasn't involved in Emma's disappearance but he needed to confirm this—and deliver a message to the Chinese. He was sitting in a bistro on Granville Street three blocks from the Chinese embassy, waiting to meet with the Chinese chief of intelligence in Vancouver, a man named Chan.

Smith had never met Chan but he knew from surveillance photos what he looked like. From Smith's window seat in the bistro he saw Chan now, across the street. He was a heavyset, bald man with an affable expression on his face. He was wearing a well-made tan-colored suit with jogging shoes. He started across the street to the bistro but then stopped abruptly, turned around, and walked into a store. The store had skinny mannequins in the window and the mannequins wore black-and-red underwear—the type of underwear that only twenty-year-old models can wear. It was called La Vie en Rose, which seemed to be Canada's version of Victoria's Secret.

Chan spent ten minutes in the store and came out holding a plastic bag. *Cross-dresser or a gift for his mistress?* Smith wondered.

Chan entered the bistro and went up to the counter and ordered a latte. As he was waiting for his drink he looked around, spotted Smith, and nodded pleasantly to him. There were four other customers in the restaurant but Smith was the only one wearing a suit—and apparently the only one who looked like a spy.

The Chinaman walked toward Smith's table, blowing on his latte to cool it, when he stopped suddenly and stared at Smith. He laughed loudly—more loudly than he had probably intended—and the other customers in the coffee shop looked at him. When he sat down at Smith's table he said in accented English, "Can you hear me now? Good!" and started laughing again.

Smith felt like shooting the bastard.

Smith began the meeting by saying, "Chan, what in the hell do you guys think you're doing?"

The meeting went exactly the way Smith had expected it to go: the Chinese spy denied everything.

He denied that they were running operations in Bremerton and particularly denied that they were involved in the shoot-out on East Pender Street and the kidnapping of Emma.

Smith found Chan's English interesting. Most times it was heavily accented, like a fry cook in a takeout place, but at other times he'd slip and Smith would hear perfect English with a hint of upper-class British accent. Whenever Chan needed time to think, he'd pretend he didn't understand, but Smith wouldn't have been surprised if the guy had a degree from Oxford or Cambridge. He was confident the guy's English was more than adequate when he used the word "hypothetically."

Hypothetically, Chan said, they might run these operations in Bremerton that Smith had mentioned. Chan gave a little shrug which meant: Hey, that's the game we're all in. What do you expect? But he said that if they were running such operations they sure as hell wouldn't go around kidnapping American agents.

"We got your gal on tape," Smith said.

"Tape?" the Chinese agent said. "What you mean 'tape'?"

Smith told Chan how Emma's phone had been on when Li Mei had kidnapped her. Chan winced at the mention of Li Mei's name.

"That's right," Smith said, "we know who she is and we know she's one of yours."

"I not understand," Chan said.

"You understand perfectly," Smith said. "And you better understand something else. If we don't get Emma back we're gonna make your lives miserable here in Canada and in every Chinese embassy in the United States. You guys aren't gonna be able to go for a walk without having our people all over you. We're gonna tow your damn cars away every time you park. We're gonna take pictures of you every time you enter a strip joint or visit a hooker—or go shopping in a place that sells slinky underwear." Chan frowned at the last comment, but when Smith said, "We might even deport a few of you clowns," the frown was replaced with a broad smile. They both knew that for every Chinese agent the Americans deported, an American agent would be deported from China.

Seeing that his threats were having little effect, Smith added, "And just maybe the American government's attitude toward your country will change dramatically. I'm talking embargoes and trade sanctions and tariffs, you understand?"

"Oh, bollocks," Chan said, and there was no accent at all when he said the word. Smith didn't know what "bollocks" meant but he suspected it was limey for bullshit—and Smith was bullshitting. International relations with the Chinese were too important to let one little spy operation rock the boat. Oh, the diplomats would make some noises, but that's all they'd do, and Chan knew it.

Communication between spies is as easy to interpret as whale songs, and only whales can sing the lyrics. Smith and Chan were old humpbacks with scars on their fins. By the time Chan had finished his latte, Smith was pretty sure the Chinese were not behind Emma's kidnapping. He couldn't be certain, of course, because Chan talked in circles, never admitting anything specifically. Smith's conclusion was based on experience and body language. In the end, he was convinced the Chinese government wanted to get their hands on Li Mei as much as the Americans did, and when the Chinese got her, her spying days would be finished. The meeting ended with Chan saying—or implying—that if by chance they found Emma they'd certainly return her to the Americans. Chan somehow managed to say this while simultaneously saying he had no idea who Emma was.

44

---◆◆◆---

There were four big cranes on the pier on Burrard Inlet. The cranes were painted a rusty red and stood on steel legs fifty feet high, their booms reaching out over the water. To DeMarco, they looked like the erect skeletons of some species of red-boned dinosaur.

Only one of the cranes was currently in service. A train had driven directly underneath the crane, between its steel legs, and about every ten minutes a cargo container would be transferred from the railcar to the deck of the Indonesian ship moored at the pier. Whoever was running the crane, someone invisible in the cab high above the ground, was good at his job. He was fast and never seemed to have to make any adjustments to place the container exactly where he wanted. Containers were stacked on the ship seven high and a dozen across.

There were *hundreds* of containers visible on the deck of the ship.

DeMarco was in a section of Vancouver called Gastown and he stood in a parking lot on a bluff above the waterfront watching the loading operation through binoculars. He'd occasionally see men in uniform, men he assumed were customs agents, looking at clipboards that he guessed held bills of lading. He never saw anyone actually open an outbound container and inspect its cargo. He figured all the security and inspections were focused on the stuff people were bringing *into* Canada and not the stuff they were sending out.

As he watched, he questioned once again the wisdom of coming to Vancouver. It sounded as if Smith was doing everything that could be done, and he had lots of people helping him. There really didn't seem to be anything for DeMarco to do. He tried not to think about the fact that he'd lost his job and had no idea what he was going to do for employment after this was all over.

After two hours of watching port operations De-Marco gave up. The container ship terminal he was watching was one of several around Vancouver, and a brochure he'd read said thousands of tons of cargo were shipped daily from the Canadian port. If Emma was in a cargo container and she had been loaded onto a ship bound for a Chinese-friendly country, there was no way in hell they were going to be able to save her. He didn't even allow himself to think that Emma was someplace being tortured.

He trudged back to his rental car and went in search of a place to stay for the next few days. As Uncle Sugar was no longer paying his per diem, he had only one criterion for lodging: cheap. He finally settled on a Best Western on the outskirts of Vancouver that charged about eighty bucks a night. Eighty bucks Canadian.

He unpacked his suitcase, hung up his clothes, and put his shaving kit in the bathroom. He then stood in the middle of the small room trying to think what to do next. It was almost six p.m. He was tired and hungry, and the only thing he could think to do was go to dinner. Hell of an investigator he was.

He walked to the door, put his hand on the door-knob, but as he did, he happened to glance down at the small desk located near the door. There was a phone on the desk and next to the phone was a little sign explaining how to make a phone call and how much it cost. The little sign also had a few words about using the phone line to make an Internet connection.

He took his hand off the doorknob, picked up the phone, and dialed a number in Washington, D.C. The phone rang ten times before someone finally answered.

45

Emma was talking about a man named Jin Zhang. She'd been talking about him for almost an hour. She liked Jin. He was an engineer who had worked for the Chinese space agency. He had a wife and a son and kept pigeons. Emma was telling Li Mei how Jin had used his pigeons to send her information.

Li Mei. Emma had been astounded by how little Li Mei's appearance had changed since Hawaii. She was still beautiful, maybe even more beautiful than she'd been as a young woman, but there was a hardness in her face, a wintry coldness in her eyes, that hadn't been there twenty years ago. The vibrant China doll was gone. Emma wanted to ask Li Mei what had happened since Hawaii but then the fog came again, the fog that wrapped around her mind.

Emma was *so* tired. She wondered when she'd slept last. And her eyes hurt because the light in the room was so bright. She'd asked the big man to turn off the light but he'd just shaken his head. She wasn't afraid of the big man, Bao. The little one though . . . What was his name? Whatever it was, there was something about the little one that frightened her. She scratched her forearm then looked down at the place that itched. My god, what were all those marks? On her other arm, too. She needed to see a doctor. And she stank. She hadn't bathed since her capture. She lifted her arm to smell her armpit, but then she realized that Li Mei was still there, watching her. She laughed, embarrassed, thinking of the sight she must have made sniffing herself.

"Stop that and concentrate! Put your arm down!" Li Mei said. "Did Jin talk to you about the rocket that blew up in Xichang in '96?" Li Mei asked.

"What?" Emma said.

"Pay attention!" Li Mei screamed. "The space center in Xichang. Szechuan Province. Nineteen ninety-six. Fifty-six people were killed. Did Jin Zhang cause the explosion?"

"Oh, I don't think so," Emma said. "There was something . . . something about the fuel mixture. I didn't understand it, but I passed on what Jin said to our technical guys. The technical guys said . . ."

Emma didn't know how long she'd been talking but she just kept talking and talking and talking. She was a real magpie, as her mother used to say. Was her mom still alive? She couldn't remember.

"Can I have a drink of water?" Emma said.

"No," Li Mei said. Then she said, "Yes. We're through for now."

"Oh, don't leave," Emma said. She didn't know why, she'd never been a particularly talkative person, but she could talk to Li Mei forever. When she was by herself she went kind of crazy. She'd talk to herself and sometimes she'd see people she knew were dead, and she'd talk to them. She was a real magpie.

"When I come back we're going to talk about submarines. Do you understand?"

"I've been on submarines before," Emma said.

"No, not your submarines. Our submarines. Chinese submarines. I want to know who you know, that works on them."

"Oh, I know . . ."

"I'll be back in half an hour," Li Mei said.

"Wait, don't go."

46

Fat Neil did a slow turn—an elephant doing a pirouette—as he inspected DeMarco's motel room. "Jesus, Joe, this place is a dump," he said. "Tell me we don't have adjoining rooms."

Neil was in his fifties, short, maybe five seven, and weighed two hundred and fifty pounds. He was the guy you didn't want to see walking down the aisle of an airplane when the seat next to you was empty. His head was balding on top but he allowed his remaining hair to grow long at the back and tied it into a grayish-blond ponytail that reached between his shoulder blades. The only attire DeMarco had ever seen him wear was Hawaiian shirts, shorts, and sandals, and that's what he was wearing today.

"It was the best I could afford," DeMarco said, responding to Neil's comment about the motel room.

"Is Uncle trying to reduce the deficit by lowering your per diem?"

"Something like that," DeMarco muttered. There was nothing to be gained by telling Neil that he was unemployed.

"Good," Neil said. "Someday I'll be eligible for Social Security, and it'd be nice if there was something still in the kitty when the time comes."

This was Neil's idea of a joke. If he ever needed Social Security he'd hack into a server and the government would began to spit out the largest retirement checks it had ever printed.

Neil was an old associate of Emma's, a man who made his living by collecting and selling information. He slithered—electronically—through firewalls and hacked into encrypted systems. He tapped phones and bugged boardrooms and bedrooms. DeMarco suspected that a portion of Neil's income came from government agencies and another portion came from people trying to get a leg up on the competition. Whatever the case, Emma had once saved Neil's life so when DeMarco called him and asked for help, Neil got on the first plane to Vancouver, arriving just in time for breakfast.

"Where's your gear?" DeMarco asked.

Neil didn't answer; he was still inspecting the motel room. He stuck his head into the small bathroom. "No Jacuzzi," he said. He turned toward DeMarco and raised his arms like the crucified, suffering Christ. "And my God, Joe, this place doesn't have room service."

"Neil, trust me, you'll survive," DeMarco said. "Now where's your gear?"

Neil jerked a thumb over his shoulder. "A van, out in the lot. But before I start unpacking stuff, we need to sit down and talk. And I'm hungry."

Hunger, DeMarco suspected, was a chronic condition.

At a Denny's two blocks from the motel, Neil ordered a breakfast large enough to feed Ethiopia. After half of it disappeared, he said, "We need to develop a working premise."

"A working premise?"

"Yes," Neil said. "I can't rape every database in Canada, so we need to narrow things down somewhat. We have to start by making certain assumptions, assumptions to focus our efforts. Comprende?"

"Yeah, I get it," DeMarco said. "And our first assumption is that Emma's still alive and still in Canada."

"I hope she's alive, too, Joe, but is your assumption a product of reason or emotion?"

"Reason. If Li Mei had just wanted her dead, she would have shot Emma while she was sitting there in her car. The second assumption, that she's still in Canada, is more of a reach but we gotta make it."

"And why is that?" Neil said.

"Because if Emma was packed into a box and loaded onto a ship for China, then we might as well go home and hold a wake for her. I'm not gonna do that, so we're gonna assume she's still here."

"But why Canada?" Neil said. "Maybe she's in the States by now. Alaska, if not the lower forty-eight."

"She could be, but both Canadian and U.S. customs are watching the border crossings. And it would seem to me that the last place Li Mei would feel safe would be the States. But mostly I think she's still here because, as Smith said, the Chinese government probably isn't helping Li Mei and she'd need help to get Emma out of the country. They'd have to line up a ship from a friendly country, make arrangements with a container company, fake bills of lading. Probably more than Li Mei could do on her own."

"I don't know about that," Neil said.

"We *have* to assume she's still here, Neil," De-Marco said.

Neil could hear the desperation in DeMarco's voice. "Okay," he said, "so we assume she's still in Canada. Then what?"

"Then I don't know," DeMarco said. "That's why I called you."

Neil started to answer, stopped and ate another slice of bacon—his fifth or maybe his sixth—then jabbed his fork at a syrup-sodden piece of pancake.

"Neil," DeMarco said.

"Have you considered *why* this woman kidnapped Emma instead of killing her, Joe?"

"Yeah," DeMarco said, "and it's not good. Smith thinks Li Mei is forcing Emma to give up stuff she knows. Classified stuff." DeMarco didn't want to use the word "torture."

"That's what I thought you were going to say," Neil said. "But let's not think about that for the moment. Let's return to our working premise."

Neil shut his eyes and pursed his lips, moving them in and out. He reminded DeMarco of Rex Stout's description of a thinking Nero Wolfe—Nero Wolfe in a Hawaiian shirt.

"Where would she take her?" Neil said.

"Well if I knew that—"

"That was a rhetorical question, Joe. You're going to have to get used to them. Now as to Emma's current location, let's see if we can narrow down the possibilities. First, I don't believe Li Mei would stash her in a heavily populated area."

"Why not? If they put her in a cellar someplace or a vacant apartment in a high-rise, who's to know?"

"I don't think so. Li Mei needs someplace she can smuggle a kidnapped person into—a person who's unconscious or being restrained. She needs someplace where the neighbors won't see a lady in handcuffs and a blindfold being carried up the stairs."

"So she smuggles her in at night."

"The kidnapping happened about noon," Neil said. "Li Mei wouldn't have driven her around all day, waiting until dark. No, Li Mei needs someplace where her comings and goings won't be noticed, where they won't be exposed when they go out for food and supplies."

"Maybe—" DeMarco started to say but Neil continued as if he was sitting alone.

"Nor do I believe that they'd stash her anyplace with a large Asian population, such as Chinatown. Li Mei and her companions might blend into such an area, but the Chinese embassy probably has more contacts among the Asian population than the Canadians do. And I imagine that by now both the Chinese and the Canadians have alerted everyone they know in Vancouver—agents in place, gang leaders, merchants, forgers—to be on the lookout for Li Mei and her two associates.

"On the other hand," Neil said, "being Chinese also poses a problem for Li Mei. Urban Vancouver has a large Asian population but the outlying areas do not. This makes Li Mei and her associates stand out—something we can use to our advantage."

"How—"

"So we'll add to our working premise that Li Mei has Emma somewhere isolated but not in an area with a large Asian population."

"Well shit, Neil," DeMarco said, "that leaves just about all of fuckin' Canada, from here to Nova Scotia."

"No, travel takes time and increases the risk of discovery. That's not what a logical person would do. A logical person would find a place close to Vancouver, someplace they could get her to quickly after the snatch. So I believe she's in an isolated area near Vancouver, but in a place where her neighbors won't notice the activities of a beautiful Chinese woman and her two thuggish companions.

"Which brings us to the thugs," Neil said, switching direction without signaling. "Who are they? Are they Chinese agents? The answer to that question is probably no, as your Mr. Smith has assumed. So they're the kind of people who work on the fringes. People like me, in other words. People with skills who operate for profit but who are not part of the government's infrastructure."

Neil sat for a second saying nothing. "Yes, I think that all sounds right." After a few more minutes of silent lip-pursing, he said, "So, that's our working premise, Joseph: Emma is alive, near Vancouver, in an isolated area with two Chinese for-hire thugs." Neil rubbed his two thick, soft paws together. "Now we have something to work with."

"What exactly do we have to work with, Neil? All you've done with your working premise is reduce the size of the haystack—but it's still a big fucking haystack."

Neil shook his big head, feigning dismay. "Allow me to explain for the slow learners in our group. We can now start looking at records for property that has been rented or sold—but I think rented—to a Chinese woman or a Chinese couple in the last two weeks. We may be able to narrow the date down even further because this operation was not planned long in advance. But for now we'll consider the time frame from the date you and Emma arrived in Bremerton until the day Emma was snatched."

"But how would you know if Li Mei's rented property? You think she'd use her own name?"

"No, but it's probably a safe assumption that they would use a name suitable for an Asian—Chinese, Japanese, Korean, something like that. Or she could have used a name that sounds both Caucasian and Asian."

"Like what?"

"Like Lee. Is Lee American or Chinese? Or Park. Is Park Korean or American?"

"I get it," DeMarco said. "But why can't they just use a non-Chinese name? Why not Jones or Taylor or Butler?"

"For a couple of reasons. One, such a name would draw attention to them. But I think the primary reason they'll use an Asian name is that these people would have false papers, and if you have false papers and you're an Asian, you don't have the papers made out in the name of Fenshaw."

"If she has fake papers," DeMarco said, "maybe the intelligence guy at the Chinese embassy would know what name she's using."

"That's a good thing to have Smith check on," Neil said, "not that the Chinese would necessarily tell him. Then there are the thugs."

"What about the thugs?" DeMarco said.

"Because they're thugs, there's a good chance they'll have police records. Or if they don't have police records, folks in the underworld—gang members, mob bosses, those sorts of people—probably know them. This would be a good thing for the RCMP to look into."

Neil started to say something else, then stopped.

"What?" DeMarco said.

"I think there's someone else we need to look for. A pharmacist."

"A pharmacist?"

"Yes. As you said earlier, Li Mei is probably forcing Emma to give her information. Now she could be pulling out her fingernails or—"

"I get the idea, Neil."

"Yes. Well that sort of interrogation isn't particularly effective, not if you want *large* amounts of information. I mean if all you want to know is where the family silver is buried, whacking off someone's pinky can be pretty effective. But to get large amounts of data, too much time is spent allowing the person being questioned to recover from the torture. And it often requires a doctor to keep the person alive while you're torturing her. And it's messy and it's noisy. But most important, it's often difficult to tell if the captive is telling the truth as the pain wears off. So if I was Li Mei, I'd use drugs. And since one of our prior assumptions is that this operation was not sanctioned by the Chinese government, where would Li Mei get these drugs?"

"A pharmacist."

"Precisely. A very special pharmacist," Neil said. Neil covered the empty plate in front of him with a napkin as if he were pulling a sheet up over the head of a corpse.

"Well, Joe, let's go back to the motel and unload my equipment. I've got enough to get started."

As they walked toward the car, DeMarco said, "Wouldn't Smith's people have come to the same conclusions we have?"

"Possibly. Assuming they're as bright as *moi.*"

"Let's assume they are."

"Well, assuming they are, they're probably going after information legally—meaning they're working through the Canadians. If we were on American soil, Smith might be inclined to run roughshod over a few privacy rights. But here in Canada, I think they're probably asking the Canadians to help them with record searches, and the Canadians—since it's not *their* ex-spy who's gone missing—are probably following the rules. Well, Joe, m'boy, I'm not following any fucking rules. I owe Emma my life."

47

Emma was crying. She was crying for Suki.

She was nine years old and it was a Saturday morning. She was sitting on the porch of her grandmother's house playing jacks. Practicing, actually—not just *playing*. At recess on Monday she was going to play Judy Parker again and this time she was going to beat her. She could now scoop up eight jacks with her small right hand. Sometimes she could get nine, but ten were just too many. But Judy Parker, who had bigger hands than hers, big *fat* hands, could get all ten almost all the time. Emma would practice until she could get ten. She'd stretch her fingers if she had to.

While Emma was practicing, Suki was playing near her. She'd chased a butterfly for a while, swatting at it with her paw until the butterfly flew away. Bored, the kitten had pushed her sweet little face into the area where Emma's jacks were and nudged them with her nose. Emma pushed her gently away. "Suki! I need to practice," Emma said.

Then she forgot about Suki, so intent on mastering the game, and the next time she looked up to see where Suki was, she couldn't see her. She stood up, on the top step of her grandmother's porch, and searched all around the front yard with her bright blue eyes. Then she saw her: the kitten was across the street, stalking a bird.

Emma didn't want Suki to catch the bird. "Come here, Suki, come here," she yelled. But Suki ignored her and crept toward the bird. Emma jumped down from the porch and ran across the street calling, "No, Suki, no." As she neared the kitten she waved her arms and the bird flew away, but when she tried to pick up Suki, to scold her for being a cat, the kitten scooted out of her arms and ran in the same direction the bird had flown—back across the street, toward Grandma's house.

Emma saw the car coming and she screamed—but it did no good. The car's right front tire broke Suki's back. Emma ran to the bleeding cat, screaming hysterically. The lady who'd been driving stopped the car and ran over and clutched Emma to her, holding her, trying to comfort her, to contain her. Emma struggled in the woman's arms and kicked at her, all the time looking at Suki, who just lay there, her eyes open, with funny stuff coming out of her nose. Emma couldn't stop crying.

"Stop crying and answer me," she heard a voice say. It didn't sound like Grandma though; Grandma never yelled at her that way.

"She killed Suki," Emma said.

"What?" the mean voice said.

"She killed Suki. The woman with the red shoes."

"Goddamnit, how much did you give her?" Li Mei said to Loc in Chinese.

"I gave her the same amount as before, just like you told me," Loc said. He didn't like this arrogant woman. "I'm telling you, it's building up in her system. You're going to fry her brain if you don't stop for a couple of days."

Li Mei ignored Loc and said to Emma, "Quit crying, Emma, and tell me about Wu Sing. Emma! Stop crying! Tell me what Wu Sing gave you before he died."

"Wu Sing?" Emma said.

Sing had worked at the Chinese finance ministry and for several years he had provided the Americans with data on how much the Chinese were spending on their weapons programs. The amounts being disbursed gave the DIA an indicator of priorities and strategies. Unfortunately, Chinese counterintelligence eventually identified Sing as a mole but before they could arrest him, he bolted. He made it as far as

Taiwan where he was crossing a street to meet Emma, the last step in a journey to freedom, when a Chinese agent ran him down. Emma remembered Wu Sing lying there on the wet asphalt, his back broken, staring up at her, his eyes begging her to save him.

"You were driving too fast," Emma said to Li Mei, her voice petulant and oddly childlike.

Li Mei shrieked in frustration and raised her hand to slap Emma, but then she stopped. She studied her prisoner for a moment: she looked terrible, her hair dirty and matted to her scalp, her face thin and haggard from lack of sleep and loss of weight. She looked beaten.

Li Mei exhaled. "Okay," Li Mei said to Loc in Chinese. "We're done. But don't let her sleep yet. Give her a small dose of the amphetamine if you have to to keep her awake, but nothing else. I have something to tell her and I want her lucid. Do you understand?"

When Loc didn't answer immediately Li Mei said again, "Do you understand?"

"Yes," he finally said. He was staring intently at Emma and there was a slight smile curving his lips, a strange light in his hooded eyes. Li Mei knew Loc was a sadist, possibly a psychopath. She wondered if she should kill him now.

48

◆

DeMarco didn't tell Bill Smith about Fat Neil, but he did tell him about the working premise they'd developed. Smith was impressed.

"That's pretty good," Smith said, "particularly the housing angle. We hadn't thought of that but I'll get Dudley's guys looking into it. We figured the pharmacist was our best bet. We thought if we could find him, we could make him give up Li Mei's partners, and that might give us some leads as to where she's hiding. Right now we've identified nine or ten guys who could have supplied her with the kinda drugs she'd need, and Dudley's pulling 'em all in."

"What else are you doing?" DeMarco said.

Smith frowned, annoyed by DeMarco's question, but he answered him. "We've got about thirty guys," he said, "watching the Chinese embassy to see if any of their people run to Li Mei. On top of that, we've cut the cables going to their computers, jammed their radio transmissions, and every time they pick up a phone we make sure they hear lots of clicks and beeps. We're sending a very strong message that if we don't find Emma, normal business is going to be difficult for a very long time."

"Is that it?"

"No. We're still watching airports and train stations and border crossings. And we've got undercover guys down on the docks. The problem is the longer this goes on, the less vigilant people get."

"So go home, DeMarco," Smith said, before DeMarco could ask another question. "We're pros and we're doing everything we can. And we're not doing all these things just because we like Emma or because she used to work for us. Emma's brain is a friggin' *vault* in which a lotta secrets are stored and we don't want Li Mei to crack it open, or if she has, we have to know what she got. And there's another thing: we think it's possible that Li Mei still has the stuff she got from Carmody and Washburn. So . . ."

"Why would she still have their files?" DeMarco said. "Wouldn't she have shipped those out of the country as soon as she got them?"

"Maybe, but maybe not. You gotta remember that Li Mei got busted once before using a courier and we don't think she'd trust FedEx to get a box of stolen, classified material to China. So we think there's a good chance she's hanging on to the stuff until she can deliver it in person. The point is, Joe, we're busting our asses to find Emma because we *have* to, not just because we're nice guys, and we're gonna keep busting our asses until we either get her or know she's dead."

Smith's cell phone rang. He answered it, said "Okay" a couple of times, and hung up. "I think we've got the pharmacist," he said.

———◆◆◆———

The pharmacist was a short, bald Chinese man in his seventies with round glasses and a large wart on the left side of his nose. He was pale and sweating profusely, and DeMarco was worried that he'd have a heart attack before he told them anything.

The pharmacist was sitting in the interrogation room at the RCMP complex near Queen Elizabeth Park, the same room where Phil Carmody had initially been questioned. DeMarco, Bill Smith, and Robert Morton were behind the one-way window watching a young Chinese woman interrogate the pharmacist.

The young woman was short, a bit on the homely side, and she looked tougher than shoe leather. She

was one of Morton's street cops. She was screaming
at the pharmacist in machine-gun rapid Chinese,
in a high-pitched voice, spittle flying from her lips.
The sound of her voice was worse than fingernails
on a blackboard, and DeMarco thought that if she'd
been screaming at him he'd have confessed just to
stop the noise.

"What's she saying?" DeMarco asked Smith.

"How the hell would I know," Smith said.

"Well," Morton said, "my Mandarin's a bit rusty
but I believe she's saying—"

"Dudley," Smith said, "since when do you speak
Chinese?"

Morton smiled slightly. "As I was saying, Mr.
DeMarco, I believe the sergeant is informing Mr.
Fong that if he doesn't tell her what she wants to
know, we're going to deport him *and* his large, extended family. She's saying we're going to put them
all into a boat and drop them a mile off the Chinese
coast, and those who *can't* swim will be the lucky
ones. She's also saying that before we deport him
we're going to freeze his bank accounts and close
down his pharmacy, his butcher shop, and his real
estate agency."

"Jesus, he's an industrious old bastard," Smith
said.

"Yes, he is," Morton said. "He's also . . . Ah,
I believe Sergeant Chang has made some sort of
breakthrough."

The pharmacist had stopped shaking his head and Sergeant Chang had stopped screaming at him. She was listening as the pharmacist spoke to her, his voice too low for DeMarco to hear. Ten minutes later, Sergeant Chang left the interrogation room.

Sergeant Chang stood at attention before Morton. She was five three and looked like she weighed about eighty pounds but she had really mean-looking, small black eyes. She was scary, DeMarco thought—like the female villain in a kung fu movie.

"He says he gave drugs of the type that could be used in an interrogation to a man named Loc Zhongyu. I know Zhongyu. He can be very, ah, *cruel*. Very brutal. When he was young he belonged to a gang. He freelances now, strong-arm stuff. We know he's killed before but we've never been able to convict him."

"But I assume we have his picture in our files," Morton said.

"Yes, sir. And one other thing. Loc Zhongyu has a cousin who helps him. The cousin isn't very bright, but he's big."

"Do we have the cousin's picture also, Sergeant?" Morton asked.

"I don't know, sir. I'll go look if I'm no longer needed here."

"How big a supply of drugs did he give this Loc guy?" DeMarco asked.

Sergeant Chang locked her black eyes onto De-Marco's face. "I didn't ask that," the sergeant said.

She sounded annoyed, as if DeMarco was questioning her skills.

But Morton understood what DeMarco was getting at. "What we need to know, Sergeant, is if Li Mei and her companions will have to be resupplied, in which case we'll stake out Mr. Fong's pharmacy."

"Yes, sir," Sergeant Chang said, and her eyes narrowed and the expression on her face changed and she walked back into the interrogation room. She took up a position behind the pharmacist, put her face about two inches from his right ear, and started screaming.

49

DeMarco entered the motel room where Neil was staying. The area where Neil's equipment sat was operating-room clean, but every other flat surface was stacked with boxes from various takeout places: Domino's, Wendy's, Tony Roma's, KFC. DeMarco noted that all the food had come from U.S. fast-food chains and concluded that Neil had no desire to expand his cultural horizon. All the boxes were empty—it was apparently impossible for Neil to order more than he could consume—but the room still smelled like the bottom of a Dumpster.

Neil looked up at DeMarco in annoyance. He was talking on the phone and DeMarco heard him say, "I miss you, too, honey. I can't stand being away from you either."

Last year Fat Neil had married. Neil—an egotistical, condescending slob—had a wife and a stable relationship while Joe DeMarco had neither. And Neil's wife was a sweet, normal person. She wasn't Hollywood gorgeous but she was cute. She was also very bright—Neil would have eaten a dumb woman alive—and she was compassionate and considerate and loving, all those attributes that men value in the women who might one day bear their children or tend to them in their feeble, sundown years.

"And I might not be here much longer," DeMarco heard Fat Neil say.

"What?" DeMarco said.

Neil jerked his thumb toward an open door that allowed entry to the room adjacent to Neil's. Shit, DeMarco thought, he's rented a second room. He would have to declare bankruptcy if this went on much longer. As DeMarco walked toward the open door he wondered if Neil had rented the adjoining space because he couldn't sleep in the landfill he'd created. DeMarco pushed open the door, and there sat Bobby.

Bobby Prentiss was Neil's protégé, the heir apparent to his electronic domain. He was a young black man who wore Rastafarian dreadlocks that hung down between his narrow shoulders. He looked about sixteen years old but was actually twenty-six. He had dropped out of MIT when the university refused to allow him to develop his own eclectic curriculum. Neil said Bobby was the best hacker he knew, and coming from Neil that was high praise indeed.

"Bobby," DeMarco said. "How you doing?"

"Aw right," Bobby mumbled as he continued to look at the computer screen in front of him. Bobby wasn't much of a talker.

"When did you get out here?"

"Uh, last night."

"Well, I'm glad you're here."

"Yeah," Bobby said.

"Bobby, Neil's talking to his wife but he said something about a breakthrough. You know what he's talking about?"

"Yeah," Bobby said.

Jesus, DeMarco thought. "Well, can you tell me what it is?"

"Uh, sure," Bobby said. He stopped pecking at the keyboard, picked up an index card, and handed it to DeMarco. On the card was written an address in an area near Vancouver called Delta and the names Lili and Tian Moy.

"What's this, Bobby?"

"What?" Bobby said, lost once again in cyberspace.

"Bobby . . ."

"Quit bothering Bobby, DeMarco," Fat Neil said. "Come here and I'll tell you what we've got."

"As you'll recall, we assumed Li Mei rented a place out-side Vancouver, somewhere remote, and they rented it within the last two weeks," Neil said. "So I got back copies of real estate ads for that time period for Vancouver and the surrounding towns, and focused on locations meeting certain criteria. Single-family dwellings, dwellings on large lots not too close to the neighbors, that sort of thing. The problem is, you can only get so much information from an ad. The next step was to find out who had rented the places. In some cases, we could use databases: people would activate phones or electricity, that sort of thing. If they did, we would get names to see if they sounded Asian. The problem was that it wasn't always necessary to activate the utilities in these places. So then what I did—I'm such a sly fellow, I took . . ."

Neil had stopped speaking because he was try-ing to unwrap a piece of Bazooka bubble gum and his short fingernails were having trouble getting the paper off the gum. After he finally scraped the wrap-per from the gum, he then took time to read the cartoon. DeMarco barely suppressed an urge to jam the gum up Neil's nose.

"Anyway," Neil said, "I took the phone number in the ads and programmed a machine to dial all the numbers and leave a recorded message. The mes-sage said that if two or three Asians have just rented from you, and if one of them is a tall, pretty woman in her early forties, call this number because these people might be dangerous criminals. I also offered a reward."

"A reward! How in the hell am I supposed to pay a—"

"We got a hit about an hour ago," Neil said, and blew a triumphant pink bubble.

"Well shit, Neil! Why didn't you call me?" De-Marco said.

"Relax. I'm just trying to see if we can get anything else before we, I mean you, run out there on a wild goose chase."

"What else are you trying to get?"

"Driver's license pictures. We have the names of the renters and if they're legit, they probably have a driver's license. So Bobby's getting into Canadian DMV records and we're pulling up pictures. If they have licenses and they don't look like the lovely Li Mei and her two ugly companions, we'll know they're not the right ones."

"So how long is this going to take?"

"I don't know, but it'll take a lot longer if you bother Bobby."

Bobby came into Neil's pigpen two minutes later. "They don't have driver's licenses," he said. "At least not legitimate ones."

"So they could be our guys," DeMarco said.

"Maybe, but not necessarily," Neil said. "They could just be a pair of illegal immigrants renting the place."

"Let's get the damn landlord on the phone again," DeMarco said.

The phone rang six times before a woman's voice said, "Hello?"

"Ma'am," DeMarco said, "this is Chief Superintendent Robert Morton, RCMP. I'm calling about the people who rented your house."

"Does this mean we get the reward?"

"Possibly, ma'am, but we need to get a few more facts."

"Oh, okay."

"Can you describe the woman?"

"Well, she's Asian, Oriental, whatever."

"Yes, ma'am. But is she Chinese, Japanese, or Korean?"

"I don't know. How can you tell the difference?"

"Jesus," DeMarco said under his breath.

"What?" the woman said. "I didn't hear that."

"Uh, never mind, ma'am. Was the woman who rented from you tall?"

"Sort of."

"How tall are you, ma'am?"

"Five two."

"And she's taller than you?"

"Yes, quite a bit taller."

Neil muttered that anyone over five six would seem tall to her.

"And is she pretty, ma'am? The woman we're looking for is very pretty."

"Well, I guess. Sort of."

"Christ," DeMarco muttered.

"I'm sorry," the woman said, "I didn't hear that."

"What about the woman's husband, ma'am? What can you tell me about him?"

"Well, he's Asian, too."

"We know that, ma'am, but can you describe him. Is he a big man?"

"Sort of. He's about as big as my husband."

"How big is your husband, ma'am?"

"Jack?"

"Yes, ma'am. How big is Jack?"

"Oh, he's five eight and weighs almost two hundred pounds. He really needs to lose some weight."

"And this man, the renter, he weighed as much as your husband?" DeMarco said.

"I guess. Maybe a little less."

DeMarco wondered if the woman's description of the male renter was accurate. One of the men the pharmacist had identified, Loc Zhongyu, was five seven but skinny. And his cousin, the man they thought was with Loc, was over six four. But he wasn't sure he could trust the woman's memory.

"Have you been to your rental house since these people moved in?" DeMarco asked.

"No. The house is about twenty miles from here. Maybe my husband has, but I haven't. I don't drive."

"Okay," DeMarco said. "Now this is what I need you to do, ma'am. I need you and your husband to stay away from your rental property. Don't go near it until we contact you again. We're not sure that your renters are the people we're looking for, and until we are sure, you need to stay away from them."

"When will we get the reward?" the woman said.

"When we're sure, ma'am," DeMarco said and hung up.

"Lovely, bright woman," Neil said.

DeMarco ignored him and called Bill Smith's cell phone. Smith didn't answer. DeMarco left a message for Smith to call him as soon as possible. He called Morton next. A man at Morton's office told him that Morton had taken emergency leave.

"Emergency leave?" DeMarco said. "What's wrong with him?"

"A family matter, sir. I can't discuss the details with you."

"I need Morton's cell-phone number. Or his home number."

"I'm sorry, sir, but we don't give out that sort of information over the phone."

DeMarco started to scream into the receiver, then realizing the futility of it, left a message that if Morton called in he should call Mr. DeMarco.

"Would you like Bobby to get this Morton person's numbers?" Neil said.

DeMarco thought for a minute. He could call Glen Harris and get help from the FBI, but the Bureau would form a committee and hold ten meetings before they made a decision. Plus Harris pissed him off. DeMarco had called Diane when he'd arrived in Vancouver, hoping he'd be able to see her, but she'd been sent back to Seattle. Harris had assigned her to a desk job until he could finish debriefing the shoot-out in Chinatown. Diane was still shaken by Darren Thayer's death, and now she was worried that Harris was going to torpedo her career. Yeah, Harris really pissed him off.

"Yeah, get Morton's number," DeMarco said, "but I'm not going to wait. I'm going out to this place to see if Emma's there."

"You're going alone?"

"Yeah."

"Do you have a gun, DeMarco?"

"How many people has this woman killed already?"

"Six."

"Six," Fat Neil repeated. "And she's with two known criminals who are probably armed. I think you should wait for—"

"Call me when you get Morton's number," DeMarco said.

50

———◆———

Li Mei opened the bedroom door. Emma was sitting on the floor in a corner, idly scratching at her left arm. Loc had just given her another injection, a small upper to keep her awake. Li Mei studied Emma's face. She looked weak, of course. She hadn't slept for days. Her body was limp and her head lolled on her neck like a drunk's. But her eyes were less dilated, more able to focus, an indicator that her mind was beginning to function a bit more normally. This was important to Li Mei; she wanted Emma to understand everything she was about to tell her.

"Look at me," Li Mei said. "I'm going to tell you a story."

Emma just nodded. She was too tired to do anything else.

"Look at me!" Li Mei screamed. Emma raised her head.

"I'm going to tell you what happened to me after Hawaii, after you killed Zhao. Or have you forgotten his name? It was Zhao Zhenyan."

Emma nodded again. Even in the state she was in, she knew who Li Mei meant: her handsome lover, the one with the beautiful gymnast's body—the one whose face she'd blown off.

"We were new agents," Li Mei said, "but we gave our agency some of the best intelligence it had ever received. Yes, you caught me, but I should have been treated like a hero when I returned home and Zhao, he should have received a warrior's funeral. But that didn't happen. They considered me weak for breaking down under your interrogation, and for getting caught, they called me a reckless fool. And because you made me talk, men in other places were captured, other operations were blown. I was disgraced and my lover was dead, all because of you. Then do you know what happened?"

Emma shook her head.

"Then *they* interrogated me, *my own people*, with more drugs. They had to make sure, they said, that I hadn't been turned by *you*, that I wasn't going to double for *you*. And I was raped. Raped! They didn't plan for that to happen. It was a jailer who got out of control."

"I'm sor—"

"But that wasn't the end of it. Do you know who Zhao was?" She didn't wait for Emma to answer. "He wasn't just my lover, he was the son of one of the most powerful men in Beijing and he blamed me for his son's death. He wanted me shot but instead I was sent to Lanzhou in Gansu Province for four years. Do you know Lanzhou, Emma, what a lovely place it is? We have a gaseous diffusion plant there for our nuclear weapons program, and I worked in the kitchens and in the rice paddies. I worked like a slave. After that they sent me to a listening post on the North Korean border and I lived in a hut without plumbing and hot water for three more years. It was like being in prison. But that wasn't enough for Zhao's father.

"My parents, my poor parents, they lost their apartment in the city. Zhao's father made that happen. And my younger brother, he was a student, just a sweet boy, but he was taken from school and put in the army. He died on a training exercise. All this happened because you killed Zhao."

"I'm sor—"

But Li Mei wasn't finished. "But I haven't told you the best part. I had a baby eight months after you finished with me. His tiny brain had been destroyed by all the drugs. Your drugs, their drugs. They said he was stillborn, but who knows. They may have just destroyed him when they saw his condition. My baby!"

Emma tried to say "I'm sorry," but she couldn't form the words fast enough.

"Zhao's father finally died and I was allowed back into intelligence again. My language skills were too good for them to lose me. *I* was too good. So for ten years I took every miserable assignment they gave me and most of my assignments involved sleeping with men to gain intelligence. I had *such* a bright future. I was an Olympic athlete; I speak four languages; during training, I was always at the top of my class. If it hadn't been for you, I would have been *directing* Chinese intelligence operations by now. Instead I stayed a lowly field agent. I became a sex lure, a perpetual honey trap, forced to use my body to succeed. But they gave me no choice. And in spite of how successful I was, they still didn't trust me completely. The fact that I had failed in Hawaii was always in the back of their minds. So to advance, I started having affairs with my superiors. I had to *fuck* my way back into their good graces, to be given an important assignment in the West."

"I'm sor—" Emma said.

"Quit saying that!" Li Mei screamed. "But at last I was accepted. Twenty years after Hawaii, twenty years after you destroyed my life and my career and everyone I loved, I was given two operations to run in America: penetrate the shipyard and lure John Washburn to China. And I was succeeding. But then *you* showed up. You're like a bad penny that just keeps coming back, and you were about to destroy everything I had worked for again. Again! But then I came up with a plan. I decided to take *you*. I would give *you* to my superiors."

Li Mei had been standing, talking down at Emma as she sat on the floor. Now she squatted so she was eye level with Emma. Lowering her voice, she said, "I have thirty hours of tape, tape that shows how valuable your knowledge is. You kept me from getting Washburn out of the country but I have his files. And I have the files Carmody copied. And now I have tapes of your interrogation and I have you. My superiors will be happy. This time I'll be treated as a hero and not a failure."

Emma shook her head. "They won't," she said.

"They will!" Li Mei said. "They'll take me back and they'll help me get you out of the country, back to China, to finish your interrogation. They'll torture you for *months* until they've bled you dry. Then they'll shoot you."

Emma shook her head again, but she was just too tired to speak, too tired to form the words to tell Li Mei how wrong she was.

Li Mei stood and looked down at Emma for another moment, her eyes triumphant. "I've beaten you," she said, her voice almost a whisper. Then she opened the door to the bedroom and called out, "Loc! Bao! Come here."

The two men came to the doorway, Bao puzzled, Loc irritated at being summoned so rudely.

"I have to contact the embassy in Vancouver," Li Mei said in Chinese. "It will take a couple of days to set up a meeting. While I'm gone, I don't want her out of this room. Keep her handcuffed to the bed. Let her sleep. If she wakes up, give her something to make her sleep some more. She's very dangerous. Do you understand?"

"Yes," Bao said.

Loc didn't say anything. He wasn't looking at Li Mei, he was staring at Emma. Li Mei noticed that he had that odd light in his eyes again. She couldn't tell what the man was thinking but whatever it was, it wasn't good.

"Loc," Li Mei said. She waited until he made eye contact with her and said, "If she's not here when I return, I will kill you."

"She'll be here," Loc said. His lips twitched briefly as if amused by Li Mei's threat.

"And don't hurt her. I need her in good physical condition."

"Of course," Loc said.

Loc knew ways to hurt the woman that would never show.

51

The house was a run-down rambler on a two-acre lot. It was set well back from the road, and surrounded by wild blackberry bushes and evergreens. Behind the house was a small creek and beyond that a fenced-in pasture occupied by two cows. The nearest neighbor was at least half a mile away. Isolated, as Neil had predicted.

DeMarco drove by the place a second time then parked a block away, in a spot where his car wasn't visible from the house. But he didn't immediately exit his car. He did *not* want to go up against three armed people by himself. He called Bill Smith again, and again got no answer. Goddamnit. How could a friggin' DIA agent not respond to his cell phone?

So now what? He couldn't approach the house from the front because of a picture window, or from the rear, through the pasture, because there was no cover. He could approach from either side using the foliage for cover. He flipped a mental coin and decided to go in from the east side.

He jogged in a crouched position in the direction of the house and as soon as he could see the house through the trees, he got down on his belly and started crawling. As he crawled, he used the barrel of his newly purchased twelve-gauge shotgun to part the bushes in front of him. The shotgun was loaded and the safety was off. He hoped like hell it didn't accidentally discharge as he crawled through the brush.

DeMarco had never fired a shotgun in his life and he had fired a handgun only once, which was pretty ironic when he thought about it. His father had been a Mafia enforcer and here was his son, a man whose only knowledge of firearms came from television. Or maybe it wasn't ironic. Maybe his ignorance was the expected and desired result of good parenting. His father had not wanted his son to follow in his footsteps and he had never exposed his child to the tools of his trade—and had he ever tried to, DeMarco's iron-willed mother would have undoubtedly intervened. Whatever the case, his educational gap when it came to guns had never really bothered him—until now.

He had bought the shotgun at a pawnshop. He didn't know Canadian gun laws but he figured it would be easier to buy a shotgun than a handgun— and he figured that he'd have a better chance of hitting his target with a shotgun. He had walked into the pawnshop, a wad of cash visible in his hand. He pointed at the shotgun with the biggest bore and said, "How much?" The pawnshop owner, an Indian with a beard and a turban-wrapped head, didn't ask for ID nor did he require DeMarco to fill out any forms. DeMarco didn't know if the absence of paperwork was lawful and standard, or just the owner's way of making sure he didn't lose a sale. The pawnshop guy didn't sell shells for the shotgun though. He said he didn't have any. A more likely explanation was that he figured that if he sold a customer both a gun and shells for the gun, it was possible the customer might shoot him. DeMarco purchased shells in a sporting goods store ten minutes later. He had to ask what type of shell would blow the biggest hole in a target, a question that earned him a strange look from the clerk.

He was now within fifty yards of the house and he could see two small windows, probably bedroom windows. Both windows had the curtains closed. He took a breath, rose quickly, and ran toward the house, dropping back to the ground as soon as he was beneath one of the windows. He waited a couple of seconds then stood up and looked through the window. He had been hoping for a gap in the curtains but there was none.

He decided to crawl around the house to see if he could find a point of entry or at least get a glimpse of the occupants without being seen. As he was crawling, his cell phone vibrated. He looked at the caller ID screen: it was Neil, probably calling with Morton's phone number. It was too late for that now.

When he reached the back of the house he saw a crudely built patio made of flat cement blocks and on the patio was a rust-encrusted Weber barbecue. A sliding glass door exited the house onto the patio.

DeMarco hadn't been sure how he was going to enter the house or if he would enter at all. He had been thinking that he might be able to draw one of the occupants outside in some way, get the drop on him, and then use that person as a hostage to get to Emma. His other option was to kick in a door and take them by surprise. He thought this a really dumb option as someone would assuredly get killed—and it would probably be him. He also wasn't certain how easy it would be to kick in a door. What looked easy on TV could be problematic in real life. But now he *had* an entry point. All he had to do was bash in the sliding glass door with the butt of his trusty shotgun.

The smart side of DeMarco's brain said he should wait for the cavalry, call Morton and request some backup—professional backup from people trained to do stuff like this. But he wasn't going to do the smart thing; he couldn't. He needed to know if Emma was inside the house. So he inched forward, cautiously, until he came to the sliding glass door, then quickly poked his head around the edge of the door to see if he could see Emma's captors—and that's when a woman screamed.

Oh, Christ. Hold on, Emma.

Then he thought: God help me—and swung the butt of the shotgun at the glass.

52

Loc opened the bedroom door and then stood in the doorway, looking at the white woman handcuffed to the bed. She was groggy but she wasn't sleeping yet; the drugs hadn't completely worn off.

Loc had been trapped in the house for a week, the whole time taking orders from an arrogant woman. And the white woman, he could tell that she was arrogant, too. She would not be so arrogant when he was done with her.

He walked over to the bed and looked down at her. That she was handcuffed excited him. That she was so helpless excited him. He reached into a pocket and took out a knife. He pushed the button on the handle of the knife and a four-inch blade leaped out.

He'd cut off her clothes; that would be easiest. He reached down and grasped her blouse and placed the knife blade below the top button. Then his nose wrinkled. The woman smelled *horrible*. He knew that she hadn't bathed in a week, but it was worse than that. It must have been all the drugs that they'd given her that made her smell so bad.

Loc put the switchblade away and unlocked the handcuff on Emma's wrist. "You get up," he said in English. "You take shower. You smell bad."

"What are you doing?" Bao said in Chinese. "Li Mei said not to uncuff her."

"I'm going to have some fun, cousin. You can have some, too, when I'm finished."

"What?" Bao said.

His cousin was always confused, Loc thought. If he wasn't so big, he'd be completely worthless. Ignoring Bao, he said to Emma, "Get up! Take shower now!"

Emma didn't respond. She was beyond exhaustion but the residual drugs in her body kept her mind spinning, her thoughts coming in meaningless, fragmented bursts. It was as if there was a little man with a small cattle prod inside her head, and every few seconds he'd give her brain a jolt. But she could tell that the effects of the drugs were beginning to dissipate. The jolts were becoming less frequent. Sleep seemed like it might finally be possible. But now the skinny Asian, the one with the pockmarked face, the one who hurt her when he gave her the injections, he was saying something to her, something about getting up. No. She wouldn't move. She had to sleep.

Loc reached down and grasped Emma's left arm and yanked her to her feet. "You take shower!" he screamed, and then he pushed Emma in the back, propelling her toward the bedroom door.

A shower, Emma thought. A shower would be *so* good.

"You move faster," Loc said, and he pushed her from behind again, out the bedroom door and down a short hallway toward the bathroom.

The push helped. Walking helped. The fog was rising from her mind.

As Emma walked toward the bathroom, the big man said something in Chinese.

Bao had said, "You're going to get us in trouble. Li Mei said not to take her out of the room."

"Li Mei is an arrogant bitch," Loc said. "I'll do what I want." Loc laughed and said, "You can watch if you want, cousin, so you'll know what to do when it's your turn."

"I'm not going to touch her," Bao said

Loc ignored Bao and shoved Emma again. "You move faster," he said in English.

They reached the bathroom. Loc was behind Emma, his hand on her back. Bao was standing in the hallway, frowning, uncertain what to do.

"Take off clothes," Loc said to Emma.

"What?" Emma said.

Loc cuffed the back of her head, not hard, but hard enough to get her attention.

"You take off clothes!" Loc screamed. "You take shower."

Emma nodded. She started to unbutton her blouse, the one she had been wearing since her capture. Then she realized the bathroom door was open. She turned slowly to close the door, but Loc's hand slammed into it.

"No!" he said. "Leave door open."

"Okay," Emma said, completely docile, but her mind was beginning to function. Finally. She continued to unbutton her blouse.

"You hurry," Loc said.

"All right," Emma said, but she didn't move any faster. As she undressed she looked around the small bathroom, then she looked back at Loc. He smiled at her, his lust transparent. She looked away from his face and down at the pistol in the shoulder holster he was wearing. She assumed the big man was armed also, but she hadn't seen a weapon on him. She looked about the bathroom again. Nothing. Nothing to use for a weapon. Nothing to use to her advantage.

She finished taking off her blouse and looked at Loc again, more defiantly this time.

"I want privacy," she said. Her words came slowly but they were less slurred than they'd been a minute earlier. And she was thinking clearly now—or as clearly as one can think when deprived of sleep for days.

"You shut mouth. You take shower," Loc said.

Emma thought that if she didn't move, if she didn't obey, the man would slap her again. When he did, he'd be close enough for her to reach the gun in the shoulder holster. But she didn't trust her reflexes. She knew that before she could get her hands on Loc's gun, the big man would be there to help him.

She finished undressing and heard Loc say something in Chinese.

"She has a good body for her age," Loc had said to Bao. "Very firm. A little skinny but firm. Good ass."

Bao just shook his head. The naked white woman disgusted him; his cousin disgusted him. "I'm going to make some tea," he muttered. He wasn't going to be part of this.

Loc laughed. "Good. Tea will give you strength. It will put some iron in your cock."

Emma stepped into the shower, closed the glass door, and turned the faucet handles.

Loc started to tell her to leave the shower door open, but then he realized he liked the way her body looked behind the glass. It was like watching a movie. In some way he found it more erotic than watching her with the door open.

The water felt wonderful, Emma thought, absolutely wonderful. And it helped to further revive her. She washed herself thoroughly, taking her time.

She was in no hurry, and she was so tired her arms could barely move. She saw a bottle of shampoo on the window ledge. As she reached for the shampoo, she felt the razor—a small, pink disposable razor. She poured the shampoo from the bottle and massaged it into her scalp, then rinsed her hair. Then she picked up the razor.

She planned to stay in the shower as long as possible, until Loc started screaming at her again. The longer she stayed, the better she'd be able to defend herself—and delay what was going to happen next. She knew what Loc planned to do to her and she didn't think she could stop him.

Loc banged on the glass shower door. "You clean now. You get out now."

Emma continued to let the water run over her body.

"I said you stop now!" Loc yelled. "You stop or I beat you."

Emma reached out slowly with her left hand and turned the faucets, shutting off the flow of water. The pink razor was in her right hand. She turned to exit the shower, paused—then screamed as she fell through the glass shower door. She felt her left forearm being ripped open by jagged glass and there was a burning sensation on her right thigh.

Bao heard the scream in the kitchen and came running out. "What happened?" he said to his cousin.

"Stupid woman," Loc said. "Stupid, stupid woman."

Bao could see the naked woman lying on the floor of the bathroom, on broken glass.

Loc grabbed a towel and threw it at Emma. "Get up," he said.

Emma didn't move. "I need sleep," she said. And she did; she could have easily slept on a bed of broken glass.

"Shit," Loc said in Chinese. He reached down, to pull Emma to her feet, and saw the handle of the razor in her right hand. He cuffed the back of Emma's head and said, "Stupid woman" again. He jerked the razor out her hand and flung it into the shower stall, then pulled hard on Emma's left arm to bring her to her feet. She screamed again when he yanked on her arm. Loc wondered if she'd dislocated her shoulder during the fall. Stupid woman.

53

As DeMarco slammed the shotgun butt through the sliding glass door, he heard the woman scream again. He kicked one large piece of glass out of the way—a piece that was standing straight up, like a stalagmite jutting up from the floor of a cave, sharp enough to slice off his balls—and entered the house. He moved forward, pointing the shotgun at the kitchen door. He was going to kill the first person he saw, blow his head off with double-aught shot.

The first person he saw was a short Chinese woman in her fifties. She was standing there, apparently frozen in place, her hands up to her mouth. When she saw DeMarco coming toward her, the shotgun aimed at her face, she screamed a third time, spun on her heels, and ran.

"Aw, shit," DeMarco said. "Wait," he yelled at the woman.

The woman had reached the front door of the house by then. "Wait," DeMarco yelled again as he ran after her—holding his shotgun.

The woman was pulling desperately on the doorknob, trying to open the front door, but unable to do so in her panicked condition.

"It's okay," DeMarco said, lowering his voice. "I'm not going to hurt you."

The woman was now talking rapidly in high-pitched Chinese, probably praying, as she tried to open the door.

DeMarco reached the front door and put his hand on the woman's shoulder. This caused her to collapse to the floor, at DeMarco's feet. She put her hands over her head to protect herself and began to sob—huge, air-sucking sobs.

"I'm not going to hurt you," DeMarco said again. He hoped she could understand English. While he said this his eyes were searching the house, waiting for the woman's husband to appear. He hoped her husband didn't have a weapon.

"I'm sorry," DeMarco said to the bawling woman. "I've made a mistake."

Neil had been wrong; the landlord's wife had been wrong. The crying woman at his feet was four inches shorter than Li Mei and about as pretty as a waffle iron. He had broken into the wrong fucking house.

"Who are you," the Chinese woman yelled in accented English. Seeing the look on DeMarco's face—the look of a guilty idiot as opposed to that of a sex-crazed serial killer—the woman's fear changed to anger. She leaped to her feet and began screaming at DeMarco in Chinese, reminding him immediately of Morton's little interrogator, the one with hit-man eyes. DeMarco didn't understand Chinese but he could imagine what the woman was saying. He hoped he had enough cash to pay for the door he'd just destroyed.

"Why did you scream?" he asked the woman.

She said something in Chinese, something that sounded like a curse, then said, "Because I saw you at door holding gun, you stupid white man."

"You saw me?" DeMarco said.

The woman pointed at a mirror. DeMarco realized that if he moved about three feet to his left, he would be able to see the patio—and the now shattered sliding glass door.

Then she started yelling at him again in Chinese.

DeMarco was beginning to appreciate that Chinese was an excellent language for a woman to use to berate a man.

54

With a towel wrapped around Emma's bleeding forearm, Loc pushed her out of the bathroom and in the direction of the bedroom where she'd been kept captive the last week. As he pushed her, he admired her backside. Yes, she was in very good shape for her age.

He'd have to stop the bleeding though. He didn't want to get blood all over himself while he fucked her. He told Bao in Chinese to see if he could find some Band-Aids in the bathroom. He pushed the naked woman again. She moved slowly. He was becoming very aroused.

Emma heard the big man curse and in her peripheral vision she saw him walk toward the bathroom, pausing as he looked at the shattered glass on the floor.

When they reached the bedroom, Loc said, "Let me see cut."

Emma turned around slowly.

Nice tits, Loc thought. Little but nice. His girlfriend was younger than this woman but his girlfriend's body was nowhere near as firm.

"Let me see cut," he said. "Move towel. Let me see cut."

Emma looked confused.

"Move towel!" Loc screamed. Couldn't this woman understand anything?

Emma nodded, then she whipped the towel off her arm, temporarily blinding Loc, and drove a shard of glass from the shower door deep into his throat. She cut her hand as she stabbed him, but she cut Loc worse. Much worse.

Loc let out a strangled cry and reached for his throat. Emma grabbed the front of his shirt, kicked his legs out from under him, and pulled him to the floor on top of her. Loc tried to free himself from her grip but Emma slammed the side of her hand into his throat, cutting her palm but driving the glass deeper into his throat. Blood was shooting out of his throat now, covering Emma.

Bao walked into the bedroom, carrying a box of Band-Aids in his hand. He saw Loc lying on the woman, the woman's legs spread wide for him, blood all over the ground. He could hear his cousin making wet, grunting sounds. So disgusting, he thought. His pig of a cousin couldn't even wait until he'd bandaged the woman's arm. He couldn't watch this. He wasn't going to watch. As he reached out to shut the bedroom door, he saw the barrel of a gun. Loc's gun. The gun was between his cousin's left arm and his rib cage. It was pointed at Bao's face.

Bao didn't hear the shot that killed him.

55

DeMarco's cell phone vibrated. It was probably Neil calling again. He pulled the phone off the clip on his belt and said hello, but he couldn't hear what the caller was saying. He'd given the Chinese woman three hundred dollars to pay for the sliding glass door. He figured that should be more than enough, plus it was all the cash he had on him. But she still wasn't happy. She had followed him out of her house and was now yelling at him to tell her his name. She probably wanted to sue him for traumatic stress disorder.

"Hello," he said again into his cell phone, pressing it harder against his ear.

"It's me," a voice said. He could hardly hear the caller. He checked the signal on his phone. He was getting a good signal. He pressed a button to increase the volume.

"I can't hear you," he yelled. "Who is this?"

"It's Emma. Help me."

"Jesus Christ! Where are you?"

Emma mumbled something but he missed it. The Chinese woman had been saying, "What your name? What your name?"

DeMarco put his hand over the phone, spun around, and said to the woman, "Shut the fuck up!" The woman backed away holding her hands in front of her. DeMarco hadn't meant to, but when he turned to face the woman, he had pointed the shotgun right at her. The Chinese woman ran toward her house, screaming her head off.

"Emma, where are you?"

"Don't know," Emma said. "Gas station. Store."

She was mumbling and her voice was slurred. DeMarco wondered, at first, how she knew he was in Canada, then realized she probably didn't. She sounded so out of it; she had probably just called the first number she remembered.

"Emma is anyone near you?" DeMarco said.

"Yeah. Guy."

"Put him on the phone."

The phone went silent. She'd hung up—or somebody had made her hang up.

"Goddamnit," DeMarco said. "Goddamnit." He pressed buttons on his cell phone to redial the last number that had called him. He hoped the number wasn't blocked. A man answered the phone.

"Hello."

"Is there a woman there? A woman who just used your phone?"

"Yeah. Some crazy, drugged-up bitch."

"Now you listen to me. That woman—"

"Listen to you? Who the fuck do you think you are? This crazy bitch—"

"Five hundred bucks."

That got the guy to stop talking.

"What?" The guy said.

"Five hundred bucks. I'll give you five hundred bucks if you help that woman. I want you to hide her somewhere. Put her in the restroom, a storeroom, someplace where people can't see her."

"Be glad to do that. The bitch is naked, she's only wearing a blanket, and she's covered with blood. I was gonna call the cops."

"Don't call anybody. You get her out of sight, and I'll get there as fast as I can and pick her up."

"Man, I don't know."

"Where are you?" DeMarco asked.

"A Shell station on the King George Highway."

"What city?"

"Surrey."

"I'm in Delta," DeMarco said. "How long will it take me to get to your place? I'm not from around here."

"About . . . Aw, shit. It looks like she's passed out."

"She's hurt. Now how long will it take me to get there?"

"About fifteen minutes or so."

"Shit. Give me directions."

The guy did. Fortunately they weren't complicated.

"One last thing," DeMarco said. "If that woman's there I'll give you five hundred bucks. If she isn't there, I'm gonna beat the livin' shit out of you."

The guy's reaction surprised DeMarco: he laughed. Then he said, "I kinda doubt that, muthafucker, but you're welcome to try." He laughed again and hung up.

56

DeMarco parked in front of the Shell station and ran inside. The man behind the counter was black and the size of an industrial refrigerator. He had to be six five and weigh in at three hundred pounds.

"Is the woman still here?" DeMarco said.

The black guy smiled. "Ah, it's the dude who's gonna beat the shit out of me."

"Forget that," DeMarco said. "Is the woman here?"

"Yeah. She's in the can, lying on the floor. Completely fucked up."

"Where?" DeMarco said.

"I'll show you," the black man said, a smile on his face, still amused by DeMarco's threat.

The black guy unlocked the door to the bathroom and let DeMarco in. Emma was lying on the floor, a blanket covering her. Her arms and shoulders and throat were smeared with blood. DeMarco could see a cut on one of her forearms and two cuts on her right hand. Maybe that was the source of the blood, but there was an awful lot of blood. He knelt down next to her and felt her pulse. He could feel one, but he didn't know if the pulse was strong or weak. She seemed to be sleeping. Ignoring the black guy standing behind him, he pulled the blanket off her and looked quickly to see if there were any other injuries. There was a long scratch on her right thigh but it wasn't bleeding. He didn't see any other cuts but then he noticed the needle marks on the inside of her arms. She had the punctured arms of a heroin addict.

He pulled her to her feet, then picked her up in his arms. The store manager held the door open for him and helped DeMarco put her in the backseat of the car. When he saw the shotgun lying on the backseat, he said to DeMarco, "Whoa! What's that for?"

DeMarco turned to face the man. "About the five hundred. I don't have it on me but I'm good for it. I just need to get her to a doctor."

The black guy looked down at the shotgun again. Then he took a closer look at DeMarco's face. "Forget the five hundred," he said. "I used to be a junkie, back in the day. There were times when I wished I'd had somebody to come pick me up."

"No," DeMarco said. "I'll get you the money. And this woman isn't a junkie. She's been . . . Something bad's happened to her. But I'll get you the money."

"Sure, bro. I'll believe it when I see it."

DeMarco looked at Emma again. She looked the same. He wondered if she was in a coma. He needed to get her to a hospital. He was about to ask the black guy where the nearest one was, when his cell phone rang.

"DeMarco," he said into the phone.

"It's Bill Smith," the caller said. "You called me."

"Smith, you piece of shit, where in the hell have you been?"

"Busy," Smith said. "I was—"

"I've got Emma," DeMarco said.

"What!"

"She needs a doctor. Tell me where to take her."

"Does she need emergency treatment?"

"Yes, goddamnit!"

"Okay, okay. Calm down. Where are you?"

DeMarco told him.

"Hang on," Smith said and DeMarco could hear him talking to someone.

"Okay," Smith said "You take her to Surrey Memorial. It's right on the King George Highway, where it intersects 96th Avenue, less than five minutes from where you are. We'll call ahead so they won't give you a bunch of shit about insurance forms, or whatever they do up here. I'll meet you there."

———◆———

"I've sent blood samples to the lab to do a tox screen. Her respiration and pulse are slightly abnormal, but not unduly so. She's not in a coma. She's sleeping."

The doctor was a slim guy in his thirties and De-Marco thought he looked a little like a young Kevin Costner. He wore running shoes, jeans, a white shirt, and a loud tie covered with Disney characters. De-Marco had noticed that doctors often felt the need to wear silly ties.

"Can we wake her up?" Smith said.

"If it's an emergency, you can try. It won't hurt her," the doctor said. "But she didn't wake up the entire time we were examining her, including when we drew her blood. The best thing to do is let her sleep."

"We need to talk to her," Smith said. "It's important."

The doctor led Smith, DeMarco, and a uniformed Canadian cop to Emma's room. Smith went over to the bed and gently shook her arm. "Emma," he said. "Emma, wake up."

She didn't.

Smith shook her harder.

"Don't," Emma muttered.

"Emma, we have to talk to you," Smith said.

"Sleep," Emma said.

"I know, Emma, but we need to talk to you. Emma, wake up! Emma, where are the people who took you?"

"Dead," Emma said

"Is Li Mei dead?"

"Gone," Emma said.

"What's that mean?" Smith said to DeMarco. "Does that mean Li Mei's dead or she's disappeared?"

"How would I know?" DeMarco said.

"Emma, is Li Mei dead?" Smith said. Emma didn't respond. Smith shook her again. "Emma! Emma! Wake up! Is Li Mei dead?"

"Leave her alone," DeMarco said. "We can try again in the morning."

Smith turned to the doctor. "Is there something you can give her to wake her up?"

"Fuck you, Smith," DeMarco said. "You can see by her arms that she's been pumped full of shit. You're not giving her—"

"Your friend is correct," the doctor said. "Until we get the tox screen back, sir, I'm not giving her anything. And that's final." For a guy with a cartoon tie, he sounded damn serious.

"How long will the tox screen take?" Smith said.

"Four hours, if we rush it."

"Well rush it. This is a national security issue."

"Which nation's security are we talking about?" the doctor said, smiling slightly.

"Fucking Canadians," Smith muttered. He handed the doctor a card. "Look, just call me as soon as the tox screen is complete or if she wakes up. Okay?"

"I'll do that," the doctor said.

"Come on, DeMarco, let's go get something to eat and you can tell me what the hell you did."

"Wait a minute," DeMarco said. He pulled out his cell phone and called Fat Neil back at the motel. "I've got Emma," he said. "She's okay but she's in a hospital recovering."

"Thank God," Neil said. "So she was at the address I gave you."

"No, Neil, she wasn't at the address you gave me. At the address you gave me there was an old Chinese woman who I scared the crap out of. But never mind that. I picked Emma up at a Shell station on the King George Highway in Surrey. She walked there from wherever she was being held. Look at all those rental addresses again, and see if there's one close to the gas station."

"Can't Emma tell you where she was?"

"No. She's all drugged up."

"Okay. I'll see if we can find something. What's the zip code there?"

"How the hell would I know, Neil! Look it up!"

"Who were you talking to?" Smith asked DeMarco.

"Somebody who's been helping me."

"You've been a real busy beaver, haven't you, DeMarco?"

There was no IHOP near the hospital, but they did find a Denny's. It seemed lately that DeMarco had eaten nothing but chain-restaurant cooking and he was getting damn tired of it. While Smith was eating eggs and a piece of cow advertised as steak, DeMarco told him what had happened.

"You pointed a shotgun at this poor woman?" Smith said, laughing.

"Yeah. She was damn lucky I didn't kill her, I was so keyed up."

"Why didn't you call me?" Smith said.

"I did call you! I got your voice mail."

"Oh, that's right. Well you could have called . . ."

DeMarco's cell phone rang.

"There are two addresses near the gas station that fit the profile," Neil said.

"I'm not too sure about the profile anymore," DeMarco said, "but give me the addresses." He motioned for Smith to give him a pen and wrote the numbers on a napkin. He hung up on Neil and said to Smith, "Tell RCMP to check out these two addresses, right away. One of them might be the place where they were holding Emma."

"What makes you think so?" Smith asked. De-Marco ignored him and ate his French toast. With enough maple syrup anything was edible.

Ten minutes later, Smith had convinced the Canadians to dispatch SWAT teams to the two houses to see if Li Mei and her companions were at one of them. Thirty minutes later, about the time they were finishing their meal, Smith received a call.

"They found the place," he told DeMarco. "Two guys were inside. Dead. One of them had a piece of glass jammed into his carotid artery. The other guy had been shot in the head. That Emma. She's somethin' else. They also found a bunch of videotapes. They looked briefly at one of them. They're tapes of Emma being interrogated. I gotta get over there and pick up those tapes. Right away. God knows what's on 'em."

"What about Li Mei?"

"No sign of her. I told the Canadians to grab all the tapes, leave the bodies, and get out of sight and watch the house. If Li Mei comes back they'll pick her up."

57

"Emma, wake up," DeMarco said.

"Go away," Emma said.

Her voice sounded much stronger. The doctor said they'd found lots of different chemicals in her body—sodium amytal, scopolamine, thiopental sodium, amphetamines, and a few things that their lab didn't recognize that might be Chinese herbs or designer drugs—but nothing that required them to take any immediate medical action. Depending on the amount she'd been given, one of the drugs could cause liver damage, the doctor said, but it was too soon to tell. She'd need to have her liver tested every month for the next six months.

"Emma, wake up," DeMarco said again, this time giving her shoulder a little prod.

"If you don't get away from me, Joe," Emma mumbled without opening her eyes, "I'll break your big nose."

"Emma, we have to talk about Li Mei."

"Joe, I swear . . ."

Emma suddenly sat up in bed. She was still groggy but she was now remembering what had happened to her. "Where am I?" she said.

"A hospital."

"I can see that. What city?"

"Vancouver," DeMarco said. "Surrey, actually."

"How long have I been asleep?"

"Fourteen hours."

"Well, it wasn't enough. Now get out of here while I go to the bathroom and wash up."

"I better make sure you can walk," DeMarco said.

Emma arched an eyebrow. "It feels like I'm wearing one of those hospital gowns that's split up the back. If you look at my ass, I *swear* I'll break your nose. I mean it."

DeMarco wondered what she'd do if she knew that he'd seen her naked.

"I promise I won't peek," he said.

Emma pushed back the bed covers and slowly lowered her feet to the floor while DeMarco held on to one of her arms. She took a couple of steps and said, "I'm fine. Now get out of here and come back in . . . Oh, my God! Does Christine know what happened to me? Does she know I've been found?"

"Yeah," DeMarco said, and he explained.

After Emma was kidnapped, DeMarco had been preoccupied with finding her and it hadn't occurred to him to call Christine and tell her what had happened. The media had, of course, become aware of the debacle in Chinatown, and the U.S. and Canadian governments were both putting the best spin they could on what had happened and why, but Smith and the FBI had decided not to go public with Emma's kidnapping for a number of primarily self-serving reasons. But then Christine had called DeMarco after she hadn't heard from Emma in several days, and he'd been forced to tell her what had happened. He'd emphasized that a large number of highly trained people were doing everything they could to get Emma back, and he had called her every day after that to keep her apprised of what was happening, sounding as optimistic as he could, knowing that no matter what he said it wasn't going to make her feel any better. While Emma had been sleeping, he'd called her to tell her that Emma was safe, and as Christine sobbed in relief, DeMarco had wondered what it would be like to be loved that much.

"Well, give me your cell phone," Emma said. "I need to call her right now. Oh, and I'm hungry, too. Get me some food."

"Yes, ma'am," DeMarco said. He could tell she was recovering rapidly.

———◆◆◆———

"I remember killing the two men," Emma said. "Li Mei called them Bao and Loc. I don't know if those were their real names or not."

"They were," DeMarco said. "Loc Zhongyu and Bao Jiang," he added, stumbling over the pronunciation of the Chinese names. "They were a couple of lowlifes—cousins—who freelanced for the Asian gangs in Vancouver."

Emma was sitting up in bed, and her hair was combed. She still looked tired and her face was pale and painfully thin. Her cheekbones were like knife blades. But she was alert and she was mad.

"Anyway, I remember killing them," Emma said. "But I can't remember too much else. I know Li Mei interrogated me, but I don't know what I told her."

"Smith said they found tapes in the house where you were being kept."

"They found the house?"

DeMarco filled her in on how they'd found it.

"Neil's here?" she said.

"Yeah, and his assistant, that little guy Bobby with the dreadlocks."

"Damn it," Emma said. "Neil will never let me forget this."

"Anyway, they found the house, the two guys you killed, and a bunch of tapes. But Li Mei wasn't there."

"I think Li Mei was trying to contact the Chinese," Emma said. "She was going to convince them to transport me to China to finish the interrogation. She may have given them a transcript of what I told her. If she did, that's not good at all."

"Do you have any idea what you might have told her?"

"Not really. I remember some things, but it's all scrambled inside my head. Sometimes I babbled like a . . . like a magpie for hours. We have to find her."

"Right now you have to recover."

"No, we have to find her. The last time we talked, she said she still had John Washburn's files and the stuff Carmody got from the shipyard. We have to find her before she turns all that over." Emma paused then added, "if she hasn't turned it over already."

"Smith's looking for her, Emma. So are the Canadians and the FBI. You don't have to do anything right now."

Emma was silent for a minute. "Did Smith give you the background on Li Mei?" Emma said after a moment.

"Yeah."

Emma nodded. "This whole thing here in Vancouver, kidnapping me and torturing me, that was as much about revenge as intelligence collection. It was about humiliating me, disgracing me." Emma sighed.

"Joe, she's insane. Literally. She's been driven over the edge. And she's going to come after me again."

"Don't worry. Smith will—"

"I'm not worried. I want her to come after me. It's the only way we'll get her."

Emma shook her head sadly. "Ah, Joe," she said. "We screwed her up so badly. We just *destroyed* her, and it didn't have to be that way. I feel so bad for her."

58

"It's not too bad, Emma," Smith said.

Smith and Emma were sitting in a small visitors' lounge down the hall from Emma's hospital room. Emma was wearing a borrowed robe and sitting in a wheelchair. The wheelchair wasn't necessary but Emma had decided to use one in case anyone was watching.

"I've got six people transcribing the tapes and they're almost done. What they're telling me is, you just babbled about half the time. You told her about operations that happened twenty years ago and mixed those up with ops that happened five years ago. The good news is, since you've been retired almost three years, you didn't have anything too current to give her."

Smith didn't know that Emma hadn't *completely* retired, but all she said was, "Plus, my last five years, I was mostly on Mideast ops."

"Yeah," Smith said. "And sometimes you lied, whether intentionally or not; we couldn't tell. I really got a kick out of you telling her we used carrier pigeons for sending messages. They'll probably wipe out the entire pigeon population in China when they hear that."

"So I didn't give her anything vital?" Emma said.

"I didn't say that. I said it wasn't too bad. So far we've picked up three things, things that if the Chinese heard those tapes and interpreted what you said correctly, could cause problems. We got one guy out of the submarine base at Qingdao last night just in case and we're disbanding a team in Beijing that we've had in place for almost a decade."

Smith took a sip from a bottle of ice tea he was drinking and grimaced. "I hate this fruit-flavored ice tea," he said. "I go to the damn vending machine down the hall there, and I can't read the whole label on the bottle. But I figure, tea's tea, so I push the button and I get this raspberry-flavored shit. Christ, why do they have to screw everything up?"

"Bill," Emma said, her impatience showing. "What else?"

"Well, there really isn't anything else. We listened to the tapes real quick, and now we're transcribing them so we can go over them in detail. You're going to have to work with us on that, Emma. You know, review the transcripts and see if you can tell us where you lied and where you didn't."

Smith paused. "She really wasn't a very good interrogator. Certainly not a pro. If she had been, she'd have known that it'd take at least a couple of months to get what she wanted, to duplicate questions and cross-check your answers. And we think she over-doped you. A lot. You're really jacked-up on some of those tapes. A pro would have used smaller doses but taken longer to debrief you. Li Mei knew the basic technique—what drugs to use, sleep deprivation—but she didn't have the experience. Or the patience."

"Do you think she could have transcribed the tapes and given the transcripts to the Chinese?"

Smith shook his head. "We don't think she had the time to transcribe them and we didn't find a computer or a typewriter in the house. But she may have made duplicates and we're pretty sure one tape is missing. She recorded the dates and times of the interrogation sessions on the tapes, and there's a gap. So she may have taken that tape with her to impress her bosses, to show them what a gold mine she had in you."

"Goddamnit," Emma said, hoping that the missing tape didn't contain anything vital. "Where do you think she is right now?"

"If I had to guess," Smith said, "I'd say she's out there in the wind. I went to see the head spook at the Chinese embassy while you were getting your beauty rest, and I don't think they have her. If they did, this guy would have looked, you know, *relieved*. But he just looked frazzled, like his bosses have been screaming at his ass every day to put this thing back in the box. So, it's just a guess, but I think she's still on the loose."

"That's what I think, too," Emma said. "She could quit while she's ahead, but she won't. She could give them Carmody's and Washburn's files and go back home and take her medicine but—"

"Hah," Smith snorted. "Her 'medicine' is going to be a bullet in the back of the head, that bullshit she pulled in Chinatown."

"There's that, but there's something else. Bremerton was Li Mei's chance to restore her reputation, to become a star once again in the Chinese intelligence community. But she failed. Again. She had to close down Carmody's operation in Bremerton prematurely because of me and then we caught Washburn before she could get him out of the country. So she was going to give them *me* to make up for all that, but now she's failed at that, too."

"It's like you're her . . . what's the word? *Nemesis,*" Smith said and laughed.

"You may think you're joking, but that's exactly what she believes. I'm the source of everything bad that's ever happened to her. She's not going to leave until she kills me or kidnaps me again."

"Maybe," Smith said, "or maybe she'll just decide to run for her life."

"No, Bill, she's not going to run away. That's not in her makeup."

"Am I sensing that you have a plan?" Smith said.

"I do. We'll tell the newspapers that a woman my age was found wandering along the King George Highway, out of her mind, no memory, no ID, and she's here at this hospital. We'll make it sound like it's just your typical lost lunatic, no big thing, but Li Mei will realize it's me because of the location and maybe she'll bite."

"I like it," Smith said.

"But your team is going to have to be invisible. She may not be an interrogator but she's a hell of a field agent. She proved that when she snatched me and killed those agents in Chinatown. She'll spot the guy lurking in the janitor's uniform, Bill, and she'll get by him—or kill him."

"What do you shoot these days, Emma?" Smith asked, his eyes bright behind the lenses of his glasses.

———◆———

"Go home, Joe," Emma said. "I'll be fine."

"You're being used for bait, Emma."

"Exactly. And I'll be protected by trained killers, using the latest technology and the most sophisticated weapons in Uncle's arsenal. You, on the other hand, don't even know how to use a shotgun."

"Do, too. Scared the hell out of that old Chinese woman."

Emma laughed. "Joe, I really appreciate what you did for me. I'll owe you forever. But go home. I don't need you and by now Mahoney must have something devious and underhanded he needs you to do."

"Uh, not exactly," DeMarco said.

"What does that mean?"

"Mahoney fired me. I told him I was coming back here to look for you and he said to let Smith take care of it, and when I said I was going anyway, he fired me."

Emma's response to DeMarco's fiscal and professional tragedy was: "Good. It's about time you were rid of him. Let me know if you have a hard time finding a job. I know some people who might be able to help."

"Emma, I'm a lawyer who's never practiced law. I'm a guy who works in the basement of the Capitol and does things that I can't put down on a résumé. Then there's the small fact that I have a number of years invested in a federal pension."

"Oh, you'll be fine."

"Yeah, you bet. I can just see me in my new job right now. Would you like some fries with that, ma'am?"

59

DeMarco took a seat at his usual table in the restaurant on Capitol Hill where he had breakfast almost every day. Still a young man, but he'd become a creature of habit, a fact he found both troublesome and comforting. There were two things that were different this particular weekday morning though. The first was that he had *The Washington Post* open to the classified ads instead of the sports section. The second was that he was dressed in jeans and a golf shirt instead of one of his dark suits.

After breakfast he'd go over to the Capitol and find out what the procedure was for getting fired from a government job. There had to be a bunch of forms to fill out. There were always forms to fill out. And he had to find out about the money he'd paid in to his pension. The problem was that he didn't know who to ask and he didn't want to go to Mahoney's office to find out.

He did notice that his paycheck had been deposited in his bank account, like it always was, during the time he'd been in Vancouver. Maybe that was his severance pay. If it was, his golden parachute was the size of a doily.

He saw one ad for a job as a process server. Oh, yeah. He could just see himself creeping up the stairs of a roach-infested apartment building that did double duty as a bordello and crack house. He'd knock on a door which would be answered by a guy wearing no shirt, his torso covered with jailhouse tattoos, and the guy would be the size of a defensive end. A pit bull would be standing at the guy's side, its tiny, mean eyes fixed on DeMarco's crotch. Then the guy would smile and say, "Get him, JoJo."

Jesus, there had to be some office job he was qualified for, something that paid more than thirteen bucks an hour. What he really needed was a government job; he did *not* want to lose his pension. The post office hired crazy people. He'd go see them first.

His usual waitress came to his table and noticed he was out of uniform.

"Joe, honey, what is it? Casual Tuesday over at the Capitol?"

"Hey, Betty," he said, ignoring the question.

"So what's with the jeans?" persistent Betty said again, but before DeMarco could answer, Betty—a dyed blonde in her early fifties—said, "You know, you look kinda hunky in them jeans. You oughta wear 'em more often, give all us girls a thrill. So what are you havin' this mornin', sweetie? Your usual?"

"Just give him coffee," a gruff voice said. "He's got things to do. And bring me a cup, too."

"Oh, Mr. Speaker," Betty said, and she unconsciously reached a hand up to fluff her hair. For reasons DeMarco could never understand, Mahoney had that effect on any woman over fifty—and many under fifty. "I'll get your coffee right away, gentlemen," Betty said, bustling away.

Mahoney sat down heavily at DeMarco's table. He started to say something then glanced at the newspaper lying on the table. He pushed the classified section aside with a thick finger and looked at the headlines on the front page of the sports section.

"Fuckin' Red Sox," he said. "They finally win a series, but here they go again. Nine goddamn games behind the Yankees and it's August already. And can you believe they traded Mendoza? I'm tellin' you, Joe, if I ever get tired of this job, I'm gonna apply for general manager of that team."

Betty arrived with their coffees. "Here you go, Mr. Speaker," she said.

"You're a darlin', m'love," he said as he placed a thick paw lightly on one of Betty's motherly hips.

He pretended to look around as if afraid of being overheard and added, "Do you think, sweetheart, just maybe you could sneak back there into the bar and add a little jolt of Bushmills to that cup?"

"Of course, Mr. Speaker. I'm sure, for you, Jimmy wouldn't mind at all."

Mahoney gave her hip a little squeeze, then his eyes widened in mock surprise. "What's this? Betty, are you wearing that thong underwear again?"

"Oh, Mr. Speaker!" Betty squealed, slapping him on the shoulder and blushing fire-engine red. "I'll be right back with your coffee, you devil."

Mahoney squared himself to the table and looked down at the sports page again, scanning the box scores. While he read—or pretended to read—he said to DeMarco, "You remember that state house guy Cochran, the one I told you was acting up?"

"Yeah," DeMarco said.

"I sent Perry up to see him, you bein' busy. He handed Perry his head. I swear, Joe, I think he made him cry. That's one tough old son of a bitch up there. So anyway, I still need you to take care of that."

"I'll leave this morning," DeMarco said. "I'll be on his ass before noon."

Thank you, Jesus, thank you.

"And another thing . . ."

"Here's your coffee, Mr. Speaker," Betty said.

Mahoney took a sip. "Ah, Betty, there's only one thing better than a good morning toddy." He paused dramatically, pumped his eyebrows in nasty Groucho fashion, and added, "And we both know what that is, don't we?"

"Oh, Mr. Speaker!" Betty said for about the third time and ran away to relay Mahoney's bawdy comment to her coworkers.

"You were saying?" DeMarco said. "There's something else you need."

"Oh, yeah. While you're up there, go talk to Hanreddy. I haven't heard from him in some time. You might tell him that the asphalt business can get pretty fuckin' tough with some of these air admission things they're talking about."

"Got it," DeMarco said. He knew Mahoney meant air emissions and that not having heard from Hanreddy meant his contributions to his favorite politician had not been forthcoming.

"Can you believe this?" Mahoney said, looking down at the paper again. "Some Russian gal just pole-vaulted over sixteen feet. Sixteen two. I think a woman who could pole-vault sixteen feet would scare me."

DeMarco didn't say anything.

"I hear you got Emma," Mahoney said, still pretending to read the paper.

"She mostly saved herself," DeMarco said, speaking to the top of Mahoney's big head. DeMarco then told him what was going on with Emma, the primary point of this discussion being to convey that he had dutifully come back to D.C., leaving Emma on her own to catch Li Mei.

"We'll probably read in tomorrow's paper," Mahoney said, "that that Chinese broad went to that great rice paddy in the sky." Mahoney paused and added, "I wonder how high Emma can pole-vault."

Mahoney finished his coffee. "I gotta get goin'," he said. He rose from the table, glanced down at the sports page again, and said, "Fuckin' Red Sox. Some things never change."

No, they don't. Thank God they don't.

60

Zhi Chan, the man in charge of Chinese intelligence operations in Vancouver, walked slowly away from his mistress's house. There was a content, peaceful look on his broad face. The situation with Li Mei had been very stressful, and he had needed these few hours with his Canadian friend, not so much for sex but simply to relax, to laugh, to talk about trivial things.

He stepped into his Mercedes, the car sagging to one side under his weight. He had been working so late the last two weeks that he didn't even need to think of an excuse to give his wife. He hit the control for the CD player and the sound of Nat King Cole's voice filled the car. He particularly enjoyed the song "Unforgettable," the duet the dead Mr. Cole sang with his daughter. He liked the idea of ghosts singing with the living. Zhi Chan believed in ghosts.

He had just had that thought when he felt a hand on his shoulder. He jerked in alarm, making the Mercedes swerve dangerously to one side.

"Relax," said a voice from the backseat. "I'm not going to hurt you."

Chan looked into the rearview mirror and saw the man who had been lying on the seat sit up. And then he did relax.

"Ah, Mr. Carmody," Chan said, smiling broadly, his teeth square and white in the rearview mirror. "I was wondering when we would hear from you. I'd have preferred something less dramatic, but . . . well, you're here."

"I want to help," Carmody said. "With Li Mei."

Chan nodded. "Exactly the right answer, my friend. You are a wise man."

"Do you have any idea where she is?" Carmody said.

"No. She mailed us a tape from her interrogation of the female American agent, but after the woman escaped—"

"I don't know what you're talking about," Carmody said. "The last time I saw Li Mei she was trying to kill me."

"Yes, so I heard. You're lucky to be alive."

"So what has she done? For me to help, you need to fill me in."

Chan did. As he talked, he drove his car into Stanley Park; there would be few people driving through the park at this time of night and he would be better able to tell if he was being tailed. In ten minutes, he gave Carmody Emma's history with Li Mei. He also told him about John Washburn, the other operation Li Mei had been running in Bremerton, and how Li Mei had kidnapped Emma and interrogated her and then how Emma had managed to escape.

"Did you know that she intended to kidnap the American woman, Carmody?" Chan said.

"Yes, but she didn't tell me everything. She told me to come to Vancouver, allow myself to be captured, and blame the Bremerton operation on the North Koreans. And she told me to tell the Americans that I was meeting my control in a certain restaurant in Chinatown. She said she planned to capture this woman, Emma, while I was in the restaurant, but she said that afterward, she would demand the Americans exchange me for her. Instead she tried to kill me."

"Hmm," Chan said. He decided that he believed Carmody. Carmody had no reason to lie and many reasons to tell him the truth. "As I was saying earlier," Chan said, "Li Mei sent us a single videotape from her interrogation of the American woman. It contained some things of interest. Unfortunately, Li Mei's plan failed. Just as she failed to deliver

John Washburn, she failed to deliver the American woman—not that we would necessarily have taken her. And now Li Mei is out there, somewhere. We have no idea what she plans to do next, but she has Washburn's files and the files you gave her and she has broken off contact with us."

"So what do you want me to do?" Carmody said.

"We want you to find Li Mei and retrieve the files she has in her possession, of course. I'm glad you came to me tonight because we would really prefer to use you rather than our own people; we don't need another embarrassing incident on North American soil."

"Is that all?"

Chan laughed. "I'm sure you know that's not all, Mr. Carmody."

"And if I succeed?" Carmody said.

"No, no, Mr. Carmody, this is not the time to begin a negotiation. You may have been simply following Li Mei's orders, but at this point you are part of the problem. You want to become part of the solution. So just do as we ask, and if you're successful . . . well, let's just say that then we may be more amenable to whatever you might propose."

And the voice of a ghost filled the silence in the car.

61

DeMarco waited patiently outside the Massachu-
setts State House on Beacon Street. Denny Cochran
should be coming through the building's doors any
moment now. Like Mahoney, Cochran was an alcoholic, and every morning at ten thirty he went to
a bar and had breakfast: two eggs over easy, bacon,
hash browns, toast—and a boilermaker.

A moment later a man in his sixties wearing a
rumpled brown suit exited the building. He wasn't
that short but he seemed shorter than he was because
his legs were stumpy and he weighed more than two
hundred pounds. His hair was reddish gray and cut
short on the sides, and he had the mug of an Irish
brawler: a nose smashed flat by more than one fist,

fleshy jowls, and a pugnacious, in-your-face chin. His eyes were small and mean and blue.

DeMarco waited until Cochran reached the bottom of the steps before he yelled, "Hey, Denny, c'mere a minute."

Cochran smiled automatically when he heard his name called—a political facial tic that exposed his teeth. The smile disappeared when he saw the speaker was DeMarco.

"What do you want, DeMarco? Mahoney already sent Perry Wallace up here to talk to me, and I'll tell you the same thing I told him: kiss my fat Irish ass. I'll vote any fuckin' way I want to."

DeMarco nodded his head as if agreeing with Cochran. "Yeah," he said, "I heard you were real mean to Perry. That wasn't nice."

"Fuck you, tough guy. What do you think you're gonna do? Put a bullet in me?"

It always bothered DeMarco when people said things like that to him.

"No, Denny, I'm not gonna do that. What I am gonna do is ask you why you've been doin' what you've been doin', and you're gonna tell me. You voted against a school lunch program last week, you piece of shit! You know how Mahoney feels about things like that. So tell me who has their hooks into you, Denny, and don't try to feed me that bullshit you fed Perry."

"And if I don't?" Cochran said, looking up at DeMarco, tilting his fleshy chin defiantly.

"Denny, you're up for reelection next year."

"You think I don't know that."

"You've been in this job, what, eighteen years? It's the only thing you know how to do."

"I'll win. I've explained to my constituents—"

"Oh, shut up, Denny, just shut up. You know Michael Farleigh?"

"Farleigh, that kid at the DA's office?"

"Yeah, Denny, that kid. The one who looks like Robert Redford and who's won every case he's ever tried."

"He'd lose money if he took my job," Denny said.

"Yeah, but he's rich, Denny. And next week the party's going to back him for your job. Very strongly. Half a million dollars will be earmarked for his campaign. People all over town are going to start talking about the need for change."

"I'll beat him. I got friends everywhere."

"Yeah, you do, Denny, and they love you because you get them jobs and loan them money and listen to their complaints. And your friends don't read the paper, except for the sports page, so they don't know how you've been voting lately. But they watch TV, Denny. And half a million can pay for a lot of TV ads, ads that'll tell all your friends how you've gone over to the dark side. And the ads will show pictures of Farleigh with his movie-star smile and his knockout of a wife, and next to him will be a picture of you exiting a bar, looking like the fucking dinosaur that you are."

"He won't run," Cochran said.

"Yes, he will, Denny. He'll run because Mahoney will ask him to and because Mahoney will promise to make him a congressman in a couple of years—or governor, if he doesn't want to move to D.C."

"How come Mahoney never backed me for governor?"

"Get serious, Denny. Now tell me who has their hooks in you, and I'm not going to ask you again."

Cochran stood there a minute, his stubborn Irish face not giving an inch—then his features crumbled into surrender.

"Let's go get some breakfast," he said.

———◆◆◆———

Cochran slammed back the shot of bourbon, then banged the shot glass down on the table in front of him. "Give me another, Tommy," he called to the bartender.

"Sure, Denny," the bartender said.

"It's my daughter," Cochran said, taking a sip of his beer. "She was in an accident two months ago. She hit this old lady's car and then she fled the scene."

"Was the old lady hurt?"

"Not too bad. A couple of bruises. But I'm sure if somebody slipped her a few bucks she'd put on a neck brace in a New York minute. Anyway, my daughter isn't two blocks from the scene when a cop pulls her over. There was a witness and he called 911."

"A witness, too," DeMarco said.

"Yeah. Next thing that happens—and this is within fifteen minutes of the time the cop pulls her over, Mary Ann's still sittin' in the backseat of the damn squad car—I get a call from Morgan."

Hadley Morgan was the minority leader in the state senate.

"He tells me that if I don't start playing ball the cops are gonna book her. DUI, hit-and-run, resisting arrest, the whole fuckin' nine yards."

"She was drunk, too?"

"Oh, yeah. When my daughter fucks up, she does it right."

"Jesus. So why didn't you tell Morgan to go to hell, Denny? We'd have gotten her a lawyer, she'd promise to go to counseling, and life would go on. She's got two kids, doesn't she? She wouldn't have done jail time, not if the old lady wasn't hurt that bad."

Cochran shook his head. "It's not about my daughter. It's about her kids, my grandkids. Mary Ann's divorced and the asshole she was married to has been looking for an excuse to take the kids from her. Not that he wants the kids; he just wants to put the screws to her. And he lives in California to boot. Plus this isn't the first time Mary Ann's been caught drivin' drunk, either. Don't get me wrong. She's a good mother and she works her ass off in this job that doesn't pay for shit, and every moment she's not workin', she spends with her boys. But she's human, so every once in a blue moon she gets together with her girlfriends to let off some steam. The problem is she's unlucky. She's got to be the unluckiest woman I've ever known."

The bartender brought Cochran his second bourbon. "Your eggs'll be up in just a minute, Denny," he said.

"Ah forget the eggs today, Tommy. Just bring me another beer."

"So that's it," DeMarco said. "You're worried that if the case goes to court, your daughter will lose her kids?"

"Yeah. Morgan told me that's what would happen. No doubt about it."

"How the hell can they charge her this long after the accident?"

"Easy. The witness will say his conscience has been bothering him, and he just decided to come forward. He won't mention that he got paid two months ago *not* to come forward. And the bartender at the place where she was drinking'll say, yeah, I remember her like it was yesterday because she looks just like my sister, and when she left the bar she had about six daiquiris in her and could hardly walk. And the cop'll say how he had to chase her for six blocks with his siren blarin' and he gave her a DUI—funny how that got lost in the system for months—but he didn't know she'd just hit the old broad. Then they'll drag out her record."

DeMarco shook his head. "How'd they get to Morgan so fast?"

Cochran coughed a bitter laugh.

"I told you Mary Ann was unlucky. The cop was Morgan's brother-in-law."

62

DeMarco glanced nervously at the two Doberman pinschers. They in turn stood there, side by side, still as statues, eyes as lifeless as marbles—*staring* at him.

"Will you quit worrying about the dogs, Joe," Emma said. "They're not going to do anything."

"Then why are they staring at me?"

"Because that's what dogs do. Just ignore them."

They were outside, on Emma's patio, drinking coffee. Emma had been home for a week but this was the first time DeMarco had seen her since Vancouver. She looked completely recovered. She'd regained the weight she'd lost, her eyes were clear, and her muscles were, if anything, more toned than usual.

DeMarco noticed her English garden had lost some of its luster since the last time he'd visited. The flowers were still in bloom but they were now a bit faded, somewhat forlorn, like a prom queen after the dance. Other changes had occurred at Emma's house as well. Security cameras were mounted on the eaves and *all* her windows and doors were alarmed. And there were the dogs, of course, borrowed from some Armageddon-ready nut she knew.

"Where do you think she is, Emma?"

Emma's right arm swept a large semicircle in the air. "Out there. Somewhere. Waiting."

The trap Emma had set in Vancouver for Li Mei had failed. She'd been too smart to be drawn in.

"And you think she's on her own, not being supported by the Chinese?"

"Yeah. She's on her own."

"So how's she existing? Does she have access to funds?"

Emma laughed. "You could say that," she said. "Ten days ago a woman robbed a bank in Bismarck. The bank's cameras showed a blurry picture of a woman wearing a baseball hat and sunglasses. Witnesses, those not scared into complete amnesia by the gun she pointed at them, think the robber was Asian."

"She's robbing banks!"

"Joe, there are probably fifty bank robberies a day in this country, most of them committed by morons. How hard do you think it would be for a government-trained agent to rob a bank?"

"So if she robbed a bank in Bismarck, she got out of Canada and is here in this country."

"Yeah. Which isn't surprising, considering her skills."

"And all this stuff—the cameras, the killer puppies—you think that'll make her give up and go away?"

Emma smiled. Arctic ice was warmer than that smile. "The security here isn't intended to make her go away, Joe. It's designed to make her try for me at a spot of our own choosing."

"What are you talking about?"

"I beefed up the security around my house not to make it impregnable—there's no such thing as impregnable—but to make this place a harder target. Now I'm establishing a routine. I'll get groceries the same day every week. I'll go to my club at ten a.m. every other day: I'll visit my hairdresser each Thursday. And I'm already jogging *every* day. The bottom line is, we're making sure that the most attractive location for an attack is while I'm jogging."

"How?" DeMarco said.

"When I go to my club or the hairdresser, I'm not exposed for any length of time and there are always people in the vicinity. Here, I'm alone, but there are neighbors—and the puppies. But when I'm jogging, I jog on busy streets until I reach the two-mile point, then I cut through a section of woods on a trail that hardly anyone uses. It's a perfect spot for an ambush."

"And while you're jogging, you're armed?"

Emma lifted the bottom of the blouse she was wearing, exposing an ugly, short-barreled automatic tucked into the waistband of her shorts.

"What if she gets a rifle and shoots you from two hundred yards away while you're sitting here on your patio?" DeMarco said. Just saying this made him look around nervously for places where snipers might hide.

"Then I'm dead. But I don't think that's going to happen. She—"

"You don't *think*!"

"She needs to confront me, Joe, to see the fear in my eyes. She needs to tell me one last time how much she hates me. And I still think she might try to kidnap me again."

"You hope."

Emma shrugged.

"How's Christine taking all this?"

"Not well. She's living in a condo in Falls Church with a friend. I haven't seen her since I got back because I'm afraid Li Mei might follow me and use her against me. I can't allow that." She smiled sadly. "I guess if a relationship can't endure a long separation, it probably wasn't much of a relationship to begin with."

DeMarco wasn't the right guy to give advice on relationships.

"So when you go jogging," he said, "does Smith have agents all over the place?"

"No. His manpower is limited."

"That's crap, Emma. He must have pulled thirty people into Vancouver after Li Mei snatched you."

"He did that because he had to, because he was afraid ongoing operations had been compromised. Vancouver involved national security; my death doesn't."

"Then what about the FBI? She killed one of their agents and made them look like clowns in Vancouver. And they're the ones responsible for catching her. Are they protecting you?"

"No."

Emma explained. The FBI, meaning the agent in charge, Glen Harris, wasn't convinced that Li Mei was still in the country. He figured that, after blowing both the shipyard operation and Emma's kidnapping, Li Mei would have fled the country and the Chinese government would have helped her. Harris's logic was based heavily on the assumption that Li Mei still had in her possession Carmody's and Washburn's files. He believed the Chinese would have helped her escape just to get their hands on those files.

"Harris doesn't believe it's *me* that Li Mei wants," Emma said. "He says she'd be insane to come after me. What he doesn't understand is that she *is* insane."

"Smith says the Chinese government wouldn't have sanctioned what she did in Vancouver," De-Marco said. "Doesn't Harris understand that?"

"Harris," Emma said, "is a thickheaded ass. And there's a, ah, *bureaucratic* issue, if you will, when it comes to protecting me."

"What's that? Are they arguing over who should pay?"

DeMarco had been kidding when he said that and was therefore surprised when Emma said, "Well good for you, Joe. You're finally beginning to understand the inner workings of your government. The FBI thinks protecting me is a DIA responsibility and they're not going to spend their budget or their manpower on it, at least not until they have some evidence that Li Mei is actually in the area. They are looking into the bank robbery in Bismarck though, and—"

"Well that's big of them."

"—and trying to track her down here and overseas, but my protection isn't a priority for them."

"Shit," DeMarco said. "So in other words, the Bureau and Smith, that four-eyed little bastard, just hung you out to dry."

"Not exactly. Come with me. I want to show you my new Weedwacker."

"What?"

DeMarco followed Emma to a large tool shed at the back of her yard. The shed was partially and artfully hidden by tall, thin stalks of bamboo. She opened the door and there, sitting in a lawn chair, was Clint Eastwood—or at least a guy who looked like Clint did when he was playing Rowdy Yates in *Rawhide* fifty years ago.

The man was a lean six foot four. He was dressed in tight-fitting jeans, a sleeveless T-shirt, and cowboy boots made from a reptile's hide. His dirty-blond hair was long and elaborately combed, and when he saw DeMarco, he flashed him a killer smile. All he was lacking was an unlit cheroot in his mouth, a thin, twisted one like the real Clint chewed in those spaghetti westerns.

Then DeMarco noticed other details. There was a small periscope penetrating the roof of the shed so the man could observe Emma and her home without being seen. On a sack of fertilizer was a pair of night-vision goggles, and leaning against the wall, within easy reach, was a rifle with a banana clip. In a shoulder holster, the man carried a revolver that looked like it weighed ten pounds and had an eight-inch barrel.

"Joe, this is Rolf," Emma said.

Rolf rose to his feet, having to duck because of the low ceiling in the shed. He extended his right hand and said, "I am very pleased to meet you, Yo."

Rolf even had a Western accent—western Russia.

DeMarco shook Rolf's hand. There were a lot of calluses on the hand.

"Rolf freelances for Bill at times," Emma said. "You've heard the expression about being able to shoot the eye out of a june bug?"

"Yeah," DeMarco said.

"Well, Rolf can."

Rolf smiled again when Emma said this, but this time when he smiled he didn't look like a movie-star wannabe. He looked like a guy who had climbed over the Iron Curtain using the bodies of his enemies for stepping-stones.

"I don't know, Emma," DeMarco said. "I'm sure Rolf here's as good as you say . . ."

Rolf nodded.

". . . but I think Smith oughta be doin' more than this."

"Like I said, Joe," Emma said, "Bill's got man-power problems."

Before DeMarco could protest, she explained that Rolf was always nearby when she went somewhere, staying out of sight as he was doing now, but if Emma was approached by anyone he'd be there. Or close enough to shoot someone—and he didn't have to be all that close.

"And when I go jogging," Emma said, "Rolf's at the ambush spot ahead of me."

"Yeah," DeMarco said, "sounds like a pretty good plan."

But he was thinking he might have a word with Mahoney about all this, see if he couldn't get him to land like a ton of bricks on the tightfisted shit who ran the DIA.

63

---◆◆◆---

"His *grandkids*?" Mahoney said. "They're usin' his grandkids against him?"

"Yeah."

"What the fuck's wrong with those guys? You never go after family."

To DeMarco that sounded like something the people his father used to work for would have said. Then again, maybe there really wasn't all that much difference between politics and organized crime.

DeMarco hadn't seen Mahoney in a week, and this was the first opportunity he'd had to tell him how Denny Cochran was being blackmailed by Hadley Morgan. The president had decided to take a diplomatic swing through South and Central America and

Mahoney had accompanied him. Mahoney didn't particularly like to travel, and he really didn't like to travel with the president, but he'd made the trip so he could have some one-on-one time with the Man and tell him how to run *all* the Americas, North and South.

"And how long did they think they could keep this up?" Mahoney said. "I mean, hell, at some point what Denny was doing would become news and he'd lose his job." Mahoney paused a minute. "I guess, when you think about it, that's not a bad result either. While he's there he votes their way for a while, and with his clout gets a few other guys to vote with him. Then, come election time, they plaster his record all over TV and the best thing that happens is one of their guys replaces him, and the worst thing that happens is he gets voted out and somebody new with no influence gets the job. Christ, what a mess. If Denny wasn't such a good guy I'd just let 'em sink him."

"Replacing him with Farleigh wouldn't be all that bad," DeMarco said.

"Aw," Mahoney said, "Farleigh would never take a job like that. He wants Ted's seat."

"Ted" was Senator Edward Kennedy.

Mahoney chewed on the stub of an unlit cigar for a moment, turning the tip of the stogie all wet and brown and nasty. "You think the daughter's ex-husband would really take the kids?" he asked.

"I don't know," DeMarco said. "He's a lowlife who sells cars out in Oakland. He's got a girlfriend who's younger than him and the last thing he probably wants is two kids running around their apartment— but he'll take his ex to court to get the kids because Morgan'll pay him to. At least that's what Denny thinks."

"Shit," Mahoney said.

"Maybe the best thing to do is play it straight," DeMarco said. "Get the daughter a good lawyer and take the initiative. Have her turn herself in and throw herself on the mercy of the court."

Mahoney didn't say anything. He just gnawed on his cigar as he looked out the window of his office. For some reason a large flock of seagulls was circling the Washington Monument like it was a five-hundred-and-fifty-foot bird feeder.

"Nah," Mahoney said at last. "First of all that's a crap shoot, and second, that doesn't pay Morgan back for pullin' this shit. Let me think on this a bit. You go think, too. I wanna spank Morgan hard for this."

DeMarco got up to leave Mahoney's office.

"Hey, what's goin' on with Emma?" Mahoney said.

DeMarco had been hoping he'd ask.

64

I don't appreciate what you did one damn bit, De-
Marco," Bill Smith said.

Ignoring Smith, DeMarco turned to the hot dog
vendor and said, "Polish sausage. Just mustard and
onions, no sauerkraut."

The hot dog vendor said, "Yes, sah. One dog,
onion, no kraut." The vendor was one of those
scrawny little guys who weighs about ninety pounds
but has forearms corded with muscle. He wore a
blue vest over his grease-stained white apron, and
the vest was covered with political campaign buttons. McGovern, Humphrey, Carter were all given
space. DeMarco figured the hot dog guy for a die-
hard Democrat—kind of dangerous for business in

a truly partisan town—until he turned around to get DeMarco's hot dog. The back of the vest gave the Republicans their due.

"No sauerkraut!" Smith said. "That's like eating peanut butter without jelly, like having lox without cream cheese, like—"

"I get it," DeMarco said. "I just don't like sauerkraut."

They were standing by the Court of Neptune fountain in front of the Library of Congress. The fountain, directly across the street from the Capitol, depicted a muscular, naked Neptune holding his trident; two faintly sinister-looking guys, also naked, standing on either side of Neptune; and two nude, extremely well-endowed women riding on creatures that were half horse and half fish. DeMarco was surprised that some of the more conservative members of the legislature hadn't demanded that a sheet be thrown over all the naked people.

Smith shook his head in disgust at DeMarco's culinary barbarism then said, "So why'd you have Mahoney bust my chops over Emma? I mean, you coulda just called me."

"Yeah," DeMarco said. "And assuming you'd have returned my call, you would have given me some bullshit about manpower shortages."

"It's not bullshit," Smith said, spitting bits of sauerkraut from his mouth as he talked. "You don't have any idea what we're up against right now. We're trying to spy on the entire Muslim world, DeMarco! Don't you get it?"

"You're right, Bill, I don't have any idea what you're up against. Furthermore, I don't care. All I care about is Emma. You remember Emma, don't you? The lady who busted up a spy ring in Bremerton when you didn't think one existed? The lady who was tortured and almost—"

"Enough," Smith said, raising a hand in surrender. "But the fact that it's Emma doesn't change the fact that I can only spare so many agents to protect her."

"You spared one, Bill! One! And he's not even an American."

"Rolf's good, Joe. I'd tell you exactly how good but that's classified."

"I don't care if he's James fucking Bond. One guy isn't enough. Now what are you going to do?"

"Well, after Mahoney badgered my boss's boss's boss . . . Who the hell did he talk to anyway, DeMarco? The Secretary of Defense?"

"Probably. He tends to start at the top."

"Well, whoever he talked to rattled the whole chain of command. Anyway, we're gonna provide a guy to relieve Rolf so that she has round-the-clock protection on the outside of her house or wherever she is. Right now Rolf's only working a sixteen-hour shift because he's gotta sleep sometime. We're also putting a gal *in* her house and the gal will be with her 24-7. The gal we got looks like her . . . whatever you wanna call her, the cello player."

"Now that's good. I like that."

"I'm glad you approve, DeMarco, being the expert at personal protection that you are. We don't think Li Mei's ever seen Emma's, uh . . ."

"Her lover, Bill. You can say it."

"Yeah. So we got a tall gal—had to fly her up from Panama, thanks to you—and we'll jam a blond wig on her head and have her carry a cello case into Emma's house. Maybe we'll have Emma, uh, you know, smooch her a couple of times out in the open."

"Is she any good?" DeMarco said.

"She came in fifth in the biathlon in the '98 Olympics."

"Great." DeMarco said. "So if Li Mei shoots Emma and takes off on skis, this gal'll get her."

65

Emma saw DeMarco standing outside her club, his gym bag near his feet. Without breaking stride, she pointed a finger at him and said, "You. I want to talk to you, you jackass."

Accompanying Emma was a woman with a blond ponytail. She was wearing white shorts, a white polo shirt, and court shoes. She was in her thirties, as tall as Emma, and looked a bit like Christine except she was more muscular. Actually, DeMarco realized, she was much more muscular than Christine: she looked like she lifted big weights several days a week and she had thighs that would crack your ribs if she wrapped her legs around you. She wasn't as pretty as Christine either—not by a long shot. She wasn't ugly but her face was hard and unfeminine, like those East German swimmers before they started testing their urine. Come to think of it, she didn't look at all like Christine.

Emma walked past DeMarco and into the health club without another word. The other woman stared at DeMarco as if memorizing his face for future reference and followed Emma through the double doors. DeMarco emitted a long-suffering sigh, picked up his gym bag, and followed the women.

Emma's health club catered to the wealthy in the D.C. metro area and was appropriately pricey and ostentatious. There was an Olympic-size pool, two indoor tennis courts, four outdoor tennis courts, a half-court basketball court, steam and massage rooms, two racquetball courts, one squash court, and an exercise room with every machine designed by Precor. There were also two bars—one for the alcoholics and one for the carrot juicers—and a small cafeteria that looked out onto an emerald-green, nine-hole golf course. The cafeteria served egg-white omelets with shiitake mushrooms that were so light you felt as if you were eating air.

Emma approached the front desk and was greeted by a tanned young man with a body that could have posed for Michelangelo's *David*. Emma signed in and walked about twenty feet down the hall in the direction of the women's locker room before she stopped and spun around to face DeMarco.

"What are you doing here?" Emma said.

DeMarco hoisted his gym bag. "Just thought we could play a little racquetball."

"Bullshit. You came to check out my security."

"Okay, I did. And I'm not impressed. Where the hell's Rolf?"

"Oh, so you didn't see Rolf," Emma said.

"That's right. Where is he?"

"You didn't see him, because you're not supposed to see him! Jesus, Joe." She started to say something else, then realized that the Christine double was standing there, glaring at DeMarco.

"Joe, this is Carla. Carla, this is . . . oh, never mind who he is but the next time you see him, shoot him."

"Yes, ma'am," Carla said, sounding completely serious.

"Carla, I've told you . . ." Emma took a breath to calm herself. "Carla, I need to talk to this fool for a minute alone."

"Yes, ma'am," Carla said. "I'll check out the locker room." As Carla walked away, DeMarco noticed that her back was almost as broad as his.

"Jesus, will you look at her," Emma said. "Why doesn't she just wear a damn sandwich board that says 'Bodyguard'? And I've told her about fifty times to quit calling me 'ma'am' but she's ex–Secret Service and just can't seem to make the adjustment."

"Well, she's better than noth—"

"No! She's not better than anything. I had this set up just the way I wanted it. The idea was to draw Li Mei *out,* to make her come after me. All I needed was Rolf. But now I've got Carla walking next to me every minute of the day. And Christ, she's living with me! Can you imagine the kind of houseguest that woman makes?"

"Sorry," DeMarco said. "I just thought—"

"Did you bring your racquet?"

"Sure. I told you I—"

"Good. I'm gonna whip your ass something horrible. Go get changed."

———◆———

DeMarco didn't like playing racquetball with Emma. Not only was it bad for his ego—the most points he'd ever scored against her were eleven—but it was also bad for his health. She ran him ragged, making him dive or jump for every point, and she delighted in hitting the ball as close to his head as possible. And that's when she was in a good mood. He was going to get killed today.

DeMarco's humiliation was also liable to be public. One of the racquetball courts was designed for tournament play. The top half of the back wall of the court was made of glass and there was a gallery with benches so spectators could look down onto the court. DeMarco was relieved that there was no one presently seated on the benches, but as Emma was the club's reigning female racquetball champ, a small crowd could gather at any moment to watch her play.

DeMarco took his time warming up. The only reason he'd come to the club was to see if Smith had augmented Emma's security—a subterfuge she'd immediately seen through—but now he was stuck. He thought of faking a pulled hamstring after a couple of points, but knew that wouldn't work. Emma would just stand him up against the front wall of the court and use him for target practice.

She won the first game 21 to 7. His T-shirt and shorts were drenched with sweat and he had a bruise on his ass that was going to be the size of a grapefruit tomorrow morning. Emma had driven the ball into his butt with all the force she had, standing less than three feet from him. She apologized, acting as if the shot had been an accident, but he knew better.

The score in the second game was now 6 to 1, and the one point he scored had been a complete fluke, the ball going off the wood of his racquet instead of the strings and hitting the front wall about an inch from the bottom. DeMarco took his position to serve for the first time in the game. He stood at the back of the court bouncing the ball as if planning his shot. Actually he planned to bounce the ball until his heart stopped hammering.

Emma, of course, realized what he was doing and spun around to face him. "Are you ever gonna . . ." Then she stopped and looked up at the gallery, and her shoulders seemed to slump in . . . what? Resignation? DeMarco turned around to see what she was looking at, expecting to see Brunhilda, the bodyguard.

"Joe, don't move," Emma said.

DeMarco ignored her. He couldn't see up into the gallery as close to the back wall as he was standing, so he moved a couple feet toward the center of the court. It wasn't Brunhilda. It was Li Mei—and she was pointing a long-barreled pistol at Emma's heart. There was a silencer attached to the barrel of the pistol.

"Get back against the wall," Emma said to Joe, while still staring up at Li Mei. If DeMarco stayed flat against the back wall, Li Mei couldn't shoot him from the gallery above. The glass prevented her from getting the right angle to make the shot.

But DeMarco didn't move. He just stood and watched in horror as Li Mei smiled—then pulled the trigger.

66

Mahoney hadn't been back to Boston in almost two months. He loved Washington but he missed this place, the city where he'd been born and raised. He could still remember, with Technicolor vividness, the first time he returned home after being gone for two years. He'd stepped off a Greyhound bus, supported by crutches, medals covering his chest. His parents had stood there in the terminal waiting for him, both as stout as Mahoney was now. He could see the tears streaming down his mother's plump cheeks, sobbing in relief that her boy had made it home from that horrible place. And his father, his face bursting with pride and his chin trembling as he willed himself not to cry. Men of Mahoney's father's generation didn't cry; neither did Mahoney.

Mahoney sat now in one of his favorite bars. The bar hadn't been there when he was a young man, and had it been, he couldn't have afforded it. It was on the top floor of a building owned by an insurance company and it looked down onto the ballpark. He loved this angel's view of the diamond. He loved it when the team was playing and the stands were filled with people, but he liked it better when the stadium was empty and there was nothing to see but the crosscut green grass and the worn-out bleachers.

They talked periodically of replacing the ballpark with something grander, something with skyboxes and fancy restaurants and seating for sixty thousand fans. But they never did. Everyone knew that to raze Fenway would be the same as destroying a holy place—which in many ways, to many people, it was.

"Mr. Speaker," a baritone voice said from behind him.

Mahoney grimaced, irritated at the interruption even though he'd been the one who'd called the meeting. Before turning he fixed a grin on his face—not the friendly one, but the other one, the one that made you think he was going to eat you in a single bite.

"Ah, you're here, Morgan," Mahoney said. "And you only kept your betters waiting ten minutes."

Hadley Morgan, minority leader of the state senate, was a grim, gray man: gray hair, gray suit, gray eyes, and a prim, disapproving mouth. Mahoney suspected that the Puritans who had hanged the witches at Salem had looked like Hadley Morgan. Now Mahoney, intermittent Catholic that he was, knew that had he been at Salem he would have been more inclined to have bedded the witches than to have hanged them.

"It was the traffic," Morgan said, making no attempt to conceal the lie.

"Yeah, it's terrible, the traffic," Mahoney said. "And who's this?" he said, gesturing with his big chin at the young man standing behind Morgan dressed in a blue suit and holding a briefcase.

"Robert Fairchild, Mr. Speaker. My aide," Morgan said.

"Your aide," Mahoney said and nodded as if he approved. "Well, Bobby," Mahoney said to Robert Fairchild, "I want to talk to your boss in private. So haul your yuppie young ass on outta here. Walk over to the ballpark," Mahoney added with a gesture toward the stadium below him, "and place your head up against the great wall and pray for God to forgive you for working for a man like Morgan."

Fairchild opened his mouth to say something, but Morgan silenced him with a raised hand. "It's okay, Robert. I'll meet you in the car." To Mahoney, he said, "Should we get a booth, Mr. Speaker? Or maybe a small, private room. I'm sure they'd find one for us if we asked."

"Nah," Mahoney said. "Let's just sit here at the bar. Pull up a stool." Mahoney ignored the look of distaste on Hadley Morgan's face—Morgan wasn't a stool-sitter—and waved to the bartender.

The bartender was a redhead in her early forties. When she was younger she had danced topless in drinking establishments with lower prices and lower pretensions. "Another bourbon, John?" she said with a smile. Mahoney loved that smile, both sexy and nostalgic. It was a smile that said: *Oh, the times we had*.

Mahoney could see that Morgan was shocked that the waitress would address Mahoney so familiarly, clearly troubled that a member of the working class would dare speak to a man of his position with so little respect. And this proved to Mahoney that Hadley Morgan had no understanding of what it took to earn respect.

"Of course, sweetheart," Mahoney said. "And what's your poison, Morgan?"

"I don't drink, Mr. Speaker."

"Now why doesn't that surprise me?"

"I can bring you a club soda, sir," the bartender said to Morgan. "Or coffee or a soft drink, if you'd prefer."

"Bottled water," Morgan said, not meeting the woman's eyes.

"Yes, sir," she said—then she patted Mahoney's thick paw, winked at him, and said, "I'll be right back with that drink, sugar."

As the bartender walked away Mahoney said, "That's one good-lookin' woman, Morgan. You should have seen her when she was twenty."

"I'm sure," Morgan said.

Mahoney waited until the bartender brought their drinks before saying, "You know, Morgan, puttin' Denny Cochran's nuts in a vise to get his vote, there was nothin' wrong with that. That's the way the game is played."

"I don't know what—"

"But usin' his grandkids for leverage . . . Well I gotta tell you, that's when you stepped over the line."

"Mr. Speaker, I—"

"I've been giving Denny's situation a lot of thought lately, bein' fond of Denny as I am. I figured paying you back in kind wouldn't be easy though, you bein' the paragon of virtue that you are. I mean, Jesus, you're boring, Morgan. You don't drink, you don't gamble, and you're too rich to take kickbacks, at least the old-fashioned, stuffed-envelope kind. And, of course, you don't chase women. Yeah, I figured you'd be a tough nut to crack, I did. Then it occurred to me. A man as . . . what's the word . . . as *antiseptic* as you, what vice would you have?"

Mahoney drained his bourbon and pulled out a cigar. Morgan started to say something but

Mahoney raised a hand to silence him while he completed the ritual of lighting his stogie. After blowing a cloud of noxious smoke over Morgan's head, he said, "The other day, I was talking to a young associate of mine. I was telling the lad how he needed to be more careful with those e-mails he's always sending, telling him how everything you do on a computer stays in there somehow, hiding in the wiring or something. Did you know that, Morgan? Did you know that you hit that little Delete button and those e-mails *pretend* to disappear, but they really don't? They just hide in your machine, those wee sneaky electrons, but if you know where to look, you can find them. And that's when it occurred to me, Morgan."

It didn't seem possible, but Hadley Morgan's gray complexion grew even grayer.

"I have another young associate," Mahoney said, "and he has an associate. One of those weird guys who hunts on the Internet the way I used to hunt ducks from a blind. Well I asked this fellow, this computer fellow, to look into *your* computer, Morgan, to see what you've been hiding. And can you guess what he found?"

Morgan didn't say anything. Mahoney wasn't sure that he could.

"The computer guy, he said something about being able to trace visits made to Internet sites from your computer, Morgan. And he made a record of your visits, something that proves that you were the one doing the visiting. I don't know how he did it—maybe that young aide of yours can explain it to you—but it seems you've been visiting these sites in your spare time, sometimes for several hours at a time. Well, I had him print me out a copy of one of the pictures you see on those sites. I was gonna bring the picture with me but I was terrified I might get hit by a bus and that picture would be found on my dead body. But you don't need to see a picture, do you, Morgan? You know exactly what sorts of pictures they have on those sites?'

"No," Morgan said, "I don't need to see a picture."

"I thought not," Mahoney said. Then he leaned forward so that his big face was an inch from Hadley Morgan's, and said in a harsh whisper: "Now you listen to me, you sick fuck. If you take Denny Cochrans grandkids away from him I'm gonna send every paper in the state a copy of your computer logs. And for what you're doing on the Internet, Morgan . . . well, let me put it this way: if you *ever* decide to indulge your sick fuckin' fantasies in the flesh, if you *ever* go near a child in person, I'll send you to jail, as God is my witness, I will. Can you imagine jail for someone as gray and frail as you, Morgan? Can you imagine how you'd spend your nights?"

Mahoney turned away and called to the barmaid, "Sweetheart, could you be a darlin' and bring me just one more?" To Morgan he said, "Get the hell outta here. But by the day after tomorrow, I better read in the papers that you've decided to retire."

Morgan's dry lips parted to say something but nothing came from his mouth. He slipped off the bar stool and moved slowly toward the exit, walking carefully, as though he wasn't certain that his legs would support him.

The redheaded bartender brought Mahoney his drink, then leaned down, placing her forearms on the bar so Mahoney could enjoy her cleavage.

Mahoney smiled at her. She smiled back.

"I love it," Mahoney said, gesturing with his head, "the way the lights shine down on the ballpark, on all that green grass. Can you remember, sweetheart, the first time you made love on the grass?"

67

---◆◆◆---

The viewing window above the racquetball court exploded into a million shards and glass rained down onto DeMarco's back and head. When the glass stopped falling, he looked up and saw Li Mei still standing in the gallery overlooking the racquet-ball court, her pistol still extended. He looked back toward center court where Emma had been standing, expecting to see her lying on the floor. She wasn't. Emma was unharmed, in the same position she'd been in before Li Mei had fired. Either the thick glass of the viewing window had deflected the shot or Li Mei hadn't intended to kill her with the first bullet.

DeMarco swiveled his head and looked up again at Li Mei. She was now aiming the gun at him, not Emma. With the glass out of the way she could shoot directly down at him, even if he was pressed up against the back wall of the court.

She was going to kill him first.

As Li Mei was about to pull the trigger, Emma screamed "No!" and then flung her racquet at Li Mei's head. Li Mei ducked, and the racquet sailed over her, and she trained her weapon again on DeMarco.

And then two gunshots boomed out, fired by an unsilenced weapon. Li Mei spun to her right, toward whoever had fired, and began to shoot her automatic. DeMarco could hear the little "puffs" her gun made each time she pulled the trigger. He didn't know how many bullets Li Mei's weapon held, but it sounded to DeMarco like she fired five or six shots. Then she stopped firing and turned and ran to her left, in the direction of one of the stairways leading down from the gallery. As Li Mei ran, someone fired at her two more times, one shot chipping plaster from the ceiling of the gallery.

While Li Mei had been shooting, Emma had sprinted to the corner of the racquetball court. She had placed a small purse in one corner of the court and now she removed an automatic from the purse. She chambered a round into the weapon and pushed against the door to the court. The door should have swung outward but it didn't move. It appeared that Li Mei had wedged something beneath the door.

"Joe, help me," Emma said.

DeMarco and Emma slammed their shoulders against the door until it opened far enough for them to slip through. They probably wasted two minutes, maybe three, opening the door.

Emma ran without hesitation toward the set of stairs that led down from the gallery, the stairs that Li Mei would have used to escape. She didn't bother to go up to the gallery. She knew that by now Li Mei had already descended. She ran instead toward the nearest exit and slammed a foot into the bar that opened the door. She held her weapon in front of her in a two-handed grip and swept the grounds with her eyes and the gun. Li Mei was gone. Emma stood there a minute, continuing to look for a target, then relaxed her pose. She turned to DeMarco and said, "Go call . . . Oh, shit! Carla!" She pushed past DeMarco and reentered the club.

It took DeMarco a moment to remember who Carla was, then it came to him: Brunhilda, the bodyguard. He found Emma on the other set of stairs that led to the viewing gallery. Carla was lying facedown at the bottom of the stairs. There was a gun near her left hand and the hardwood floor beneath her head was awash in blood.

"Ah, Christ," Emma said. "You poor, poor thing." Emma rose slowly to her feet. "She died saving my life," she said to DeMarco.

"Emma," DeMarco said, looking down at the body, "it looks like she was shot in the back of the head."

"Yeah," Emma said. "She was probably spinning away after she fired at Li Mei." Before DeMarco could say anything else, she said, "I'm going to see if Rolf's still alive." The way she spoke, she didn't sound as though she expected him to be. "Call Bill Smith," Emma yelled to DeMarco as she ran down the hall. "Tell him to try and get here before the cops do."

As Emma sprinted away, DeMarco thought back on the sequence of shots. Li Mei had fired her silenced weapon first, breaking the glass above the racquetball court. Before she could fire a second shot, someone fired two shots at Li Mei with an unsilenced weapon. Li Mei then turned and let loose a volley of shots, five or six, then ran for the gallery stairwell. Then two more unsilenced shots were fired.

The first thing that occurred to DeMarco was: How did an Olympic biathlon contender miss a stationary target with two shots? The second thing that occurred to him was that if Li Mei had shot Carla in the head, who had fired the last two shots?

DeMarco called Smith then left the club to find Emma. She was standing over Rolf's body, which was lying behind a shrub near the club's parking lot. The bullet that had killed him had entered the back of his head and the exit wound had made his face unrecognizable. Emma said that Li Mei had been less than a foot from Rolf when she fired, and from her tone, it sounded as if she couldn't imagine how she had gotten so close without Rolf noticing.

To DeMarco's untrained eye, the gunshot wound in Rolf's head looked similar to the one in Carla's.

The next two hours were organized chaos. Patrol cars and ambulances roared into the club's parking lot; medics put bodies into bags; forensic technicians crawled on their knees near the racquetball courts looking for clues. Club members, all dressed in expensive athletic wear, were herded into a cafeteria and then led out one at a time to be interviewed by detectives. Most of the members were quite shaken—gunshots had been fired in their exclusive club, people had been killed. Their faces all seemed to say that their dues were far too high for something like this to have happened in a place where they played.

Bill Smith finally arrived and managed to convince the local cops that it would be okay for Emma and DeMarco to leave with him. As they'd each brought their own car to the club, they left the parking lot in convoy fashion, Smith and DeMarco following Emma. She led them to the first bar she could find.

No one said anything until they all had drinks in front of them. DeMarco swallowed most of his drink immediately and noticed that Emma did the same.

"She didn't do what I expected," Emma said.

"The bitch never seems to," Smith said.

"I figured she'd try for me while I was jogging," Emma said. "Instead she picks a place filled with civilians."

"Do you think she planned to nab you again or just kill you?" Smith said.

"I don't know," Emma said. "She could have killed me right after she shot the viewing window out but she aimed for Joe instead. Then before she could fire, Carla started shooting."

"Thank God for Carla," Smith said, raising his glass in a small toast to the fallen.

"Yes," Emma said. "Did she have anyone? A boy-friend, a husband, kids?"

"I don't know," Smith said. "I didn't know her."

"Well, find out," Emma snapped. She finished her drink and waved at the bartender for another round.

"I'm not sure Carla saved you," DeMarco said. He hadn't spoken until now. Emma seemed completely recovered from the gunplay that had occurred but DeMarco was still shaken by what had happened.

"What?" Emma said.

DeMarco told them about the sequence of shots and the fact that Carla had been shot in the back of the head.

"You're saying someone else was shooting at Li Mei?" Smith said.

"I don't know. I could be wrong about the shots."

"You are wrong," Emma said. "If somebody else had been there we would have seen him."

DeMarco shrugged. There'd been a lot of shots fired and glass had been raining down on his head and his heart had been beating a zillion times a minute. And Li Mei had used a silenced weapon so maybe she'd fired more shots than he had heard. But it still bothered him that Carla had missed Li Mei with the first two shots. When he said this, Smith said, "Well, firing at paper targets and firing at a human being are two different things."

"No," Emma said, "I think Joe has a point." She reached out and pulled a piece of glass from De-Marco's hair. To Smith she said, "Call the cops at the club. Ask them to see if the clip in Carla's weapon is still full."

Smith nodded, took out his cell phone, and made the call. DeMarco noted that when Smith talked to the cops his voice took on this I'm-a-government-heavy-hitter tone. They all waited, sipping their drinks, as Smith held the phone to his ear.

"Okay," he finally said into his phone. "Thanks."

"She never fired a shot," Smith said to Emma.

"Then who shot at Li Mei?" DeMarco said.

"There's only one answer to that question," Emma said. "The Chinese. They must have sent a team here to watch for her and to watch me. They must have seen her this morning when she followed me to the club."

"So why didn't they try to capture her?" Smith said. "Or kill her before she got inside the club?"

"I don't know," Emma said. "Maybe they didn't spot her until just before she entered the club. She's good."

"No shit," Smith said. He paused a moment to sip from his drink then said, "So in addition to Li Mei, we got a fucking Chinese hit squad on the ground, right here in the Capitol, trying to catch one of their own agents."

DeMarco opened his mouth to rail at Smith, to tell him that if he'd had the right manpower guarding Emma, *his* guys might have spotted Li Mei and the Chinese. But before DeMarco could say anything, Smith said, "Well, the good news is that the FBI will jump all over this now that we know Li Mei's here. *And* they can't give me any more crap about how protecting Emma is a DIA problem."

"You know," DeMarco said, "I'm getting pretty goddamn tired of all this interagency, bureaucratic bullshit. You guys need to—"

"I'm leaving the country," Emma said. "I'm going to get on a plane using a false name and switch planes a couple of times before I get to where I'm going. Li Mei doesn't have the resources to find me."

"Then what?" Smith said. "You stay in exile for the rest of your life?"

"I don't know," Emma said. "But I do know that no one else is going to get killed because of me."

Smith snorted. "I got a better idea," he said. "We'll set you up someplace—like a cabin on a beach with good lines of fire. We'll make sure she knows you're there, I don't know how yet, but we will. Then we'll surround the place with snipers in gillie suits. I'll be there myself. And when Li Mei shows up, I'll put a bullet right through her fuckin' heart."

DeMarco's first reaction to Smith's statement was: *Why didn't you just do that in the first place?* He also realized at that moment that Smith was a cold-blooded killer. He talked about waffles and looked about as lethal as the late Mr. Rogers, but DeMarco suddenly realized that affable Bill Smith was a member of the same lethal club that Emma belonged to. He'd kill Li Mei without hesitation and not lose a wink of sleep afterward.

"I don't want her killed, Bill," Emma said. "I want her off the streets but I don't want her dead."

"Are you nuts, Emma?" Smith said. "That woman has killed—how many?—seven, eight people since this thing started? And she's going to kill you for sure the next time she gets a chance."

"We made her what she is, Bill. Me and the damn CIA. Those bastards."

68

Mahoney walked out of the bar, drunk but not too drunk. He laughed at that. The Irish in him said there was no such thing as *too* drunk

As the elevator descended to the parking garage, Mahoney thought that it had been a grand evening, putting that rat Morgan back in his cage. And seeing Myra again. She'd aged well; she looked great. He had thought about asking her to meet him at his hotel for a drink after her shift ended, but he didn't. He didn't want to put her on the spot. And maybe, he thought, just maybe, he was getting too old for that sort of thing.

Nah. He laughed out loud.

The elevator doors opened. Now where the hell had he parked his car? He should never have driven to the bar; he should have driven back to his hotel, parked the car there, and taken a cab to his meeting with Morgan. But he'd been late, so he had driven straight to the bar. Normally, Mahoney would never have rented a car at all. He would have had someone drive him, but when he came up here to squash Morgan he also scheduled a lunchtime speech to a bunch of Rotarians or Shriners—some group like that—and after the lunch he met with a couple of guys, guys he needed to open their wallets, but not guys he wanted people to know he was meeting. So he'd driven himself—and now here he was, half in the bag, and stuck with a car he couldn't find.

He checked the markings on the pillars in the garage. Yeah, he was on the right level. He'd just have to wander around until he found the damn car. It was a big, black Lincoln. It shouldn't be that hard to find—he hoped.

As he searched for his car, his knee started to ache. Damn shrapnel. He hoped the little motherfucker that had planted that mine was crippled with arthritis. That was funny, now that he thought about it. He didn't want the guy dead, whoever he'd been. That war had been a long time ago. His enemy was now as old as he was, maybe older, and Mahoney wished him well—well with a limp.

Where the fuck was his car? Ah, there it was. Big as life. He reached into his pocket and searched for the keys. Now where were the keys? Jesus, he was losing his mind. He hoped he hadn't left them up in the bar. Ah, there they were. He was a lucky man. Yes, he was.

He started to insert the key into the lock when he felt something hard pressed into the middle of his back.

"Get in van, old man," a voice said. The voice sounded young and foreign.

Aw, shit. Mahoney turned to see who was speaking: a young guy, probably Vietnamese, five foot six, and maybe all of eighteen years old. He was holding a Glock.

Mahoney was entitled to security and could have it any time he wanted. His security was normally provided by the U.S. Capitol Police but sometimes, because he was third in line for the presidency, the Secret Service insisted he take their protection. If the national threat level was high, or on those rare occasions a threat was made against him, or like last year when the vice president had his bypass operation, they didn't give him a choice. But most times, Mahoney avoided bodyguards; they tended to cramp his style. And on this particular trip, he hadn't wanted anybody with him. So as fate would have it, the one time he drives himself and doesn't bring his security, he gets held up by a little Vietnamese punk in a parking garage. Fate obviously didn't know his rank.

"You go to van," the Vietnamese kid said again, jerking his head in the direction of a black van that was two parking spaces away.

"Son," Mahoney said, "do you know who I am?"

"Don't care," the kid said. "You go to van or I put bullet in your . . . in your foot."

"Come on," Mahoney said. "Just take m'damn wallet. It's in my back pocket, left-hand side. There's probably three hundred bucks in there. Credit cards, too."

"Look at me," the kid said. Mahoney looked down, into the kid's eyes, then nodded his head and walked slowly toward the van.

And it had been such a grand evening up until now.

69

DeMarco sprinkled the Parmesan cheese, making sure it was evenly spread. The sprinkling of the Parmesan— not too much, not too little—was the last step, the bow on the package, the signature on the painting.

The lasagna recipe had been passed down to him from his father who had inherited it from his mother who had inherited it from her mother. As DeMarco had no children, the possibility existed that the recipe would go with him to his grave. But DeMarco wouldn't allow such a thing to happen. He could not be that selfish. If he never fathered a child, he would, in his final years, find a worthy recipient. He would search the globe to find this person. It would be the last, great quest of his twilight years.

This made him think: What if he collapsed from a sudden heart attack? He needed to have his will revised and a copy of the recipe placed in a vault. No, a mere recipe would not do. A list of ingredients and mixing instructions and cooking times could never capture the process of creation. He'd have to record himself on video as he made the dish. Yes, he would pass on his knowledge from beyond the grave. In fact, that's the way he'd start the video: "If you're watching this, I must be dead. But I bring to you from beyond the grave the taste of paradise."

DeMarco covered his lasagna with aluminum foil and checked the oven temperature. The oven was ready, preheated to the exact, required degree. He placed the lasagna carefully inside the oven, precisely in the center of the cooking box, and set the timer. The lasagna would cook covered for forty-five minutes. When the timer sounded, he would remove the aluminum foil and it would bake another ten minutes, until the Parmesan was golden brown. Then the dish would be taken gently from the oven and allowed to *rest* for fifteen minutes. He hoped Diane Carlucci was punctual. He would be annoyed if she was late and he had to reheat his masterpiece in the microwave. Such an act could end their relationship before it was ever consummated.

Well, maybe not.

DeMarco was really looking forward to seeing Diane. She had called two nights ago and said she had been transferred back to D.C. and would be there for the next six months. DeMarco had dated a woman who worked at the Department of Interior for four months last year, but that relationship had gone the way all of his other recent relationships had gone—due south—and there had been no one since then who had really mattered. Maybe this time things would work out differently. That Diane looked and sounded like his ex-wife—a point that Emma had made the first time she saw her—was a fact which DeMarco chose not to dwell upon.

He checked his watch. While his lasagna cooked he'd have just enough time to shower and shave—and change the sheets on his bed in case he got lucky. And he was feeling lucky. He opened a bottle of wine, a strong red that two Italians could appreciate, and headed for the shower.

Thirty minutes later he was back in his kitchen, squeaky clean and perfectly groomed. He put on an apron—a plain blue, manly one—and poured himself a glass of wine. The wine was perfect. He was glad he had bought two bottles. He made a salad and was just starting to set the table when the doorbell rang.

She was early. This was good. They'd share a glass of wine before dinner. He started to take off the apron as he walked toward the door then changed his mind. Nothing wrong with a man in an apron. He opened the door, a smile on his face—a smile which collapsed when he saw Phil Carmody standing there pointing a gun at his chest.

"Move back," Carmody said.

DeMarco did. Now it bothered him that he was wearing the apron. For some reason he felt that it gave Carmody an advantage—an absurd thought, considering that the man had a gun and had been trained by the U.S. Navy to kill in multiple ways.

"What's cookin'?" Carmody said. "Smells good."

"Lasagna," DeMarco said.

Carmody looked at the set dining-room table. "You're expecting company. When's she arriving?"

"Any moment now."

"That's not good," Carmody said.

"What do you want?"

"I want you to set up a meeting between Li Mei and Emma."

"Fuck you."

"Yeah, I thought you might say that." Carmody pulled a cell phone from his pocket and, while still pointing the gun at DeMarco, punched a single button. "It's me," he said after a moment. "Put the big guy on."

Carmody handed the phone to DeMarco. "John Mahoney is on the other end of that phone. Ask him where he's at right now."

Oh, shit. DeMarco took the phone from Carmody. "Boss?" he said.

"Yeah, it's me. Do you have any idea what's going on?"

"No."

"Ask him where he is," Carmody said.

"Boss, where are you?"

"I'm in a van with three Vietnamese punks. We're on 95 South heading toward D.C. But I don't know what the hell's going on."

"Give me the phone," Carmody said and De-Marco handed it back to him. "Mr. Speaker," Carmody said into the phone, "this is Phil Carmody. As long as DeMarco does what I want, you'll be in your office in the morning. I promise. Now will you tell him to obey me, sir?"

"Kiss my ass," Mahoney said.

Carmody laughed and hung up.

"What are you doing, Carmody?" DeMarco said.

"I told you. I need you to set up a meeting between Emma and Li Mei. I had the Chinese embassy out here do a lot of research on you. They found out you worked for Mahoney, so I figured if I had him, you would be a lot more inclined to cooperate."

"Are you insane, Carmody? He's the Speaker of the House. Do you think you can kidnap him and walk away from this?"

"Yeah, I do. We've got about ten hours, DeMarco. That's how long it'll take Mahoney to make it back to D.C. If we're done in ten hours, he'll be set free, right on the steps of the Capitol. No one will even know he was kidnapped unless he tells them."

"And if I don't cooperate?" DeMarco said.

"Don't go there, DeMarco. Like you said, he's the Speaker. You don't want to risk his life. You *can't* risk his life."

Before DeMarco could answer, the doorbell rang. Diane Carlucci. Right on time.

Goddamnit.

❖

"Joe, I'm busy packing," Emma said. "What do you want?"

Emma, always the charmer.

"Emma, Carmody's here in my house. He's pointing a gun at me and Diane Carlucci."

"Who?"

"Diane Carlucci. The FBI agent I met in Vancouver?"

"What does Carmody want?"

"I'll let him tell you. But Emma, there's something else you need to know. He had some guys kidnap Mahoney."

DeMarco heard Emma suck in a breath. "Put him on, Joe."

Carmody took the phone from DeMarco. "Ms.—" Carmody started to say.

"What do you want?" Emma said.

"I want you to meet with Li Mei."

"So she can kill me."

"No. So I can capture her."

"What?"

"You heard me. I don't want you dead and I don't want Li Mei dead. But I can't get close to her. So I want you to set up a meeting with her, and when you do, I'll take her."

Emma didn't say anything for a moment. "You're working for the Chinese government, aren't you, Carmody? You're the one who saved me at my club."

"We don't have time to get into that now," Carmody said. "Now listen to me. There's a lot at stake here. DeMarco, this young lady from the FBI, and the Speaker. Are you willing to sacrifice all of them?"

"What do I have to do?" Emma said.

Diane Carlucci looked mad enough to kill.

She was tied, hand and foot, to one of DeMarcos kitchen chairs, and she was gagged. And the chair was tied to the refrigerator so she couldn't move it.

"I'm sorry about this, Ms. Carlucci," Carmody said. "I truly am. But this'll all be over in a few hours, and then you and Mr. DeMarco can enjoy the dinner he made you."

The sounds Diane made then were muffled by the gag, but DeMarco could guess what she was saying.

Carmody had been the complete gentleman. He'd let Diane get a drink of water and go to the bathroom before he tied her to the chair. And he'd allowed DeMarco to turn on the small television in the kitchen so she'd have something to watch while she sat there. He'd even allowed DeMarco to take his lasagna out of the oven and put it in the refrigerator.

You couldn't ask for a nicer kidnapper.

DeMarco looked apologetically at Diane, which made that about the millionth apologetic look he'd given her.

"Okay," Carmody said, "let's get this show on the road."

70

"I gotta take a piss," Mahoney said. He could see out of the front windshield of the van. They had been driving for two hours now and had just passed Hartford, Connecticut.

There were three young Vietnamese gangsters in the van. The driver, a guy in the passenger seat, and the little bastard with the hard eyes sitting in the back of the van with Mahoney. The kid in the back leaned against the back of the passenger seat looking at Mahoney through bored, hooded eyes. He held the Glock loosely in his right hand and didn't seem particularly concerned that Mahoney would try anything.

The three kidnappers were all kids; Mahoney doubted that any of them was even twenty. The guy in the passenger seat—the passenger—was particularly young, maybe fourteen or fifteen. God-awful rap music was coming from the radio and the driver and passenger were bantering back and forth in Vietnamese. If they were worried that they had just kidnapped one of the most powerful politicians in America, they didn't show it.

Mahoney could see how Carmody had set up the kidnapping. The lunchtime engagement with the Elks, or whoever that group was, had been written up in a couple papers and posted on Web sites. The Vietnamese guys probably picked him up at the luncheon then followed him until they found a good place to snatch him, the parking garage being ideal. Mahoney was also pretty certain that these immigrant kids had no idea who he was. He may have been a recognizable figure in his home state, but get more than ten miles outside the D.C. Beltway and most Americans couldn't *name,* much less identify, the Speaker of the House. To these immigrant kids he was just some fat, old white guy they'd been told to kidnap.

"Hey! Did you hear me, you little prick?" Mahoney yelled. "I said I gotta take a piss."

Mahoney wasn't restrained in any way. He was sitting with his back against the double back doors of the van. The back doors were locked so even if he wanted to jump out of a vehicle going sixty miles an hour, he couldn't. He held a bottle of bourbon in his hand. A full one. The kidnappers had given it to him. Carmody had obviously researched him enough to know some of his habits but not enough to know his preferred brand. Mahoney was guessing the three punks had been told to buy him a bottle and let him get drunk and pass out, figuring he'd be less trouble that way. It really pissed him off how little respect the bastards were showing him. Not respect for him as the Speaker—but respect for him as a man. They had no doubt that they could easily handle an unarmed, overweight guy with white hair—as if he were no more of a threat to them than a ten-year-old child—and that pissed him off more than the kidnapping itself.

"Hey!" Mahoney yelled. "I said—"

"You shut up," the little Vietnamese gunman said. He turned and said something to the driver and the driver and the passenger began to laugh, the passenger pounding the dash board as if he'd just heard the funniest joke of his young life.

"If I piss my pants, I'm gonna kill you all," Mahoney said. And he wasn't kidding.

"You shut up," the gunman said. "We stop in a minute." He paused then added, "We told not to hurt you, but you call me prick again, I pistol-whip you. You understand?"

Mahoney smiled.

Five minutes later the van took an exit off the highway. They drove five more minutes then stopped on a dark, isolated section of road near a fallow field. The driver pushed a button and Mahoney heard the back doors of the van unlock. The driver and the passenger exited the van and the driver opened the rear doors so Mahoney could get out.

The gunman said, "You piss fast."

Mahoney started to say that with his prostate that wasn't possible, but decided not to say anything. The gunman barely spoke English and he'd had no indication the other two kids spoke any at all. His prostate joke—not that it was a joke—wouldn't be appreciated.

He stepped from the back of the van with some difficulty. His joints had stiffened while he was sitting and his shrapnel-damaged knee was aching like a bitch. He wandered over to the side of the road and unzipped his pants. The driver and gunman stood behind him. The third kid, the passenger, stood beside Mahoney and peed with him, as if they were old drinking buddies.

Mahoney looked up at the sky. There were a lot of stars in the sky, visible now that they were away from the smog of the city. That always amazed him, how many stars there were. He remembered looking up at the stars during the war and experiencing the same sense of wonderment. He'd been afraid back then, lying in a foxhole or near some rice paddy, waiting for guys that looked just like these kids to sneak up and kill him. He'd been a kid himself then.

But he wasn't afraid now—and was surprised he wasn't.

He just wished he knew what the hell was going on.

71

DeMarco had been told to take the Metro. He exited the subway at Gallery Place and passed under the great, colorful arch on H Street that marked the entry to Washington's Chinatown. He could feel that he was being watched as he walked down the street.

He walked a block. As Carmody had told him, on one side of the street, the side he was on, was a Red Roof Inn. Across the street were four run-down row houses in a white brick structure. Three of the houses had red doors; the fourth house, the one closest to the corner, had a green door. He crossed the street, walked up to the green door, and turned the doorknob. It was unlocked. He started to open the door but before he did, he looked behind him.

There were three Chinese men and they were less than ten feet away, staring at him. Where in the hell had they come from? It was as if they had just materialized out of the steam coming from the grate in the sidewalk.

"I'm here to see Li Mei," he said to the trio. "I'm not a cop," he added.

The men didn't answer; they just continued to stare.

Jesus, he thought—or maybe he was praying. He opened the door and saw a set of stairs that ascended to the second story of the house. He started up the stairs. If they shot him in the back, he hoped they killed him. He didn't want to end up a quadriplegic.

Carmody had told him that Li Mei had been using a Chinese gang to watch Emma. That's why Emma and Rolf had never seen her near Emma's place. The gang, there were about twenty of them, half of them teenage boys and girls, would take turns watching Emma, following her, and reporting back to Li Mei. Carmody suspected the gang didn't know who Li Mei was, just a woman with lots of cash willing to pay them for easy work.

"But I can't approach her," Carmody had said. "I could kill her—a long shot with a rifle—but I can't

get near her. She has the gang all over the street acting as lookouts."

Carmody didn't tell DeMarco that he had imi-
tated Li Mei's strategy and hired kids from a Vietnamese gang to kidnap Mahoney.

Carmody had told DeMarco to be careful approaching Li Mei. "One-celled organisms have more
conscience than these gangsters. They'll kill you and
go eat dinner afterward, and not give it a thought."

What Carmody hadn't told him was exactly how
he was supposed to be careful.

At the top of the stairs there was another door.
Chinese symbols were painted on the door, which
DeMarco naturally couldn't read. He knocked,
waited a few seconds, and knocked again. He turned
and looked down the stairs. The three Chinese were
halfway up the stairs. Two of the men were in their
twenties; the third, a man wearing a Redskins jacket,
was older, maybe in his midthirties. The one in the
lead had a gun in his hand now, held down by the
side of his leg. DeMarco turned back to face the door;
he thought he saw the peephole darken.

The door opened. It was Li Mei.

This was the closest DeMarco had been to her,
and he had two immediate impressions. The first
was that he was standing a foot away from the most
lethal person he had ever known, a woman who had
killed eight people and who would kill him without
hesitation. The second was that she was stunning,

and he could understand how John Washburn had been captivated by her.

"Who are you?" she said.

"You know who I am," DeMarco said. "I'm the guy who was with Emma in the racquetball court, the guy you tried to kill." He wondered if Li Mei really didn't recognize him, if Emma was the only one she could see.

"How did you find me?"

"Emma followed one of your pals," DeMarco said, jerking his thumb in the direction of the three men on the stairs.

"You're lying," Li Mei said.

"Emma wants to meet with you."

Li Mei smiled at this.

"Think about it," DeMarco said. "If she wanted you dead or captured, I wouldn't be here. The cops would."

"Maybe they're on the way," Li Mei said, but she didn't look nervous.

"You know they're not."

Li Mei nodded. "Why does she want to meet?"

"I'm not sure exactly," DeMarco said. "To clear this up, I guess."

Li Mei laughed, her laughter sounding a bit hysterical to DeMarco. "To clear this up!" she said. "What does that mean? What the *hell* does that mean?"

"I don't know," DeMarco said. "All I know is that Emma said too many people have died and she doesn't want to be responsible for any more deaths. She wants to meet and talk. Like I said before, if she wanted you dead the FBI would be here instead of me."

That was the strongest argument DeMarco had.

"And where does she want to meet?" Li Mei said.

"You pick. She said if she named a place, you'd think it was a trap. Pick any place you want except here in Chinatown."

"Why are you acting as her messenger?"

"Because she asked me to. I'm her friend."

"Has it occurred to you. . . . What's your name again?"

"DeMarco."

"Has it occurred to you, DeMarco, that you may be a dead man?"

"Yeah. But if you kill me, you'll never see Emma again. She said if you didn't agree to the meet, she'd disappear and you'll never find her. And she said that if I wasn't at the meeting, alive, she wouldn't show herself. She's not going to let you use me for a hostage."

Li Mei laughed again, then said something in Chinese. DeMarco heard the men behind him thunder up the steps. He began to turn to face them, but before he could, one of them slammed into his back and drove him into the apartment. He hit the floor hard and felt his face burn as it skidded along a linoleum floor.

72

Mahoney heard the driver say something to the gun-man in the back of the van and then the gunman and the driver started arguing. The passenger chipped in and the gunman screamed at him, too. The three kids yelled at each other for a couple of minutes, then the gunman appeared to give in, capitulating to whatever they were haggling about.

Mahoney twisted the cap off the bourbon bottle and took a small sip, his first drink since he'd been given the bottle. He needed to keep his head clear but one sip wouldn't hurt. He wondered what the murderous little shits were fighting about.

Fifteen minutes later, the van took an exit. They were someplace in New Jersey, not too far from

Trenton, but Mahoney didn't know exactly where; he'd missed the exit sign. They took a left off the exit and drove a couple of blocks until they reached a McDonald's. The driver started to park the van near the entrance to the restaurant but the gunman said something, and the driver drove to the rear of the restaurant and parked near the Dumpsters.

Mahoney was relieved. They'd been arguing about stopping to eat, or maybe where to eat. Either one was better than them debating about where to dump his body.

"You hungry, old man?" the gunman said.

"Yeah," Mahoney said. And he was, which surprised him. "I'll take a Big Mac, fries, and coffee. Two creams, two sugars in the coffee."

The gunman smiled at this and said something in Vietnamese to the kids in front. They all laughed.

"You pay," the gunman said.

Mahoney swore and reached for his wallet. He took out a twenty and tossed it to the gunman. The driver made a gesture with his fingers and Mahoney tossed him another twenty.

The driver killed the engine, then he and the passenger started to exit the van. Before they did, the gunman said something and the driver put the keys back in the ignition and turned on the radio. As the driver and passenger headed for the McDonald's entrance, the kid guarding Mahoney said, "You make noise, I shoot you in gut."

Mahoney almost said: How would anyone hear me over that shit coming from the radio? But he didn't. Fuckin' rap music; it was driving him nuts.

Mahoney figured it would take the other two guys about ten minutes to get the food. He looked over at the guy guarding him and the kid stared back dispassionately. What a cold-blooded little son of a bitch he was.

Mahoney was sitting down, his legs stretched out in front of him. The gunman was maybe five feet away. Mahoney picked up the whiskey bottle and started to twist the cap, but the bottle slipped out of his hands, rolling to the other side of the van. "Shit," Mahoney said. The Vietnamese kid sneered. Mahoney couldn't reach the bottle sitting down so he got awkwardly to his knees, his joints stiff from sitting. From a kneeling position he leaned forward and grasped the bottle, grunting at the effort. Still kneeling, he twisted the cap off, raised it to his lips— then let the bottle slip out of his hand.

When the bottle fell, Mahoney pretended to make an effort to grab it but he actually pushed it toward the gunman. The kid shrieked something in Vietnamese. The van was new and clean. And it was carpeted in the back. Mahoney imagined the kid didn't want his fancy van stinking of cheap bourbon. The kid lunged toward the whiskey bottle, to upright it, and the gun in his hand was momentarily pointed toward the floor. When the kid lunged, so did Mahoney. He doubted he'd be fast enough, but if he wasn't, he was betting the kid had orders not to kill him. As he fell toward the kid from his kneeling position, the kid looked up, eyes wide, and Mahoney hit him in the face with a fist the size of a small ham. Mahoney heard bones in the kid's face break.

"There, you son of a bitch," Mahoney said. He was lying on top of the kid because his lunge had propelled him forward. He got off him, picked up the gun, and tossed it to the front of the van. He also picked up the whiskey bottle and checked the level. About half the bourbon had spilled out. He put the whiskey bottle in one of the cup holders between the front seats. Waste not, want not, as his mother used to say.

The kid stirred and Mahoney raised his big fist to hit him again—he couldn't afford to have him regain consciousness—but then he lowered his arm. The kid was out cold; he wasn't going to wake up anytime soon.

Mahoney had to get out of the van but the rear doors were locked. He tried to get to the front seat but he couldn't get his big ass over the top of the seats or his gut through the space between the seats. He looked down at the kid again to make sure he wasn't coming to. On the driver's side door he could see the button that locked all the doors. He lunged and almost reached the button. He lunged again.

He must have looked comical, his broad butt in the air, straining to reach the locking mechanism. He hit the mechanism on his third try and heard the lock on the van's back doors release. He scooted to the back of the van, opened the double doors, and stepped out of the van.

He needed to hurry. He reached back inside the van, lying on his stomach, stretching, until he could touch the unconscious kid's feet. He pulled the kid straight out the back of the vehicle, letting the bastard fall hard to the ground, his head bouncing off the asphalt.

"Little asshole," Mahoney said to the unconscious kid.

He pulled the Vietnamese kid to one side, so he wasn't in the way of the rear tires, and hustled to the front of the van. He started to get into the van but then stopped and went back to the kid and searched his pockets until he found the cell phone he'd seen him using earlier.

Mahoney opened the driver's side door and hopped into the van. The seat was so close to the steering wheel he could hardly move but he didn't want to take the time to adjust it. He turned the key in the ignition and started the van. He had to study the gearshift knob to figure out where reverse was, finally figured it out, put the van in reverse—and stalled the van.

"Son of a bitch," he muttered. He started the van again and this time backed it up.

As he pulled out of the McDonald's lot he let out a whoop.

He felt great, maybe the best he'd felt in years.

73

Emma drove to DeMarco's place and found Carmody sitting nonchalantly on the front porch. He
walked calmly to Emma's car carrying a gym bag in
his right hand. He opened the passenger-side door
of the Mercedes, tossed the gym bag onto the floor,
and entered the car. "Hi," he said to Emma.

Hi—like they were buddies commuting to
work. Emma wondered what it would take to rattle
Carmody.

"Now what?" she said.

Carmody explained. He concluded with, "Now
we wait until Li Mei calls you."

"She may not call," Emma says. "She'll be afraid
of a trap."

"She'll call. She's obsessed with you. And when she does call, for your friend's sake—and for Mr. Mahoney's sake—you better convince her to meet with you."

They sat in silence for a few minutes before Emma said, "Why are you doing this, Carmody?"

"My employers want her back. She's become an embarrassment."

"Bullshit," Emma said. "The Chinese want the files she has but then they want her *dead*. You want her alive for some other reason."

Carmody shrugged.

"I've met you before, by the way," Carmody said.

"Oh?" Emma said.

"Yeah. You briefed a SEAL team one night, ten, twelve years ago. We were on a sub off the coast of Libya. We were all wearing wet suits with hoods, so you wouldn't have gotten that good a look at us."

Emma studied Carmody's face. "I don't remember you but I remember that op. One of you died."

"Yeah, but we got the target."

Emma nodded; SEALs always got the target.

"When you showed up in Bremerton, I recognized you. You have a memorable face. I figured maybe you'd switched jobs, but going from spy to congressional staff seemed pretty unlikely."

"So you're the one who put Li Mei onto me."

"Yeah. She was my control. But I didn't know about her history with you at the time. The Chinese told me about that after she tried to kill me in Vancouver."

"Why'd she try to kill you?"

Carmody shrugged. "She didn't need me anymore. I guess she was just making sure the Americans wouldn't have time to interrogate me in depth and find out more about her and the shipyard op. But who knows with her."

"How'd you find her here in D.C.?"

"The Chinese and I figured she'd go after you, so the Chinese watched you while you were in the hospital in Vancouver. When you left the hospital, they helped me get out of Canada. Then I watched you until I spotted Li Mei's guys."

"Her guys?" Emma said.

"She recruited a Chinese gang to help her. They're helping her now."

Emma shook her head. *She* should have spotted Li Mei's people *and* she should have spotted Carmody. The fact was, she had lost her edge. Everything that had transpired in the last month had shown that she wasn't as good as she'd once been. Or maybe Carmody and Li Mei were just a lot better.

"How did you set up this thing with Mahoney so quick, so soon after what happened at my club?"

"I didn't set it up that quick. I've been watching Li Mei for a week, trying to figure out some way to separate her from that gang, and I came up with the idea of using you. And Mahoney. But she took me completely by surprise going after you at that fancy club today. It's like her cork just popped. I was lucky I got there when I did. I could have killed her but she got away before I could capture her. But after the thing at the club, I had everything in place to take Mahoney."

Carmody was as good as anyone Emma had ever worked with. "Carmody," she said, "how'd a man like you ever become a traitor? And don't tell me it was the money."

Emma's cell phone rang before Carmody could answer.

—◆—

Mahoney drove to the next exit on the highway, about five miles from the McDonald's, and stopped at a gas station. He spent a couple minutes finding the lever that allowed him to move the friggin' seat back, and then took a sip from the whiskey bottle that he'd placed in the cup holder.

Now what?

The smart thing to do would be to call the cops. The problem was that Carmody had DeMarco and Mahoney had no idea where they were. So if he called the cops, would that endanger DeMarco? Maybe, but probably not. The Vietnamese kids, if they hadn't already, would soon call Carmody. Mahoney had the one kid's cell phone but all the little bastards had cell phones these days. And if they told Carmody that

Mahoney had escaped—that old, fat, white-haired Mahoney had gotten away from them—would Carmody kill DeMarco? Yeah, possibly, but not right away. Carmody had those punks kidnap him to make DeMarco do something, so they needed Joe alive, at least for a while.

So he'd call the cops. Immediately. If the cops could catch the Vietnamese kids—they were probably walking around near the McDonald's right now looking for a car to steal or hijack—then maybe the cops could make them talk, make them tell where Carmody was. Remembering the hard eyes on the little shit that he'd knocked out, he didn't think so, but maybe.

Mahoney took another sip from the bottle. It was lousy bourbon but tonight it tasted as good as any he'd ever had.

Now who should he call? He could call anyone: the governor of New Jersey, the director of the FBI, the attorney general. The problem was he didn't know their damn phone numbers. He could call Perry Wallace, his chief of staff, and get the numbers or get Perry to call, but that would take time. He needed to get those kids picked up right away.

So Mahoney did what any other citizen would do: he called 911.

———— ◆◆◆ ————

DeMarco's hands were duct taped behind his back. Li Mei and her three friends had hustled him through the apartment to a closet in a bedroom. In the back of the closet was a concealed door. The hidden door in the closet led to a hallway in the adjacent, connecting row house, and from that hallway they took stairs to the roof and then down a fire escape into an alley where a late-model, full-sized sedan was parked. Li Mei was making sure that if DeMarco had brought people with him, or if Emma was watching, they wouldn't be followed.

They drove away from Chinatown, through the District, and crossed the Potomac via the Fourteenth Street Bridge. DeMarco was in the backseat sandwiched between two of the Chinese guys. The third man drove while Li Mei sat in the passenger seat, staring out the window. The Chinese men never said a word to him or each other. They were hard, silent, and unemotional—pros just doing a job. The man sitting next to DeMarco was wearing a long-sleeved shirt but DeMarco could see tattoos banding the man's wrists, and he figured the tattoos went all the way up his arms. DeMarco bet that if the guy took off his shirt there'd be a big damn dragon tattooed on his back.

The driver merged onto the George Washington Memorial Parkway and five minutes later took the exit for the Columbia Island Marina. The marina was at the southeastern end of Lady Bird Johnson Park and bounded on one side by the George Washington Parkway and on the other side by a small tributary off the Potomac called the Boundary Channel. The Boundary Channel was the path the boats took from the marina to enter the main section of the river. DeMarco could see why Li Mei had picked this place to meet Emma: it was only fifteen minutes from downtown D.C. but at ten p.m. the marina was closed to the public and was dark and deserted—and the Potomac made for a nice place to toss a body if one were so inclined.

They drove down a short access road and into a large parking lot. At the end of the parking lot was a building containing a snack bar and offices for the people who operated the marina. On the left side of the parking lot was an area suitable for sunbathing and picnicking, planted with grass and small shrubs and trees. In the center of this grassy section was a public restroom, a low brick structure. On the right side of the parking lot was the Boundary Channel, and seven or eight piers, each about sixty yards in length, jutted out into the channel. There were a couple hundred powerboats docked at the piers. The driver drove to the end of the parking lot then turned the car around so it faced the access road. The marina concession stand and offices were now behind the car, about fifty yards away.

They pulled DeMarco from the backseat, then Li Mei spoke to the three gangsters for a couple of minutes in Chinese. As she talked, one of the men took weapons from the trunk of the car. The weapons were identical, as if the gang had stolen a crate of them from an armory or a gun shop. They were stubby-looking guns, machine guns DeMarco thought, something like Uzis. When Li Mei finished talking, the men walked off into the darkness, one in the direction of the picnic area, and one toward the marina offices so he'd be protecting Li Mei from the rear. The third man walked down the pier that was closest to Li Mei, and as he walked he broke the lightbulbs illuminating the pier.

The next thing DeMarco heard was the sound of wood ripping—as if someone was prying open a door or hatch cover with a crowbar. The sound came from the now unlighted pier. A moment later he heard diesel engines—the burbling, low-throated, rumble of big, twin inboards. It appeared that Li Mei's man on the pier had broken into a boat and hot-wired it. The engines were soon turned off and the marina was quiet again.

Why did Li Mei need a boat?

Once her men were in position, Li Mei pulled out a cell phone and called Emma at the number DeMarco had given her. Her dark eyes were feral, and like a cat's seemed to glow in the dark.

"Meet me at the Columbia Island Marina," she said into the phone. "Do you know where it is?"

There was silence as Emma responded.

Li Mei could have called Emma from Chinatown but DeMarco realized she wanted to make sure that Emma didn't get to the rendezvous ahead of her.

"How long will it take you to get here?" Li Mei said.

Another pause. "An hour! Bullshit!"

Another pause. "Okay, one hour, no more. If you're late, I'll kill your friend. If you're not alone, I'll kill your friend. If the police show up instead of you, I'll kill your friend."

Jesus. Was there some scenario where he didn't get killed?

Li Mei closed the cell phone and said to DeMarco, "You better hope she does what I told her. Now go stand there, at the front of the car."

Li Mei called out in Chinese. DeMarco was guessing she was telling her companions that Emma would be a while.

DeMarco leaned his butt against the hood of Li Mei's car, his hands still taped behind his back. He could hear the Potomac River—which made him think of shrouded bodies being carried out to sea by current and tide.

———◆———

Carmody and Emma stopped on the parkway, a hundred yards before the marina exit. It had only taken her ten minutes to get there, driving at breakneck speed from DeMarco's Georgetown home. Her meeting with Li Mei was scheduled to start in fifty minutes.

Carmody opened the gym bag lying at his feet. He pulled a tube of camouflage paint from the bag, streaked his face and hands with the paint, and put on a black watch cap. All his clothes were black: black cap, black turtleneck sweater, black jeans, black boots. The next thing he took from the bag was a knife in a scabbard; he strapped the scabbard to his right leg with Velcro straps. After the knife came a silencer, which he screwed onto the barrel of the .22 pistol he had been holding. Then he took another pistol from the bag, a backup gun. He shoved the backup weapon into his belt behind his back. He executed the move so quickly that Emma wasn't able to identify the make of the second weapon. The last item Carmody took from his gym bag was a pair of night-vision goggles.

"Just like the good old days, isn't it, Carmody?" Emma said.

"No," he said. "Back then I did this for my country." There was an ache in his voice that surprised Emma.

"I need an hour," Carmody said.

"I'm supposed to meet her in forty-five minutes," Emma said. "She said she'd kill Joe if I wasn't on time."

"I need at *least* an hour," Carmody repeated.

"That's going to make her nervous. She's liable to bolt."

"Well, you better hope she doesn't."

Carmody reached up and pressed a switch so the dome light in Emma's car wouldn't come on when he opened the door. He placed his hand on the door handle but didn't open the door. "By the way," he said, "in case I don't get out of this alive and you do, tell the navy that the Chinese didn't get anything good from me."

"What are you talking about?"

"The basic technology on navy nuclear ships is pretty old at this point. The first Nimitz class carrier was built in 1972. The first Trident, in '79. The Chinese have had a lot of time to collect intelligence on our ships and there probably wasn't much that I gave them that they didn't have already. But when I got the CDs from the shipyard I went through them before I passed them on to Li Mei. I deleted the new stuff, particularly any mods made in the last four or five years. And I changed a lot of information in the manuals so some of what they got wasn't accurate. Anyway, the Chinese got a lot of stuff, maybe some stuff they never had before, but none of the recent modifications to propulsion plants or weapons systems. On the operational side, I gave them absolutely nothing of any value. They would have learned more from reading press releases. Tell the navy it was the best I could do and still . . . and still do what I needed to do."

"But *why* did you do it, Carmody? It wasn't for money, was it?"

Carmody ignored her question and opened his door. "If you want to get out of this alive, give me an hour," he said.

He was stepping from the car when Emma said, "The bottle rockets."

"What?" Carmody said.

"That stuff in the box we found in your house was for a kid. It was for *your* kid, wasn't it, Carmody?"

Carmody looked into Emma's eyes for a minute but he didn't answer her question. He shut the car door quietly and walked into the night.

"Where the hell is she?" Li Mei said.

"She'll be here," DeMarco said.

"She's ten minutes late."

"Where was she coming from?" DeMarco asked.

"She said Manassas. But she was probably lying."

"She wasn't lying; that's where she went after you tried to kill her at the club. It would take at least an hour to get here from Manassas because they're doing construction on Route 66. That would have slowed her down, even at this time of night."

That was a lie, about the construction. DeMarco didn't know why it was taking Emma so long to get to the marina but she—or Carmody—had to have a reason. But Li Mei didn't look satisfied by DeMarco's explanation. She was agitated, probably trying to figure out what sort of trap Emma was setting. He wondered how long it would be before she decided to kill DeMarco and abandon the rendezvous.

Time passed with agonizing slowness, and while the minutes crept by DeMarco wished for a number of things. He wished that he could smoke a cigarette; at this point lung cancer was the least of his worries. He wished that he had called his mother recently and told her that he loved her. He wished that Diane Carlucci hadn't been caught up in all this. He wished that he had taken that trip to Europe rather than just talking about it all these years. He wished that his marriage had lasted and that he had a kid. He wished. He wished. He wished.

A car turned onto the access road leading down to the marina. The car stopped for a moment at the head of the parking lot, then proceeded forward slowly, stopping again about a hundred feet from Li Mei's vehicle. It was Emma's Mercedes and her headlights were blinding DeMarco.

Carmody lay on the ground and peered through the night-vision goggles at the piers where the boats were moored. The boats—their hulls, their cabins—were all fluorescent green.

He didn't know how many people Li Mei had brought with her, but he was guessing three. The car that had transported Li Mei and DeMarco to the marina had bucket seats in the front and wouldn't comfortably hold more than five. This was assuming, of course, that another car hadn't transported more men and then parked somewhere else.

So far he'd found two of Li Mei's men. He found the first one almost immediately, hidden near the public restroom on the left side of the parking lot. He had guessed that a second man would be hidden near the marina office or snack bar, using the buildings for cover. The third guy would be on one of the piers behind Li Mei; that was the only place he could be.

It had taken him almost half an hour to get to the second man. He had to slither on his belly, using the sparse foliage around the marina for cover, and that took time. And to get to the marina office he had to pass within fifty yards of Li Mei's car. If Li Mei had turned to look in his direction while he was crawling she might have seen him. But she didn't turn.

He had just shot the second man in the back; he'd been hiding behind a Dumpster near the snack bar. Carmody studied the piers for a few minutes searching for the third man. He was most likely on the pier closest to Li Mei, but Carmody couldn't see him. He turned his head to look at Li Mei and DeMarco. DeMarco was still standing at the front of Li Mei's car, his butt resting against the hood. His hands were behind his back, and Carmody assumed they were tied or handcuffed. Li Mei was behind DeMarco, on his right-hand side, holding a pistol in her hand.

Carmody looked at his watch. Emma would be here any moment. To get the third man he had to search the piers and to do this he would have to go into the water. He didn't think there was time to get the third man before Emma arrived. He crawled to the river's edge.

Just before he entered the water he saw headlights at the top of the access road.

———◆———

Emma checked her watch. It was time. She turned the key in the ignition and switched on her headlights and pulled back onto the parkway. She exited at the marina access road and drove to the head of the parking lot. At the other end of the parking lot she could see a car and a man standing in front of the car. She assumed the man was DeMarco. She drove slowly through the empty parking lot and stopped a hundred feet from Li Mei's car. DeMarco was now clearly visible in her headlights and the expression on his face was grim. Grim and angry, but not afraid.

She couldn't see Li Mei.

Emma slouched down so her head was partially hidden by the steering wheel, then she opened the driver's side window and called out, "Li Mei, let Joe go. Let him walk up to the parkway. When he's out of sight, I'll get out of the car and we can talk."

Li Mei laughed, the sound coming from someplace in the darkness off to DeMarco's left. Li Mei must have moved as soon as she saw Emma's car start down the access road.

"And after he leaves, he calls the FBI," Li Mei said.

"No. As Joe told you, if I wanted you caught, the FBI would have arrested you in Chinatown. Or they would have been here by now. I just want to talk."

"About what?"

"Let Joe go, Li Mei. If you don't, I'll back this car up, block the access road, and call for help. Lots of help."

"You move your car and I'll kill him."

"But you won't get me. Now let him go."

DeMarco was thinking that Emma didn't realize that Li Mei had people hidden nearby. If she tried to move her car, the Chinese guys would shred her tires with their damn Uzis. And if Li Mei let him go to appease Emma, her men would certainly kill him before he reached the parkway. Li Mei wouldn't allow DeMarco to roam the parkway, trying to flag down a cop.

Emma—and DeMarco—waited for Li Mei's answer. She finally spoke, her voice now coming from a place on DeMarco's right. She was moving constantly so Emma couldn't be sure of her position.

"Go on, you," Li Mei said to DeMarco. "You can go."

DeMarco didn't move. Where was Carmody?

"What are you waiting for?" Li Mei said. "Move."

DeMarco still didn't budge. He couldn't help Emma—unarmed and with his hands taped behind his back—and if he walked away, one of Li Mei's people would come out of the dark and knife him as soon as he was out of sight. He needed a plan.

"Joe!" Emma said. "Just walk up to the parkway and keep walking. Don't call anyone. I'll be all right."

DeMarco thought Emma sounded surprisingly confident—but then she always sounded confident. Not knowing what else to do, DeMarco walked toward her car. As he neared her car he said quietly, "She has three guys with her. They've got machine guns."

"Don't stop," Li Mei yelled from the darkness.

"Keep walking, Joe," Emma said.

"Where's Carm—"

"Move, Joe!" Emma said.

Emma waited until DeMarco's figure disappeared into the darkness behind her, then she took a breath and stepped from her car. She had had a good life, an incredible life in many ways. If it all ended this night, here by the Potomac, in sight of the Pentagon, so be it. There were worse places to die.

She walked slowly toward Li Mei, her hands in the air to show she wasn't armed. She was wearing a tight-fitting pull over and jeans. She did a slow turn to show Li Mei she didn't have a gun behind her back.

"Turn off your headlights," Li Mei said. "A cop might see the car from the parkway and come down here. You don't want to be responsible for any more dead cops, do you?"

"No," Emma said, "you've killed enough people." She walked back to her car and reached through the open window to shut off the lights then turned and continued toward the sound of Li Mei's voice. She had yet to see Li Mei.

She had walked fifty paces when Li Mei said, "Stop."

Emma did.

"I know if I raise my head right now, I'll be shot," Li Mei said. "You have a sniper out there somewhere, don't you?"

"No," Emma said. "I came alone like I said I would."

Li Mei laughed. "You think I'd trust you?"

There was nothing to say to that.

"Why did you want this meeting?" Li Mei said. "Why didn't you have me arrested in Chinatown?"

Where was Carmody? Emma was running out of things to say.

"Because I don't want anyone else to die because of me, and if I had sent the FBI to Chinatown, a *lot* of people would have died. I came here to make you an offer, an offer to live. If you give up Carmody's and Washburn's files, and agree to cooperate with our intelligence agencies, in a few years you'll be free, free to live wherever you want, free to begin a new life."

Emma had no authority to make such a deal but that didn't really matter. She was just stalling.

Where are you, Carmody?

Li Mei didn't answer for several seconds. Then she stood up and walked toward Emma, a pistol in her hand.

"You're a fool to think I'd accept such an offer," Li Mei said. "And you were an even bigger fool to come here tonight."

Emma didn't say anything. She'd run out of words.

"There's a trawler waiting off Cape Henry," Li Mei said. "My people still want what's inside your head. So you're going to take a cruise. On your way to China, you'll be interrogated and tortured and probably raped. When you reach China you'll be interrogated and tortured some more. You'll betray your country and you'll die alone, debased and humiliated. *That* will make up for Hawaii."

Emma assumed that Li Mei was telling the truth: that she'd contacted the Chinese at some point in the last two hours and made a deal with them to take her if Li Mei could arrange delivery. But Emma also imagined the Chinese wanted Li Mei more than they wanted her.

"If you try to hand me over to your people they'll kill you, Li Mei."

"Maybe. Or maybe I'll make the exchange and survive. What I won't let them do is capture me. And if I die, I'll go to my death with the satisfaction of knowing that you'll suffer for months, maybe for years. That's enough for me."

Keep her talking.

"My God, Li Mei, you're still a young woman. Is that all you want from life, for me to suffer?"

"Yes," Li Mei said.

That was all, just "yes." Nothing mattered to her anymore than destroying Emma.

"One more thing," Li Mei said. "Your friend dies, too."

Li Mei suddenly called out in Chinese. She screamed, "Kill the white man." Emma's Chinese was too rusty to understand her but it didn't matter, she knew what Li Mei meant.

"No!" Emma screamed.

A moment later there was a burst of gunfire. It took Emma a few seconds to realize the shots had *not* come from behind her, the direction that DeMarco had taken, but from one of the piers.

———◆———

DeMarco had walked through the parking lot and started up the access road, toward the parkway. He turned his head once to look back at Emma and saw her standing near her car. He couldn't see Li Mei.

He looked around, into the darkness. Where the hell was the Chinese guy? He knew one of the men was on the pier near Li Mei and one was near the concession stand, but one had to be close to him, hidden somewhere on the grassy strip. And that big bastard Carmody, where was he?

He didn't think the Chinese gangster would shoot him; that would make too much noise. But any minute now, as soon as he was completely out of Emma's sight, and before he could reach the parkway, the guy was probably going to come out of the bushes and put a knife into his gut. He knew it. He had to get his hands free. Fast.

He looked behind him again. He could barely see Emma. Twenty yards away, there was a bend in the access road and there were trees near the bend. He walked toward the bend as fast as he could. He didn't think Li Mei would be able to see him there—the trees should block her view—but the Chinese guy on the grassy strip probably *could* see him. As soon as reached the bend he went for the nearest tree and started to scrape the tape binding his hands against the bark of the tree. He rubbed frantically, peeling off more skin than tape, and it hurt like hell—but finally the tape came free.

Now what? Run up to the parkway and try to flag down a car, or stay with Emma? The smart thing to do would be to run to the parkway before one of the Chinese guys could get to him. So he ran toward the parkway—but he wasn't going to abandon Emma.

DeMarco's idea was to run toward the parkway but before he reached it, he would double back. If the Chinese guy on the grassy strip was watching him, he'd think DeMarco was fleeing. So if he went toward the parkway and then looped back, he might be able to get behind the guy. Probably not a very good plan—probably a really dumb plan—but he didn't have a better one. He needed to find a big stick or rock, he thought, and then he started running.

DeMarco couldn't see well in the dark and he couldn't find Li Mei's man. He was moving slowly now, cautiously. Three or four minutes passed, maybe more, and he was almost back to the parking lot and he still hadn't seen the bastard. With his luck the guy was some kind of ninja who could make himself invisible. He continued to move forward, probing the darkness with his eyes. He hefted a big rock he'd picked up, ready to throw it if he saw the guy. And then he saw him.

He was lying on the ground near the public restroom, but he didn't seem to be hiding because he was lying on his back. DeMarco moved quickly forward, intending to launch himself at the man if he moved, but he didn't. He reached the man and touched him. He didn't move. He wasn't cold yet, but DeMarco thought he was dead. He didn't bother to check for a pulse; there wasn't time. Instead he searched the ground around the body with his hands. He found the man's gun, the Uzi or whatever the hell it was.

Now he was ready. He was pissed off and he was armed. Armed with a gun he didn't know how to shoot, but armed nonetheless. He started moving forward toward Li Mei's position. As he walked he tried to figure out where the safety on the gun was. He found a little switch near the trigger guard, but he didn't know which way to flip it and it was too dark to see any markings on the gun. Would the guy have had the safety on or off? DeMarco wondered. DeMarco bet the safety was off. If it had been him, the safety would have been off at this point.

And then he heard the sound of another Uzi firing.

Who the hell had they killed: Emma or Carmody?

Carmody let the current pull him along until he was next to the pier. As he floated he searched the pier through the night-vision goggles. A movement caught his eye and he finally saw the man on the pier. He was hiding behind the bow of a boat that jutted out over the pier. The man was in a position where he could observe Li Mei and Emma, and was maybe fifty yards from Li Mei's car.

Carmody noticed that this man was bigger than the two men he'd already neutralized, almost as big as him. He pulled off the night-vision goggles and let them sink into the river. He dove and swam past the man on the pier, past three moored boats, and pulled himself up onto the wooden planks of the pier. He was behind the man now.

He looked over toward the parking lot. Emma was out of her car and standing about twenty paces away from Li Mei. Li Mei was holding a pistol. He could hear the women talking but couldn't understand what they were saying.

Just keep her talking a minute longer, Carmody thought.

He crept up behind the man hiding on the pier, extended his right arm, and shot him in the back. Carmody's gun made no noise; just a puff of air, like a BB gun firing. That should have been it, game over, but the man had been holding his weapon with his finger on the trigger. When Carmody shot him, the Chinese gangster pulled reflexively on the trigger of his weapon and the Uzi gave off a noisy ten-round burst. Bullets skipped across the Boundary Channel, some hitting the wooden hull of a boat on the next pier.

Goddamnit, Carmody thought, and he immediately stood up and said in Chinese, "Everything's okay. I made a mistake." Then he started walking down the pier toward Li Mei and Emma. He hunched over a bit to minimize his height. It was dark on the pier and he figured that if he walked calmly, Li Mei might think, at least momentarily, that it was her man approaching. He only had to fool her for a few more seconds, just another thirty yards, until he was close enough to fire the pistol and be sure of hitting her.

Li Mei turned toward the sound of gunfire and heard Ming say everything was all right. But was that Ming?

No! The man was too big. Li Mei had excellent night vision. She could see the man now. It was Carmody!

She didn't know how he had gotten here—she thought she'd killed him in Vancouver, but she obviously hadn't. He wasn't dead; he was coming toward her. *He* was Emma's ace in the hole.

Li Mei immediately raised her pistol and fired— and she saw Carmody stagger.

Before Li Mei could fire a second shot at Carmody, Emma leaped forward, throwing herself at Li Mei. She drove the Chinese woman to the ground and was able to grasp Li Mei's right hand, the hand holding the pistol.

Emma struggled to get the gun away from Li Mei, but she was losing. Li Mei was stronger and younger—and insane. She was going to break Emma's grip any second.

Carmody picked himself up off the pier. Li Mei's weapon had struck his body armor—right where his heart was. He saw Emma and Li Mei wrestling and he smiled. He ran toward the women, his gun hand extended, and stopped about ten yards from them, close enough so he wouldn't miss. It didn't really matter to him which one he shot first. He started to pull the trigger.

At that moment, DeMarco burst from the darkness, wild-eyed, the Uzi in his hands. DeMarco was scared. He thought there were still two Chinese guys out there somewhere armed as he was, but instead he saw Carmody. Carmody was holding a pistol and it was aimed at Emma and Li Mei, and the two women were on the ground, fighting. Carmody was the immediate threat.

"Carmody!" he yelled. "Drop the gun."

Carmody spun in DeMarco's direction, the pistol in his hand now pointing toward DeMarco.

DeMarco didn't hesitate. He pulled the trigger on the weapon. He figured the gun shot so many bullets that some of them had to hit Carmody no matter how bad his aim. But when he squeezed the trigger nothing happened. The goddamn safety was on; he'd guessed wrong.

Carmody fired back immediately and hit DeMarco. DeMarco looked down at his chest in amazement and said, "Aw, shit." The Uzi dropped from his hand and he collapsed, his legs folding under him. He could see the Uzi, only a foot away, and he reached out for it but his arm was leaden, a useless deadweight attached to his shoulder.

Just before he disappeared into the void, DeMarco saw Carmody fire two more times.

First he shot Li Mei in the throat.

Then he shot Emma in the heart.

74

Mahoney shoveled a forkful of scrambled eggs into his mouth. He felt like a million bucks. Hell, a *zillion* bucks. He was practically grinning, even with his mouth full.

He looked across the table at Emma and De-Marco. Sourpusses, the both of them, sitting there glumly, barely touching their breakfasts. In Emma's case, breakfast was half a grapefruit and unbuttered toast. Life was just too short to eat that way, Mahoney thought.

"Yeah, you guys got your asses kicked on this one," Mahoney said. "But cheer up. You busted up a spy ring and took one very nasty bitch off the board."

Neither Emma nor DeMarco responded, but Emma looked at Mahoney like she might take her little pointed grapefruit spoon and shove it into his thick neck.

Carmody had beaten them all. He'd shot everyone—DeMarco, Emma, Li Mei, and Li Mei's three men—with tranquilizer darts. The dart gun had been Carmody's second weapon, the weapon that Emma hadn't recognized. He took Li Mei with him in Li Mei's car. The car was eventually found in Baltimore, near the harbor, and in the trunk of the car were the files that Carmody and Washburn had stolen for Li Mei.

Carmody also must have called the police at some point and told them about the unconscious people at the Columbia Island Marina. When DeMarco came to, there were both cops and paramedics looking down at him. DeMarco, Emma, and the three Chinese gangsters were lying together in the parking lot, handcuffed with plastic ties. The cops didn't know what had happened at the marina but when they found three Uzis, one of which had been fired, and a boat with bullet holes in its hull, they decided to treat everybody as criminals until they could sort things out.

The first thing DeMarco told the cops was that Mahoney had been kidnapped. The cops told De-Marco that the Speaker had escaped his captors. In the three hours that DeMarco had been unconscious, every law enforcement agency on the eastern sea-board had become aware of Mahoney's kidnapping and was looking for the three Vietnamese kids who had snatched him. The teenage gangsters were never found. They had hijacked a car just as Mahoney had thought they would, and vanished into the New Jersey night. The cops suspected they drove to a Vietnamese conclave in Trenton or New York and would hide there until they could be shipped out of the country.

DeMarco had asked the cops to get word to Mahoney that he and Emma were in their custody, and half an hour later they were free—embarrassed but free. DeMarco had been conscious almost an hour before he remembered to tell someone that Diane Carlucci was tied up in his kitchen.

But Carmody and Li Mei were gone. The FBI and all the three-initial spook shops were looking for them, but they had vanished.

"This guy Carmody," Mahoney said to Emma. "So you think there was a kid involved."

"Yes," Emma said. "The shoe box we found in his basement made me think of it, and yesterday I did something I should have done weeks ago: I contacted some people Carmody knew in Hong Kong when he worked for that security company over there. They told me he kept to himself and nobody knew him all that well, but they said he was involved with a local woman. One of them said he thought Carmody had a kid, a son. He wasn't sure, but he thought so."

A man like Philip Carmody wouldn't have betrayed his country for money. Emma's theory was that the Chinese government had used Carmody's Chinese wife and son to force him to spy on the shipyard in Bremerton, and he did as little damage to the navy as he could while still giving Li Mei enough to keep his family safe. Emma thought that the reason Carmody had captured Li Mei instead of killing her as the Chinese desired, was that he wanted her for a bargaining chip. He would have told the Chinese that he'd exchange Li Mei for his family, and that if the Chinese government didn't agree, he'd give her to the Americans. The Chinese would not want the publicity that would result from the capture of their rogue agent, but more important, they would be afraid that under interrogation she would tell the Americans things they didn't want told. One man and his small family just wasn't worth it.

"He's out there somewhere," Emma said, "setting up the exchange of Li Mei for his family. And then he'll disappear."

"And what do you think the Chinese will do with her?" Mahoney asked. Before Emma could answer he said, "Where the hell's the damn Tabasco?"

Mahoney's head was swiveling around to find a waitress when Emma said, "They'll kill her."

Mahoney shrugged. "After what she did, killing so many people to get at you, I say hooray for the Chinese."

"You just don't get it," Emma said, looking directly into Mahoney's eyes. "If the CIA hadn't bungled the capture of those two young people in Hawaii, her lover would never have died. He didn't have to die. And this woman was a *soldier*. If we had treated her humanely, if we hadn't tortured her, she wouldn't have lost her child. That's the thing that bothers me the most: her child. We talk about human rights then we act like barbarians. The CIA did it in Hawaii twenty years ago and we continue to do it in places like Abu Ghraib and Guantánamo Bay. We *have* to learn to act better than our enemies, Mr. Speaker."

Mahoney grew serious for a moment and said, "I get it, lady, and I feel bad about her kid, too. But she was a spy and a killer and madder than a hatter. She bad to be put down. But I agree with you: it's too bad, all the stuff that happened to her."

Before Emma could respond, Mahoney signaled a passing waitress. "Hey. sweetheart," he said, "could you find me a little Tabasco when you get a chance?"

"Oh my gosh yes, Mr. Speaker," the waitress gushed, and ran off to find the Tabasco sauce at a speed she would have normally used only to save her children from a fire. She returned within seconds and handed the small bottle to Mahoney, almost curtsying as she did so. He took the bottle from her, then took her work-worn hand in his and said, "Alice, if I wasn't married, I'd . . . well, it'd make you blush if I was to say what I was thinking."

Alice's plump face went beet red, her eyes fluttered like she might swoon, and you could almost see her stout heart hammering in her chest. Mahoney—old, overweight, and alcoholic—a man who said things so corny a screenwriter for a soap opera wouldn't use such lines, and women found him irresistible.

DeMarco, on the other hand, was pretty sure he wasn't irresistible. He'd called Diane a couple of times—she was still in Washington taking the FBI training course—but so far she always had an excuse for not seeing him. DeMarco believed, as irrational as he thought it was, that Diane considered him bad luck, like it was *his* fault that Carmody had tied her to a chair. He thought she was beginning to come around though; he'd sensed a little more warmth in her voice the last time they'd talked. Maybe one day in the near future he'd make his lasagna for her again. He hoped so. He needed someone like her in his life.

The only happy person was Mahoney. He was delighted he'd escaped his captors on his own accord, taking a gun away from a kid one-fourth his age. He was in the pink—and he didn't really care that they hadn't caught his kidnappers. And the press coverage for what he had done—hell, it had been better than all the paid advertising in the world. Letterman had called yesterday and asked if he wanted to be on his show. He was thinking about it; he liked Dave, thought he was a hoot.

"Oh, and I forgot to tell you," Mahoney said to Emma, as he shook Tabasco sauce onto his scrambled eggs, "the navy looked at those classified files Carmody copied. He told you the truth: he altered the files, took out the important stuff. The navy says that if the Chinese had gotten their hands on those discs, it might have actually set their program back a decade."

Emma just nodded, her mind still preoccupied with Li Mei's fate. "Is there anything else?" she said to Mahoney.

"I guess not," Mahoney said. "I just thought you'd want to know what Carmody did."

Emma's lips parted as if she had another lecture to deliver to Mahoney, but then she stopped and turned her head away. DeMarco thought he saw a sheen of tears glaze her pale blue eyes. He'd never seen Emma cry—and he wasn't going to see her cry now.

"Good," she said. "I have to go." And without another word, she rose and departed.

"She'll get over it," Mahoney said to DeMarco as they watched her walk out the door. His normally gruff voice sounded surprisingly gentle.

"I don't think so," DeMarco said.

Emma had once told DeMarco that governments could always rationalize what they did in the name of national security. But that noble objective—preserving a nation—always seemed to be realized in an endless accumulation of individual tragedies:

Li Mei's stillborn child; the young FBI agent who had died in an alley in Vancouver; the young woman, Carla, who died protecting Emma. And individuals would go on dying and suffering because the people who governed just weren't smart enough or humane enough to find a different way. DeMarco knew the next time he saw her, Emma would be her old self, as tough and cynical as ever, but he also knew she'd never forgive herself for the part she had played in turning a young woman into the person Li Mei Shen became.

Mahoney didn't know what DeMarco was sitting there stewing about, but he did know that it was time to get the lad's mind focused on something else.

"Well, I gotta get back to work," he said, sounding like a guy taking a smoke break from a factory instead of being the chosen leader of the House. As he was putting on his suit coat, he said to DeMarco, "I heard something about Hutchinson, the other day." Hutchinson was the minority leader in the House, a man Mahoney despised.

"Seems his kid has gotten himself into a jam, something that if it gets out, will embarrass that weasel pretty good. Now *that* I wouldn't care about, but I'm thinking of Hutchinson's wife. She's a nice gal, I like her, and a mother doesn't need to hear this sort of thing about her son. I was thinking . . ."

Outside the restaurant, as they were about to part company—Mahoney to return to the Capitol to try to turn partisan interests into good laws, DeMarco to go visit a man with a wayward son—Mahoney gestured with his square chin at a car parked at the curb.

"Didn't I see you drive up in that thing?" Mahoney said. "You get a new car?"

"Yeah," DeMarco said.

"What is it?"

"A 2005 Toyota. Only has twenty-four thousand miles on it. Gets over twenty miles to the gallon."

Mahoney, whose personal car was a classic twelve-cylinder Jaguar Cabriolet, shook his big head in dismay. "Jesus, Joe," he said, "you gotta learn to live a little."

DeMarco nodded, then his mouth turned up in a small smile as he pushed the button on the cool little beeper thing that unlocked the doors.

EPILOGUE

———◆◆◆———

Carmody watched as the black Mercedes pulled to a stop.

The Chinese man who stepped from the Mercedes was wearing a suit, but he looked like a man who normally wore a uniform. The man was as big as Carmody and he looked just as tough. He and Carmody stared at each other but neither man said anything. The Chinese man opened the back door of the Mercedes and a slender woman and a young boy stepped out.

Carmody nodded at the Chinese soldier and pointed at a Buick with a dented fender. The Buick was parked twenty yards from where Carmody was standing, halfway between him and the soldier. The soldier said something to the woman, and she took the boy's hand and they started to walk slowly toward Carmody. As the woman and boy approached him, Carmody tossed a set of keys to the Chinese soldier.

The boy and his mother had only walked a few paces when the boy suddenly pulled his hand free of the woman's and ran to Carmody. He swept the boy up into his arms and held him so tight that he was afraid he might break the child's ribs. When the woman reached him, he encircled one arm about her, pulling her close, kissing her on the lips.

The Chinese soldier looked briefly over at Carmody, his face expressionless. If he was touched by the family reunion he didn't show it. He walked over to the Buick, and taking the keys that Carmody had tossed him, opened the trunk. He stood for a moment, looking into the trunk, then reached down and touched the woman's throat, to make sure she was still alive. She was. She was such a lovely woman, he thought. It was a shame.

The Chinese soldier looked at Carmody and nodded, then he surprised Carmody and gave him a quick smile and a two-fingered salute. Carmody couldn't tell if the soldier was being sarcastic or if the salute was a gesture of respect—and he didn't care.

He had everything he wanted.

AUTHOR'S NOTE

The author ensured that all information in this book related to the United States Navy, naval shipyards, and nuclear-powered ships was already publicly available information and not classified.

The loss of controlled removable electronic media (CREM) discussed in this book is based entirely on events that occurred at the Los Alamos National Laboratory in July 2004. The loss of CREM at Los Alamos was documented in numerous newspapers and Web sites.

The fact that information for nuclear-powered ships exists in an electronic format, and the existence of reactor plant and steam plant manuals, is discussed online at a number of official navy Web sites. Similarly, discussions of submarines being used to collect foreign intelligence, and discussions related to noise-silencing and submarine-detection technology came from a number of online sources as well as the book *Blind Man Bluff,* by Sherry Sontag and Christopher Drew.

The discussion of physical security at naval shipyards in this novel—such things as employee badges, barbed-wire-topped fences, perimeter monitoring cameras, and guards—is generic and even intentionally inaccurate in a number of areas, as my friends at the Puget Sound Naval Shipyard will certainly recognize. (Marines don't normally guard the gates, and classified materials are protected in other ways than discussed in this novel.)

Read on for the opening pages of *House Rules*,
the next Joe DeMarco thriller.

"I was absolutely delighted to discover
Mike Lawson. . . . This smart political thriller
offers readers both a wild ride and
thought-provoking issues."
—Nancy Pearl, *Pearl's Picks*

Available in paperback now!

PROLOGUE

They had no idea how big the blast might be.

The techs, those useless dorks, said the bomb could take out just the garage or just the surrounding homes—or it could flatten structures as far as a quarter mile away. It all depends, they said. It depended on how the bomb was constructed, if it was shaped to blow in a particular direction. It obviously depended on how much ammonium nitrate the bombers had. It all depends.

No shit, had been Merchant's response, *and thanks for all your help.*

But Merchant knew, no matter how big the bomb might be, that he couldn't evacuate the nearby homes. If he started an evacuation, the two guys inside the garage might notice all the lights going on at three in the morning and then would see people running like hell, dressed in their pajamas. Or, with his luck, one of the good citizens they were trying to protect would call a radio station, and the bombers would hear that they were surrounded by fifty FBI agents. And once they knew that, they'd probably blow the thing right where it was, and Merchant and his guys, hiding less than twenty yards from the garage . . . well, they'd be toast. Literally.

If the bomb did explode and a bunch of civilians were killed, the media weenies and the politicians would naturally second-guess the hell out of his decision not to evacuate. They'd call him reckless and irresponsible, and his bosses would blame it all on him to save their bureaucratic butts. But then what did he care? He'd be dead. No, the smart thing to do was to forget evacuating anybody and go in now. And as for trying to negotiate with the guys in the garage. . . . Hell, even the suits at the Hoover Building agreed that would be useless. You can't negotiate with people who are willing to kill themselves in order to kill you.

What a way to spend Labor Day.

He spoke softly into his mike: "Alpha to Bravo Team Leader. Any sign of a third man yet?"

"No, sir."

The two men assembling the bomb were in a garage that was fifty feet from a two-story house. Merchant had overall tactical command of the operation and command of the five-man squad that made up Alpha Team. Another senior agent commanded Bravo Team, also a five-man squad. Bravo was on the opposite side of the garage from Alpha. Charlie Team, which consisted of almost forty agents, was protecting the perimeter, making sure no one entered or left the site. Charlie also had the snipers. The snipers would shoot anyone they thought needed shooting—and they wouldn't miss.

Merchant and his men were dressed in SWAT gear: combat helmets with face shields, black fatigues and body armor, headsets so they could hear and talk to Merchant, night-vision goggles, and an assortment of assault rifles, shotguns, and .40-caliber pistols. They were dressed for war, a war they were going to start.

"Alpha to Charlie Team Leader. What about you? Any sign of the third man?"

"No, sir."

The reports they'd received said three guys were involved, but there might not even *be* a third guy. The intelligence on him was weak. Maybe the third guy was in the house sleeping, or maybe he'd left to get something. Whatever the case, it was time to move. They had to move before daylight and the longer he waited the higher the likelihood that the guys in the garage would see his men or, even worse, drive the truck out of the garage. If that happened he'd be dealing with a *mobile* bomb, and that would be no fun at all.

"Alpha Team Leader to all personnel. We're going in. Bravo, are you ready?"

"Yes, sir."

"Charlie, are you ready?"

"Yes, sir."

Merchant nodded, although no one could see the gesture. He couldn't rely on the intelligence and he couldn't rely on the techs—but he could rely on his guys. He spoke into his mike again. "Remember, we want these assholes alive but I don't want any of you people dyin' to keep them that way."

Merchant took a breath, flipped the safety on his weapon, and felt the adrenaline start to squirt into his bloodstream. "On my go," he said. "Three. Two. One. Go!"

The garage had two doors: a normal door, like the door to a house, and a slide-up garage door operated by an electric garage door opener. There were also two small windows. On Merchant's *go!* the men from both teams belly-crawled forward until all ten agents were pressed up against the walls of the garage. Merchant tapped one of his men on the shoulder, and the agent placed four small C-4 charges on the large garage door, each charge at the corner of an imaginary six-foot square. A fifth charge was placed in the center of the square. Merchant took a breath and whispered into his mike a second time. "On my go. Three. Two. One. Go!"

Three things happened simultaneously: flash-bang grenades that produced a horrific amount of noise and light were shot in through the two windows; a door knocker—a heavy piece of pipe with a plate welded on one end and equipped with handles—was slammed into the small door, ripping it open; and a button was pushed on a remote control and the five small charges on the garage door exploded, blowing a hole in the door. Merchant's men were inside the garage in less than three seconds, screaming like banshees out of some urban nightmare.

It went down perfectly, like a training exercise at Quantico. The two men inside the garage were both on the floor, knocked down by the concussion of the door being blown open. They'd been blinded by the flashbangs, had their fists pressed against their eyes, and were wondering why their ears didn't work. Merchant's guys had handcuffs on the mutts less than a minute after they breached the building.

Jesus, Merchant thought, they're just kids. Then he looked inside the truck. Holy shit! That was a *lot* of fertilizer. There had to be at least a ton, maybe two.

"Merchant to Charlie Team Leader. Garage secure. Perps in custody. Get the bomb techs in here now, *right* now, to tell me if this goddamned thing is armed." Turning to the agent in charge of Bravo Team, he said, "Harris, take your people and do a quick sweep of the house and make sure the third guy's not in there. Clemens, you take these bastards to the command vehicle and stand by. I'll wait here until the bomb techs show."

Merchant looked into the truck again. Man, that was one big bomb! He wondered what—or who—these guys had been planning to blow up.

———◆◆◆———

He was two blocks away when he saw all the flashing red and blue lights. He stopped the car and took the binoculars from the glove box. There were so many lights that he could see the scene as clearly as if it were noon instead of 4 A.M. He could see a fire truck, two ambulances, and more than a dozen marked and un-marked police vehicles. There were also two armored trucks, one truck looking like something a bomb disposal squad might use. The other truck, with the satellite dishes on the roof, was probably a command and communications center. There were uniformed men milling about and men wearing windbreakers over white shirts and ties. FBI, he assumed. Stand-ing off to one side was a group of men dressed in helmets and black clothes, shaking hands, patting each other on the back, acting like athletes who'd just won a game. There were also a lot of people standing outside their homes wearing robes or clothes they'd just thrown on, wondering what was happening in their peaceful American neighborhood.

What had those fools done wrong?

He had to leave immediately; he was particularly vulnerable now. He hoped he hadn't left anything inside the house or the garage that would identify him, but if he had there was nothing he could do about it. They could have cars patrolling the area and if they stopped him he had no doubt they'd detain him because of the way he looked. He made a slow turn into a driveway, backed up, and began driving in the direction from which he'd come, forcing himself to drive slowly.

His right leg was on fire; it always hurt when he'd been sitting for a long time. He needed to get out of the car and walk around a bit, but he couldn't do that. He would bear the pain—as he'd always borne the pain—until it was safe to stop.

He headed in the direction of the freeway. With God's blessing, he'd be in Philadelphia in two hours. There he had a place to go, a place set up in advance. There he *might* be safe.

What had those fools done?

———◆———

Myron Clark was good at his job because he was smart and because he was patient, but most of all because he was tireless. He was absolutely indefatigable.

He always looked fresh whenever he conducted an interrogation: his shirt wrinkle-free, his tie in place, face clean-shaven, hair carefully combed. He looked as if he'd just stepped from a shower after a full eight hours of peaceful sleep. The truth was that he was surviving on catnaps, but he would never allow the prisoners to see this. They had to think that Clark could go forever, that he'd never stop. And he wouldn't.

Clark was interrogating the two men captured in the garage in Baltimore. He'd been interrogating them for twenty-six straight hours, and he could tell that the one named Omar al-Assad was going to break first. In fact, he was going to break the next time Clark talked to him.

Clark was an ordinary-looking man in his forties, five-nine, receding hairline, carrying twenty pounds he ought to lose. He wasn't physically intimidating and he knew it—that's why he had Warren Knox for an assistant. Knox was six-four, heavily muscled, and kept his hair cut close to his big knobby skull. He had a particularly brutal face, the kind you'd expect to see on a tattooed felon, and he always looked like he was just barely suppressing an incredible amount of rage. The truth was that Warren Knox was hardly violent at all; Clark had killed more men than Knox.

Omar had asked for a lawyer when the interrogation first began, and Clark had nodded to Knox and Knox had grabbed Omar by the throat and slammed him up against the wall of the interrogation room. As Omar was pinned against the wall, choking, his feet no longer touching the floor, Knox said, "If you say *lawyer* one more time I'm gonna kick your teeth out."

That's when Omar began to fully appreciate his situation. This wasn't like TV. It wasn't like all those

Law and Order shows where the cops yelled at the prisoners but never touched them—and stopped yelling as soon as they asked for a mouthpiece. No, Clark and Knox had made it clear to Omar that he had no rights. He wasn't going to be allowed to see anyone. Not a lawyer, not his partner, not his mother. He was completely alone.

If they took these clowns to trial, the fact that they'd trampled all over their rights as citizens could be a problem. The government's lawyers would spout legal gibberish to minimize the damage, but *convicting* these guys wasn't a priority, not at this point. In London, in Spain, in India, the subway attacks hadn't involved just a single bomb; the terrorists had set off four or five bombs simultaneously. Clark needed to know if Omar and his pal had accomplices, and if he had to cause Omar a little discomfort to find this out . . . well, too bad for Omar.

So for twenty-six hours Omar wasn't allowed to sleep. He'd be allowed to almost fall asleep, but just as his head would hit his chest, Knox would slam open the door to the interrogation room, cuff him on the back of the head, and tell him to go stand in the corner as if he were a truculent five-year-old.

And Omar was given no food and a lot of coffee. The coffee not only kept him awake but the caffeine in his empty stomach compounded the condition of his already jangling nerves. Yes, Omar was ready. Omar's partner—who was just a bit dumber than

Omar and didn't have Omar's imagination—would last a bit longer, but not much.

Clark checked his appearance in the mirror near the interrogation room door and entered the room. He took a seat across the table from the prisoner and looked for a moment into his bloodshot eyes, his terrified young face. "Well, you've beaten me, Omar," he said, shaking his head in mock disappointment. "My boss says we gotta send you someplace else, to see if some other guys can do better than me. We used to send people like you to Gitmo, Guantánamo Bay, down there in Cuba. But Gitmo became a fishbowl, Omar. Too many pussy liberals always watchin' over our shoulders, always tryin' to make us play by the rules. Well, my friend, we've gotten a lot smarter since Gitmo. Now we use an island off the coast of Maine."

Clark smiled sadly at Omar, as if he truly pitied him.

"The army used to use the island for testing biological weapons. They have a facility there, and they have cages in the facility. The cages don't have a lot of headroom because they used to keep monkeys in them—you know, the monkeys they used for the experiments. The monkeys are all dead now, but the cages are still there. But the best part isn't the cages, Omar. The best part is that nobody knows about the island. And nobody knows what happens there."

Omar al-Assad stared at Clark for a moment, maybe looking for mercy, but knowing by now that there was nothing merciful about Myron Clark.

"We were going to explode the bomb in the Baltimore Harbor Tunnel," Omar said.

In the next hour, Clark had the whole story. Omar al-Assad and his friend Bashar Hariri were American-born Muslims. They were eighteen years of age, from low-income families, high school dropouts, and unemployed. Neither young man was particularly religious, and their tastes and style of dress were typical of Americans their age.

One Saturday evening, they attended a lecture at a local mosque. The main reason they attended was because it was cold outside, and free food and coffee came with the speech. The title of the lecture, which neither young man could remember exactly, was "The Impact of American Imperialism on the Muslim World." Something like that, they said.

The lecturer told the two Americans that his name was Muhammad—he might as well have said John Smith—and he was from Yemen, was an imam, and was traveling around America preaching to the faithful. He instantly became the two young Americans' new best friend, spending hours with them, buying them dinners and hammering into their weak brains a message of hate. After a month he convinced them that blowing a hole in the Baltimore Harbor Tunnel, killing several hundred people, and disrupting commerce up and down the eastern seaboard would be a good and noble thing to do. *And* they'd each be given ten thousand dollars after the job was done.

Muhammad gave the young men the money to purchase a truck and the other ingredients they needed to make the bomb. He had been helping them assemble the bomb until just before Omar and Bashar were captured. All Omar knew—and ultimately, three hours later, Myron Clark believed him—was that Muhammad had to leave the garage to call someone, but Omar didn't know who.

But the most important thing Omar told Clark was that Muhammad had an artificial leg. That's what allowed the Bureau to find Muhammad in their files and determine who he really was—an honest-to-God al-Qaeda operative.

"How did you catch us?" an exhausted Omar asked.

Clark didn't tell him, but they'd caught Omar and his buddy because a fertilizer seller hadn't liked their looks.

They had needed two major ingredients for their bomb: ammonium nitrate fertilizer and a racing fuel composed primarily of nitromethane. At one of the places they'd purchased the ammonium nitrate, the fertilizer supplier had asked the young men why they needed it and Omar had said that they operated a landscaping business. The supplier was used to dealing with beefy white farmers, and the two men purchasing the fertilizer were obviously of Middle Eastern ancestry, too young to be likely principals in any business and visibly nervous during the purchase. He was on the phone to the FBI before the young men and their truck had exited his parking lot.

But instead of answering Omar's question, Clark asked one of his own. "Why did you and Bashar decide to become martyrs? I mean, do you guys really believe all that virgins-in-paradise bullshit?"

"Martyrs?" Omar said. "We weren't going to be martyrs."

Then Omar explained. Their plan had been to drive the truck and another car—the car Muhammad had escaped in—into the tunnel, punch out the tires on the truck so it couldn't be easily moved, and flee the scene in the second vehicle. They would have been miles away when the bomb exploded.

That's when Clark unveiled the part of Muhammad's plan that Omar obviously didn't know.

"Omar," he said, "your pal Muhammad had set the timer to detonate the bomb two seconds after you armed it."

Mike Lawson, a former senior civilian executive for the U.S. Navy, is the author of six novels starring Joe DeMarco: *The Inside Ring*, *The Second Perimeter*, *House Rules*, *House Secrets*, *House Justice*, *House Divided*, and *House Blood*.